SMOKE

WHITE COLLAR CRIME

PAUL EBERZ

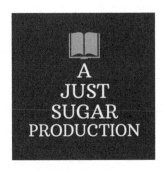
Cover Design - Paradox Book Cover Designs & Formatting

Line Editor - Carrie Murgittroyd

Printed in the United States of America

First Edition 2020

Copyright 2020 1-8914959101 Smoke - White Collar Crime

Paul Eberz

Smoke – White Collar Crime – a Just Sugar Production

Ebook ISBN 978-1-7352566-9-6

Paperback ISBN 978-1-7352566-7-2

Hardcover ISBN 978-1-7352566-8-9

Website: BooksbyPaulEberz.com

DEDICATION

To my wife Veronica – The source of my encouragement, and the rock of my foundation.

CONTENTS

ACKNOWLEDGMENTS

The Working Writers Workshop – The Critique Group Extraordinaire.

Phil Walker, Diane Dean, David Bishop, Barbara Rein, Mary Ann Weakley.

Beta readers – Johanna Zorn, Karen Naughton, Karen Cobb, Walt Griffin and Jo Soehl.

Patti Roberts – Paradox Book Covers & Formatting – A cover designer who can make a concept reality.

SMOKE

PAUL EBERZ

I

INTERVENTION

1

The sound of footsteps in the distance caused the Thin Man to drop and crush his cigarette. He unbuttoned his perfectly tailored grey suit jacket and slipped his hand around his Berretta. He gripped the handle, leaving it in the holster, gently rubbing his thumb up and down the handle.

The footsteps came closer.

He pushed his face forward, peering around the corner of an ancient stone wall, straining to see down the dimly lit cobblestone street.

A man, head down and covered by a fedora, approached slowly.

The Thin Man pulled his face back to where no light shone, and where no shadow was cast.

The footsteps got closer.

Thin Man drew his pistol and held it at his side.

The footsteps stopped.

He slid his thumb, clicking the pistol's safety off.

The man stood in front of the steps then turned slowly, the tip of the fedora raised upward when he peered into the shadow.

He brought the gun to his chest.

The man started up the steps.

He pressed tight against the wall.

The man stopped and spoke. "Did you have a good trip?"

The Thin Man clicked the safety back on. "Yes, I did, Father. Nice of you to ask." He stepped out of the shadow.

The man in the fedora followed, parted his coat, and removed a pack of cigarettes. He held out an offering. The dim light reflected off the small patch of white at the man's collar.

He glanced past the priest. No one followed him. They were standing a few steps up from the typically tourist-packed cobblestone street. It was a good meeting place—easy to find, even in the dark of night. He lit his own cigarette which illuminated the entrance to Torre delle Ore, the ancient clock tower in Tuscany's oldest walled city, Lucca.

"I read the newspaper. It said the woman was a victim of a robbery." The priest struck a match and lit his cigarette. Its glow showed his ghostly white face.

The Thin Man blew a cloud of smoke. "I've always been impressed with your English. It's excellent. Almost no accent. Much better than my Italian."

"I studied in the states for a few years before returning to Rome. Was there anything not reported in the paper that I should know?"

The Thin Man tapped ash to the ground. "It went as planned, no problems. Do you want to hear the details?"

"Do I need to?"

"No, but I can't talk about it with anyone else, and I do so enjoy my work."

The priest remained silent, giving assent.

"I used a butcher's boning knife so the blade would be long enough to reach the heart but wouldn't break if I hit a rib." He took another long drag. "She was so afraid, she didn't scream, and when I slid the knife inside her, she couldn't." He smiled.

The priest didn't react. The Thin Man was disappointed, his smile fading.

The priest put his hand inside his jacket. The Thin Man's eyes followed the movement, but he didn't react.

"Final payment, ten thousand euros." The priest held out a brown envelope.

Thin Man took it and put it in his pocket. He felt no need to count it. The priest had never shorted him before.

The priest dropped his cigarette, crushing it with a polished shoe. "I've been transferred to the United States. I leave for Philadelphia in a week."

"I guess your success in silencing this problem resulted in a promotion?"

"If I need to get in touch with you, should I use the same email?"

"Yes, it's encrypted. You remember the address, of course?"

The priest nodded, pulled his jacket closed, and started to walk away.

"Did you ever hear the legend surrounding this clock tower?"

The priest stopped and turned to listen.

"According to a seventeenth-century legend, a wealthy noblewoman bargained with the Devil to remain young and beautiful throughout her life. The Devil agreed and told her their agreement would end on her eightieth birthday. Her life was as she bargained. Her appearance remained young and beautiful, but as her eightieth birthday approached, she became terrified of eternal damnation. Then just before midnight on the night before her birthday, she went up the tower steps to try to stop the clock. She wanted to stop the Devil from hearing the bell ring and mark the hour of her death. She failed. When the clock stuck midnight, the Devil came and collected her soul. The next morning an old woman was found at the top of the tower, her gnarled hands gripping the chain on the bell clock."

"Interesting. Is there a point?" the priest inquired.

The Thin Man looked at his lapel and brushed something away. "Do you believe in the Devil?"

The priest flipped his collar up. "I believe in power. I want it, and you sometimes help me get it."

"But Father, you didn't answer the question. Do you believe in the Devil?"

The priest started walking away. His back turned; he spoke into the echo of the alcove. "If I get an offer to sell my soul, I'll include you in the bargain."

The Thin Man waited on the landing until Father DeFrancisco walked up the street. He pulled his coat tight, then stepped into the street and walked the other way.

He heard his own footsteps, but not the Priest's.

2

H enry Smokehouse lay naked, face up on his bed, exactly where his head came to rest six hours before. Sleepless nights were not unusual. He'd overcome his affliction by learning to relax his body—lying motionless, resting muscles. He stared at a crooked crack in the ceiling that had been there since he moved-in, years ago. His mind worked like a pendulum, each thought fueling the next, and that thought the next, and the next, and the next.

The long, irregular break in the yellowing plaster functioned as a sundial. It tracked time via a narrow stream of sunlight beginning its journey halfway up the wall. The beam of light nearing the center of the ceiling crack told him the hour to be about noon.

The night was long gone, and his body protested his first movements. He swung his legs over the bedside and put his feet flat on the floor, preparing for his morning routine. He felt the discomfort almost every day; the aching thigh was from a through and through bullet. Another had damaged only muscle in his calf. His back was a different story. It had demanded six surgeries in which the doctors had removed eighteen pieces of shrapnel and screwed a hunk of metal onto his spine at the juncture of $L_5 - S_1$.

He placed a hand on either side of his leg, rotating his left knee back and forth. It snapped, crackled, and popped back into operational condition. Next, he rubbed the two scars on the opposite sides of his right thigh and then two more on the calf of his left leg. When he finished, he stood up, testing function. He reached up, extending both arms, palms together in a modified prayer pose. To his surprise, pain from the four-inch metal bar screwed to his spine didn't happen today.

Yawning, he stumbled toward the bathroom scratching and straightening out his business. He opened the mirrored door on the medicine chest and removed an amber bottle. His breakfast was one white and three large blue oval pills that he downed with a handful of water from the faucet.

Besides the war wounds, he also had very noisy shoulders. The injuries that caused the awful cacophony had no war stories attached. The damage to cartilage was older than the battle scars, the result of youthful baseball abuse.

Smoke walked to the shower rotating his neck side to side. He heard it crack as he pulled back the shower curtain and turned on the hot side of the shower faucet.

The meds began their magic act.

A cloud of steam filled the bathroom, and rivulets of condensation ran down the tile walls. Hot water poured over his head, soothing muscles and diminishing brain fog.

He toweled dry, then squared away the debris, restoring the bathroom to order. He pulled a t-shirt from a hanger and jeans from a drawer in the dresser. He didn't own much of anything because he didn't want much of anything. What he did possess was neat and either hung up, folded, or carefully stowed. Nothing he owned was fashionable; serviceable would be a better description. His only 'wardrobe rule' anomaly was a black suit coat, a white shirt, and a striped dark grey tie. He'd worn them only once.

His two-room apartment was neat and decorated in unfashionable functional. Two by twelve's on cinderblocks functioned as bookshelves. Scores of books on a vast range of subjects lined each plank. There were two sources of color in the room. A framed poster of a Santana concert he attended in 1990 had a special place. Also adding color were two original acrylic oil paintings. A white house on a lake in New England and a Caribbean seascape of three empty boats hung frameless on an otherwise bare wall. They were a payment from his first client. He didn't like the paintings, but they covered a hole in the wall left by the previous tenant.

The only thing of value in the entire apartment was an embossed silver frame on the nightstand next to his bed. In it was a photo of Helen. In a drawer under her picture were a matching frame and another memory.

He owned a bed, a couch, and a TV that sat on a dresser. He had cable TV, but only because he occasionally needed a baseball fix. There was a small efficiency kitchen in one corner with a couple of cabinets and a cooktop. Under the sink, cleaning supplies and a plunger shared space with a well-worn souvenir of college life—an El Producto cigar box once used to remove seeds from pot. Written in black magic marker on the box, the word SMOKE identified its owner. The word was what had been in the box and the name he preferred.

He had never been fond of his surname, Smokehouse. As a kid, he was skinny and short, and teased until he wasn't short and skinny anymore. He didn't like his given name either. He understood the family name followed every descendant, but someone had to choose to name him Henry. It was his grandfather's name, which caused him mixed emotions. Young Henry thought Grandpop to be a righteous dude, but to Smoke, the moniker should have been on a gravestone, retired, not on him.

There was no pot inside the box under the sink. There hadn't been since—forever. The crusty brown box contained a broken pipe, half a pack of Zig Zags, two paper clips, and an empty disposable lighter. Tony Taylor's Philadelphia Phillies 1960 baseball card was a keepsake and a tool he had used to clean the pot. Also, amongst the antiques, was a piece of red, white, and blue ribbon attached to a gold cross. On the front was a flying eagle and the words FOR VALOR engraved on the back.

It was an odd place for someone to keep the Distinguished Service Cross. The medal meant something to him, but he wasn't sure what. So, he put it where he didn't have to think about it.

He picked up the book he was reading from the bed and marked the page in Hemingway's *Garden of Eden*. He pulled the bedsheet tight and centered his pillow. On the only chair in the apartment, he sat and put on a pair of broken-in boots. He did a quick inspection before he closed the door on his way out. He didn't lock it. There wasn't anything to steal; nothing to protect, only some memories that he couldn't forget.

At the bottom of the stairs, dead leaves swirled upward in a mini-cyclone. The fall crop remained in the alley refusing to leave and continued to evade capture. He passed the ballet and emerged from the shadow of the old brick building into the warming afternoon sun. He blinked, squinted, then covered his eyes with dark sunglasses. They were black frames with large mirrored lenses, obnoxious, but a tool. When placed on a table, they functioned as eyes in the back of his head—the best kind of partner, a silent one.

He did another mini stretch-out when he reached the sidewalk—legs, knees, and shoulders. A big, rugged-looking man, Smoke stood six foot two and walked a straight steady pace that matched a fixed gaze. It was a stature that stood out in a crowd. It was more than his size— it was the attitude. A lot of guys had similar builds. The difference was the subtle, leading-man way he walked, the way he sat at a table eating dinner or reading a newspaper in a chair. One stranger's impression of him might be that he was quiet. Another might say he seemed unpredictable. To some, he appeared volatile or dangerous.

He was aware of people's cautionary attitudes toward him. In most circumstances, he found it useful. In general terms, he didn't like people and preferred his days to be quiet, with as little human contact as possible. It took a while, but he found the persona that accommodated that need. It involved keeping people at a distance, much like a big dog no one wanted to pet.

He was cautious. His role as the tall, silent type was part of finding the pace he needed so he could do what he needed to do. It was his business. It was what he did, and it was what he had become. He had no personal life. There were friends. He didn't see them often—or speak to them—but they were there. They would always be there.

A Philadelphia SEPTA bus making one of its last stops on the Market Steet run rolled up on him and stopped. A small, gray-haired woman carrying an oversized handbag climbed down. The driver hit the accelerator as soon as the door closed. The diesel engine coughed a cloud of toxic black fumes as it power-sputtered its way up Frankford Ave.

He closed his eyes to the assault of the dark cloud. Coughing, he waved his hand in front of his face then exhaled an equally foul curse.

The bus spit out another black cloud.

"Fuck me," he said, coughing again.

Smoke looked up and saw a young boy, about ten or eleven, staring at him from the back window of the bus. There was no promise in his eyes, either.

Cold chills rushed from his head to his toes and then back up his spine. He shook his head, trying to rid his mind of the images that haunted him. He ducked his head, pushed his shoulders forward, and followed the trail of the bus and the boy. The boy and the memory disappeared in the traffic.

He raised his eyes, re-gripped his attitude, and fixed on his goal in the distance ahead. He started walking, then stepped up the pace to double-time. Within fifty yards, his heart rate leveled out, and he felt a pounding in his chest and a burning in his thighs. His heart rate leveled over the next hundred yards, the pain sliding down to his calves. He kept up his pace, pumping his arms for the last hundred yards. He hit the corner of Frankford and East Girard like it was a finish line.

He put his hands on his hips, taking several deep breaths to slow his heartbeat. He billowed his t-shirt, cooling his body. His workout concluded; he went to a cool-down pace, walking past the buildings on the street he knew so well.

He passed a storefront window where he used to watch a jeweler fixing watches and rings. A stout black-haired woman was there now working an old sewing machine. Surrounding her were countless thimbles and hundreds of brightly colored spools of threads. A Russian family, the newest immigrants to the street, now owned the store.

He passed the old Five and Dime Store. It used to sell everything from clothes to clothespins, and from pinwheels to pincushions. It was now a consignment store. Instead of new unique junk for sale for a nickel or a dime it had old antique junk for sale for a dollar or two.

It was Philadelphia, and like every major city, its neighborhoods evolved. The Great Northeast was no exception. English, Irish, German, Italian, Puerto Rican, African American, Asian, and now Russian, all mixed into the melting pot. They immigrated with high hopes and lofty dreams, holding tight to their most valuable possession—enthusiasm. They sought a new home and a new beginning. Somehow, despite their limited resources, they survived.

He kept walking, three blocks to go.

3

"Cann I be getten ye a whee draft, Lewtenant?"

"Na... I don't think so." Police Lieutenant Robert Aimer eyed the front door.

The Scotsman looked around his almost empty bar. "Were empty jus now. A whee pint counldna be hurten anything." Without waiting for consent, Jim flipped a large brown mug into the air then snatched it by the handle. He poured a cold draft instead of coffee.

The lieutenant looked to the door again.

"He'll be along soon enough." Jim lingered, wiping the bar top in bartender fashion. "So, I've been knowing our boy, Mr. Smoke, going on eleven years, now. How long have you been known' him?"

"Longer than that—since High School. Almost thirty years." He shook his head as he sipped. "A long damn time ago." The lieutenant turned back the clock smiling at his memories. "He was something back then; one of the best athletes I've ever seen, football, baseball—captain of both teams."

Jim listened intently.

"Smart too. Smoke did his homework on the bus and got an A. I studied for hours and got Bs. I fucking hated him."

Jim smiled. So did Smoke's friend.

"If someone figured out how smart he was, he would have wound up at Harvard or Stanford, but no one did."

"Aye, pure dead brilliant, then."

"He stayed local, at LaSalle."

"Aye...up North Philly off 20th Street. Good school."

"He was in pre-law and did well. He met Helen, and they were perfect together. He also played baseball...and... from a school that never had a Major League draft pick before—he got picked by the Red Sox in the sixth round."

"No, schidt."

Aimer figured the Scotsman meant 'no shit' and continued. "Life was going great. Then everything changed." The lieutenant sipped his beer. "He was a senior when the Gulf War happened. He said no to the Sox and enlisted in the Army right after graduation."

Jim scratched his head. "That bee sounden odd to me. The Sox's is a pretty good organization? He gave up playing baseball to be fighten' in a war?"

"Jim, back in the day, the guys in this neighborhood joined up when there was trouble. It wasn't like a political statement or anything. It was, just the way it was. Kinda hard to understand unless you came from here. They joined up to fight in spite of the politics not because of it."

Aimer wasn't sure a Scottish immigrant would understand something he barely understood himself.

But Jim surprised Aimer. "I get it. Their da's did...so, they did. Pretty much the same in Scotland. We are not real fond of the Brits, but we always signed up when there's a fight, all the same."

"He had a degree so Smoke could have gone in as an officer. However, that meant a year of ROTC, then a four-year hitch as an officer. He went for two years as a private. It all became part of a grand plan. Helen would get a teaching degree. He would not get killed. Then, after his hitch, they would go to South Carolina. He would play baseball for the Sox and Helen would teach. The Red

Sox agreed to give him a shot when he got back...so...that was the plan. Then..."

Jim and Aimer both knew what happened next.

Neither spoke of it.

Loud laughter came from the backroom, followed by a crash of breaking dishes. Both their heads turned to the noise.

"Fishtown." Jim frowned and shook his head.

Smoke reached his destination and took the four well-worn stone steps to Jim's Ale House two at a time. He pushed open the door, and the darkness was like a flashbulb going off in reverse. He pulled off his sunglasses. His eyes watered but even dark-blinded, he knew the direction and how many steps he needed to take.

His destination was the bar.

Jim's bar needed some paint here and there, but it was clean and profitable. It was successful because Jim was a bartender's bartender, and Connie made the best corned beef in the city.

A cold glass of Schlitz arrived at Smoke's usual stool at the same moment he did. It was one of the smallest pleasures one could have in life, and it was one of the most satisfying—the first cold sip of his favorite beer.

"Oyee," said his friend Jim.

"Ehey, Jim." Smoke smiled just a little.

"How ya doing on this fine day?"

"Not too bad. How's Connie?"

"She's been busy in the Kitchen, corned beef special tonight..." There was a loud bang followed by laughter from the pool table area in the rear of the bar. Jim looked but only shook his head without any comment on the commotion.

Smoke, transitioning from sunlight to bar light, was not able to see into the backroom but his vision had cleared enough to see

Lieutenant Aimer sitting at the far end of the bar. Smoke nodded recognition, got off his stool, and headed in Aimer's direction.

Another loud bang followed by a heavy thump accented by a crash of glass stopped him.

A smallish woman with red hair pulled back in a tight bun burst through two swinging doors behind the bar. She carried a galvanized metal bucket in one hand and had a white-knuckled grip on a mop in the other. She wore a long apron, white Adidas sneakers, and a scowl.

Connie flew past Smoke, mumbling to herself, "Pericks from Fishtown." She had the same thick accent as her husband, but he understood every word.

Jim looked confidentially at Smoke. "Ther a bunch a' idiots working the demo on the tire shop that burned up last month. Dinna bother aboot them. Conni will settle it din."

Unconvinced of an assured outcome, Smoke stopped walking and returned to his seat. Trouble was brewing.

There was another crash and more laughter.

Jim and Aimer reacted and both started down the length of the bar headed towards the noise. They arrived at the far end at the same time, coming up on either side of Smoke.

Smoke held up two stop sign palms.

"Jim, you don't need this. I hear at least three voices back there, maybe four. That's too many for you. And...," looking to the cop, "you're not supposed to be in a bar while on duty. I suppose you've had a beer?"

He lowered the stop sign. He put one hand on each of their shoulders, pushed them backward. "I have a plan." Smoke winked then walked toward the laughter.

Jim and Aimer followed a few steps behind Smoke taking positions on either side of the entryway.

Connie, her back up against a wall, was holding a mop handle defensively across her chest. Two large athletic types had her flanked like bookends. They were several inches taller and many pounds heavier than Smoke. A smaller man stood in front of her and was working hard at what he thought was a hysterical comedy routine. The trapped foreigner was his punchline.

A shadowy figure resembling a pregnant tick remained seated, enjoying the show.

There were four.

The standup comedian said, "Mickey and Stan were just having a good time there, sweetie. So, the light got broke. So what?" He pointed at the debris on the pool table. "It's a piece of shit anyway."

He laughed loud—too loud.

The matching Bookends tried to follow the leader but were a little slow on the upbeat.

Connie, pinned against the wall, was red-faced with anger. "Yeah, well then, you be breakn' it, so you be payin' for it."

The Bookend on her right joined in as the arrogant piece of shit he was. "We're not going to pay for the light, and we're not gonna pay for the beer either."

The Bookend on her left added a pithy, "Yeah."

Connie tried to escape again, pushing the mop handle hard into the Comedian.

He pushed it back, then doubled down. He threw his mug of beer in Connie's face.

The drunken men's laughter had reached its peak. Their ability to laugh was about to disappear—for about six months.

The lieutenant's cell phone beeped when he pushed the first two digits of 911. He put his finger on number "1" and waited.

Connie pushed the handle forward catching the Comedian under the nose. He rubbed it, and red-faced said, "Fuck you...you Irish bitch."

"She isn't Irish. She's Scottish."

The Comedian turned around fast. He spotted the shadow outline in the doorway. His eyes then darted side-to-side looking for assurances of his comrades' commitment.

A moment of silence followed as the group sized up their

opponent. Smoke saw the silent communication, and surmised it wasn't the first time they had acted up in public.

They looked at him, then each other, and nodded a game-on grin.

"One minute," said Smoke.

Their expressions changed as doubt crept in.

The Comedian stammered out, "What...what did you say, old man?"

"One minute," Smoke repeated immediately.

The Comedian laughed again—loud—too loud.

"You will put fifty dollars on the table for the broken light, and the beer, then leave. You have sixty seconds—and—I mean, sixty seconds. All four of you...all the way out the door."

The Comedian pointed a boney finger. "We will leave when we fucking feel like leaving...old man." He glanced at his Bookends, signaling them into action.

Bookend Left grabbed a chair and threw it in Smoke's direction, yelling, "Ahhhhhhhh." He charged, intending to drive Smoke into and through the wall.

Smoke assumed a defensive stance. He squared shoulders, feet spread apart, hands rolled into fists. He stood still, not moving a muscle.

Another voice rose up a few seconds later. Bookend Right echoed his partner's, "Ahhh," and followed two steps behind.

The first on-coming rhino lowered his head and his eyes, preparing to deliver a crushing blow. When the hunched-over body arrived, Smoke shifted his weight slightly to the right pivoting on his front hip. Using his left forearm and the open palm of his right hand, he pushed the incoming body off its direction. Bookend Left had missed his target and was now out of control, off-balance and falling forward. Smoke punched straight down, hitting Bookend Left's kidney with the full power of his right fist. The bully's knees folded. He face-planted the floor, sliding headfirst into the wall.

One down and out.

Smoke returned to his Karate defensive ready position in anticipation of the second incoming body. Bookend Right was also leaning forward, head lowered, eyes down, unable to see the target. He didn't see the pain coming, either. Smoke pivoted, guiding the victim's energy offline.

This time, instead of a kidney punch, Smoke drove his elbow down onto the back of Bookend Right's head. The body also face-planted the floor, joining his partner. He was not unconscious like his buddy, but he was writhing in pain.

Right rolled over and tried to stand.

This one's not a quitter. Good for him.

Smoke ended the gallant effort with a leather heel that changed a bleeding nose into a broken nose.

Two down.

The police lieutenant's phone made another sound when he pushed the one button again.

The Comedian, now white-faced, backed up and tripped over the broken light fixture. His arms flailed wildly, trying to regain his balance.

There was a whistling noise as a cue stick generated speed. Jim broke it over Connie's beer-throwing attacker's back. The Comedian went to the floor hard. The blow didn't knock him out, but he wisely stayed down.

Three down. One to go.

"43...44...45." Smoke went from a silent to a verbal countdown.

"I get it, one minute...that's for me, right?" stammered the Tick. The last party animal struggled to his feet and headed for the door. He knocked over a chair, which offered no resistance, and walked past his fallen comrades.

"54...55...56."

The Tick almost got there.

The last creep standing heard "60" when he was a step away from the door. What he didn't hear was the cue ball that hit him in the back of the head.

Four down. Game over.

Lieutenant Aimer appeared on Smoke's right looking impassively at the body by the door. "Still got the fastball."

"Nah," said Smoke, "If I still had it, he wouldn't get up."

Jim was comforting Connie, who was still mad as hell.

Aimer put his cuffs on Bookend Left and a plastic cuff-tie on The Comedian.

Bookend Right did not need cuffs. He was holding both hands on his bleeding nose and weeping.

Two patrolmen came through the door answering the lieutenant's call. The swinging door hit the Tick who was still lying where he dropped.

The lieutenant pointed to the body, "Hey, cuff that guy."

It took an hour to escort the party animals out and to complete the reports. After the police left, the regular crowd came in fast. The regulars couldn't wait to hear what happened. They wanted a cold beer, Connie's corned beef, and the story.

Smoke's street rep would grow exponentially.

A tall, cold beer was waiting when Smoke returned to his seat.

Connie appeared at his side. Taking hold of his shirt, she pulled him down. She grabbed both sides of his head and kissed him hard, full on the mouth. It didn't have tongue, but it had length and feeling.

She let go of the lip lock and his face. "Yourn' a white freeken knight, laddy boy. My white freeken knight."

"Uh-huh," he said, slightly embarrassed and without much enthusiasm for her accolade.

She reacted to his lack of appreciation by punching him hard in the chest.

Smoke rubbed the injury, wincing.

Aimer, laughing, slapped Smoke on the back. "Four men down and not a scratch. Then, a five-foot one woman lands a blow, center mass."

Smoke looked at the cop with his best scowl and, still rubbing, changed the subject. "So why are you looking for me?"

"Your girl—McKee—has been looking for you. When you didn't return any of her calls, she called me and asked for help. I said I would. Actually, I said I would...try...to locate you."

"Why?"

"I'm not a messenger," Aimer said, annoyed. "Call her and find out yourself." He took a sip of beer. "Anyway, it's better coming from her, directly. You do still have a phone, right?"

"Not why, her—why, you? How did she get you to carry her water?"

"Why me...oh? Well, she helped me out with something, and I owe her."

"What?"

"Why—What—Who? You know any other words?"

"Yes."

The lieutenant smiled a little and changed his tone. "Look, Smoke, I've known you for a lot of years, right?"

Smoke did not respond.

"Right." The lieutenant pushed forward undaunted. "Okay, right to the chase. My—why." Aimer took a moment to formulate his answer. "Somebody in the print business threatened to blow me up over a bullshit charge. It wasn't true. The department left me hanging. I was on my own. McKee got to the bottom of it and did what the department wouldn't and the union couldn't. She could have made a lot of enemies in the department, but she didn't care. She went bulldog on everybody. Now, I'm clean and green. Free of all baggage. In short, I owe her big time, and I always pay my debts. So, when she asked me for help, I said, 'Absolutely'. In the payback department, finding you wasn't even a down payment. However, even if she hadn't helped me out of that jam-up, I would have done it anyway. Not for you mind you, for her, she's good people...you know...a friend."

"Okay, so...you found me. Now what?"

"Will you meet her?"

Smoke didn't answer. He picked up his glass and drank some beer.

"Smoke, you can be such a son of a..." Aimer didn't get to finish.

"When?"

"Soon as you can. McKee filled me in a little bit on what she needed, but I can't help her officially or otherwise. When she tells you what she wants, you'll know why she needs your help and not mine."

There was another pause while Smoke decided. "Okay."

The lieutenant breathed a little sigh of relief.

Smoke pushed the empty glass away. "Ralph's—Wednesday—two o'clock."

"Okay, sure thing, BOSS. You do realize I'm a fucking homicide police lieutenant, not your secretary."

Aimer got off his stool and put his hand on Smoke's shoulder. "You need me...call...anytime."

He didn't take his hand away until Smoke nodded.

"Till next time, Jim." Aimer waved goodbye.

"Till next time Lewtenant—And haste ye back."

Jim turned to Smoke, "A whee pint more?"

"No thanks, Jim." Smoke reached into his pocket.

Jim immediately lost his nature. Red-faced, he slammed his hand on the bar.

"Don't you be insulting me now, Mr. Smoke. You're a powerful man, but if'n you place a coin on this bar I'll be puttn my hands on you."

Smoke nodded, stood, drained his glass, and placed it on the bar.

He walked to the door and pushed it open into the light.

4

From a window in a building facing Doctor Olivia Bennet's seventh-floor office, a man was watching.

His job was to report when the man they were looking for showed up. It wasn't an easy job. They told him he would be going to a certain office. It was the only office that opened at ten a.m. and closed after seven p.m. He was to observe the traffic going in and out of the building. The employees were easy. They all arrived around the same time, so it wasn't difficult to photograph and print their pictures. Other people came in and out of the building at random times throughout the day. The doctor's appointments always came in about ten minutes before the hour. He always watched but only used the bathroom on the half hour.

Daylight reflecting off the office windows shuttered the world inside the building making it impossible to see who was in the office, so they gave him heat sensor lenses for his camera. The optical equipment provided blurry red and blue images. It helped determine when more than two people were in the office.

Once a day, at dusk, the sunlight dimmed, providing an opportunity for the watcher to look for his quest without electronics.

The thirty minutes between dim and dark permitted him to photograph the private life of Dr. Olivia Bennet. Her life was visible as long the blinds were open.

He sat in the only chair in the small, one-room vacant office. His long-lens camera rested on a cheap folding card table as he positioned a tripod equipped with high-power binoculars. After sixteen days, he was able to distinguish the heat glow figures of the doctor and her secretary, but images had no faces and no personality.

He made a note of every client arrival, every lunch break, and every mail delivery. He needed to identify the new blurs appearing through the office door so he developed a system. He knew patients' appointments started on the hour and lasted an hour. When a blur left the office at the top of an hour, he picked up the camera and walked to the one window that opened. From there he could see who came out the front door. The blur became a full-face picture four and a half minutes after it left the office.

The last blur leaving the office was a woman, blond, mid-thirties. He took the picture, sent it to the printer, then added it to the logbook.

They wanted everything, all the details. As much information as he could gather.

They were looking for a man—a particular man.

The pen moved across the paper with precision—each stroke etching words with the same care as the thought that produced them. Balanced lines flowed from margin to margin on unlined white paper. It was careful, precise, and with little need for correction.

She never began a sentence unsure of its end.

Documenting her impressions immediately after a session was essential to the patient's treatment. It was as necessary a tool as the taping system that recorded the sessions. Facial tics, rapid muscle movement, even nose wrinkling, often contradicted the spoken word. Her notes were the keys needed to unlock hidden truths.

It was part of her routine, her procedure, her process.

"Mrs. Daniels is here." A voice from the intercom announced the curtain was going up in five minutes.

She placed the pen east and west to the closed file. She ran her hands across the uncluttered surface of her command center. Her desk looked like an antique because of its polished rosewood finish and artful carvings. However, it was new and custom built to her specifications. Beneath the beautiful finish, it had hidden compartments concealing state of the art technology. Wireless communication and switches that controlled lighting and the taping system were out of sight. Her desktop computer screen lowered into a hidden compartment with the push of a button.

The doctor spun her high-backed chair towards a full-length mirror. She rose up and stretched. Standing tall, she lifted her arms toward the ceiling, rising on bare toes like a ballerina. She was taller than average and possessed a slim athletic figure. A short but intense daily exercise regime kept her fit. The doctor was mature, confident, and in shape.

She ran her fingers through her hair. It was short, parted in the middle with one side longer than the other. The cut was purposeful. She could command one's attention with her eyes front or, with a flick of her head, conceal herself behind a dark shield.

She looked into the mirror and adjusted the collar of an Eskandar red silk blouse. She liked it and not because of the name on the tag or that it cost thirteen hundred dollars. She loved it because it was beautiful. Her publisher gave her the blouse because he knew what the press photographers wanted at a book signing, expensive clothes, attractive authors, and big toothy smiles.

She smoothed the skirt, snapped a fashion runway pose. She was aware she was attractive, but she was not a slave to appearance nor a prisoner of its preservation.

Picking up a lip pen, she leaned toward the mirror and ran a thin line of red across her lips. It complimented the stark contrast between deep dark brown hair and her alabaster skin. She glowed. It was like her face generated light rather than reflected it.

She sat back down, closed her eyes, and began five minutes of meditation.

Loretta offered the patient a choice of either coffee or water.

Mrs. Daniels chose the latter, but without drinking it, nervously screwed and unscrewed the cap. "I am curious to find out about—the —I mean... How did she get the...?"

"Nickname?"

"Yes, I don't have the nerve to ask her—but what's with that?"

"Okay, I'll tell you, but it needs an explanation." Loretta took the seat next to Ms. Daniels. "The New Yorker, the London Review, and the New York Times published great reviews when her book came out. A lot of nonfiction gets good reviews so critical recognition alone doesn't always mean instant success. It was the Celebrity/Gossip magazines like People and Cosmo that put her face on the front page. That's what drove the book up the bestseller list."

"Ahh...the nickname?" pressed the patient.

"Right—okay, but before I tell you, you need to hear this." Lo took a copy of the book from a shelf, opened the cover, and read the inside leaf. "Dr. Olivia Bennet earned a BA in Psychology from Harvard. She received a Master and Doctorate in Social and Cognitive Psychology from Stanford. The doctor then completed a Fellowship at the Sorbonne and also became fluent in French. In addition to her private practice, she provides profiling for law enforcement, including federal and state agencies. Dr. Bennet is a nationally recognized authority in her field."

Lo closed the book and held it straight out in demo mode.

Appearing on the front cover of the book was a silhouette shadow portrait of an embracing naked man and woman. New Times Roman bold black lettering announced the title, SEX *and* *the* ENLIGHTENED MIND.

She flipped it around. The back cover had the same silhouette and color. It had a different title written in bold red lipstick, RELEASE THE BEAST.

"The title Doctor O wanted is on the front. The publisher didn't love it and insisted on the different title. He said a catchy title would transform a small audience textbook into a bestselling classic. Obviously, he was right. Release the Beast got everybody's attention. It shot up the chart and was number one after only three weeks."

The patient checked her watch.

Loretta could see Ms. Daniels was becoming impatient. The patient wanted the inside scoop on the nickname before her appointment began. But that wasn't going to happen without a full explanation.

Loretta started reading again. "The subject matter in this book is sound medical and psychological fact. Its foundational premise is elementary. Despite the overexposure to sexual content in movies, music, and advertising, people in the US are statistically the most repressed and sexually unaware audience of any developed nation in the world. The remedy is a personal journey, not an event. Embracing new and sometimes-foreign concepts is essential. There must also be a willingness to discard outdated and harmful taboos. Enlightenment occurs when reason and individualism replace shame."

The patient coughed, still waiting for the inside scoop.

Loretta relented. "Okay—here is the lowdown on the nickname. The Post ran a story with the headline, Doctor Orgasm Goes to Number One. In the first line of the article's copy, the author abbreviated it to Dr. O. The name stuck like super glue."

The patient smiled, now in the know.

Her oft-repeated speech complete, Loretta returned to her desk. She looked at the clock. Two minutes.

Her patient was silent—again. The only sound she made was the nervous drumming of her fingers to the beat of a song only she could hear.

Dr. O studied the young woman sitting across from her. Her assessment began with a great deal of admiration for her determination.

This songbird needed to summon up massive amounts of courage to confront her issues.

The silence persisted for a full minute.

Dr. O broke the tension. "He doesn't understand. That's the biggest problem. He doesn't understand."

Startled, the young woman sat up straight and crossed her legs. She wore a loose, charcoal skirt that covered her knees and a simple white blouse fastened with white buttons.

The doctor continued in a lower voice, "The problem is his, not yours."

The young woman's eyes widened then looked back down to the floor.

The doctor was giving her permission to let go of guilt. She wanted her patient to lose the anger and open up.

Using firm eye contact, the doctor tried to make her patient engage. "What I am about to say is important." She paused and waited until the woman looked up. "You need to focus on the future. Explore what might work instead of dwelling on the past and what hasn't."

The woman looked curious and sputtered out an, "Okay."

"You have taken a step forward. It is a big step—a good step—but only the first. Your husband is agreeable but hesitant to join you. You feel that progress will stop and that frustrates you."

The patient nodded.

"His acceptance of a new path of discovery will be contingent on your approval. He will be looking for permission every step of the way. He will need reassurances."

The patient nodded again.

The doctor folded her hands on her lap. "Sexual energy is a divine, all-encompassing life force. It sleeps within us. It permeates our universe and affects everything from birth to death. As a sexual being, we can raise that energy. We can pull it up and use it to experience alternate or even mystical states of consciousness."

Dr. O had her patient's full attention.

"Your current sex life is leaving you unfulfilled and unsatisfied."

The woman nodded and shifted around in her chair.

"You came here to see me. You are choosing an unexplored path, which means this journey will not be mistake-free. It is not only normal, and expected, but also unavoidable, and necessary. Our understanding of sex comes from personal experience and acquired knowledge. We learn behavioral norms from social and religious rules of behavior. Those rules, society's views on sexuality, are constantly evolving. Like all change, sometimes it is painful. One has to growwith or without and sometimes in spite of what surrounds you. On your journey, if you want to pause or stop, stop. If you don't, then don't. What is most important is to continue to learn and experience. Like every other quest for knowledge; read, learn, seek advice but don't let anybody tell you what is right for you."

The doctor took a beat, then continued. "You want to have sex with your husband more often. You desire more originality, and more spontaneity. You want to try more sexual positions. You may want to introduce toys that might enhance your enjoyment. You even fantasize about role-playing. You have decided this is important. It's your choice. It is your path, your willingness to experiment, to expand your horizons."

The patient was nodding with eyes wide, her mouth slightly opened.

"Your husband has agreed, and accepted your invitation but only in theory. He is unprepared for the responsibility of his part. The position you have asked him to accept challenges him. You want him to begin precoital interaction, foreplay, and intercourse. You want him to be more masculine. You hope his understanding of your desires will bring you both greater satisfaction."

Dr. O paused, allowing her words to penetrate.

A few seconds went by. The woman, her head down said softly, "Right."

Dr. O was unsure if anything she said had hit home.

Then the patient raised her head, and boldly said, "I want him to nut up."

The doctor couldn't help a small smile.

The patient was thirty-five, although she seemed much older. She had her hair pulled straight back in a tight bun and wore very little makeup, not even lip-gloss.

Dr. O continued, "It is almost a hopeless task to undertake this journey without guidance. Even the most intuitive and romantic man will not be able to understand the psyche of a woman. Much as it is also true in reverse, of course. Men are as big a mystery to women."

Dr. O had lowered her tone from a doctor's directive, to that of a friend giving advice. "This situation is not your fault. It's also not his. It is a reflection of our society. You have had very little guidance for embarking on a sexual journey of discovery. Sexual experiences or fantasies often fall outside a narrow view of social tolerance. But remember you are the captain of this ship. He will follow if you lead. You must also remember that you can always question what you and your partner do, but never, why you are doing it."

The grimace on the patient's face returned, her eyes going back to the floor. She straightened her back, and her face grew tight with tension. A look of hopelessness was creeping across her face.

The doctor saw the hesitation to take on the responsibility. Her advice was not going to break the pattern.

"Have you heard of Tony Robbins?"

The patient's head turned like a terrier at a closed front door. "Ah, uh."

"Have you heard of the fire walk—walking on hot coals as a confidence builder?"

"No. Not exactly."

"It is an exercise about pushing through any and all limitations and becoming a new version of yourself."

"Okay, but what does that have to do with..."

Dr. O commanded, "Stand Up."

The woman reacted, sitting straight up in the chair.

"I said, Stand Up."

The woman stood immediately.

"—I—"

"Don't talk."

The patient stopped. She was looking down at the floor, but she remained standing almost at attention.

"Don't look down."

The woman's eyes came up.

Dr. O saw that they were blue, wide open, and were now sparkling.

"Take off your blouse."

The woman flushed a bright red. She reached for the top button as instructed, then hesitated.

Seeing her pause, the doctor commanded her again. "Take off your blouse."

The woman unbuttoned, leaving the blouse on and opened to her belly.

"Take it off," the doctor commanded.

The patient shrugged her shoulders, and the blouse fell to the floor, revealing a simple white bra. It fastened in the front with a clasp that had a small-embroidered red flower attached.

"Unhook your bra and take it off."

Again, the woman flinched.

"Now."

The woman unhinged the flower. Her breasts spilled out, freed from their confinement.

Dr. O was a little surprised at the unexpected beauty. "Turn around."

The woman turned and saw herself appear in a full-length mirror.

"Look at yourself."

The woman concentrated on the reflected image.

Dr. O stepped closer. Standing behind her, she looked over the patient's shoulder. Her face and her patient's face were inches away.

From down deep, the patient sighed. Her shoulders slacked with the release of tension.

Dr. O watched the woman gain confidence. Her tone changed back to that of a friend. "You are beautiful. You are attractive. You are desirable. You are woman."

The patient exhaled again—a long deep breath.

Dr. O raised her hand alongside the image in the mirror. "You desire to experiment. You want to become uninhibited. Your desire to release yourself is completely normal and productive. You want this for yourself and your husband. To not share your desires is destructive behavior. You cannot achieve that goal as a couple if you do not feel desirable. You must be a—human—sexual—being."

The patient's shoulders straightened.

"You want a man who is as confident as you are. He will need to step up to your responsiveness. You can help him fulfill his sexual life as well as yours, and bring you both to new levels of awareness."

The small smile returned to the patient's face.

Dr. O moved a half step right of her patient. She pointed at the image in the mirror. "Watch me looking at you."

When her patient complied, the doctor slowly looked up and down the woman's body. Dr. O then looked into the patient's eyes. "You watched me look at your body. It wasn't a doctor looking; it was a woman who was admiring your beautiful body."

The woman's cheeks flushed.

"Now look at yourself like I looked at you."

The patient's eyes went back to the mirror. She pulled her shoulders back and lifted her head with pride.

"Now, tell me. What do you see?"

The patient's voice cracked, "A beautiful..." her words trailed off. The woman shivered.

"Tell me, what do you see." The doctor was forceful but smiling.

The patient's eyes widened, her hands clenched, "I see...a...a... A BEAST!" The woman exploded with laughter and spun around and surprised her doctor with a huge bear hug.

"I am a BEAST." The patient pushed away but held onto the doctor's shoulders.

"Good for you." Dr. O. was a little uncomfortable in her grip, and disappointed in herself. She should have seen this reaction coming. She gently pulled away. Stepping back, she grabbed the bra with the red flower from the chair, and tossed it to her patient.

"I would suggest that you have some long, detailed conversations with your husband. I would also suggest both of you come next week."

"We'll be here." The patient hooked, and buttoned quickly.

"Good—good for you." The session was over. She glanced at her watch, 6:52. Two minutes over. She took her pen from the center desk drawer.

The patient turned, smiled, and waved goodbye.

The red flower on her bra clasp was peeking out above the unfastened button on her blouse

...ctor noticed her patient's departure from the 'button to the neck' look.

Make a note of that. Progress.

"Are you almost ready to go?" Loretta's voice ended her quiet moment.

"Almost, I need about five minutes."

"I'll call for the car."

Dr. O pushed the button, and the computer screen disappeared into the desk. She put a file in the drawer then walked to the window to close the blinds. She grasped the bottom of the stick in one hand, and began twirling with the other. She almost walked away. Instead, she turned and pinched back the blinds. She felt very uneasy.

She knew something was wrong.

It was just the darkness—just the night—

But maybe it was.

She shook off the thought.

There was movement everywhere, cars, buses, and people. She pushed the blinds opened a little further and looked out at the New York night and into the darkness.

She looked up from the street to the building across from hers. It was a mirror of her office building. It had black metal around long windows in half-lit offices like missing teeth in a giant mouth.

Something's wrong.

She spun the stick, shutting off her thoughts and closing the blinds to the night.

5

There were only a few unopened cardboard boxes. They held books Dr. O couldn't part with but had no home in her new loft.

Her West Village condo was spacious and expensive. She asked Lo to decorate every room but the bedroom. That sanctum belonged to Dr. O. She used soft pastels on the walls and multi-colored rugs on the floor. But they were hardly noticed. Floor-to-ceiling windows looking out over the Hudson River were breathtaking. Her bed faced the view, and the first thing she saw when she awoke was the river and the shore of the mainland United States—also known as Jersey.

It had been a long day. The calendar at the office had been full, but her business wasn't done. Staring into the mirror, she raised a brush to her hair, drawing the fine bristles down. Her hand was slow and steady. Something in her eyes made her stop. The window to the soul had a doubt.

She blinked it away and concentrated on her preparation.

Long thin silver earrings split the distance halfway from lobe to shoulder. Three bands of silver thread formed a choker around her neck.

Except for the jewelry, she sat naked in front of the mirror.

A red dress draped across her bed. It had spaghetti straps securing a plunging neckline. The open back dipped to centimeters above the crest of her bottom. Matching high-heeled shoes were side by side on the floor. Next to the dress was a pure white Mardi-Gras masquerade mask. The color of the feathers sprouting from the top matched the red on the mask's lips.

The mouth, sealed in silence, had no opening.

She was attending this masquerade party alone; unescorted would be a better description. Lo would be there as always—but not with her—watching her.

The Fat Tuesday party was a function of an exclusive private club. It was complete with the most exceptional food, flamboyant costumes, and very adult entertainment. The hedonism tonight would honor Hedone, the Greek goddess of pleasure.

The club had a single purpose and served a group of like-minded people. The members were demanding, and the club always met expectations. Most members of Club 423 were in mid-life. Those who bordered either side of the median group were very mature young-uns or very young oldies. Membership was expensive, but most members looked upon it as comparable to box seats on Broadway. The difference was that there was no curtain, and the show encouraged audience participation. The finest gourmet chefs catered to the events. The food was terrific, and of course, unlimited access to the finest libations from around the world. The entertainment, professional, and amateur, always fulfilled the price of admission.

*. was well run, tightly controlled, and extremely profitable. Doctor ~lned, referring her rich and famous friends and some of her clients. For service, she received two considerations. She and Lo were guests of the ι. ~ and she was able to 'prescribe' a one-time free pass for patients.

She placed the brush back on the ~ ¹~ stood, and walked to the four-poster bed.

Lo came into the bedroom from the great room. "Are you still going tonight?"

Dr. O turned around, unabashed.

Lo had taken a firm position on bailing on the evening's festivities, and over the past three hours, presented five different reasons why the doctor should pass.

"Yes, and for the last time, I'm going." She knew Lo's concerns were valid, but she believed observing her patients in a clinical environment important. She wasn't canceling just because Lo was worried about something that might not be real.

But giving up was not something that came naturally to her friend and bodyguard. "You don't have to do this. There could be dangerous situations that I can't always—"

"Yes, I know." The doctor cut her off in mid-warning. "You can't always be there to save the day." Dr. O wheeled around, picked up the dress, and slipped it on.

She adjusted a strap in the mirror. "MDs treat symptoms. Most often, treatment with correct medication is successful. Our patients have particular needs that prescriptions cannot address. When I recommend a healing path, I need to observe progress. Sometimes, I need to get into the ditches to use your vernacular."

"Trenches," corrected Lo.

"What?"

"Getting into the trenches, not ditches."

The doctor had reached her limit and dismissed the comment with a flick of her hand. "Loretta, I'm going."

Dr. O snatched up a roll of fashion tape and tore off a piece.

Lo pointed to a specific location on her breast. "Right here—near the nipple. Last time you used tape, you put it on too low, and everything was showing."

"Thank you." Dr. O placed the tape as advised by her well-meaning friend.

"I'll have the car in front at 1800." She turned to the door, her face reflecting defeat.

37

Dr. O calculated the military time conversion. "Better make it 1830. I don't want to be early, but I won't be staying long. I'll be in and out in one hour."

"Ah, uh. Sure, you will." Lo said this at the door because it listened better.

At the far end of the doctor's block, a four-door sedan was parked next to a hydrant. The Thin Man behind the wheel had smoked a half a pack of cigarettes. Waiting wasn't a problem for him. It was part of the job. What he did hate was pissing in a bottle.

A limo drove past and pulled to the curb in front of her house. The chauffeur got out and opened the back door. He leaned against the car and waited.

Thin Man shifted his weight in the driver's seat, anticipating movement. The man watching her office gave him no new information on their quarry. He had to use the Little Round Man, as he called him because he was free labor. His client also insisted, keeping the cost down. Good for them, bad for him. The Little Round Man was an amateur—and bonus—annoying.

Maybe she was going to meet his quarry tonight?

The front door opened, and the secretary came out, bounding down the stairs.

TAP...TAP...TAP.

The noise coming from the passenger side startled the Thin Man. He turned and looked but didn't see anything.

TAP...TAP...TAP.

A nightstick appeared on the rear passenger window. Holding the stick was a policeman. The cop had taken an excellent defensive position at the back window and was peering at him, squinting in the darkness.

Nothing suspicious. I look like I have a reason to be here. I am an Uber waiting on a fare.

The Thin Man nodded at the cop.

The cop waved his baton. "Move this car. You're on a hydrant."

He started the car but didn't put it in drive.

"Let's go. Move it."

The doctor came down the stairs and resolved his parking problem.

The secretary went around and jumped into the passenger side seat without looking down the street. She got in without checking her six. She was the bodyguard, a former MP.

Didn't even glance my way. That was sloppy, Marine.

The Thin Man rolled down the street and turned on the headlights after the limo made a left at the corner.

6

———

The deserted New York City street, wet after an evening shower, glimmered in the yellow glow of the streetlight. It resembled a scene from a French art-noir movie, black asphalt surrounded by up-scale antiques and art galleries. Above the stores were a few apartments, most of which were dark. Now long past closing, the picturesque streetscape had little traffic and was void of pedestrians.

The Doctor's car headlights momentarily disrupted the calm. The black Mercedes stretch limousine drove halfway down the block and stopped, and the driver opened the door. Quarry-cut stone steps led up to an enormous black wooden door. It was the only opening on the windowless first floor of the hundred-year-old former bank.

She extended her leg. It held a momentary pose, hesitating to touch the wet sidewalk as she gathered the hem of her red gown. A white glove reached down and took her hand. Feet planted, she waited as Lo, who had also jumped out of the limo, rang the doorbell.

A vintage light fixture glowed above the door. 423 was stenciled in black on a dome of white glass. It was the only light on a building half a block long and six stories high. Halfway up the edifice, a line of gargoyles peered down from the masonry scaring off evil spirits. Dr. O followed Lo up the steps. The door clicked and swung open. They walked past giant bodyguards, who could also scare evil to the curb.

They passed through a foyer, and as the Doctor entered the great hall, she placed the white mask over her face. She came through a high-arched opening into a long rectangular room. The exact height of the room was hard to determine; the ceiling disappeared into black shadows. Soft yellow light from wall sconces accented crimson red walls. There were high-backed couches and chairs placed around the room. Multi-colored Persian rugs added color, and the air smelled of jasmine.

A waiter wearing a white long-tailed jacket arrived almost instantly with a tray containing chilled flutes of fine champagne.

People mingled in small groups. They were chatting, laughing, drinking—all had darting eyes. Everyone fantasizing.

He came at the Doctor at a half run from across the room.

Felix Upton Grant wasn't wearing a mask— hiding wasn't his thing. He wore a silver-sequined jacket, matching pants, and a huge smile.

Her very good friend was a silver tank standing six foot three and weighing more than 250 pounds. Two fire hydrant-sized legs supported a triangular torso. On square shoulders was a head of short, spiked white hair. Multi-colored tattoos protruded from the neckline of his shirt and from the cuff of the be-speckled jacket. He had resisted face ink, though the temptation was strong. He tweaked that rule to include fine lines of a cobweb. The ink threads extended from his shoulder up the back of his neck to his left ear. His arms had no boundaries. Tats continued out from under his sleeves, the right arm featuring the green head of an Iguana. Its long red tongue tipped the end of his middle finger.

She could not help but smile and reached up for a kiss.

"Darling...where have you been? I've been holding back the

troops so you wouldn't miss the show." Felix mimed, pushing back an imaginary crowd.

He was loud and proud.

She smiled. "Did my guest arrive?"

"Yes, she did—and I might add—she dressed very well for a newbie. You saw to that. I could tell."

"Fel—"

He interrupted her before she could finish. "And..." He dropped to a lower tone. "You were right about her. She looked very nervous. She looked like she might bolt, but I followed your instructions, and I guided her to Gia." He flicked his wrist and pointed the tongue finger. "They are having drinks over there."

"Thank you, Felix. You're a dear."

She reached up, and pulling him closer, kissed him on the cheek.

He smiled, stepped back, and bringing his hands together in a Yoga prayer pose, bowed. A big man with glowing red cheeks from one small kiss was a little comical.

She had not noticed the back of his hand before, a bald eagle on a black chevron. She knew he had served, but had forgotten he was Airborne.

He spoke softly with reverence. "At your service, my very, very, lovely lady." A twinkle came to his eye. "By the way, you look fabulous." Then—he was gone disappearing into a crowd of costumes.

Dr. O sipped her champagne as she walked across the room to observe her patient.

Lo, also in costume, followed behind her charge at a distance. Black leather pants, a matching sleeveless vest, and a featherless black mask completed her don't-hit-on-me look.

The Doctor looked for and found the two women. They were oblivious to their surroundings—fingers touching, hair tossing, laughing. Flirting.

Her patient was a recently divorced mother of two. She was a suburban housewife, drove an SUV, and was the definition of the term soccer mom. She also had never been heterosexual. She was the product of an affluent suburban, relatively happy family. After college, she married a boy she had known from grade school. She had a model home lifestyle, and everything she ever wanted, right up to when she didn't. She drifted into depression, self-medicating with alcohol. Then she read *RELEASE THE BEAST*. She made an appointment, and Dr. O became her mentor in recovery, her sanity, and her future.

The woman with her client was the stimulator. Gia was a hostess at the club, and her job was to inspire the members. She was a sexual muse. She liked this job, and she was a skillful employee.

Gia's daytime job was trying to make it as a professional dancer. She had stage presence and possessed tremendous stage confidence. She was good, but not quite good enough to be the lead—yet. She maintained hope that the next audition would be her big break, and her job at the club made that dream possible. Felix was an excellent boss, and she was paid very, very well.

The Doctor found her to be a very interesting +3 on her mental health scale. In observing her over the past couple of years, the job did not appear to be a stretch of Gia's morality or principles. She exhibited no sexual inhibitions, none, ever. She loved men and women. She seemed to have no prejudice against race, or weight, or age. Her participation only required kindness of spirit and respect for others.

Gia possessed another gift from life's genetic spinning wheel. She was beautiful. She told Dr. O that her mother was French and Indonesian; her father, African American and Irish. The blended ancestry had produced a statuesque beauty that grew up with a global personality and a dancer's grace.

A hairy-chested employee wearing brightly patterned tights shuffled a newbie couple to a group near the bar. Another employee carried goblets of champagne on a silver tray. Her costume was matching silver high heels, G-string, and strapping around her breasts. On her head, in keeping with Mardi Gras, she wore a tri-colored crown hat. Wherever she stopped, she accepted adoring caresses with a huge smile.

The Doctor also noticed three couples standing near the Doctor's patient and Gia. The women wore black cat masks with pointy ears—cattails dragged behind their skintight bodysuits. The men had made little effort adding only Lone Ranger masks to black suits.

The six stood in a tight group, talking, but their attention was directed toward Gia. Their conversation accented with smirks and pointed fingers.

Dr. O looked for and then found Lo in the corner opposite the grouping. She nodded sideways, directing Lo to move closer to her patient and Gia.

The music that had been in the background lowered.

"Ladies and Gentlemen." A voice low and clear came over a speaker system that was, like everything else, perfect.

The announcer waited as the crowd's collective voice lowered to a murmur of anticipation.

The baritone announcer continued, "We have an extraordinary treat for you
tonight."

The lights dimmed.

A single spotlight suddenly lit the center of the room. A piano and a bass began to play a New Orleans Jazz backbeat.

"Now for your viewing pleasures. Here tonight...direct from Amsterdam's most infamous nightclub—The Moulin Rouge. We are proud to present...three acts that will amaze and astound."

A short round of applause came from the crowd who closed in on the light.

"Our first act is the world-famous ensemble, The Body. Following them will be Vivaca, who will perform the legendary audience participation, Banana Game. Our feature performance tonight will be a one-act play. In the starring roles are Alicia, as the maiden, and Gigantis, as the marauder. But first, ladies and gentlemen, from The Moulin Rouge, Club 423 is proud to present... *The Body.*"

The single light on the floor became eight bright concentric circles. A body appeared in the center of each, four men and four women.

The bodies stood as still as statues. Slowly, as the music rose, they began moving. Bodies began executing powerful combinations of dance and gymnastic movements. Each moved in their own circles of light, but then they broke the circular barriers of the spotlights. Eight became one. Moving together, they touched, then grasped, then embraced, and then entangled. They became a single body of torsos and arms and hair and hands. Choreographic perfection sent an individual body's ripple of energy from one side of the mass to the other.

The crowd was dead silent. Eyes were moving in unison as the dancers progressed through their routine. The energy from the stage reached into the audience stimulating every cell and every id.

The Doctor was struggling with the lights. She lost sight of her patient. She also couldn't see Lo. The program was short, lasting less than ten minutes, but as time passed, her anxiety rose.

The single circle of light turned back to eight. The bodies separated and returned to their spotlights. The music died; seconds later, the soft lights rose in the room. The dancers were gone.

Applause rose, as did the lights.

The background music resumed. Several employees with fresh trays of refreshments began circulating.

The Doctor looked over to where she last saw her patient. The three felines were walking towards the stairs without their husbands —and without their mouse. Doctor O saw her patient and Gia had moved to a couch near the back wall. It had a high back, big pillows, and a false sense of privacy.

Gia was nuzzling the soccer mom's neck and had her hand halfway up her thigh.

Her patient had her back pushed into the couch, her head laid back, eyes staring at the ceiling. Her face was alight with pleasure.

The Doctor scanned the room again, and Lo was missing in action.

"Hey baby, wanna fuck?"

The husbands of the three felines had descended on the Doctor. They had drinks in hand and attitude abundant.

"No, thank you." She did not look at them.

"Hear that boys? This one is playing hard to fuck," the fatter man said with a drunken laugh.

The taller man chimed in. "What a MILF. Look at those tits. Wow."

The last man in line was trying hard to match his buddy's vulgarity. "I'll bet she could suck the chrome off a bumper."

"Boys, boys, boys." Felix's voice came from behind. "This lady has entertained your attractive offer and declined. I would suggest you move along."

The fatter man looked at Felix with rich-man arrogance and without fear. His two buddies fell in line behind him.

Felix responded to the look with a steely-eyed stare. "You won't like it if you forfeit your membership fee. I believe its about thirty-k."

He gripped the first man on the shoulder and squeezed. "You are all new members, so this time I will caution you not to press your luck. Now do what I ask, move along."

The backup husband looked at his leader, who had turned and walked away. He ducked his head and followed.

"Where is your Lo?" Felix looked around, concerned.

"I don't know. Usually, she's first in line for any trouble."

"I saw her before the show. She was making sure your patient had privacy."

Just then, Lo appeared, breathless, "Sorry, I was—"

"No worries. Felix came to the rescue, no problem."

"I...had to use the ladies."

"Forget it. Please, both of you get back to business. I'm kind of working here." She nodded toward the couch in the corner.

Lo went back across the room, and Felix magically disappeared, again.

Gia was now holding her patient's hand and leading her to a chair that had a small drapery surrounding three sides.

The Doctor followed them, walking to a corner of the room where she could watch unobserved.

Standing in front of the patient, Gia began to remove her top. Soon the dancer wore only the thin G string. She began a slow, rhythmic lap dance. Her legs moved against the patient's thighs. Up— then down—then releasing the pressure completely. The patient was moaning, and her head was flying back and forth with pleasure.

Gia stepped back, legs spread, her hands on her hips, her eyes challenging the patient.

The woman was now staring up at Gia—her eyes wide open.

Gia put her thumbs in the little strings and began to peel off her G-string.

The patient exhaled loudly. She shot both her arms forward. Her hands reached out and gripped Gia's bottom. She pulled the dancer to her, and the patient plunged her face into a place she had only dreamed about.

"Look at this, will you, Billy? This one tells me she doesn't want to fuck, and here she is watching two dykes getting it on."

Two of the husbands were back.

"I told you no." Her head swiveled around looking for Lo. "And in here... at this club...that means something."

"Not to me," said the fatter man, calmly. He reached out and grabbed her by the hair. "Come on, baby, let's go upstairs and party."

The Doctor spun and slapped his face hard.

He stepped back. His face was red from the slap and anger.

His face contorted then he slapped her. Hard. The impact spun her around, and she fell backwards into his buddy.

47

The buddy laughed loudly and gripped her breasts from behind. "These are really great tits."

Lo threw an overhand right cross that instantly re-assembled his face, interrupting his moment of joy.

Blood poured from his nose.

Several screams came from onlookers.

Lo had her attention on the man on the floor, making sure he wasn't getting up.

The fatter man froze for an instant then did something that surprised the Doctor and caught Lo off guard. He retrieved a five-inch long serrated cheese knife from a plate nearby.

He brought his arm high in the air. It paused for a second then plunged down toward Dr. O's face.

Lo took a step and dove. She caught the blade's downward thrust with her open hand. The blade went completely through her palm, the hilt flush against her flesh.

She had stopped the attack.

Her knees buckled, and she started to fall. As she went down, she delivered a roundhouse punch to the attacker's stomach.

The force of her punch caused his cheeks to expand, and his fat lips to pucker as the air left his lungs. The pain made his grip on the knife tighten. His legs went to rubber, and he started to fall. The blade ripped the flesh of Lo's hand from side to side.

The third husband, wearing only boxer shorts and colored clown shoes, watched from a distance. He, by association, was guilty and got upended, his feet flying, by a charging silver bull.

"Are you okay, darling?" Felix was frantic.

"I'm fine. I'm fine. Please, take care of Lo...Please!"

"An ambulance is already on the way."

Felix tried to recover his composure—and almost did. He stood, hands-on-hips; face still flushed with anger. He took a breath then kicked the attacker in the nuts.

The man on the floor screamed in pain.

"Nobody is coming for you shithead. Crawl if you must...but...get out. And I do mean now."

He looked over at the man holding his nose—took another breath —then kicked him in the nuts.

His scream was louder.

Felix was a little less angry.

The fatter man had gotten up on all fours.

"Take this pile of shit with you, Fucknuts."

Felix then looked hard at the third husband who had righted himself.

He didn't stop to help his downed friends. He turned and ran for the door.

Lo was sitting up, holding a bar towel full of ice on her hand. The knife wound was so long and wide that the knife fell out onto the floor.

Felix bent down and took over first aid. He wrapped the wound tight and pressed hard above her wrist. Stopping the blood flow was the number one priority.

Lo could see the blood continuing to seep through the cloth and shook her head.

Dr. O sat next to her friend, amazed her Marine wasn't reacting to the injury. Lo's blood had turned her red satin dress brown.

"I'm pretty fucked up, Doc. You're going to need a new hand for a while." Lo smiled weakly at her inadvertent joke.

Dr. O shook her head, dismissing that concern. "Don't think about anything now. We'll work this out. This is not a problem."

Felix elevated Lo's hand. He was quiet for a moment, in deep thought. He looked at Lo, then the Doctor. "I got somebody."

"I said, we don't need any help. We will get along fine."

"Who?" Lo was not listening to her boss.

"A guy I served with. His name is Smoke. He's very, very good."

"Served?" Lo had a momentary lapse of memory.

Felix flipped his hand over, showing her the Airborne tattoo.

"He saved my ass twice, once in Iraq, and once in Afghanistan."

"Sorry," she said, embarrassed, and then added with reverence, "I forgot you served."

"A Lesbian Marine dissing an Airborne Queen. Shame, shame, shame." He smiled then looked at Dr. O. "No worries, Doc. I'll have him here in forty-eight hours."

She began to protest again. "I told you I do not need—"

"He's exactly what you need." Felix overruled her objection. He got up and watched two of his doormen helping the husbands out —hard.

He then lowered his voice and said to himself, "And you're exactly what he needs."

Thin Man sat in a Lincoln with blackout windows. He watched as the ambulance arrived and the EMTs rushed up the steps of number 423.

He had watched three men bounced out of the building by men in tuxedos. Their shirts were half-buttoned, and only one was wearing shoes. Of the three, one was holding his face in the air with a towel over it. Another was also holding a bag between his legs and limping. The last man had no pants but had on what looked like clown shoes.

Walking behind them were three women who had cattails dragging on the ground. They were shouting at each other, and at the men, they were following down the street.

The EMTs then left with the secretary on a gurney. She was sitting up but in obvious pain.

The Doctor came out at the same time and looked completely out of sorts. A man in a suit of sequins put her into the limo and then jumped in beside her. The limo followed the ambulance.

He was a little confused at this extreme departure from the usual routine. But he had a hunch whatever had happened in there would work in his favor. If the secretary were out of commission, the Doctor would change her day-to-day schedule. That might present different opportunities. It might be easier to extract the object of their surveillance when he showed up.

He drew the last drag on his cigarette and flicked it out the window.

The evening's activities were over.

There would be no contact tonight.

Thin Man started the car, put it in gear, and drove down the dark street back into the shadows.

7

The Italian Market in Philadelphia is an anachronism—it is the past and the present, a megastore, and a neighborhood shop.

Every day at dawn, vendors offer the best fruits, vegetables, meat, and fish available. Loops of sausage lay in shop windows of hundred-year-old stores. Suckling pigs, ducks, and chickens hang from butcher's hooks. One can handpick the reddest tomatoes, hottest peppers, and juiciest oranges. Cheese that defies imitation is displayed just inside shop doors. Anything needed, in any recipe, is available on Ninth Street in South Philadelphia.

The Market survives, in part, because it's a neighborhood. South Philadelphia is work and home for its evolving family. It has a rich history and definitive rules. Today, there is more diversity than in the original godfather era, but its atmosphere still harkens back to the Capo's who set the tone for protecting its own.

Smoke got off the Broad Street bus and walked eight blocks east to 9th Street. His destination was the oldest family-owned restaurant in America. Ralph's Italian Restaurant was his favorite, and it was a place where he had friends.

Today he was to meet Bonni McKee, Esq. She was his sometimes employer and, at least in her mind, more than a friend.

He was still undecided.

"How yous doin'?" JP greeted Smoke from behind his podium.

"How yous doin'?" Jimmy in the back?"

"Nah. The boss won't be in till six."

"Tell him I said hey."

"Absolutely." The wall phone rang. "Ralph's." JP pointed.

"I see her. Thanks, JP."

JP had seated Bonni at a table in the corner, on the back wall. He kept the surrounding tables open for their privacy.

"It's about fucking time." She looked at her watch. "If I don't get something to eat quickly, somebody's going to get hurt."

Smoke looked up at Ben, a waiter who was passing by with a full tray. Smoke nodded; her urgency silently communicated.

"Why do you always take the bus down here? Also, why won't you meet me downtown? My office is there, and I have to take a cab and—" She stopped, her objections falling on deaf ears.

He allowed a calming second or two to pass. "How you doing, McKee?"

"Fine."

"You're buying, right?"

"Of course."

"It's cash only." He quickly held up his hand to stall her attack. "I'm just reminding you."

She almost got angry. The expression indicated that her wheels were turning.

"Right, I did forget. Thanks." She started to reach into her purse, then stopped. "No...its okay. I got it." She sighed relief; crisis averted. She stared at him, regaining control of the narrative.

He didn't say anything.

The bread arrived.

She hit it hard.

He wanted some but dared not reach. "What's with you?" He pointed to her heavily buttered roll.

"Yeah, well, I'm hungry, okay? Actually, my hunger relates to why you're here."

"Okay?" His brows wrinkled.

Ben arrived to take their order. "Ready?"

She responded immediately. "Mussels red, chicken cacciatore, side of spaghetti, a house salad."

Smoke did not need a menu. "Usual."

"Veal Picante, side of spaghetti." Ben didn't need paper.

The second basket of bread was disappearing. "Jesus, McKee, when did you eat last?"

"Okay, enough. I'll explain it." She pushed the bread away. "A few weeks ago, I finished up a case that was a real butt-kicker. It started okay. Big retainer. But I was working a hundred hours plus a week, and it wore me out. I got the verdict on a Friday morning, and that afternoon I booked a flight. The next day, I was on a plane to Costa Rica. I went to a Yoga retreat for a detox and cleanse."

It was involuntary. Smoke's face momentarily reacted to detox and cleansing. The nanosecond after he flinched, he regretted it.

"Oh, you don't like clean living? Are you judging me and my life choices?"

He lifted one hand and made a calming gesture.

Damn, another mistake.

It immediately made her madder. She looked up, saw the other customers looking over, and must have remembered why she was there. Instead of pursuing his lack of appreciation, she just stared daggers at him.

"How did it come out?" he asked, trying to repair the moment.

"What...how did what come out?"

"The case?"

She cocked her head and gave him a well-that's-a-stupid-question look.

"Of course, you won." His voice trailed off.

He had faced enemies in combat who were trying to kill him all day, every day. He was careful but not afraid. Bonni McKee made him nervous, and he was slightly scared of her. He might do okay head-to-head on a battlefield, but in court, defeat was a certainty.

She cocked her head and started again.

He noticed the dimple in her cheek.

Very nice.

"I booked into a retreat called Shambhala. The name means a peaceful place." She paused a moment, eyes searching the ceiling for the right description. "It was off the grid, no phone, no Internet, no TV. Nothing."

"Okaaaay, and why are you telling me this?"

"There is a point. Wait for it." She started in again. "I was there for meditation, yoga, and a cleanse. A cleanse is an all-liquid diet. That, combined with some other things, cleanse the digestive system."

Smoke mulled a second, then said, "I know enough not to ask what 'other things' are."

The mussels arrived.

She sneered at him while grabbing three mussels. "I was five days without solid food. I guess I've been catching up since then."

"Right, that explains the feeding frenzy. Now, please tell me why I am here."

"There is a woman who works there, a native Costa Rican. She administered the enemas—."

Smoke reacted to TMI.

She rephrased. "I mean...we became close."

"I'll bet." Smoke smirked.

"Moving on." She returned the smirk. "One day, she asked me where I lived. I said Philadelphia, and she immediately broke out crying. I mean like, hysterical crying. She told me she had a daughter named Valentina, who worked with her at the retreat. She said about a year ago, a woman from Philadelphia was a guest. The woman became friendly with her and her daughter."

Smoke nodded.

She ate the last mussel.

"At the end of the woman's stay, she offered Valentina a job as a domestic. If her daughter performed, they would sponsor citizenship for mother and daughter."

Lunch arrived.

"Luciana said she, very reluctantly, approved. She felt the opportunity was just too great to pass up. It started well enough. Luciana received a letter from her daughter every week. Luciana didn't have access to a phone." Bonni was eating and talking.

"Six months ago, Valentina's letters suddenly stopped. The mother's letters came back stamped *Addressee Unknown*. She sent letters to the woman in Philadelphia and got no response. She has tried the police in Costa Rica, but they say they have no jurisdiction."

"What do you want from me?"

She gave him the 'I'm not done look.' At that moment, he suddenly realized he knew quite a few of her looks.

"I got into it as soon as I returned. The woman is—THE—Mrs. Roberta Howard of Bryn Mawr. Her husband, Dwight, is the owner of a chain of discount tire stores and a concrete business. His big money came from partnering real estate with some Philadelphia upper-enders. They own one of the old mansions up on the Main Line. It has everything, a million rooms, a pool, and servant's quarters."

He said goodbye to the last bite of Picante and signaled Ben for more coffee.

"I checked around my firm to see if anyone knew him. Fortunately, one of the partners represents one of the husband's partners in an industrial park. He told me Mr. Howard was smart, rich, and lived large. He also said he was a lowlife. Howard pushed people around and did what he wanted whenever he wanted. The thing was though—he was cautious—he pushed hard but only against those who couldn't push back. He was careful not to piss off the wrong people."

She ate her last bite of cacciatore with the last spin of spaghetti. "The partner said he was a rainmaker in land deals, and he made them money, so they put up with him."

She changed the tone of her voice, then the look in her eyes.

"There was a rumor he bought off a couple of women who worked at the tire stores who had alleged sexual assault. The partner also indicated there was a squashed rape complaint."

She looked down at the empty coffee cup. Magically, it became full.

"With all that background, I called the Howard house, and to my surprise got the Mrs. Howard on the phone. I asked if I could make an appointment to talk about the whereabouts of Valentina. She said it was not convenient. I asked when it would be convenient, and she said it wasn't necessary. She said Valentina ran off, and she had no idea where she went."

Bonni leaned over the table. "I asked if they filed a police report. Now get this—she said, 'of course not and besides, you know how those people are, she probably ran off with the gardener.' Naturally, I had to come back—so I said—'So the gardener is missing too?' She started screaming at me, saying she meant some gardener, not her gardener."

Bonni leaned back. "I had broken her down, and she was off-script, but she didn't hang up. Everything else Mrs. Howard said to that point seemed rehearsed."

He could tell Bonni was a little disappointed that he had no visible reaction to her brilliant cross-examination.

"I didn't let up and pressed on. I asked if Valentina took her belongings with her when she left? She seemed confused and said she didn't take her belongings. That was a big mistake, and the Mrs. knew it. She began stuttering and stammering. Finally, trying to recover, she said the stuff Valentina left was a worthless pile of junk."

Smoke knew that was terrible news for Valentina.

"I jumped on it. I said great, and I would drive there immediately to examine what Valentina left behind. I said that maybe there was a clue to where she went."

Bonni tilted her head again and pointed her finger at him, "She said not to come there because she threw it all out."

"Hmmm."

"There's more." Bonni added facts to her case.

He waited for the worst.

"He's dead."

"Who's dead?"

"The husband. Mr. Howard. Corpus delicti."

He pushed his chair back and put his hands behind his head.

"Died of a massive heart attack six weeks ago."

She paused after divesting the last of her information.

Smoke looked down. He now knew why she wanted to meet. He took a sip of coffee and computed the possibilities.

She watched him and waited.

"It is obvious that something horrible happened to this girl. It is also obvious that you suspect the husband in her disappearance. You also suspect that Mrs. Howard knows what happened. However, the trail is as cold as the husband. Which means finding out what happened to the girl—"

"Valentina." McKee corrected.

Smoke, undaunted by the interruption, continued. "Which means finding out what happened to—Valentina—is almost impossible. None of her possessions exist; there is no evidence of a boyfriend; there are no relatives in the States; so, there is no place to run to. Also, there is no forensics because there is no crime scene; there are no witnesses and no circumstantial evidence. Not to mention—there is no motive."

"Apparent—no apparent motive," she again corrected his summary of the facts.

"Right, no apparent motive."

"Okay. You got it." McKee dropped her spoon like a rock star drops a mike. "Check, please."

"Wait...What?" He was genuinely surprised.

"What, what?"

He extended both hands, stopping her from standing. "What do you want from me?"

"You know exactly what I want. Find out what happened to Valentina."

He was stunned.

She began to fumble for her wallet.

"No."

She stood up and shook her finger in his face. "Don't say no to me when I say yes to you."

She smiled, and flicked his chin with a painted nail.

"Just how am I supposed to do that?"

"You know. Do that private investigator stuff you do so well."

He pushed back in his chair, exasperated. "I am not a licensed investigator."

"Why do you keep saying that? Every time I ask you to do something, you say the same thing. I keep telling you that it doesn't matter. I've always paid you as a consultant, not an investigator. However, now that you mention it."

"Wait. We didn't talk fee yet."

She lowered her head, pretending to search for her wallet. "I had to open a file on this. That is the firm's policy, even if it's pro bono. It is also an office policy not to hire consultants on freebies."

She started tapping her foot. "Stop fucking whining...and, yes, this one is on the cuff." She broke character for a second. "This girl needs you, Smoke."

"Ah, uh." His shoulders dropped, defeated.

"I can expense three dinners and three lunches."

Without any options, he nodded acceptance.

She pulled some money from her wallet and, while counting, said,

"Oh—one more thing. I think I can give you a place to start. When the husband was alive, they attended St. Marks Roman Catholic Church every Sunday. Their financials itemized sizable donations for the building fund, feed the poor, the usual. However, something has changed. Since his funeral, the wife has been going to church three times a week, ...and...this is the head-scratcher part...she doesn't go to St. Marks. She goes four or five times to one church then switches to another."

McKee dropped a pile of bills that included a healthy tip on the table. "Bye. Bye. Call me when you get something."

She stopped, leaned over the table, and patted his cheek. "Another time, another place." She spun on her heels. The meeting was over.

He finished his coffee, said goodbye to JP, and followed her footsteps into the bright afternoon light.

Just as he hit the sidewalk, his phone rang. It was Felix again. He'd been ducking his calls, but it was Felix. He couldn't hide forever. "What's up?"

"I need you up here, buddy."

"In New York? What for?"

"Someone needs protection."

"Come on, Felix. You know I'm too old for that shit. I'm not that guy anymore."

"This is not straight bodyguard stuff. I know a ton of man-meat that could scare the red off the Devil, but what I need is that crazy instinct of yours."

Smoke stopped walking and leaned against a brick wall. He could use a paycheck. "What's the job?"

"A friend, I love, needs help. Her bodyguard is out of commission, and I need you to look after her."

"Her?"

"Don't be a dick."

"I'm not a dick—I'm curious. What woman do you love?"

"Have you heard of Doctor O?"

"Doctor who?"

"She's a famous doctor and author. Google her. You know what Google is?"

"Google is a close personal friend of mine."

"Seriously, Smoke, I know something is going on, and I'm not sure what it is. Something or someone has her scared. She won't talk about it or acknowledge it. I'm asking you—please—will you help me help her?"

He couldn't say no to Felix.

"When?"

"Now."

"I can't now. I just took something on."

Felix barked loud. "Hey—I need—"

"Two days. The best I can do is about two days."

There was silence while Felix considered his options.

Smoke broke first. "Can you handle security for now?"

"Yes, I guess. I have a few people, but they will only be reactionary. They won't see it coming till it does."

"Understood."

Felix had to ask. "Is what you're doing related to...I mean, is it part of... I mean, is it related to what happened?"

There was an extended silence, and Felix left his question unanswered. "Okay then, two days, right?"

"Two days—probably."

Smoke pushed the button and ended the call. He had few friends, and treated them all the same, badly. His friends understood why, even if he didn't.

He started walking again.

He took long steps.

He wanted to get where he was going fast.

He just didn't know why.

8

L o had her elbow propped up on the desk. White plaster immobilized her hand from her elbow to the second joint of her fingers. Adding pain to her jazz hand were eight chrome pins. They stuck out from the cast at odd angles and secured steel wires to each finger. Silver threads enabled the surgical repairs to take hold. She angled the cast and the antenna array to twelve o'clock. Her theory was the position would reduce swelling or get a better Internet signal.

She soon found recovering at her apartment was not an option. She was alone; trying to manage using one hand, figuring out a remote control from hell and, of course, there was the pain. She also became convinced that daytime talk shows were one of the leading causes of mass shootings. The Sergeant could have dealt with adversity, but Lo was struggling with her broken heart. Dorothy left her four months ago, and everything in the apartment brought back the memory of their good times together. Three days was all she could take. Bored to distraction, she needed action and work.

Surgery repaired most of the damage, and the prognosis was optimistic, with reservations. The surgeon said with rehab she would recover 75 percent mobility. He also told her not to strain the injury by doing something stupid like going back to work.

Giving Doctor O only the semi-good news, she talked her way back, pleading boredom and the likelihood of falling victim to the mass-shooting thing. She had made it through her first day without an incident but in the waning hours had banged the cast twice. Both times the eyes of the lean, mean former Marine welled up in pain.

Lo pushed the intercom button. "Ms. Johansson will be here in five. Do you need anything—coffee?"

"No, no, Lo, thank you. How are you making out?"

"I'm fine. No problem."

"Okay, when she arrives, let her sit a while. The new ones always come in charged up. Tell her where the coffee is, but, please do not get up and get it for her."

"Of course. Sure thing." Lo stayed in Holly Golightly character, which was almost as painful as her hand. She reached over and pressed the off button on the intercom, tilting her cast as she leaned over. The ends of the pins hit the metal lampshade.

"Motherfucker." She shrieked in pain.

The patient opened the door at that exact moment. "Oh, wow. Are you okay?"

Lo looked up and responded through a clenched jaw. "Yes. No—I mean yes, I'm fine." She forced the I'm-fine look onto her face. "Have a seat. The doctor will be right with you."

The woman pointed to the cast as she walked to the couch. "Actually, motherfucker would have been the only thing that would have worked for me."

Märta Johansson picked up an issue of Psychology Today from a black walnut coffee table. She looked around the office and smiled. "I like the interior. Who did the design?"

"Me." Lo pushed back in her pride chair. "Dr. O calls this Comfortable Clinic."

"Catchy." Märta continued to survey the room. "I like the art."

"The bronze by her door is Hans Retzbach's "*Male Nude*." Those two paintings are Paul Gauguin's *Two Tahitian Women* and Mary Cassatt's *The Long Gloves*."

The patient pointed to the most significant painting. "I really like her."

"That is Edouard Manet's *Olympia*. It's great, isn't it? It reminds me of the *Mona Lisa*. The expression on her face...you know...like, what is she thinking?"

"Yes, I see what you're saying."

"I look at it as if it were a scene in a movie. I see a beautiful woman with a flower in her hair and a black ribbon around her neck lying naked on pure white sheets surrounded by pillows. She is lifting herself up from the bed with one arm. Her head is up, and she looks as if someone just walked into her room. But instead of surprise or embarrassment, she seems relaxed. She makes no effort to cover herself. Her expression is not of surprise or embarrassment. Is it self-confidence, or perhaps defiance or maybe pride? I can't figure it out."

"That is a powerful painting."

"An art buff told me the model was almost certainly a prostitute. He said in Manet's time, only ladies of the evening wore ribbons around their necks."

"No, kidding? A prostitute? Really...no way."

"Right. That's my thought as well. But being sensitive to having a painting of a hooker hanging in the office, I asked Dr. O if I should replace it. She said the *Olympia* represented a woman who would be very comfortable in today's world and would be welcome in this office."

Märta Johansson nodded then went back to the magazine, her expression changing from curious to uneasy. She shifted her weight in the chair, then crossed her legs. The patient kept knees tight, and the gap between bare skin and the fabric of her skirt to a minimum. She wore a quality navy blue business suit. The only departure from the business work apparel was a periwinkle blue silk blouse.

Lo was struggling, trying to update the doctor's calendar with one hand. She decided to curse under her breath instead of shooting something. A small red light on the desk near the phone blinked twice.

"Ms. Johansson, you may go in now."

The patient rose, smoothed her skirt, and placed the magazine back exactly where it was on the table. She walked over, stood in front of the door, inhaled, and walked in.

"I find dimmer lights more conducive to conversation." Dr. O was seated in one of the two chairs in the center of the room. She gestured to the armchair opposite her. "Please, get comfortable."

Märta blinked her eyes, adjusting to the dimmer light. "Thank you. I read your book...twice in fact. I enjoyed it immensely, but I'm sure you don't need me to tell you that." Her voice trailed off.

The doctor shook her head, "No. No—thank you. I'm very pleased you liked it—twice."

"I appreciate that you found time for me. I completely understand that you're not taking new patients, and I am very grateful for this appointment."

"Not a problem. Professor Lloyd referred you, yes?"

The patient nodded.

"I first met him at a conference at the University of Texas. I have called on him several times for opinions over the years, and I'm happy to reciprocate. Shall we begin?"

"Yes, please."

The doctor paused then began the session. "First, do you have any questions for me?"

"Actually, I do." The patient shifted into work mode and began a checklist. "Your book deals with sexual awareness and growth. I appreciate that...believe me...I do...but I have a more serious problem than having more or better orgasms."

The doctor listened without expression.

"Professor Lloyd told me you could help me with my issue."

"I hope that you will find that to be true."

"I have a unique situation, and I am wondering if you might tell me about your experience. Your credentials are impressive, but I want to be sure I'm doing the right thing before I open the door to my private life."

"Of course. You know me because of the book, but it was kind of a fluke, to be honest. I started to write a textbook as a diversion from my daily routine. The expansion of one's sexual awareness was not the primary focus of my practice. I began as a clinical forensic psychologist for the FBI. I am private practice now, and I still work with State and Federal Law Enforcement profiling and testifying as an expert witness."

The patient was listening carefully.

"It was difficult to deal with extreme psychological disorders every day. I need positivity in my life as you do in yours. So, I began to write a book about the positive side of the balance scale."

"Balance scale?"

"Yes. Let's say that everyone's mental health is measured on a scale from minus five to plus five. Assume qualities like emotion, sexuality, ambition, love, even physical and mental capability contribute to our mental health. We acquire these abilities through genetics, education, and socio-economic background. These qualities are fluid and can grow or diminish. Therefore, a person with minus five personality disorder could easily murder and a plus five would run into a burning building to save a stranger's life. Okay so far?"

"Yes...completely."

"Professionals in psychology spend ninety percent of their efforts dealing with the people who are on the minus side of the zero. However, the plus side of the scale needs the same attention. This is not a new thought. Immanuel Kant, Ponty, John Russin, these philosophers dealt with the interpersonal process. It embeds meaning into our most basic functions: eating, sleeping, sex, and so on. Some work on the plus side of zero today, Tony Robbins, Wayne Dyer, Brene' Brown, and Simone de Beauvoir to name a few. There are too many snake charmers preying on the people's vanity, and they have too much influence on the most vulnerable segment of our society."

The patient's expression went from thoughtful to a smile. "Yes, I get that. Actually, I'm surprised I haven't heard it said like that before."

"I have been working on expanding my practice. Previously my practice dealt with the minus side. The book has attracted plus-sided patients, and I'm very grateful."

The patient shifted a little. She was getting antsy.

"You look a little uncomfortable. Would you like me to hang up your jacket?"

The patient smiled again. "Yes, thank you."

"So...Märta, are we good to move forward?"

The patient's expression changed. She re-engaged.

"Yes."

"Good. Please, relax and go at your own speed."

The patient blurted out, "I'm in trouble, and I don't know what to do."

"Why don't you start from the beginning?"

Märta raised a hand and smoothed a loose hair back into place. The forty-something patient had braided blond hair pulled back into a tight bun. It appeared that her hair was very long.

Raising her head, she said suddenly in a loud voice, "I'm a submissive."

Dr. O didn't blink.

"I have to start there so you will understand my predicament."

The doctor nodded. "Go on."

"I'm forty-two, never married, and I like my life. I don't need a man to be fulfilled. I love children, but I am aware I wouldn't be a good mother. I know that is some kind of big admission, although I don't understand why. On the positive side, I believe openness about my single life preference makes me more of a commodity in a male-dominated business world."

"What is your profession?"

"I'm an accountant. I have a Masters from the University of Texas, and I work for a national accounting firm. I am paid very well because I manage the most complicated accounting in the business, Multipliable Element Arrangements, and Software Revenue. Only one of the partners has even a basic understanding of what I do. In fact, I expect a partnership offer."

Dr. O studied her face, not much makeup. She had short nails, no polish, and had been biting her bottom lip.

"The job is intense and requires a lot of hands-on management with both employees and our clients. If either doesn't follow my procedures, we part ways. I have highly trained personnel who do not have time to babysit problem clients."

Dr. O watched the patient stiffen her back as she became commanding.

"After work, I'm at the gym three days a week where I do one-hour intense workouts. On Saturdays, I run in the park in the morning and then do four hours at the office. Sunday is for chores, shopping, and visiting my seventy-five-year-old mother, upstate, which I do once a month."

The patient wiggled her bottom in the chair, preparing for what was next.

"On the second Friday of every month, I have sex."

She wriggled again but lifted her chin bravely. She kept going as if she were reading a financial report.

"It took a while to accept my preference. I know submission may appear to be not politically correct, but to me, it is feminism when I can act on what I feel is right for me."

She ended her sentence without a question mark but was still looking for agreement.

Dr. O nodded.

"I like men better than women, although I have had sex with women. Both are enjoyable. But the women I have met eventually demand commitment, and there's all that— talking."

Dr. O smiled slightly.

"Anyway, I can now afford to act on my desires. I have an arrangement with two men who I call Donner and Blitzen."

"Sorry to interrupt, but two questions. Do you have any security...any backup?"

"Yes...they know it's a two-hour session and I need to make a phone call, or the cavalry arrives."

"Is that true? Is there a cavalry?"

"No...but they don't know that. What's the other question?"

"Why did you call Professor Lloyd? Does he know about your proclivity?"

The patient looked surprised.

"Hmmm...that's good," she said. "I thought I would not have to reveal that, but you asked...so...yes, he does. I had an affair with him. It was a long time ago, but he remains closer to me than any other person in my life."

"Please continue."

"I have two men in these sessions because I have sex once a month, and I want to orgasm four or five times in a session. I haven't found one man who has the stamina. So, I hire two, it's really just math. Four hands are great but, as I said, I want to be satisfied when I leave, and one man has never cut the mustard."

She looked for approval again. This time she received half a nod.

"Anyway, I like the total power exchange of submission and giving up control. Sometimes, I get so high that it becomes almost an out-of-body experience. I lose all contact with everything logical. I lose all sense of time and almost float in what I can only describe as a haze of pleasure."

She took a long breath and said, "In my regular life, I have a ton of responsibility. The release of control feels like removing a huge weight... like I can step away from myself and be less anxious and more fulfilled. I value the opportunity to know what I want and then go out and get it. It's me fulfilling my sexual nature."

"Tell me why it's now a problem."

The patient's eyes came up. Tears had begun to well.

"The last time Donner showed up with a new man. I should have known better, but I had a tough week, and I was ready for a night of fun. I let lust win out over better judgment."

She shifted again, and the doctor knew it wasn't because the chair was uncomfortable.

"It started very well. The new guy had a great body and was very well endowed. He seemed to know about submission and was firm but respectful. It was great for about an hour or so. Then towards the end, I was tied up over an armchair. The new guy hit my ass hard with a belt. I yelled, 'RED.' Everything is to stop if I say red. But he didn't. He hit me again, harder. Donner jumped in, stopped him, and untied me. I ended the session."

The patient took a breath.

"Märta, this is where you tell me why you are here."

"Three days ago, I received an envelope at the office. It contained a picture of me tied up, naked over the chair."

Her face became bright red. "In the picture...I was...admiring the new guy's schlong." She gulped, took another breath, recovered, and continued. "Yesterday, I received another envelope. There were two more pictures and a note. It said his silence would cost $10,000."

"Obviously, this is the new guy... yes?"

"I think so...yes."

"I understand your problem, but why did you come to see me? I don't deal with blackmail."

"Please, doctor, try to appreciate my situation. If I go to the police...it will get to the firm and I lose my job. If I pay, you know as well as I do it won't stop and it will get to the firm, and I lose my job."

She leaned forward, hands in the air like praying in a church. "No matter how I calculate this, I lose. The most likely situation is, I lose my job, and my career turns to shit. I wouldn't be able to get a job in the fast food industry."

She was now almost frantic. "The first option is out. I called Georgie...I mean Professor Lloyd. He suggested that you might know someone who could help me. Someone that you trust."

Dr. O lowered her head, hiding behind her shield, thinking. She looked up—half a decision made. "I need to ask you to do something."

"What?"

"Would you allow me to examine you?"

"Of course."

"Hold out your hands."

The patient obeyed and stood.

Dr. O stood up and inspected her hands. "Turn them over." Dr. O pulled the sleeves back. "Turn around."

The patient obeyed.

"Pull your skirt up."

She cocked her head and smiled sheepishly. She was not wearing underwear.

Angry welts crisscrossed both cheeks.

"Okay, thank you."

The patient straightened her skirt and sat down.

"Why did you ask me to do that?"

"Forensics. Your problem needs a speedy solution, and for me to help you, I needed to know what you're telling me is the truth. The marks on your wrists and the welts show that you were recently abused."

The patient wrung her hands and pleaded. "Doctor, I know I have to stop this kind of behavior. It's dangerous, and I need your counsel for that, but I was hoping that I could get your help to solve this problem now."

"What behavior?"

"You know...being submissive."

"Submission is not a problem; it's a choice. It's completely normal for you now, and you will continue to evolve. You should not interrupt your journey because of another person's actions. However, I am strongly recommending you eliminate the risks you're taking."

The patient waited silently.

Dr. O rose and slowly walked toward the door. She grasped the

71

handle and stood with her back to the patient making the second half of the decision. "Okay, I'll see what I can do."

The patient sighed loudly.

"Thank you, thank you—"

"I said, I would see if I could help."

Dr. O opened the door.

"Thank you again, and again. This is the first time I have been able to breathe in a week."

Lo watched the accountant close the office door behind her.

Dr. O started back into her office then turned. "When is that guy Felix recommended supposed to be here?"

"Four days ago," Lo smirked with disapproval.

"Shit." Dr. O shook her head. "He's turning out to be a real big help. Do you know anybody else that could help out?"

"Doing what for whom?"

"The same shit I always agree to do. More than I should."

Lo smiled at her boss. "I talked with Felix again today. He said that his guy would be here soon. I have to say he seems to think this guy is the shit and...I guess...Felix has never let you down before."

Dr. O nodded, but her frown spoke of doubt.

"Felix told me this guy is the real deal, like a Jason Statham/George Clooney combo. You know what I mean? Like, not just a tough guy, but smart and resourceful."

Dr. O didn't want to tell her friend that she didn't know who Jason Statham was—Lo was on a roll. "Thanks. Okay, I guess we wait. Listen, you should take off now and rest that hand. I'm wrapping up and should be done shortly. Go ahead and head home."

"I'm here till you leave," Lo said flatly. "I walk you to the car, and then I go home."

Dr. O smiled. "I appreciate that, but really I'm fine."

Lo, not smiling, said again, "I'm here till you leave. I walk you to the car, and then I go home."

"Okay ...Okay... I'll be ten minutes." She paused and then added with sincerity, "Thank you."

Lo began closing down her space. Something was going on, but she didn't know what it was. Lo picked up on the moments when the doctor seemed disturbed by a shadow or a sudden sound. She closed down the computer, cleaned off the desk, and rose to lock the filing cabinet. When she stood, she reached around and re-adjusted the Glock 26 she had holstered under her blouse. A doctor's secretary seen packing artillery might not be suitable for business.

She usually would have carried a weapon without a round in the chamber. That option was no longer on the table. She would not be able to rack the slide with one hand. A bullet in the chamber was essential. Only the safety would have to prevent her from shooting herself in her ass.

She leaned against the wall and quietly said to herself, "I sure hope this guy is as good as Felix says he is."

9

Smoke promised Felix he would get to New York in two days—four days ago. If this new lead didn't bear fruit, finding Valentina would have to wait until he returned.

McKee didn't get any useful information from Mrs. Howard. He knew if a lights-out attorney failed, a poorly dressed stranger without a badge wouldn't get past the gate.

What comes after a failed interview in the PI handbook? Bug the phone.

He connected an audio tap into the phone panel box on the outside wall of the garage. Fortunately, Mrs. Howard burned up the phone wires hooked to her Main Line mansion and not a cellphone. She talked for hours to her bridge buddies. Mrs. Howard never mentioned Valentina, but Smoke got a sense of her and her husband's life. It was clear she and her dearly departed husband lived in the clouds far above the peasants below.

The only other person gaining her attention was her priest.

The first calls between a recent widow and her priest seemed reasonable. He gave consolation and instructions about what services she attended. What he heard at the end of the last call left Smoke fascinated.

The subject matter discussed was difficult for him to understand. Raised a Catholic, he attended parochial schools and a Catholic University. All the clerics he encountered along the way alleged the church had the only true path to heaven. What he had never heard from a turned-around collar was a ticket to paradise could be purchased. He asked his pal Google for the definition of Plenary Indulgence.

His friend had instant answers. Plenary Indulgence was forgiveness meant for martyrs. If one gave up one's life as a matter of faith, granting a little slack for prior indiscretions seemed fitting. Its honorable intentions digressed into rampant abuse during the Middle Ages when greed and scandalous behavior of the clergy caused unrest amongst the faithful. The final straw came when the Pope started an indulgence campaign as a building fund. Martin Luther rose up in protest, and the Protestant Reformation was born. The church reacted and shelved the golden ticket—gone but not forgotten. Popes over the next centuries rolled out Indulgences for special occasions. The latest ticket did not have the same clean slate option as its predecessors.

It seemed to Smoke; the Monsignor was selling a more comprehensive forgiveness package. He closed down the Internet and re-opened his voice-recording app to listen to the last call again.

Mrs. Howard's voice made the indicator on his screen squiggle. "So...I have completed all the tasks."

"All of them?" The other voice was a deep, slow-talking male.

"Yes, Father."

"Monsignor," he corrected politely. "Excellent. We will finish up tomorrow. There is a timeline, as you are aware. There are no extensions for this blessing."

"I understand...Uh." She stammered slightly, then after a moment, her full voice rose, and she continued. "Listen, I want to be sure everything goes away...you know...everything."

"I understand. I knew Dwight, and he was a good man, worthy of forgiveness. The pilgrimage, novena, confession, and your offering will assure his soul's ascension into heaven."

"Yes...the offering." There was a pause, and her diminished voice said again, "The offering."

The male voice responded in a steady monotone. "Yes, your offering completes the requirements. I will expect you at confession tomorrow."

"Okay...Yes. All right, I'll be there tomorrow night."

"God bless you." The male voice made a significantly bigger squiggle line on the screen.

"Thank you, Father." There was the sound of a phone hanging up.

"Monsignor." His objection went to dead air.

Smoke pushed stop and leaned back in his chair. He put his hands behind his head and thought about what to do next.

He wouldn't get much more from the phone tap. He decided on one more night; one more shot to find out what happened to a girl he had never met.

Smoke waited till dark, removed the bug, and headed for City Line Avenue and St. Marks.

The cargo bay of a beat-up, 2005 Chevrolet van was Smoke's office. He resettled his butt in his comfortable desk chair. It rolled up to his command center, a piece of plywood bolted to the floor. There was a laptop, headphones, and a receiver with glowing dials. The rest of the tools of his trade were stacked and racked on the walls of the van/office. Despite its aesthetic flaws, the van was perfect for his needs. Unnoticed—nothing unusual. Like him, it was unique but possessed the ability to hide in plain sight.

He placed a cup of coffee poured from his industrial-size thermos on the desk. He adjusted the knobs of the KSUN 5800, 60-Watt receiver. The goal was to keep the signal indicator straight up on the yellow tinted dial. It was not state-of-the-art, but he knew where to kick it when it stopped working. When he got onto something he couldn't quit, he slept on a folding cot. A drywall bucket became a spot-a-pot, and he lived on Spam, apples, and coffee. Aside from a smell that would not go away, he was quite content to stay hunched over for days waiting and listening.

He waited, listening for the moment of weakness when every bad guy has to vent or boast or in this case—confess.

He turned on the receiver and the speaker hissed. He dialed the nob of the GSM gHost SC microphone, and the noise stopped.

Before dawn, he entered the church, picking the lock of a basement door. He hard wired the electrical leads of a microphone to low voltage feeds inside a smoke detector. He could hit a switch and listen in the dark like a priest—without having to grant forgiveness.

Above the plywood workstation, clipped to a screw head was a picture of Valentina and her mother. They were arm in arm, leaning against each other, matching each other's smiling eyes. They were unable to see the darkness ahead.

He pushed the photo, and it rocked back and forth.

Monsignor Patrick Fleming emerged from the arched oak door of the sacristy. He walked the expanse to the black iron gate in front of the yellow oak pews. He stopped, genuflected with textbook reverence and blessed himself with his trademark dramatic flair. In his opinion, many of his counterparts took traditional rites too lightly.

He gained recognition and promotion by keeping his parish solvent. Leaning on the Archdiocese for financial support was never right. He did the usual things; charity drives, carnivals, and cake sales. However, he found the Sunday offering was the most effective. He developed topics for his sermons that motivated the best contributors who also received personal attention.

His sermon on the Sunday following the funeral had a specific point. "To come to God and salvation, one needs to repent, have faith, and be baptized. If one commits a mortal sin, one needs to ask forgiveness for their sins in confession."

Mrs. Howard was in the first row.

"The modern world demands a lot of time to manage our lives and business. Sometimes we get too busy to do what's necessary for our entrance into heaven, like confession." He went fire and brimstone on the congregation and Mrs. Howard. "Remember—should one who is not in the state of grace die suddenly... there is little to be done." He thought he had delivered the line perfectly. He paused, looked around the church, focused on Mrs. Howard, and cast the line. "It might still be possible to gain entrance, but only if the departed loved ones truly believe."

The priest walked to the confessional, glancing at those waiting in the pews. Mrs. Howard sat in a pew nearest to his box, purse clutched in her lap, impatiently waiting. He entered the small oak chamber and sat on a red satin pillow.

He switched on the light above the door.

His store was open.

The microphone inside the confessional picked up the sound of the door opening. Smoke dialed the knobs, adjusting the red arrow to center. He heard a soft crunching sound as the screen connecting the two confessionals slid open.

"Bless me, Father, for I have sinned."

He recognized her voice immediately.

"The Lord be in your heart and upon your lips so you may truly and humbly confess your sins. In the name of the Father, and of the Son, and the Holy Spirit. Amen."

"Ah, ...ummm...I don't know where to begin Father."

"Monsignor," corrected Fleming.

"Monsignor. Yes, of course, Monsignor. I mean—I don't know how this works."

"I will begin. There are a few required questions."

"Okay."

"Do you desire a Plenary Indulgence for your husband?"

"Yes."

"Did you complete the tasks assigned?"

"Yes, Father."

"Monsignor."

"Please, forgive me, Monsignor. Yes, I have completed all the tasks assigned to me."

"Have you made a pilgrimage to the Shrine of St. Rita of Cascia in Philadelphia?"

"Yes, Monsignor."

"Have you made the novena at St. Theresa's?"

"Yes, all six days."

"Do you now hold the interior disposition of complete detachment from sin, even venial sin?"

"Yes, Monsignor."

Smoke wondered if she understood the question. He didn't.

"Have you received the Holy Eucharist?"

"Yes, Monsignor."

She had managed three Monsignors in a row. Smoke bet she wouldn't make four.

"Have you prayed for the intentions of the Pope?"

"I have Fath...I mean, Monsignor."

Smoke smiled. *I should head to Vegas.*

"Very well. Now, I must review what the Indulgence is, so you will completely understand the benefits."

"Of course."

Smoke heard paper rattling, and he assumed the priest was reading.

"If a penitent did not die in the state of grace, the eternal loss of the presence of God is the consequence. If I grant Indulgence, it will purify the soul and allow it to rise to the glory of God."

Smoke listened intently.

"It is the tradition from its inception for the repentant to offer an act of charity which we have discussed. Yes?"

"Yes, Monsignor."

"Son of a Bitch," exclaimed Smoke loud enough to echo in the van.

"Good. Good. I will be expecting your act of charity by close of business tomorrow."

"Yes, Monsignor."

Smoke heard the kneeler creak.

Damn it. She's leaving.

"I will now hear your confession," said the low voice.

"What? My confession? I haven't done anything. I thought all I had to do was to give you the mone—"

"I have a solemn duty that I am bound to do. Your confession must be heard for the sins of the husband to be forgiven."

"Yes. There it is." Smoke yelled it out like he just heard the sound of a baseball about to leave the ballpark.

She grunted. "Okay, Monsignor. Where to start, where to start? I am concerned there is—"

"It's all right. Please tell me what happened."

"You know, we have a big house, and it requires a lot of maintenance. Obviously, this requires reliable help. The local people want at least a minimum wage, and then there are the taxes and the benefits—I mean what a bother. Anyway...a few years ago, Dwight came up with a great idea. He said he wanted to import help. He sent me to resorts in countries that...well...you know..." Her voice lowered. "Where there are those third world people...you know...poor people." Her voice went back to normal. "We wanted a girl to cook and clean. Not an old one, mind you, a young one who would work hard and not be a burden."

She cleared her throat. "It worked pretty well because Dwight had connections and he got work permits for them easily."

"Go on," said the priest with no emotion.

"I had to repeat the trip three times because, after a year or two, they would leave without a word and put us in a bad spot. You know how those people are. Give them a couple of bucks, and the next thing you know they run away, have a bunch of babies, and collect welfare."

"I understand. Please continue."

"I always tried to help my husband, especially now when he can't help himself. I mean because he's dead and all. So, this all happened about six months ago. I was at the club playing bridge. I had a headache and came home early. Dwight was sitting in a chair in his office having a drink. I startled him, and when he stood up, I could see he had blood all over his shirt. He said the girl...Valentina...had tried to kill him."

Smoke slapped the plywood.

Valentina.

"I followed him to the servant's quarters. She was on the floor, dead. He told me he went into her room to get her to make him some lunch, and she came at him with a knife. He said he had to defend himself, so he hit her. She must have hit her head on the table when she fell...anyway, the little whore was dead."

"Whore?" The Monsignor sounded surprised.

"Oh...please. Whore is exactly what she was. You know how those girls walk around so provocatively and...you know...how they are so foreign."

"Ah, uh."

"Dwight said we couldn't have the police at the house. He said they would make a mess and of course there would be no way to keep the story out of the papers." Her tone changed to endearing. "He was so thoughtful. All of those people disrupting my life would be intolerable."

She got back on track. "Dwight asked me to help him. He said we had to get her out of the house. He said nobody would miss another immigrant whore."

"Ah, uh."

"He told me to cover her up and—"

"Wait, you covered her?"

"Why do you think I'm calling the little slut a whore? Dwight told me she was naked when he walked into the room. He said she wanted sex, and when he refused, she attacked him. I told you that already."

"No, actually you didn't."

"Oh... didn't I? Oh my, I guess you're right. I forgot to mention it. Sorry."

"Go on."

"Well anyway, we wrapped a sheet around her, not a good one mind you. Then he put her in the trunk of his car. We drove to his industrial park, where he had started a new building. A loading dock was getting concrete the next day, so he put the body in the foundation and covered it with stone."

Her tone brightened. "So, it all worked out...no police...no press. So thank God for small favors."

Smoke looked at the monitor. It was on, but there was no sound.

"Is that all Monsignor?"

Still, only a low hiss came from the speaker.

"He gets the Indulgence now...right? So, you can see it wasn't his fault. You know, I always had to look after him. Even now...after he's dead."

"No." The voice was abrupt. "I'm not finished, yet."

"Really? The singers are on TV tonight, and I need to get home by eight."

Smoke heard papers turning again.

"Plenary means the most grievous sins are wiped away with unconditional forgiveness. It applies to the afterlife, and any penalty for sin on earth would be Temporal Punishment. The sinner would still be subject to civil law."

"I understand, Monsignor."

"Since Mr. Howard can't make reparations on earth," he coughed. "Dwight's sins...will be...forgiven."

"You mean by close of business tomorrow, yes?"

"Yes...close of business," his voice meeker.

"Fine."

"Mrs. Howard, one more thing. How many girls did you bring into the country?"

Smoke thought some higher power-seeking justice made the Monsignor ask that question.

"You mean like total—including the last one?"

"Last one?"

"Well, yes, of course. There were three before, and this one is number four. I just got back from Panama...you know...the house didn't get any smaller. I still need help."

Smoke waited to see if the priest would kick this crazy bitch to the curb or buy a new furnace for the school.

He got the answer.

"In the name of the Father..."

The sound of the door opening and closing drowned out the rest of his blessing.

Smoke pushed open the van's panel doors and got out. He walked to the front of the church and leaned against the stone wall guarding the steps to the front door.

Mrs. Howard opened the door and came down the stairs quickly. He had seen her before but only from a distance.

He wanted to see her up close and look into her eyes.

She looked like she came from central casting—a county club grandmother, sociopath.

She hit the last step and looked up, catching his eye for a second.

He stared at her as she went by.

She gave him the same cold, unfeeling stare he judged she must have had on her face when she saw Valentina on the floor.

He watched as she walked to the parking lot and got into her Mercedes.

He heard the door close with a mechanical click.

He smiled, turned, and walked to the van and his phone.

She had no idea what was coming.

10

The cell phone rang, but Smoke did not answer. There were too many people in too small a space to have a conversation. Bonni McKee would have to wait.

The elevator's five-dollar speaker was criminally assaulting a classic song—a song he never thought he would hear in muzac. Dylan's *Tangled Up in Blue* ricocheted around the vertical tramway.

"But all the while I was alone
The past was close behind."

He escaped the torture when the door opened at seven.

The hallway, well-appointed and long, held his objective—the last door at its end. Now alone, he reached for his phone and hit redial. The lawyer answered on the first ring.

"Thank you." McKee's voice sounded meek.

Smoke didn't say anything.

Instantly disappointed he did not react kindly to her meekness, she reverted to normal speak. "I said thank you, asshole. The least you could say is you're welcome."

He remained silent.

Unsuccessful again, she retried meek. "Listen Smoke, I cannot believe what you did. I owe you big for this."

"I don't know what you're talking about." She hadn't caught on yet, which surprised him.

"Are you kidding me? Not only do I not hand out compliments but...Wait a minute..." She stopped, awareness creeping in. "If you tell me that you were the source...then..."

Smoke could almost hear the wheels grinding. "Okay, I got it."

He couldn't acknowledge her thought train's arrival.

Now aware of the problem, she began her summation. "I opened a file on this case in my office. I asked you to investigate. I am also an Officer of the Court. If you tell me you provided the anonymous tip, I would have to reveal your name. Because you're not my client and do not have the client-attorney privilege."

She took a beat.

He knew she knew.

"You would be called to testify at Mrs. Howard's trial. You would then have to reveal how you obtained the information that led to the discovery of the bodies. If you obtained it through illegal means, the evidence would be the fruit of the poisonous tree. Everything, including the discovery of the bodies, the DNA evidence, and her confession would be inadmissible. The entire case would get tossed."

He could but would not respond.

She developed tactic three on the fly.

"Okay, soooo...I will start this conversation again. Ring, ring. Hi, Smoke. Say...all the news channels are running a crazy story. Want to hear about it?"

"Absolutely." He acted curiously.

"Working on an anonymous tip..." her voice dripped in sarcasm, "The Philadelphia police, led by Detective Robert Aimer, arrested Roberta Howard, 56. The tip led to the discovery of three bodies at the industrial park owned by Dwight Howard, Roberta's husband. The body of Valentina Juarez, 19, was discovered buried under a concrete slab. Ms. Juarez emigrated from Costa Rica to work for the Howards as a domestic. Two other bodies are also female. Police suspect they were former employees. Lt. Aimer said Mrs. Howard confessed upon her arrest and implicated her husband. The charges against her are second-degree murder, conspiracy, and aiding and abetting. Dwight Howard died of natural causes and cannot be charged."

Smoke interrupted with his own sarcasm. "The detective must have been very persuasive to get a confession."

She moved along. "The Philadelphia Daily News reported that the police discovered the body of Ms. Juarez under a concrete loading dock. Police used ground-penetrating radar and cadaver dogs to locate the other two victims. The medical examiner at the scene reported the victims died of multiple blunt force injuries."

"Sounds like Mrs. Howard might be late for her bridge game."

"Definitely, I would say about twenty-five to life—late."

It was her turn to be silent.

"I like Ralph's."

"Done—tonight? What time?"

"Can't—busy."

"Okay, but sooner or later you're going to have to tell me how you got the information."

"Later...gater."

"Does that mean you will tell me or goodbye?"

He pushed the disconnect button. He liked teasing her.

He put the phone in his pocket as he arrived at the last door on the right.

Olivia Bennet, Doctor of Psychology, was etched in elegant script on a brass plate screwed tightly to a yellow oak panel.

Classy.

He stroked his face, rubbing the day-old stubble and regretting not shaving that morning.

The stranger coming through the door startled Lo. He was wearing blue jeans and a black T-shirt. The clothes passed muster, however his boots—polished but worn didn't cut it.

"Can I help you?"

"I'm here to see Dr. Bennet."

"You don't have an appointment."

"Yes and no."

"Did you make an appointment with the doctor directly?"

"No."

He was testing her patience.

"If I didn't, and she didn't...who did?"

"Felix Grant."

She gave him a pure MP once over. "So, you're him."

"You must be Loretta?"

"I am, and you are Smoke?"

"Roger that."

She rolled back her chair, stood up, and walked towards him. The wires and pins were gone, making the cast slightly easier to manage.

He went first. "Sergeant—correct?"

"Oorah." She straightened up, just short of attention.

"That makes you a Marine. First Shirt?"

"First Sergeant."

"MP?"

"Wait there." She had enough of his Kreskin-like observational accuracy and pointed to a chair.

Dr. O was behind her desk, transcribing notes from her last session.

"He's here."

"Who's here?"

"The guy Felix recommended."

Dr. O looked up.

Lo rolled her eyes and whispered, "He doesn't look very professional."

The doctor leaned back. "Send him in please, Lo."

"I'll leave the door open."

"It's okay. You can close the door."

Lo marched back into the outer office, stopped in front of the couch, and gave one head nod toward the door.

"She'll see you now."

Smoke walked through the door instantly noticing the two rooms were very different. The outer office had big paintings and a statue of a naked guy. He expected the doctor's office to be sterile chrome and black leather. Instead, it was brown wood and comfortable chairs. It smelled good, something hippy he judged. His security assessment was less favorable than the decor. There was a danger zone near her desk. Three floor-to-ceiling windows with blinds pulled open provided a clear view for the eyes of NYC.

He walked to the desk, not knowing whether to sit or to stand.

Head down, writing, she said, "Please have a seat."

He adjusted a chair and sat.

She looked up at him.

"Mr. Smokehouse, I presume?"

"Smoke." His voice cracked a little.

"Pardon?"

"I prefer Smoke."

There was a reflective pause. "Why?"

"Why what?" was all he could manage. He was uncomfortable and feeling off-center.

"Why do you prefer Smoke? One would assume it is a contraction, but it does seem a bit—unusual."

Suddenly feeling like a patient, he answered a question he rarely answered. "Smokehouse is my last name. Most people liken it to a side of bacon or a piece of salmon."

She crossed her arms and waited.

"Actually—I'm not sure why. I just prefer it."

She nodded.

He tried to regain footing. "And I should call you Dr. Bennet?"

"Olivia would be fine, but like you, I also have a nickname." Her face brightened. "Some call me—Dr. O."

"Why?"

"As you know, my name is Olivia Bennet. I'm a Doctor of Psychology. I wrote a book about sex, and the press nicknamed me Doctor Orgasm—Doctor O for short."

He had on his doctorate-degreed stone face.

"Actually, I just prefer it."

This is fun.

He was pretending ignorance. Work history, education, and even the nickname were easy Google searches. The Internet assistant also gave him a few FBI cases to read. The information was the background. Its accuracy needed verification—like her Internet images, which failed to do her justice.

She carefully put her pen north and south to her notepad.

He sensed a change coming.

She went from people-curious to business-dismissive. "I appreciate your time and effort. However, I don't think I need protection despite Felix's well-meaning concerns. I have Lo and, even in her slightly debilitated condition, I think we can manage."

"I understand."

Neither of them spoke.

She broke first, adding some disapproval to dismissive. "Also, Felix told me you would be arriving a week ago. I simply cannot have anyone around me who is so unreliable; they can't make a phone call."

Honest, forthright, and very pleasant, even in rebuke.

A few more seconds of quiet time went by.

His granite look was having an effect.

She fidgeted a little in her chair. "I'll be happy to reimburse your expenses and pay you for your time today."

"Three days."

Her eyes got big. They were blue.

Surprise. Very cute.

"I don't understand, Mr. Smokehouse. You want to be paid three days for one day's travel time?"

"Smoke and no. I want expenses—plus—three days on the job."

"Okay...Smoke." She raised her hands in frustration. "That's all the time I have for today. Please see Loretta on the way out, and she will cut you a check for whatever you want. Thank you, and good day."

She picked up her pen and hid behind her hair.

Anger—flushed red cheeks—still cute.

Smoke pressed the picture app on his phone.

"You're being followed."

"What? I don't understand."

"Men are watching you."

He put the phone on the desk and slid it to her.

Her face went from pink to white.

Fear.

She let the phone lay in the middle of her desk. Suddenly, she grabbed it and swiped the images. Slowly, her temperature changed back to pink. She placed the phone on the desk and slid it to Smoke.

She was afraid—but now—not so much. Why?

"I don't know them, should I?" Her voice was mostly calm.

"I spotted two of them. They were in place at least four probably five or six days."

Confusion replaced the fear on her face.

"I'm calling the guy in the first picture the Little Round Man. He's in a vacant office across the street." Smoke pointed out the uncovered windows. "On the seventh floor, opposite this office."

He swiped the next picture.

"I haven't gotten a good picture of the second guy's face, but he looks like a bull in a suit. I saw him at the speech you gave at NYU Tuesday night."

She was reeling. "What...who...why?"

"Those are excellent questions. However, you missed where and when." His attempt at humor was too soon. It didn't penetrate her shock. "I don't have answers...yet."

"I don't know those men. Are they fans? Stalkers? How about paparazzi, after all, I am kind of famous."

"No, I don't think so. I believe they are hired help. The surveillance is professional."

They sat in silence again but now for totally different reasons.

A smile surprised him. The doc had recovered.

She pushed the intercom button. "Lo, could you come in here, please."

Lo came in quickly.

"You have met Lo?"

"Yes, just met. However, Felix gave me a background on your security. I know she is top gun."

"Assuming that means very good, yes, she is. Even with a broken wing."

Lo got as close to blushing as a Marine could get.

Dr. O directed her attention to Smoke. "Where are you staying?"

"City Rooms near Times Square. Clean—cheap."

Her face displayed disapproval of his accommodations. "Lo, please call the Ritz and arrange a room for Mr...I mean...Smoke."

Very, very, cute.

"Tell them he'll be a guest of ours until further notice and to bill us directly for all his expenses."

Lo looked surprised but nodded. "Of course—anything else?"

Dr. O thought a minute, a painted finger tapping an upper lip.

"Did you bring a suit?"

"No...I own a jacket but I..."

She flicked a painted nail. "Lo, please arrange a fitting with Andre first thing tomorrow morning. Tell him Mr. Smoke needs two suits, six shirts, ties, and shoes—ASAP."

Lo looked like she didn't understand why he was suddenly high on a priority list. "Anything else?"

"Yes, there is. Please sit for a minute."

Lo pulled up a second chair and joined the team.

"Smoke has discovered that two men are following me. One is watching us from the building across the street."

Lo almost jumped from the chair. "What...who...why?"

Both Smoke and Dr. O grinned.

Smoke filled in the gap. "I identified the threat, but I'll need your help to discover a motive."

Lo nodded her understanding.

Dr. O looked to him for additional guidance. "What should we do now?"

"What time will you quit working today?"

Lo jumped in, "Actually, ...now."

"Any other engagements tonight?"

"No. Not tonight." Dr. O looked at Lo, who confirmed with a nod.

"Good, don't change your routine. Whoever is watching does not know about me yet. However, we know about them. I want to hold on to the invisibility a little longer. Tonight, go home and don't go out for any reason."

The doctor wanted information. "Agreed—what about tomorrow?"

Smoke thought better moving. He stood and paced carefully to stay out of the view of the windows. "I'll be here when you arrive tomorrow. The three of us will get a protection plan together. I'll be working on discovering the what, who, and why."

He looked at the doctor. "This is important; I want you to keep the blinds closed. There is an open view of your desk from the building across the street."

The doctor nodded.

"Lo has your back. Now, she's aware of the situation, so you'll be fine in the office. Do you have public events coming up?"

Lo jumped in immediately. "Tomorrow night—the dinner at the Carlton for the Atwood Charity—the art auction, remember?"

"Are there a lot of people at this event?"

Dr. O responded. "Yes, there will be many people."

"I don't suppose you can cancel?"

She shook her head.

He shrugged. "Okay, so I guess I get to continue as Lamont Cranston until tomorrow night."

"Who?"

Smoke and Dr. O responded simultaneously. "The Invisible Man."

Dr. O chuckled. "Lo—when you call Andre, please tell him Smoke will need a black tux for tomorrow night."

She turned her attention to him. "Am I correct? I will need an escort?"

Smoke just shrugged.

"Looks like a Philly boy is having a New York City coming out party."

Lo hurried off to her office and her phone.

Smoke sat down and brushed his beard.

The apprehension showing through his façade was easy to read. "All expenses. Get a haircut and a shave. You'll find everything available at the hotel. Just charge it to the room."

A small grin appeared, and to his surprise, his face didn't break apart.

She rose from the desk and walked to him.

He stood.

His voice cracked ever so slightly. "Before I accept, I have a question."

She seemed hesitant but curious. "Okay."

"You seemed determined you didn't need help. Then you suddenly changed your mind. I don't think you scare easy—so —why?"

"Simple logic for me. Felix."

"Sorry?" Now he was curious.

"First, I trust Felix, and he trusts you. Second, you quickly uncovered a threat. Therefore, if the man Felix trusts, thinks this situation is dangerous, then I would be a fool not to take your lead."

He nodded.

"It's logical, isn't it?"

"Yes, it is."

She slipped her arm through his and walked him to the door. "I also have another reason."

"Another reason?"

"While you're here, perhaps you can provide some assistance on another problem."

"Ah...Huh?"

She took his grunt as a yes. "Good, I have a patient who is being blackmailed by a nefarious party. Perhaps you have some insight that would help."

He looked down at her as she looked up.

For some reason, he wasn't walking fast.

The elevator rose without a stop. It was 6:15 AM; it took a little less than nine seconds to reach the nineteenth floor. It was Lawrence Campbell's habit to arrive early, before the rush of the masses. If he were to come later than dawn's early light, the morning express became a commuter local where he would suffer the indignity of waiting for commoners. There were thirty-four floors in the building, and he was looking to move up. He coveted the private elevator to the penthouse office—fifteen levels higher—where there were no stops on the way to the top.

The bell rang, and he burst out, moving halfway down the hall before the door slid closed behind him. Wide gold letters spread over two glass doors indicated the office belonged to Campbell Development, LLC. The lights were on already as Lawrence Campbell marched into his kingdom.

"Good morning, Mr. Campbell." The greeting came from an enterprising new accountant who sat alone amongst a bullpen of desks stacked along a long blank interior wall.

The salt and pepper-haired man grunted an unrecognizable sound.

The new accountant/slave ducked his head into his computer screen.

Mr. Campbell's grunt was a kind of acknowledgment. He usually didn't respond to minions at all.

The President of Campbell Development, LLC was perfectly dressed, everything that was supposed to be creased was. His French, baby cashmere suit cost seven thousand dollars. A Chinese silk tie secured to a white linen shirt with a diamond pin cost more than the suit.

The new employee didn't have much appreciation for the apparel, but he did notice the man hadn't shaved. The day-old beard spoiled the corporate giant's perfect clothes. The GQ outfit conveyed style and confidence, but inside the costume, there was boiling turmoil. His head was down, and his jowls drooped. The whiskers added shadow to his chalky pallor.

In the hall, Lawrence passed a large black and white photograph of his father and grandfather sitting on the first Campbell company truck. A color photo of the company's Ohio headquarters appeared in the next frame. Third in line was an aerial picture. Fields of tall corn and short grazing grass surrounded two white farmhouses. In the foreground, a man rode a tractor, in the background, steers with their heads down were producing consumable flesh. He owned what was under the cows and crops and the lives of the farmers above—natural gas and oil.

At the hall's end were two eight-foot oak doors. Opposite, and as tall as the doors, hung a picture of—him. The shot, taken from a shoe-top level, had him grinning and pointing up at his new office. At first glance, one might assume that he built the building or at least owned it. The photo captured him, celebrating a rock bottom lease on the former office of Bernard Madoff Investment Securities.

"Good morning, Sir." Nancy Ferris sat perched, at the ready, with a wide smile.

Saying nothing, Campbell walked past his admin's desk. He pushed the buttons on the keypad lock—a passcode even the cleaners didn't have. When he heard the lock click open, he spoke the day's first word. "Coffee."

The quiet embraced him, and he relaxed long enough to take a deep breath. He needed to climb back to the top of Mount Alone, where he could think in silence. His future was out of balance. Results were slipping from certain to unknown. He had gotten used to phrases like exceeding expectations, or gains above margin. Words like unpredicted delay and unforeseen circumstances were twisting his insides into knots. They haunted his sleep. The demons woke him —uncontrollable beasts—the face of fear that shook him awake.

With only an hour or two of sleep, he had showered, dressed, and walked the eight blocks from his apartment just before dawn. He had no wife, no family, no friends—his life was this office. It was his realm and the bastion behind steel-clad doors. The walls were deep purple and the floors red Italian tile. Hand-woven rugs led to four faux-marble columns that secured each corner of a desk the size of a small battleship. Near the door to his private bathroom hung a gold-framed, full-length mirror he could see from his desk. From there he could see his trophy wall. Hung from the ceiling, on single strands of wire, were photographs framed and accented with individual art lights. In each photo, he posed with Hollywood celebrities, athletes, and heavyweight politicians. Elway and Montana, Magic and Jordan, Julia Roberts and Tom Cruise, John McCain and Rudy Giuliani and even the Donald were his big-game trophies—his dead animal heads.

The desk was the centerpiece, his command center. A Resolute design like the Oval Office, it had all the tools he needed and intricate secret compartments for some toys. One of the secret hideaways held two hundred thousand dollars in cash. It wasn't a getaway fund, or cash evading the IRS. He just wanted it there, occasionally taking it out, stack by stack, piling it neatly, and admiring the feel and smell of it. It was another trophy, another picture in a frame—one he could touch and smell.

He was rich and, until very recently, there wasn't much he couldn't afford. His wealth wasn't a surprise, or a stroke of good luck, or even due to his brilliance. He believed wealth and power to be a predetermined fact of life. He didn't pursue it. It came to him.

He came from a generational gene pool of high achievers. Father, Uncles, Grandfather all out-performed their circumstances. When the guys who donated those chromosomes died, they left the sum of their accomplishments to him.

It came to him.

In late 2007, with the economy soaring, large companies were buying up smaller firms daily. One of the national companies assessed Campbell Trucking to have substantial growth potential and possessed a healthy profit and loss statement. They viewed it as ripe, low-hanging fruit.

On February 2, 2007, Campbell sold his inheritance for 39 percent above the appraised value. His profit after taxes was 41 million dollars.

It came to him.

On September 29, 2008, the stock market fell 777 points, and the world changed. However, he had already escaped. Instead of becoming a victim of the economic depression that followed, he watched from afar. The world was going to hell in a handbasket, and Lawrence Campbell had a hold on the handle.

While millions suffered economic ruin, Lawrence Campbell saw a path to financial independence. The rising price of oil made a previously expensive oil extraction process very profitable. Fracking caught his attention. The economy was taking a beating, and so were the farmers in Eastern Ohio. With prices falling on crops, leasing underground mineral rights became found money. Fracking was an expensive process, but the demand to limit imports of foreign oil fueled lenient governmental approvals. It was a gusher.

It came to him.

The oil profit added to his power base of cash, and Campbell was ready to expand. He decided New York City, the money capital of the world, would be the home of his next victory.

NYC welcomed a man with cash in a down economy with open

arms. He bought from the desperate and sold with financing. He added Real Estate to his portfolio of mineral rights, leases, and cash.

The property management business became intense and required personnel. Campbell hated staff, and the day-to-day detail required enormous effort. No matter how big the property, they all seemed to require the same effort. The deals needed to be bigger with a more substantial reward at the end.

It was waiting for him.

He began to push destiny.

His big fish needed different bait. He began accepting invitations to attend A-list fundraisers. He donated appropriately, posed for pictures, and cast hints of his intentions to all the right people.

There were nibbles. The first suitors wanted his money but not him. They got a hard no.

Finally, a lawyer who represented a client seeking an investor/partner invited him to a Catholic Charities gala. At the event, he received an intriguing brief. He liked the concept, donated $10,000, took a picture with the lawyer and a Monsignor, and talks began.

The steel door creaked open, disturbing his concentration.

Shielding coffee like she was carrying a candle in the wind, Nancy walked to the desk. "Still steamy hot, Sir."

He didn't acknowledge her or the coffee.

She placed it on a coaster, backed away four steps, turned, and left as she entered, quietly.

He sat for a minute then checked his yellow gold, Rolex Sky-Dweller watch. 6:51 a.m.

He spun his chair around and bellowed into the intercom. "Nancy."

"Yes, Mr. Campbell."

"Get Anderson in here."

"Chuck Anderson?" She always repeated a command to be sure she had it right.

"Yes."

"Right away, sir."

He spun the chair back to the window. He couldn't believe overachieving could have had such a catastrophic result.

His coffee was still hot when the door opened again. "Mr. Anderson is here, Sir."

He saw Nancy's white teeth fill a broad grin.

"Send him in."

"Yes, sir."

"When he leaves, come back and take care of me."

She hesitated. "Yes, sir." Her white teeth had disappeared.

"Good morning." Anderson was competent and possessed, what could be described as a no-nonsense approach to reporting. The accountant did not know how to put sugar on figures. Campbell found his directness to his liking.

Campbell spun around and put his hands flat on the desk. "What's our cash position today?"

"Oil and gas futures dropped again this morning. That is the second drop this month. We are still netting 3 percent..."

"Not interested—cash flow is what I need. Where are we?"

Anderson looked up and down at his papers. He flipped a page to confirm the number, "$559,800. However, a futures drop of more than two percent will put us underwater."

Campbell tapped his fingers together in a contemplative business prayer pose. "Reserves?"

"Our cash reserve is securing our credit line. Expenses verses income is still at minus eleven percent. Your cash input last month will hold us for another four weeks—assuming we stay at current levels."

"Solutions?"

"Several. If futures on gas and oil rise, the cash crisis disappears."

"Unlikely. Next."

"Sell the leases." Anderson removed his glasses and cleaned the lenses with his tie.

"No time. A fire sale in a down market—I'll lose 40 percent of real value. What happens when the cash runs out?"

The accountant replaced his glasses then gazed at a calculator somewhere in the ceiling. "If the market drops again, we will need about five hundred thousand a month to cover the shortfall. I must also note that the projections are based on an immediate freeze of acquisitions and minimizing all expenses. We must stay at current levels."

Campbell glared. "You mean I can't buy any more properties in Philadelphia."

Anderson did something unusual. He matched the boss's emotion. "I cannot make a profit plan work if we keep buying vacant units."

Campbell called his emotion and raised. "We...? We...are buying!" He slapped the desk. "I am buying. I am buying empty units, not you. Your job—is counting—I—think. You got that?"

"Got it." Anderson ducked his head.

"You can leave...now." Campbell pointed to the door.

Anderson rose slowly.

He yelled at Anderson's back, "Tell her to come in."

The door closed and he spun the chair around to the window.

Auxiliary Bishop Michael O'Hanrand was the unexpected, the unforeseen. O'Hanrand was the one standing between him and his destiny.

The church owned most of the four city blocks bordering the FDR Park in South Philadelphia. When rezoned, it would be a prime location for high-rise towers and big mall shopping. It would be a windfall of money, but only if he could get to the finish line. His equity position with the church and pre-development expenses cost eighteen million dollars. He also had to buy up properties the church didn't own, about fifty properties in all. They required another fifteen million.

It took a lot of supervision to keep the purchases under the radar. He set up shell companies and used different real estate agents. He acted quickly and closed fast, gaining control before the transactions became public. He needed to keep the street quiet.

His partner had, so far, handled any noise—public or private. However, something was wrong. Approval dates had fallen way behind schedule.

The Archdiocese, according to some, is the largest single property owner in Philadelphia. Much of what they own is shielded and out of the public view. The properties had been on the balance sheets for decades. Packaged together, as a high-rise site; the high-maintenance, low-income asset became a cash cow. Its raw site value would explode in value from less than 10 to over 100 million.

The day the City Council voted yes to rezoning; Campbell's investment would become a king's ransom. The church would receive ten times the value of their property and a percentage of the gross if he could hang on.

He hit the intercom button again.

"Is the meeting set? Did you confirm?"

"Yes, sir. I confirmed for half past eleven. You have to leave here no later than nine."

"I want copies of the latest zoning submissions." He paused, then added a command. "And tell him not to be late, again."

"Yes, sir...of course, sir...right away, sir."

The intercom hissed. Campbell hadn't disconnected. "I'm waiting."

He stood and removed his jacket, laying it carefully on the desk. Then he undid his belt and unzipped his fly.

At 8:50, Campbell entered the elevator. The early morning express had become the morning local, servicing every floor. He stood in the back against the wall, briefcase on the floor and his right hand holding his phone.

Nancy stood on his left. She held a sheaf of papers bound with a black metal clip and his coffee, in a to-go cup. She had moved from Ohio with the company and taken a small one room in a four-story walkup. He judged her as efficient and good-looking enough to sit in front of his office. She was thirty-five naturally, had short blond hair, and possessed a trim figure. She dressed appropriately and met the demands of his schedule by staying single. Most importantly, she obeyed without objection.

Nancy wore a pure white blouse. Two unbuttoned buttons revealed a small, thin, gold chain Campbell had given her. She had unbuttoned the third button when they got on the elevator.

The elevator stopped on eighteen. Two men and a woman entered.

Campbell moved against the back wall.

She moved with him.

He glanced at her.

She leaned forward.

He could see past the fold of crisp fabric to the top of her breast where her white skin disappeared into her bra. He had given instructions on how to stand and her blouse buttons.

She followed all the instructions, including when he wanted her to lean forward.

He gave her the sign. He nudged her arm. "What time is the meeting?"

She leaned her left shoulder forward and pulled her right shoulder back, creasing the fabric into an open v.

He looked down her blouse.

"I reconfirmed for 11:30. The car is waiting at the curb. You will be in Philadelphia by 10:45. The documents you requested are in the car for your review." She started to straighten up.

SMOKE

He put his hand on her back and pushed her forward. "You need to come with me to Philadelphia. I'll want your take on the Monsignor, after the meeting."

Her face blushed red. "Yes. Of course, Sir!"

He dropped his hand behind her bottom and pushed two fingers into the divide under her skirt.

She pushed back against his hand, digging her heels into the carpet. She braced against his pressure so he wouldn't push her into the woman standing in front of her.

She wore no panties as he instructed.

She never complained.

She always did what he wanted.

He lifted his phone to read emails. He dropped his other hand behind Nancy and began working his fingers, poking and probing. It made him feel better most of the time. She performed well at most things and didn't seem to mind that he talked on the phone while she was performing fellatio.

12

Ninety-six miles away, as Lawrence Campbell hurried into his office, a sixty-nine-year-old man slept. He lay face up in the middle of an antique four-poster bed. Fine Egyptian linens and a comforter filled with Eiderdown swaddled him in elegant warmth. His sleep was deep. Demons did not wake him in the middle of the night. He was protected. He was in the demon business.

The room was his citadel. Its walls, plastered stone, its only door, solid oak. Thick curtains, drawn against the windows, created a chamber filled with silence. The eerie quiet hung in the room as if it had body and weight—a presence, old and mystical. The room wasn't always dark and soundless. In the beginning, it was a home.

The extraordinary home, located in Philadelphia's Society Hill, was built in 1831. Its architecture was Greek revivalist, and the material was cut stone and red brick with tall windows and black iron gates. The only additions were indoor plumbing, electricity, and a state-of-the-art security system.

In 1838, Cletus Ovule, a wealthy importer, died and bequeathed his fortune to his wife, Dorothy. After his death, she traveled, pursuing her passion, art. She roamed the world buying what she liked and hanging her prizes in her home. At the time of her death, she owned thirty-five paintings including several works by masters of Impressionism. She died in 1862, without any knowledge of the true worth of her collection. She had no heirs and left her entire estate, including the art, to the Catholic Church of Philadelphia.

He had the authority to redecorate when he took the position and moved into his new residence. Unhappy with his predecessor's decorating choice of Danish modern, he decided to restore the house to its former glory.

Using the Ovule's furniture, Michael O'Hanrand decorated every room. His efforts resulted in a residence done well but not noteworthy. Mediocrity was not the result of his efforts in his private chambers. From period rugs to a footlocker belonging to John Paul Jones, the room was exquisite. Ovule's art collection hung on purple walls and transformed the space into a museum gallery. He hung a landscape by Jose Ruiz y Blasco and two solid gold frames held small charcoal drawings by Degas. A Cezanne watercolor called the Blue Landscape received special lighting. A striking male nude by Taillasson, framed in black onyx, hung above his headboard.

The Auxiliary Bishop of Philadelphia slept in luxury. Inside his enclave, he was a king—on Spruce Street. His reign beyond the castle walls had not begun.

The throne he sought eluded him, but he had faith. It would be so—he believed it—it was his destiny. It was meant to be, Bishop, Archbishop, then Cardinal Michael O'Hanrand.

He had missed the first opportunity. It came when Cardinal Bevilacqua died. Under normal circumstances, he would have been next in line, but these were not normal times. The Archbishop of Denver got his job. He understood the move but loathed the delay in his predestined promotion.

The sexual abuse scandal sent the faithful packing. The Church's blue-chip stock had fallen to its lowest levels. Bringing in an outsider was necessary to re-establish black beneath the bottom line. Someone had to stop the bleeding. Someone had to insulate the institution from lawsuits. Someone had to ensure the legislature would not change the statute of limitations. Archbishop Chaput of Denver was the man for the job.

Chaput stopped all new spending immediately. He also began an active pursuit of divestment of assets. The restraint and divestment weren't panic moves, far from it. It was a tried and true business plan —pull back and wait. It was a strategy to survive even the most horrific actions taken by its leadership. In its simplicity, the plan was brilliant. Minimize the damage wherever possible then wait it out. The horrors of the Inquisition and the atrocities of the Crusades disappeared. The inhumanities committed converting 'Indigenous Peoples' got an outright pass. Wait was the watchword—wait till they forget. Joan of Arc burned at the stake, then only twenty-six years later was beatified as Saint Joan. Instead of a threat, the maiden became an asset.

Just wait it out. It all goes away.

Chaput made his career reducing overhead, cutting waste, and stabilizing income. His job was to help the Church hang on to more of what the Wall Street Journal judged to be an incalculable net worth.

Chaput stabilized cash flow almost immediately, authorizing personnel cutbacks and real estate liquidations. The quick fix stopped the bleeding but didn't stop the politicians from introducing legislation to roll back the statute of limitations on sex abuse crimes. Passage would result in a huge liability. An investment into political influence would be necessary to prevent another medieval bleeding.

The freeze on spending was a nuisance, but he saw selling the land as his opportunity.

O'Hanrand's eyes blinked open when the metallic click of the door lock penetrated the silence.

Monsignor Giuseppe DeFrancisco opened the door carrying a silver tray, coffee pot, and a white ceramic cup and saucer.

"Good morning, Monsignor."

"Buongiorno. Your Excellency." The monsignor placed the tray on the nightstand. He turned, walked to the windows, and pulled the drapes to their daytime resting place.

O'Hanrand recruited Monsignor DeFrancisco from Rome. He found Father DeFrancisco on the staff of Cardinal Camillo Bocci. The priest had gained valuable experience helping Bocci push himself to the front of the line for an appointment to Cardinal. Experience O'Hanrand desperately needed.

As a part of the deal, O'Hanrand offered to promote the ambitious DeFrancisco to monsignor. He pointed out the priest was one of six clerics serving a Cardinal who no longer needed his unique talents. O'Hanrand suggested he would fare better leading the staff working toward Archbishop—perhaps Cardinal.

The Italian priest stepped back to the bed. "May I remind you, Your Excellency, your appointment with Mr. Lawrence Campbell is this morning at 11:30."

"Yes, Giuseppe. Thank you. I'll be ready." O'Hanrand looked up at his second in command, admiring his tight curls of jet-black hair and his smooth olive skin. O'Hanrand's adventurous days were behind him, but the urges still pushed his red satin garment taut.

The monsignor turned to the bed stand and poured the coffee. "Will he cooperate?"

"My instinct says yes, Giuseppe. From what I've heard, he—now—has minimal options."

The monsignor nodded, smiled a crooked smile, and handed the cup to his charge.

O'Hanrand took the saucer, allowing his fingers to linger.

"Of course, Giuseppe," he added slowly, "and as always, I will value your insight after the meeting."

The monsignor nodded and did not move his fingers away.

13

The tailor stretched a tape across his shoulders and quietly whistled. He wrote fifty-eight and a half on his sheet.

Smoke caught himself admiring the cut of the Italian wool tux in the mirror. Lo, sitting in a chair behind him, looked disinterested, her head down checking her phone. He cocked his head a bit and turned for a side view. He stroked the sleeve. It was a moon shot away from fatigues. It had been a very long time since he had looked into a mirror for more than safeguarding a razor.

He buttoned the collar of the shirt Lo had picked. It was white linen accessorized with silver studs and matching cufflinks. He glanced down at the patent leather on his feet and shook his head. The appreciation scale tipped hard toward disgust.

He looked at the man in the mirror instead of the clothes. The image was so foreign to him that his mind immediately generated a semi-silent thought.

What a Putz!

Then, from a box hidden deep inside, her voice told him he looked pretty good.

"Hmm."

He snapped back.

Lo, across the fitting room, tapped on her lips with her fingers, "You might even pass for a human man in that get-up."

He flushed and emitted a low grumble.

She winced at the barnyard grunt. "And then there's that."

Andre strung his yellow tape around his neck, "Signore, I needa to make a small adjustment in youra jacket." He held out his hand. "Per favore."

The tailor offered same day service securing a significant sale. The tuxedo cost $2,500, and two suits at $1,500. Lo had selected six $300 shirts and $700 for shoes and 'accompagna.' Andre wrote an invoice for $8,000—not a bad morning.

Smoke stepped off the measuring platform and walked to where Lo sat, still pecking on her phone.

She looked up as he approached. "Listen...Army, you need to step up. I mean, what is with that walk? You're going to an art auction with rich people so, can you please...try...to not walk like a gangster."

He dropped a shoulder and began a hood strut. "How's this? Better?"

She lost it. Smoke's frame was not meant to hood strut. Envisioning him with gold chains and a sideways ball cap broke her up. Her laugh was spontaneous, and she couldn't pull it back.

He started laughing as well. "What you talking about this is... gangsta," he said, now exaggerating his arm swing and flashing gang signs.

"Okay, okay...I take it back...you bad. Now, please go back to your usual cock walk." She laughed again.

"I don't know how to walk any other way. Maybe it's how I grew up—a Philly swagger, I guess. So, your choice, I can walk like this or I can march."

"I choose swagger instead of gangsta."

Andre hurried across the room, holding the adjusted jacket.

Smoke slipped it on, then stepped to the chair where Lo sat. "Ready for inspection."

She stood up and walked around him.

"Straighten up, Army. Shoulders back."

"Hooah." He clicked heels and snapped to attention.

She circled him, inspected the lines, and ran a finger down his lapel. "I don't know what she sees in you—but when hosed down—not too bad, I guess." She stepped back, then dismissed him with the flick of her hand.

Andre was also inspecting. Satisfied with the jacket, he stuck out his hand. "Da pants, Pelasse Comande, uno more adjustmenta."

Smoke reached for the belt buckle, but stopped suddenly and looked at Lo.

"Don't mind me." Lo waved a dismissive hand, "There's nothing in there I want."

He shrugged and dropped the pants, revealing new purple satin boxer shorts.

"Whoa," Lo exclaimed loudly, "I take it back—now I'm hot!"

"Fuck you, Lo." He laughed.

She started laughing again and through tears pointed to his shorts, "Is that a Christmas present from Felix?"

"These are the only boxers in my size in the store. Apparently, they sell suits here and not tighty-whities."

It had been a long time since he enjoyed this kind of comradery. Somehow Lo had cracked the dark chamber door open. He was laughing, and he was surprised that it didn't hurt.

He pulled off the pants and held them straight out.

Andre grabbed them and scurried away.

He sat opposite Lo, and awkwardly crossed his legs.

She snickered then got serious. "Listen, Smoke. The walking thing... What I mean is you can't be obvious or standout. You'll look appropriate, but you're going to have to drop the tough guy thing and...like...blend."

He nodded. "I get it. I understand my role. It's a formal affair. I'm there for protection."

She smirked. "Really? You understand?"

His shoulders dropped. "Lo, I got it. I will have the doc's back."

Later, when Smoke remembered this moment, he thought it was when the understanding of their mission became cemented. They joined together with one common goal.

He crossed his legs the other way.

She smirked again because it was still funny.

Smoke boldly pressed forward. "I got a lot of info on the doc off the web, but there wasn't anything about you. What's your story?"

She mulled a moment. "Most is none of your business, Army." She leaned forward, "But one part of my history is relevant. I always wanted to be a Marine. I joined, rose quickly, and made First Sergeant as an MP. I excelled in every fitness evaluation until I arrested the wrong guy—a Lt. Colonel, who also happened to be a Brigadier General's son."

"That'll do it. What for?"

"He beat his wife—multiple times."

"A real hero."

She nodded. "Short story—I got booted."

"Why?" He already knew why but wanted to hear it.

"I got called in on a domestic disturbance. I found the wife alone and beaten. For her protection, I moved her to a motel off base. Before I could locate and arrest the husband, he found her and beat her again—badly."

"Off base? Wasn't that a local PD beef then?"

"They didn't want a beef with the base. It was a small-town dependent on the base for business. The local police passed it to me. Since it was an ongoing investigation, I arrested the Lt. Colonel."

"What did you charge him with?"

"Violations of the Uniform Code of Military Justice, Section 911: Article 111, Drunken operation of a vehicle, Sec. 924, Article 124, Maiming, and Sec. 924 Assault."

"The whole book. Good memory."

"Can't forget what almost put me down."

"Then what happened?"

"He pulled a PTS defense which was bullshit. He did Desert Storm from headquarters in Kuwait. He went into rehab/counseling and a year later got a promotion to Full Bird."

"And the arresting officer?"

The story stopped. Lo was hesitating to reveal part two. "They tried to get me to drop the charges."

"No dice. Right?"

"Nope."

There was more. Smoke waited.

"The dad star outed me as a lesbian. I was done. He came after me with both barrels, and I had no way out but out."

"This is where the Doc shows up?"

"A friend of mine reached out to her. She had left the FBI and had begun private practice. I was relieved when she agreed to represent me. Smoke, they didn't see her coming. She was awesome. I got an Honorable, a partial pension, and a compensation check from the Brigadier."

"Wow—I am legitimately impressed. That just doesn't happen."

"You're telling me. The doc pulled my ass out of the pond, dried me off, and gave me my life back. I owe her big time."

The hard facade she always wore had faded. "I have seen her in action. I've seen patients have their lives transformed. They come in conflicted, confused, and always lost. She helps them."

He knew in his gut every word was accurate.

Lo tried to recover a piece of her cover with a smile and chuckle. "Of course—the job is great, and she is a great boss. I mean...I love my job. There is something new every day."

She held up her hand cast in white plaster. "Smoke, she needs to be protected. This recon going on by the men you found is scary...and that worries me. I mean, what could they want? However, for a while now, I've suspected there is something else. Someone out there has her scared." Her eyes went to the ceiling as she rattled off a suspect list. "Maybe a patient, maybe a perp that she testified against, maybe a demented spouse."

He interrupted. "Maybe somebody from the doctor's past?"

She mulled for a moment. "Possibly."

He nodded.

"What I do know: she is in denial and is disregarding protocols. She needs protection from—whomever—but also from herself."

"Understood."

"I'm just worried I'll miss something. Some of her patients are unpredictable, and I think some could be dangerous. Don't forget; she also has a lot of time with the FBI working profiling and crime scenes."

She faced him straight on. "My challenge—our challenge—is to be ready for them."

She lowered her eyes, and he knew where she was going next.

"Obviously," she held up her cast again. "I missed the threat. I wasn't watching close enough. I didn't see it coming, and she almost got hurt—bad."

He matched her intensity. "Marine, you took a knife meant for her."

"Nah—I got there late. He should have never been that close. I lost focus."

He decided on a different approach. "And, speaking as a person who has a lot of experience in those situations, believe me when I tell you...you will...never...get over it."

It startled her. Her lips parted, and she sucked air.

"Don't listen to people who tell you differently. It never gets better—it just gets worse and worse. Eventually, it becomes unbearable."

She had bitten into the self-pity apple, but he made her spit it out. "Fuck you," She started laughing. "You're a real prick."

"Yes, I am."

Her humor recovered she pointed. "I hope you plan on carrying another weapon besides those shorts?"

"Ha...ha."

Andre appeared with the altered pants.

Smoke nodded, and the tailor scurried off to finalize the bill.

"What's this gig tonight about?"

"It is an art auction/charity event that is being thrown by Mrs. Helen Throckmorton. She is the wife of New York's junior Senator, and it is as much a campaign function as an auction for charity. The money goes to the Sisters and Brothers of the Starving Martians or something like that. The Senator and his wife get a hand-grabbing photo op that will build their email address list for re-election campaign contributions."

"How does the Doc figure in?"

"This is fairly recent. The doctor had two A-listers as clients before the book. They kept their association with a psychiatrist on the down-low. After "Release the Beast" hit the bestseller list, they started bragging. Having her as their couch doc was almost as good as a house in the Hamptons. They started recommending, but she has only taken on a few of the strata elite and then only if they are genuinely in need."

"That doesn't answer the question. Why is it necessary to go to this event?"

"The elite pay big money but half of her patients are pro-bono. So, the Richy-Rich help fund a lot of good work." She held up her cast again. "I got this at a sex club while she was observing a patient in treatment. This event, like that one, is part of a patient's treatment."

"So, this is a sex auction?"

"I thought only Squids where blockheads..." She shook her head. "I guess I was wrong."

"Sorry. I was just joking."

She missed the joke. "She is a brilliant doctor who has testified as an expert forensic psychiatrist—against very dangerous people. She also testified for some who have received treatment instead of punishment."

He did what he did best to remain silent.

"She also wrote a book. She described it to me as self-imposed therapy. If you dealt with people who had dark issues every day, you'd be looking for a positive outlook in your life too. She chooses to write about something she likes, sex."

He stared, eyes fixed forward.

"Get it?" she demanded finally.

"Got it."

Andre approached, slowly this time, carrying three hangers covered in plastic and a large shopping bag.

Lo signed a slip. Smoke relieved him of his burden, and they headed out.

When the sun hit his face, he started feeling normal again. He was out of the rich and famous boutique and back in the real world. "What's your theory on the watchers?"

"That is a mystery to me." She took a beat. "I had no idea."

He interrupted her second try at the guilt trip. "Your job is close-in security. You wouldn't have any reason to look for that kind of surveillance."

"Bullshit."

"Marine, you have a multitude of close quarter tasks, including watching her six. There is no way you would have seen the spotters. They are second-tier surveillance and beyond your field of vision." He stopped walking and turned to look at her straight in the face. "Your job was to take the bullet...and you did."

"I appreciate that. Thanks."

"Hooah." The army acknowledgment came out of his mouth with the honor he intended.

Side by side, they maintained a steady pace. They didn't have to move when people approached. The slipstream of humanity diverted around them.

"There are two possibilities," he said, suddenly breaking the silence.

"What?"

"You have described, in some intimate detail, your connection with the doc and why you're here. You've talked about her and how she got to where she is."

"And...so, two possibilities. What does that mean?"

"You only told me about the recent past. You've said nothing about her beginnings. I think you have background you're not sharing. You know there is something else."

"No comment."

"Really, no comment? You running for office?"

"No...and you are such a prick."

"That fact has been established."

She held back a grin. "Okay, straight up. There is something. Something in her past but she doesn't talk about it. You're going to have to ask her."

"Not even to you, hmmm."

"Ask her," she said again with no emotion in her voice.

He wasn't disappointed in the result of his inquiry; he wasn't really expecting an answer. He didn't think Lo would know.

He had one more question but waited until they came back together, in step.

"When I first showed up, you were less than thrilled to see me."

"Accurate. I thought you were three days late and would be unreliable."

"But you don't now...feel that way? I mean you gave me a serious stink eye then, but now we are...what is this called again? Oh, yeah...bonding."

"Again..." she said smiling, "Fuck...You."

"Funny. However, seriously, you have changed your attitude towards me. Why?"

"First, you were not late. You were working and second, Felix recommended you. To her and me, that means something." She then rapid fired, "I also called some people and got background on you."

"Service record?"

"Rodger that."

"Don't believe everything you read."

"Never did—but I respect the Silver Star. That alone was enough for me to believe you wouldn't duck if it came down to you or her."

She acknowledged the Marine way. "Oorah."

There were no uniforms, no guns strapped to shoulders, and no war ribbons on shirtfronts. They were soldiers walking. In step. With resolve.

14

I n an elegant conference room located on the Warwick Hotel's eighth floor, five feet of polished mahogany separated two business partners. The principles sat in high-back leather chairs, their seconds at their right shoulders awaiting direction. The day-to-day on the meeting's agenda went quickly and as expected. One item, under the heading New Business, remained. It was titled Schedule Interruption.

Auxiliary Bishop O'Hanrand sat in front of long windows, the city skyline at his back. He wore a full-length cassock made of red watered silk. The fabric's wavy appearance suggested movement, like a still photograph of an ocean tide. It was an illusion. His oyster white hands lay flat on the table, resting on a crisp, manila file. Except for a small tuft of unruly hair flipping with the air-conditioning, he sat motionless.

Opposite O'Hanrand sat Lawrence Campbell. He could feel the sweat under his arms, his stomach nauseous from a faint smell of incense. He repeatedly clicked his pen, waiting and staring at the unopened file. Each of the previous agenda items had manila files. There was one file left on the table.

He felt the tension building, and he knew the pause between agenda items was purposeful. He would have done the same thing—get the opponent off guard.

Campbell tried to regain a superior position. "Nancy, coffee."

She turned instantly, walked to a serving table, poured a cup, added a half a teaspoon of sweetener, returned to her position, and carefully placed it in front of him.

Campbell stirred the coffee with an upright spoon. He showed a steady hand.

O'Hanrand raised his fingers slightly, eliciting his second, the monsignor, to pour a fresh cup of tea.

The monsignor responded, and a silent minute later, he carefully placed a china cup on the table.

Campbell noticed the exercise of power and was envious.

The Archbishop nodded to the monsignor ever so slightly, and the revelations of the last item began.

Giuseppe DeFrancisco stretched out an open palm. The long fingers poked out from a black cassock accented with scarlet piping, a color indicative of his rank. The red matched O'Hanrand's. It was just thinner and less noticeable. "It seems..." he cleared his throat, "it is possible there may be a small inconvenience to the schedule. This problem...may...cause a slight delay in the approval of the project."

Emotion formed words that rose in Campbell's throat becoming grunts behind tightly gritted teeth.

The monsignor continued, "The problem is with a priest who held a position of some importance in our organization. He worked in the Office of the Coordinator of Archdiocesan Planning Initiatives. Recently, we discovered, he secretly copied confidential documents." He hesitated, then as if to dismiss the importance of what he was yet to reveal waved a dismissive hand. "It seems he plans to write a book."

Campbell added confusion to his panic. "A delay because of a book? How does this affect me? I mean the project."

The monsignor nodded. "We have reason to believe the

information he has in his possession may prove...embarrassing...for Mother Church."

"Embarrassing!" Red-faced Campbell now exploded, "I have almost 30 million dollars invested in lawyers, engineers, and architects. There are the soil studies, surveys, aerial mapping, water studies, infrastructure reports...and...let's not forget the gifts that were necessary for your influential City Hall friends. I spent that money because you guaranteed project approval by January." He slapped his hands hard on the table. "That was four months ago."

The Auxiliary Bishop moved. He lifted both hands and using a settle down gesture said softly, "You are free to withdraw at any time."

Campbell's body lifted from his chair. "Withdraw...have you lost your mind? I'm not walking away from thirty million dollars."

Nancy reached out and placed a hand on his shoulder, trying to ease him back into the chair.

He slapped her hand away.

O'Hanrand shrugged impassionately. He dropped his hands back to the table and re-installed his well-practiced stoneface.

Campbell pointed his finger across the table, "I will not tolerate another delay." His threat was empty. He was shooting blanks, and he knew it.

The monsignor seemed to be enjoying the moment. "I am afraid that you nor Mother Church have much of a choice in the matter."

"You Mother..." only half the word came out of Campbell's mouth.

"However." DeFrancisco interrupted. "There may be something that can be done to forestall the actions of this misguided man and therefore, put us back on schedule."

The monsignor walked to the server to fill his coffee cup. "We know who he is and, for the most part, we think we know what he has taken. However, more importantly, we know why. As I said previously, we believe he hopes to profit by publishing the information."

He raised a finger and introduced the solution. "We now have an advantage because we also know how he plans to make the information public. So...we can take action to stop him and the threat to Mother Church." His eyes focused on Campbell, "And this project."

Campbell was pushing through the anger. He could almost put the pieces together, but there was one big piece missing.

The monsignor glanced at the Auxiliary Bishop who nodded permission to continue.

"His behavior caused suspicion. When we started looking closely, he became more suspicious. Eleven days ago, he disappeared from his rectory. We investigated and now know what he has in his possession. Most importantly, we now know with whom he plans to share it."

Campbell digested the information from the messenger. Semi-composed, he looked directly at the principle. "Please, tell me how your problem rises to become a delay in the project's approval."

"Actually, I said it was a small inconvenience." The monsignor, maintained a low tone.

O'Hanrand raised a hand. "We don't know where he is—currently. However, we do know where he is going. We have begun—I believe it is known as a stakeout." He chuckled at his familiarity with the TV Police term. "As soon as we discovered he had left the city, I asked the monsignor to put a member of our clergy in place to keep an eye out for our prodigal son. This proved to be only a temporary situation. We have decided that while the man we assigned may be of some limited assistance, he would be rather useless in the recovery of the missing material. So, we have brought in a security firm we have used with success in the past."

The Archbishop took a delicate sip of tea and peeked at Campbell for a reaction.

There was none.

With a sudden burst of words, the Monsignor finished O'Hanrand's accounting by ripping off the bandage. "We are suggesting that you provide the administration for the team responsible for finding the man and recovering the information."

The Auxiliary Bishop pushed the new manila file across the table to the land developer.

Campbell left it unopened. "Me?"

He was shocked.

"You want me to do this? I don't understand. Why do you involve me in your mess?"

The monsignor pointed to the file. "That file contains the contact information for the firm—rather, the man—we are using. He is our only contact, and he is the only one who knows anything about what we are trying to recover. He is reliable, singularly focused, and employs a variety of techniques to achieve results. He has been successful in the past."

Nancy had her fingers digging into Campbell's shoulder through his jacket.

The Auxiliary Bishop added glibly, "Of course, you could choose not to assist, but I guarantee that an outburst of controversy following a release of the information would cause a far more significant delay than we have experienced so far...and perhaps... even...the cancellation of the entire project."

Her nails were working harder.

Campbell, looking for options, didn't bite on the bait. "You still haven't said why are you coming to me with this, and why are you not doing it yourself."

The monsignor took over. "Fair question. Since the new leadership arrived in Philadelphia, all expenditures are monitored. Drawing their attention may cause a change to our partnership arrangement. Summing up, the project becomes doubtful if the Archdiocese gets involved or if there is public release of the information."

Campbell was assembling the pieces again.

The monsignor continued, "It is the only logical conclusion. You need to work with us to handle this problem out of the eyes of the public and Holy Mother Church."

The monsignor added the kill shot. "We believe the cost should be around fifty thousand dollars. Of course, the personnel we have supplied will only need to be reimbursable for their expenses."

No one spoke for a full minute.

It seemed like an hour to Campbell. He was in a tunnel, and it had only one direction out.

O'Hanrand added a light to the tunnel's end. "I think if this matter comes to a successful resolution..." he looked at the monsignor and then Campbell. "If that were accomplished—"

"And verified," added the monsignor.

"Yes, and verified." O'Hanrand agreed. "It would be correct for you to assume that full project approval would follow within thirty days."

Campbell blew a slow breath as he thought, *Millions...that once were lost might now be found.*

Nancy eased the pressure.

Campbell said, "Thirty days...with certainty...thirty days?"

"Yes, thirty days." The Auxiliary Bishop said it with conviction.

Campbell sat back and closed his eyes, contemplating additional questions. "Why don't you know where he is?"

The monsignor, feigning sincerity said, "He is, I believe it is called, off the grid. However, we have a few key facts that will lead to his discovery. We know the information is on a thumb drive. We also know he has plans to hand that drive off to an author in New York City."

The Auxiliary Bishop piped in. "We know he contacted a publisher and arranged an interview with an author."

Campbell said, "Why a book? Why not a newspaper?"

The monsignor continued. "We can only assume it's about money."

"That's pretty good intel, where did you get it?"

"We have an internal source."

Campbell took another beat. "So...let me summarize the deal points...a priest, who worked closely with you, has information that he is threatening to publish. He has disappeared. You have to find him and recover the information before it can do damage and you can't have a paper trail. So you want me to supervise and pay for people hired to find him."

"Correct." Both clerics answered simultaneously.

"What happens to the recovered information...destroy it...return it?"

The monsignor became impassionate. "Either way."

Campbell wanted more. "And the priest?"

The Auxiliary Bishop sipped his tea. "Either way."

Campbell stood up, picked up the file. "Thirty days."

The Auxiliary Bishop nodded. "Thirty days."

15

"The Overthrow Boxing Gym at 9th and Bleeker Street."
Felix sounded determined over the phone.

Smoke started paging through the guest information book, looking for a map of the city. "Cab?"

"Nope. From the front door of the hotel, you go right six blocks to 3rd Ave. Turn left. From there its two blocks to Bleeker—number nine."

"When?"

"Still a powerhouse with the vocabulary."

Smoke didn't comment.

Felix waited a beat. "I'll be there by seven."

Smoke paid no regard to his friend's curt remark and looked at the clock on the nightstand, 6:10.

"I'll be there. Showers there?"

"Yes, but not for me. You can decide when you get there but brother-man, it is definitely not the Ritz."

Smoke disconnected.

He needed a good workout. He had been using the hotel gym every morning. He used the universal machines, free weights, and pushed the incline and pace settings on the treadmill. It helped, but it was a hotel gym—too nice, too new and too clean. Also, there was no heavy bag.

He downed his second coffee and had to look around for his dungarees. He'd regulated to suits for a couple of days, and wearing his old jeans reminded him of what was normal.

He pulled the belt through its metal buckle and hooked it into the same well-worn hole. At least he hadn't gained any weight.

At 6:28, he emerged from the hotel and looked up at the green street sign displaying West Huston and turned right.

His boyhood home was a crowded city, but it wasn't like this. It also wasn't the first time he had been in New York. The mass of flowing humanity made him uncomfortable.

Daily exposure hadn't made it any more comfortable, and he wasn't hopeful that more walkabouts would help. There was just a sea of people all moving together like schools of fish—all moving in the same direction but capable of instantaneous change. Rush hour in New York City—he just wasn't prepared.

He pushed on to 3rd Avenue, and he got behind a small woman, who he guessed, from her Sari, was from India. She was pushing a shopping cart and had far more experience negotiating NYC traffic. Choosing experience over size, he stayed close behind as she successfully glided past oncoming traffic that included a multitude of speeding yellow death machines.

Despite the odds against, he arrived at The Overthrow Boxing Gym intact. Its door wasn't just dirty—it was grizzled. The facility was worse than Felix had described. He smiled.

Perfect, a real gym.

He attempted to enter, which took effort. The door moved but took a shoulder to open.

Perhaps it was part of the workout regime.

Felix was waiting for him at the end of a dark hallway, talking to a man behind a counter. The man was well built, grey, and wore the marks of the gloves he met in the ring.

Smoke passed by fight posters plastered to the walls. Faded fighters from days long gone, yellowing with age and curling up at the corners. The posters, further along, were more recent, had younger faces, but the same eyes. It was a history of a gym. There was no graffiti, not on this wall. There was respect for the memories hung there. A brand-new poster sat on an easel near the desk announcing a fight featuring a middleweight who called The Overthrow Boxing Gym home.

It was perfume to him. Sweat and leather mixed with the dank, metallic odor of the bloodstained canvas blended with the humidity rising from muscles and minds pushed to the brink. To him, it was the smell of pure will generated by those dedicated to a goal. A goal that was always completely unpredictable.

Felix pointed to the fighter as Smoke approached. "Smoke, this is the real Rocky."

"My name is Mustafa. I fought as Rocky Estafire out of Brooklyn back in the day."

He reached out, and Smoke shook his hand. His knuckles were turned and twisted, but his grip was like a vice.

"In 1984, this man was ranked the number four middleweight in the world."

"Yeah, yeah...that was a long time ago. Now I am the owner, manager, head trainer, and janitor of this fine establishment."

"You ready for me?" Felix, held up a closed fist and mugged like Ali.

The old boxer sized up Smoke. "You'd better be careful, F-bomb. I think this guy can give you some trouble."

"Not a chance," said Felix. "I've had this guy's number for years."

"Ah, huh." Rocky winked at Smoke. "I think I'd take the other side of that line."

"F-bomb?" Smoke wrinkled an eyebrow.

"Rocky doesn't think Felix sounds tough enough so he calls me F-bomb."

The boxer nodded. "That's right. Your name is Smoke?"

"Right."

"That'll do." Rocky smiled.

"It's worked out so far. Where do I change?"

Felix, alias F-bomb, showed Smoke the locker room.

"I think we hit the speed bag, then the heavy bag, then I kick your ass in the square ring." Felix used the Ali mug again.

Smoke nodded.

"Don't worry about locking anything. Nobody touches anything in here. It's safer than Fort Knox. You change, and I'll meet you by the heavy bag."

Smoke kicked off his boots and hung up his pants, leaving the wallet in the back pocket. Before going out into the gym, he looked past a plastic curtain and decided to shower at the hotel.

Felix was hitting the heavy bag but stopped when Smoke approached. "What's up buttercup?"

"You still hit like a girl," Smoke gestured at the bag..

"We'll see about that."

Felix turned and laid a powerful punch into the bag that drove it sideways and back.

Smoke grabbed a roll of tape and started wrapping his hands.

"Give me that." Felex grabbed it in disgust. "Who the fuck taught you how to do that?"

"You did."

"Bullshit, you pussy-loving son of a bitch. I never taught you to overlap like that."

"You kiss your mother with that mouth?"

Felix stopped instantly and stared at his friend. "Oh my God— you just made a joke."

Smoke looked down to the unfinished wrap. "This ain't getten' done by itself."

Felix, smiling broadly, started wrapping again. His smile was genuine, and it broke through the bravado, momentarily. While he worked on the tape, he looked up, then down, several times.

Smoke raised a curious eyebrow. "What?"

130

"What do you think of her?"

"Who?"

"Don't make me smack you. My girl—your new boss—the doc."

Smoke didn't answer.

Felix didn't press, reserving his witty retort.

"She is..." Smoke started then stopped.

Felix picked up Smoke's other hand and started re-wrapping again, still maintaining radio silence.

"She is—pretty amazing."

"And a beautiful soul," added Felix, grinning.

Smoke nodded, "That too."

"You know I love her."

"I know."

Felix checked the tape, making sure the finger joints were secure. "I was mulling over how all of this happened. You're here because Lo took a bullet. However, you need to know I wouldn't have dragged you up here for that."

"Ah huh."

"There is something else going on. The doc hasn't been right for a while, and what happened in my club was not planned. It was a drunk but I used the attack to get you here."

"There are two," said Smoke.

"Two what?"

"Threats."

"Wait—what?"

"I did recon before I made myself known. I spotted surveillance. She is being watched."

"So that must be professional—correct?"

"Very good. Correct."

"Who and why?"

"Only know a partial who, nothing on the why yet. But you are right."

"About?"

"There are two threats. One is the watcher and one the doc is hiding. I think that is what has her acting scared."

Felix finished the tape. "Don't let anything happen to her. If you need anything—anything at all."

"I know."

Felix gestured for the gloves.

Smoke reached behind him and handed his friend two gloves that had seen better days.

There was a long pause, and the first glove got fitted and tied.

"There is another reason why I wanted you to meet her, and you know why...right?"

Smoke dropped both hands back to his knees and in a low voice. "Listen up—I have only been here a couple of days."

Felix gave him a low eyebrow.

"But," continued Smoke, "I will admit—you are not wrong; she is exceptional."

Felix finished the second Everlast glove then switched back to kick-ass mode. "You just going to sit there—pussy?"

Smoke stood, pushed the heavy bag forward, and took a fighting stance. When it came back, he hit it with a right hook, then a left, then a right, each time with more force. He danced back and forth finding his rhythm. It had been a while, but it came back—the old 'riding a bike' thing.

"Time," yelled Felix.

Smoke stopped.

"You loose?"

Smoke tapped Felix's gloves. "Yep."

They climbed through the ropes, taking opposite corners and waiting for the bell.

Rocky, now also the timer, hit the bell once.

Ring.

They both stepped out of their corners, hands at the ready and heads bobbing side to side.

"Hey, none of that Karate shit," mumbled Felix through his mouth-guard.

"None needed." Smoke returned a short jab with a sharp left to the belly.

"Uff," air escaped from Felix.

Smoke moved right and sent another jab into Felix's ribcage then missed an uppercut. He stepped back out of reach, narrowly missing a right cross.

Felix stepped back and used his forearms to pull up his shorts. He also put determination on his face.

Smoke had seen this face before and realized his friend just got serious. He needed to be very careful until the truck in front of him ran low on gas.

Felix started in and began throwing body punches. Smoke had no choice but to drop his elbows to his sides, put his gloves up near his head, and absorb the haymaker body blows on his forearms. Felix was pounding him like Rocky Balboa hitting hanging meat.

Two minutes into the round, Felix began to tire. His hands were low. He had connected with a couple of good body blows, but all of the headshots had missed.

Smoke started dancing away just out of reach.

"You better be careful, F-bomb." Rocky had his hand ready to pull the cord on the first-round bell. "You better keep your hands up."

Ten seconds left in the round. Smoke avoided a straight left jab, ducking down. Coiled low, he stepped into Felix, hit him in the solar plexus with a left jab, shifted his weight, stood up and threw a straight right catching Felix on the temple.

Felix was leaning in when the right hit his head.

The truck hit the mat with a thump. His mouthpiece shot across the canvas.

Ring...Ring...Ring.

As hard as he went down, Felix wasn't out. He got to his feet. Shook his head to clear the cobwebs and spat on the mat. He wobbled his way to a stool in his corner.

Rocky was waiting with a towel and cold water.

"If he was twenty years younger—shit—ten years younger. Ummm, Mmmm." Rocky shook his head. "That boy hits like a freight train."

"I am aware." Felix rolled his eyes and shook his head. He tapped his gloves together and yelled across the ring to Smoke. "That all you got?"

Smoke, standing in his corner waiting for the bell, did not respond.

"I think you might have pissed him off." Rocky put in Felix's mouthpiece.

"You might be right. But I still got some bad dog in this fight."

Ring...Ring...Ring

Felix got up and started in.

Smoke saw his line wasn't straight.

He dropped his hands. "I've had enough."

Felix had to step right to correct a stagger.

"What, you quitting on me?"

"Yep."

"Hey, I good. I can finish this. Let's go."

Smoke turned around and looked hard at his friend since boot camp. "I good?"

Felix put his hands down and walked back to his corner, dejected.

Rocky started untying the laces on Felix's gloves. "He got you pretty good, and you were staggering a bit. I think he's just looking out for you."

Felix, blinked to clear his vision. "He always has."

MARCH 2, 2002 - SHAHI-KOT VALLEY, AFGHANISTAN: OPERATION ANACONDA

Staff Sergeant Henry Smokehouse and Sergeant Felix Upton Grant and the rest of the 187th Infantry Regiment were ready for a fight.

Their platoon along with twenty-five Afghan troops sat waiting on a road for an attack scheduled to begin in less than one hour.

Leadership, based on best intelligence, determined Al-Qaeda and Taliban forces were in control of the entire valley. The enemy had taken up positions in caves and along ridges in the five-mile-long valley at the base of mountains that bordered Pakistan.

The platoon, along with the Afghans, was to drive the enemy from their positions. The Al-Qaeda and Taliban soldiers would retreat north where the Coalition forces would cut them off before they could escape into Pakistan.

Like every battle plan, it did not unfold as designed. Intelligence dramatically underestimated the opposing force and what was expected to be from 100 to 150 troops, in fact, was more like 1,000. It was decided, however, that even with the bad intel the objective was still achievable. A German military strategist once said, "No battle plans survive contact with the enemy." This battle plan was not an exception to that rule.

Before the ground assault, an Air Force bomb run lasting fifty-five minutes was to broadcast fear and destruction across the valley. The strafing fell a bit short of that goal. The number of bombs dropped was six. The seventh of the five hundred bombs got stuck in a bomb bay of a B1-B. The second B1-B in line waited for the first to clear. When it didn't, they both flew back to base still loaded. Then two F-15ES got bumped off their run by a misinterpreted communication. They too flew back to base, also still fully loaded.

At dawn's early light, and in view of the enemy, the assault began. Immediately, their positions were besieged by mortar and small arms fire. The units went into defensive mode and quickly spread out. They first gained cover moving cautiously looking for positions allowing for a mounted assault on the enemy positions. They couldn't move back. There was no back. Just forward. They were pinned against the mountains.

Smoke took cover under an M-ATV communications vehicle that kind of resembled a cut-off pickup truck. The driver and the

Communications Officer were lying next to him. The officer was screaming into his microphone that they were taking heavy fire and were pinned down.

Felix was behind the truck. He thought he was safe.

Smoke heard him get hit.

Smoke crawled out from under the truck and bellied his way to his friend. He flipped Felix over and saw that he had taken a 7.62 round from an AK-47 in the belly. He needed medical attention and soon.

Mortars continued to rain down, tracers and small arms fire flashed by and ricocheted off the rocks all around them. Smoke saw that most of it concentrated on the troops in the trenches behind him. There was a twenty-yard gap between Smoke, the truck, Felix, and the rest of the soldiers.

The troops were pinned down but returning fire. They were also drawing fire.

He crawled back under the truck to the other side, leaving Felix with a pressure bandage on his belly and an arm full of morphine. He crouched low then sprinted across the road, diving into a drainage gutter. Making himself as small as possible, he belly-crawled a hundred yards towards the enemy position.

There was a report filed after the battle. It was a lengthy report. The narrative began describing a platoon, pinned down under heavy fire, facing an enemy of superior number and position. Staff Sergeant Henry Smokehouse, acting alone overcame the enemy position killing fourteen enemy and wounding eight. The accounting of the battle came from the interrogation of the wounded enemy. The Sergeant obtained a high ground position and attacked with hand grenades, rifle fire, a captured machine gun, and at the end, hand to hand combat.

Two coalition soldiers suffered wounds from the mortar attacks, both minor. There were no other casualties.

Several days later, the coalition forces took the valley; however, most of the enemy had already escaped into Pakistan.

Sergeant Henry Smokehouse was found unconscious and airlifted back to base. He suffered three wounds; a 7.62 in the calf, a 7.62 in the side, and severe shrapnel wounds to his back.

He received the Silver Star for Gallantry in Action against an enemy of the United States.

Smoke gave his CO one de-briefing. He never spoke of the incident again. He mustered out of the service at thirty-four after eleven years of active duty and three tours of combat. He received two purple hearts and a Commendation Medal for his bravery in action in Iraq, a purple heart and the Silver Star for actions in Afghanistan. He was recommended for the Congressional Medal of Honor; however, the application lacked enough witnesses of superior rank. He saved the lives of his unit and with no thought to his own safety attacked and killed the enemy who had superior numbers and fortification.

Sergeant Felix Upton Grant survived his wounds without any complications; however, the doctors on staff said he would have died in the field had he not been airlifted back to base. They said he came within minutes of being irretrievable.

Smoke recuperated quickly. He left his gun and fatigues but kept the boots when he mustered out.

16

The limo cruised down the West Side Highway with surprising ease. Smoke expected a stop-and-go pace that clogged every inch of asphalt. Tonight, for some reason, The West Side Highway wasn't congested. Even the tourist traffic around the 911 Memorial had dissipated.

Steel-framed glass and white concrete buildings flew past. In every window, he saw the reflection of the world that was before. He could see the looped videos of the devastation playing on new screens.

They drove under a pedestrian walkway that was under construction.

The well-lighted Battery Park home of Goldman Sachs flew by. Their offices above the highway lit the night—there was no close of business for money. A community had risen from the debris. The memory of the horror overcome with high steel and high hope. The buildings were back, better, taller, a tribute to resilience. The people were back, walking to school, shopping in stores, jogging on paths through new parks, working in the tall steel and glass—people living their lives in a tribute to resilience and never forgetting.

A yellow cab suddenly materialized inches away from his window.

"Wow." He turned to Dr. O. "Man, that was close."

Dr. O didn't respond. She was staring out her window and hadn't noticed the yellow missile. She appeared to be accustomed to the thrill of the amusement park ride.

He wondered what was occupying her thoughts. Obviously, it wasn't dying in a burning wreck as a result of a traffic accident. He shifted his weight and turned his back to his window. Lights from the street were flashing into the backseat like erratic strobes, alternating bright white and dim yellow. In the in-between, amid the light and the dark, she was a portrait in grey shadows.

He was different, at that moment. The man in the van pissing in a jar was far away. What he was, what he had always been, wasn't in the car.

The limo broke left like a train moved on a track. The back of Smoke's head banged against the window. He winced and rubbed his head. When he looked up, she was smiling at him.

"What's this event about?" he asked, trying to recover his tough-guy image. "Lo gave me a couple of highlights, but I am not sure why this is so important to you."

She stopped smiling and didn't answer.

"Okay, but you are aware you are under surveillance by persons unknown, for reasons unknown. Yet, you decide to walk into a situation where you will be vulnerable."

She did not stir.

"You haven't told why this event is so important."

"It's not important for you to know." She turned, looking out the window.

The wave of sentiment that cracked his façade healed.

They turned right, onto Little West Avenue, into the line of limos waiting to discharge their passengers at the Ritz Carlton.

She turned and looked at him. "I apologize. I was rude, and I'm sorry."

He nodded, acknowledging her sincerity.

"It's a fraud."

"What is?" he replied.

"This event is promoting a charity."

"The charity is a fraud? How's that?"

"No. I'm sorry. Let me start over. It is a fundraiser for Senator Throckmorton."

"Lo told me. It's more of a political fundraiser than a charity, but that doesn't sound like a fraud."

"You need to listen. I haven't finished."

He hadn't been scolded in a long time.

"The fundraiser is sponsored, in this case, by a Senator looking towards re-election. The hall, food, entertainment, even the guest appearances are paid for by the charity."

"Guest appearances?"

She gave him 'the look' again.

He almost cowered.

"This event is an art auction sponsored by a gallery that is promoting several artists. They invest a lot of cash to market their artists. An A list auction and the press it attracts can transport an artist to another level. Attracting the press and high rollers includes paying celebrities' appearance fees. Tonight, I understand Christopher Walken, Uma Thurman, and Denzel Washington are attending. Nora Jones and Cyndi Lauper also but they are art collectors of sorts and are welcomed freebies. Then there's Lenny Kravitz...who just shows up at everything." She chuckled.

"Okay...however, I still don't get the fraud."

She looked at him with a stern last warning look. "Every painting has a starting bid, a reserve. It suggests a third party owns the art. But actually, the art has never been purchased by anybody. The third party is an investor secured by the gallery as an insurance policy. Most never see the piece. The auction begins, and when the art sells, and it always sells, the gallery gets the reserve. The investor gets the difference between the reserve and the auction price. The charity gets a small percentage. Everybody's happy."

"What about the artist?"

"The gallery owns the artist."

"I'm still not sure that's fraud." He knew he spoke too quickly.

This time his interruption made her pissy. "I'm not done yet!"

"Okay...Okay, geez."

"The artists gain reputation through the gallery's promotion, which in turn inflates the value of the work. It's called pointing."

She glared, anticipating.

"Once a work is sold, it has an established market value. The trick —the fraud—is how that value is increased. First, a gallery finds an artist who has potential—potential defined as that which grabs public attention. It could be the subject matter or even bad behavior— anything that gets press ink. Next, a group buys pieces and then sells them to each other, building appraisal value. Then the pieces are donated to museums as tax write-offs at the full-appraised value. What was purchased for a few hundred dollars is donated for a hundred thousand."

"So." He froze, waiting for an interruption objection. When she didn't, he continued. "They buy a lot of the artist's paintings, hold them, sell one or two to each other driving up the values of the entire collection...then donate all of them to museums for a full write-off at current market value."

The car stopped its turtle-like progression at the front door of the hotel.

She finished it. "The fraud is the gallery, not the charity."

"Okay, I get it now, but I am curious to know how you fit in?"

"Tonight's artist," she turned to look at him, "is my patient. I'm working for him and now so are you."

Her door popped open. Smoke got out quickly and walked around the back of the car in time to see her hand reach out and up to a red-coated attendant. A long bare leg surrounded by red silk emerged before her arm and slightly bent wrist.

It was one of those Doris Day movie close-ups he saw as a kid on the big screen—all fuzzy and in slow motion.

He moved quickly and replaced the attendant's hand with his arm. Smoke guided her along the sidewalk and through the gilded double doors into a beautifully appointed great hall. It was a holding pen for the waiting exhibit crowd.

Tuxedos and dresses of every possible flavor were displayed on shapes of equal diversity. Photographers hurried about making their living, the shapes pretending to be inconvenienced. A couple of snappers representing art sections of legitimate papers and one from Page six of the Post looked for cleavage shots or accidental clothing malfunctions.

In about twenty minutes, Page six would get a classic picture for tomorrow morning's lead.

He had learned a long time ago to never get comfortable in a large group because there were friends and enemies in every corner of every event. Even in a small group of those who were gathered in a common interest, what might appear to be real is more often a mirage.

Neither motive nor intention is ever displayed on a buffet table.

She moved through the crowd with ease and grace. She smiled and shook hands even occasionally agreeing to pose for a picture but always dragging Smoke in on her arm.

Smoke was genuinely surprised when Felix blindsided him with a Spielberg movie moment. He snuck up behind Smoke, extended both sequenced laden arms, then grabbed Smoke's ass cheeks with his mammoth hands.

The New York Post page six photo was a classic.

Felix was in the center of the picture. The eye was drawn first to the outrageous suit. Vibrant primary colors in geometric shapes dominated a jacket and short pants. Not part of the designer's fashion vision was two tree-trunk legs covered with tattoos finished at their root with black patent leather combat boots.

The second subject in the photo was Smoke. He had both hands raised; his cheeks puckered in surprise.

Doctor O was in the foreground. Her head tilted back in unabashed glee.

The freeze-frame action shot was the cover shot above the fold. *DR. O DATE MOLESTED* was the Page six morning headline.

"Damn it, Felix, I am supposed to be under the radar here. I'm working, remember," he said, trying unsuccessfully to regain dignity.

"Hey buddy, glad you could make it." Felix ignored the comment.

Felix turned to Dr. O. "How's he doing so far Doc?" he asked, quickly reaching for his kiss.

"He's doing fine, but obviously, still adjusting to life at this altitude." She snickered.

"You look good Smokey." Felix stroked Smoke's silk lapel. "Nice suit. A little drab for my taste, but nice—Italian right?"

"Drab?" the doctor mocked, smiling "A peacock is drab next to you."

A handsome man who was taller, thinner, and a few years younger than

Felix walked over carrying two long fluted glasses. He smiled and turned to Dr. O. "Dr. Bennet, a pleasure to see you again." He nodded courteously, handing-off a glass to the molester.

She extended her hand. David shook it.

"He's my eye candy," said Felix.

"You're an asshole." David held out a hand to Smoke. "And you must be the infamous Smoke."

Smoke took the hand. "I just met you, but I like you already."

Dr. O changed the subject. "What's the art like?"

Felix became serious. "I'm in for sixty K on a reserve for the third to the last piece being auctioned. There is a good turnout tonight, and the bidding should be spirited. I think I can turn a minimum thirty percent even after the charity takes its fifteen percent."

"Oh Felix." Dr. O appeared disgruntled. "I thought we talked about this. You know I'm not a fan."

"I know, I know, my last auction. I just couldn't resist."

David stepped forward, interrupting, "I don't think it's exactly kosher either. Immoral perhaps but definitely legal. The artist benefits, the investor, in this case, Felix, benefits, the Charity benefits. The buyers at the auction, well...they win a bid against Derek Jeter or the like. They can brag they bought the best canvas of the latest and greatest. Sometimes, because of the hype, they do."

Felix sighed. "Beautiful and smart too." He grabbed David's hand and led him away.

Dr. O and Smoke walked into the Exhibition Hall following in the vapor trail Felix left behind.

The artist being shown was a new forty-year-old painter who worked with acrylic on canvas. All of the paintings began at $50,000, the centerfold piece, a mural in the style of Picasso's bombing of Guernica during the Spanish Civil War, featured the horror of 9-11. It was reserved at $285,000.

They took their time walking from painting to painting admiring some, dissing others.

"Hi Doc." The Queen's girl from Ozone Park was all smiles.

"Hi Cyndi," responded Dr. O in kind.

"Love it or hate it?" Ms. Lauper look curious.

Smoke was surprised one of his favorite singers of all times was so small.

"A little of both."

Suddenly coming in from the left was a shrill voice that made Smoke wince, "You should be ashamed of yourself."

A prune-faced woman with a helmet of grey hair pushed her way past the pink-haired Lauper and positioned herself in front of Dr. O.

"I beg your pardon." Dr. O was polite.

"Your book is trash. Your patients are the worst kind of degenerates."

Smoke assessed the threat and then stood back and watched.

Lauper's face reddened, matching her hair.

The singer stepped into the intruder, "Listen you!"

Dr. O raised her left hand giving a halt sign.

Smoke had seen real action on two wars, had been shot at by an enemy who wanted to kill him dead. He had been torn down by drill Sergeants and beaten up by Commanding Officers both of whom made him believe dying in battle would have been an easier fate. All of those threats and attacks came with a very, very high volume.

"You should be locked up for writing that kind of liberal, godless garbage." The grey-haired woman had a high volume.

He was used to it and was curious to see if the doc was up to the challenge.

The assaulting woman was vocal but never would be physical so he stayed put wanting to see this unfold.

The helmet head stood posed, defiant, hands-on-hips, with loathing on her face.

There was quiet.

Dr. O took a step toward the woman.

The woman remained firm, but her eyes were darting back and forth.

Dr. O leaned in and whispered. Her attack was not high volume.

Smoke watched in awe.

Whispered. She actually just whispered.

The woman pulled back; mouth opened in horror. Her face turned the color of her hair. Her knees buckled a little. She took a step back—then another. She exhaled loudly, then whipped around and walked away.

No volume, a whisper.

Cyndi had eyes wide in stunned admiration. "What did you say to her?"

"Nothing much."

Cyndi looked at her with a knowing smile. "You won't ever tell me, will you?"

"No, I won't." The doctor hesitated a beat then added. "I will say that some might view what I said was...unprofessional."

The singer smiled, leaned in, and kissed the doctor's cheek. "You're my hero." She smiled at Smoke then walked away.

"I think it's time to go." Smoke nodded toward the exit.

"In a few minutes. I haven't finished looking at the exhibit."

They cruised around for another ten minutes and then headed for the door.

"Did that incident prevent you from bidding on anything?"

"I never bid." She turned to him in a sudden realization. "You're the detective. You've seen my office, right?"

"I have. No original art, only reproductions, yea, I noticed. Also, you don't get involved in these schemes, do you? Even if they are legal."

"Correct."

Smoke perceived he had answered correctly and reassured her of his Holmes-like deductive insight.

The car arrived at the door, and they began the journey back up the West Side Highway to her SoHo loft.

Ten minutes of silence went by, and finally, Smoke exploded. The curiosity too much even for him. "Okay, I give up."

Dr. O smiled brightly. "I knew that you had to know."

"So, tell me."

"No. You have to ask."

"Say what?"

"You have to ask me what I said."

He was embarrassed, "Okay...Okay...I have to know." He lowered his voice and added, "Really, I have to know. What did you say to that woman?"

She turned so her shoulders were square to his and looked into his eyes. "I said," pausing to access her attitude voice. "If you don't step off, I'm going to punch you right in your cunt."

He smiled.

She smiled.

He was in love.

17

Märta Johansson arrived on time—not one minute early—not one minute late. She had requested to meet Smoke at the restaurant next to her office building. She saw the man fitting Dr. O's description immediately after pushing open the door.

She walked to Smoke's table. "I only have thirty-eight minutes." She looked at her watch as she sat down.

"This will take as long as it takes." He paused, caught her eyes, and continued, "If you don't want my help, I'll leave." He gave her his stern face.

"No—wait—I'm sorry," she stammered, "When I get nervous, I get bossy."

"No worries."

She smiled but appeared nervous.

A waitress buzzed over to their table. She cracked gum. "You want something, Honey?"

Märta replied without looking up, "Coffee, black."

The waitress rolled her eyes and walked away.

"Doctor said you might be able to help me."

"How is it that prepositions disappear when someone speaks of a doctor?"

"What?" Märta began drumming her fingers on the table.

"Shouldn't it be, the doctor or my doctor instead of just doctor? Nurses say it all the time. Doctor will be on call later—or—you will have to ask doctor. It's like the word—the—doesn't exist."

She eyed him curiously, most likely questioning her decision to take Dr. O's suggestion for his help.

"Are you serious right now? I have a real problem. I know—doctor —filled you in. So, are you going to help me or not?"

He got what he wanted. The look was real. The accountant's emotion was genuine.

He drummed his fingers back at her. She didn't flinch. "I can. It is possible...but it depends."

"On what?"

"Doctor," he shrugged amusement, "did give me the details on your predicament." He leaned over the table. "The level of success I achieve will depend on several things. First, I'll need your complete honesty about what happened. Next, I need to determine if this is the action of one or a group. Is it a part of a premeditated plan or a crime of opportunity? Is it professional or an amateur? If the former—it's a bigger problem—if the latter not so much. I also have to determine if there are more than just pictures." He saw her flinch for the first time at the mention of the pictures but continued. "It would be better to assume that there might be videos or audiotapes."

Both hands came up to her head and covered her face as her elbows hit the table, "Shit, you're right. There could be more."

He saw tears start to well in her eyes.

The waitress placed black coffee on the table and retreated.

Märta began to stir the coffee. She was facing him, but her stare was distant.

Smoke felt the pain. He also felt sympathy.

"You know then...about my—" She lowered her voice and her eyes.

"I know that a scumbag is taking advantage of someone who has found themselves vulnerable."

She looked up.

"What you don't know is how much I really don't like scumbags. What you don't want to know is how I end this."

"So, you're going to help me, then." Her shoulders were rising with her spirit.

"Yes."

Again, tears welled up.

"How much does he want?"

"Twenty thousand dollars."

"Can you afford that?"

"Yes."

"Okay, that helps, but I have some questions."

She blanched, doubt resurfacing.

He continued without a pause, "The first question. You met them through a website, correct?"

"Yes"

"Were they ever to your apartment?"

"My house?" She corrected emphatically, "No! My apartment and never!"

"Have you seen either of them at or around your office?"

"No." Her face indicated that that possibility hadn't crossed her mind.

"How do you think they found out where you worked?"

"It must have been my phone. Yes, it had to have been my phone. They must have looked when I was tied—" She didn't get to finish the sentence because Smoke cut her off.

"You called one of them Donner and the other Blitzen, correct?"

She nodded.

"Do you know Donner's real name?"

"No, but—but—wait...I thought the blackmailer was the new guy.

There wasn't a problem until he showed up." Tears were running down her face. "This is all my fault. I was so stupid."

"Stop." He took her hand. "Blitzen didn't show up because Donner didn't call him. Donner is where I start."

"Right...Yes." Again, she wiped the tears from her face.

"When did you get the picture at your office?"

"Three weeks ago, Tuesday."

"Have you received anything else?"

"No. I haven't. However, my next...ah... ah..."

"Appointment," Smoke filled in.

"Yes, my regular Tuesday night is coming up. Should I send a text?"

"You were going to keep the appointment," he said in surprise.

"No, but then—I thought maybe it wasn't them or..." She shook her head. "I don't know what to do." She flushed again, looking frantic. "Maybe it was somebody in the next room—or somebody who just bugged the room."

"No. It was them."

"Are you certain?"

"I am."

He plowed on. "I'll need the number or web address where you text Donner."

"It is a phone number. We talked from time to time, to set the scene for the next...appointment." She smiled a little.

"I'll need that number."

She wrote it down on a notepad she had in her side pocket with a gold pen she had in her inside jacket pocket.

"Can you get me the cash by 5:00 today?"

She checked her watch...calculated the time and said, "5:25."

"Good—here 5:25—bring four envelopes with five thousand dollars in each."

"Okay. Why the four envelopes?"

He took a breath, reached across the table, and took her hands in his.

"I will end this tonight. Trust me."

"No disrespect. I don't trust you, but I do trust Dr. O."

"Okay," he smiled. "That's close enough. 5:25."

She nodded.

He nodded.

18

He had his feet up on the desk when the phone on his desk rang. Detective Robert Aimer almost fell off his chair when he saw the number.

Smoke heard a rattle then a thump when the detective dropped the phone.

Aimer settled, and then calmly said, "I know it was you."

"Fredo."

"What?"

"G2."

"What—What?"

"Godfather 2. "I know it was you, Fredo. That's the line you were quoting. Michael to his brother, Fredo, on New Year's Eve in Cuba."

"No, you jerk off. I know it was—you—who tipped me to the body we found." He paused and then corrected himself. "Actually, the three bodies. Did you think I wouldn't figure that out?"

"I have no idea what you're talking about, detective, and for the record, I admit to asshole, not jerk off."

There was silence while the humor sank in.

"Okay, Smoke, I get it you can't come forward with where the information came from—I get it, and I get why—okay?" He raised his voice again, "But I know it was you!"

"Fredo."

"Asshole."

"Correct."

"Very funny." Aimer changed his tone back to the normal Smoke exchange.

"What do you want? You do want something. That—is—why you called?"

"You are correct. Yes, I do need something."

"How may I be of service?"

"I need a last known address for Gerald Cavatina. He is a resident of New York City, late twenties, early thirties, weight 175, hair brown, eyes brown, no scars, and no tats. He will have priors, no doubt. Probably for extortion or petty theft—maybe assault, but nothing hard. With any luck, there will be an outstanding warrant."

"Sounds like a lightweight. Can I ask why you need this?"

Smoke was silent, and the detective took a beat to realize he wouldn't be getting an answer.

"I need an hour or two. This number good for you?"

"Yes."

Smoke arranged a fee for services rendered. "Two beers."

"Done."

19

S moke walked along the sidewalk in Chinatown, one of NYC's most famous tourist attractions, looking for an address. Brightly colored banners flew on long flagpoles extending over awnings adding to the legions of color. There were signs and posters everywhere, each competing for the attention of the passerby.

He was at street level where people flowed up and down and in and out—living their lives today just like yesterday—utterly unaware of how different life was on Main Street, USA.

He found the address he sought marked on a black metal door that led to four floors of apartments above a Chinese Market. Smoke crossed the street at the light and doubled back. He found a shadow where he could get the lay of the land without drawing attention.

The market was closing, and several workers were pulling boxes that had been positioned out on the sidewalk back into the market. They had long handle brooms and hoses. It reminded him of 9th street, hard-working people working hard.

No one was paying attention to the man in blue jeans and a

baseball cap. He looked like every other resident of the street, just another worker bee coming back to the hive.

He crossed over, opened the door, and ascended a narrow stairwell, stopping on four. There was what was supposed to be a fire door at the top of the stairs. He pushed through into a long hallway with two doors on either side. He winced when the odor hit him. He wasn't sure what concoction of life's discards was producing it, but he assumed there were a few he had never experienced. He was sure of one, however, urine. He took a breath and found 4B on a door that had so much grit that the original color would have only been a wild guess.

The apartment belonged to Gerald Cavatina's girlfriend who had bailed him out a couple of times. Smoke hoped the man he was looking for was still in her good graces and then by extension; she would know where he was or, best case, it would be the current address of Mr. Gerald Cavatina.

The inquiry made to the NYPD by the Philly Detective resulted in a yellow sheet on Cavatina which stipulated arrests, bail applications, convictions, and a phony current address, which was why the perp was still able to evade an active bench warrant. He was a petty thief who didn't muster much attention and, when the police were unsuccessful in retrieving him, the NYPD decided to wait until the inevitable happened. It was only a matter of time before Gerald Cavatina was arrested again and placed back in the system.

Mr. Gerald Cavatina, alias Blitzen's Substitute, had five prior arrests; one arrest for extortion with no conviction, two arrests for assault, and one conviction for B&E. The outstanding bench warrant was for failure to appear on an attempted armed robbery charge.

He was not a professional but also not an amateur.

Finding this guy was a little harder than finding Donner who was Märta Johansson regular "once a month, Tuesday night, tie me up and fuck me buddy." After Märta gave Smoke Donner's phone number, a simple inquiry on Peopleloooker.com found Mr. Harry Gardner and his home address.

Smoke had deduced from her story that Donner was in on the blackmail scheme, but to confirm this fact he needed to see the fuck buddy up close and personal. So if his assumption was correct, then he could extract the information he needed to end her problem.

He found Mr. Harry Gardner/Donner home across the river in Jersey City. He was in his two-story, family of four, white picket fence house. It took Smoke no time at all to extract the information he needed to find the mastermind of the blackmail scheme. Mr. Donner was as interested in preserving his secrecy as was Märta. He was so sincere that Smoke judged the probability of him vowing his innocence in the blackmail attempt was at ninety percent.

The fact was that Donner had no criminal record, and his mistake was allowing his 'friend' to come along on his sexual adventure.

It seems that Cavatina/Blitzen ran into his old friend Gardner/Donner and former high school buddy in a bar and after a long evening of drinking and listening to Mr. Harry Gardner/Donner bragging about his family of four—and— his once a month tie me up and fuck me liaison with Märta, Cavatina convinced Mr. Harry Gardner/Donner that it would be in his best interest to allow him to participate in the sex party and in doing so he would make sure that his once a month would never get back to his wife and kids.

Smoke knocked on 4B, "Gerald Cavatina...Cable Company."

He heard footsteps thumping towards the door.

"Who is it?" came a rough voice.

"Gerald Cavatina. Cable Company," Smoke repeated.

"What the fuck do you want?"

This time Smoke yelled, "Hey, you fuck. If you don't want your cable to work, then you can go fuck yourself. I got fourteen apartments to update with new boxes; otherwise, Cable and the Internet goes off at midnight."

There was a slight pause, but the prospect of no Internet porn must have been too much, and Smoke heard the chain come off the door.

The voice that had come from inside started to open the door slowly.

Smoke kicked it open and came in fast. He shot a straight right just above the bridge of the man's nose.

Blitzen went airborne, feet in the air, and landed on his back.

Smoke looked down the hall for the girlfriend as he slowly closed the door. Luckily, she wasn't home.

While Blitzen was unconscious, Smoke searched the apartment carefully. It didn't take long. The apartment was only two rooms and a bath, so he rummaged quickly, trying not to get too much of the filth on him. Still, he was careful, as it wouldn't have been the first time that he subdued a perp only to be attacked by a knife-wielding girlfriend hiding in a closet.

Blitzen awoke, sitting upright in a straight-back chair in the same hallway where he was knocked out.

Smoke was standing over him.

"Don't talk," Smoke said.

The man in the chair began to protest; "I—" was all he got out.

Smoke hit him with a left in the same spot just above the nose.

Blitzen went off the chair, on the floor and unconscious again.

As the fog began to clear sometime later, Smoke again cautioned Mr. Gerald Cavatina/Blitzen Substitute. "Now, again. Don't talk," he warned.

The twice-damaged man now just nodded.

"You have attempted to blackmail one Märta Johansson."

The damaged man opened his mouth.

"Un uh...I wouldn't." Smoke said, shaking his finger back and forth.

Gerald Cavatina/Blitzen Substitute closed his mouth.

Smoke put both hands in the air palms open and said, "I am going to let you stand up. Then, you will gather all the material you have on Märta, and the party you attended. You are going to give all of it to me."

Smoke looked at him to be sure he heard what he said.

"I have twenty thousand dollars with me," Smoke continued. "You will hand the material to me. I will give you the money, and you will forget Märta Johansson and me—forever."

Smoke was always fascinated when a negotiation began. The man in the chair sat for a minute, calculating.

Then Mr. Gerald Cavatina/Blitzen Substitute raised a finger asking permission to speak.

Smoke reluctantly nodded his head, doubting the outcome. "Okay—but, I had better like what I hear."

"Okay. Okay...man...I get it...I mean, I get it!"

The man moved slightly in his chair and signaled with a finger, indicating he wanted to get up.

Smoke nodded begrudgingly knowing what was going to happen.

Blitzen stood. He took slow steps towards the bedroom, turning back and looking for approval with almost every step.

"It's all in here—man—all of it, I promise! You did say you had twenty grand on you?"

Smoke followed behind, shaking his head, knowing it would go wrong.

Mr. Gerald Cavatina/Blitzen Substitute knelt, smiled up at Smoke, and slowly reached under the bed. He stretched under and pulled out a flat plastic container. He lifted its lid as it slid clear of the mattress and stuck his hand inside, keeping the top down as cover.

Smoke allowed him to fumble around in his fruitless search of the container.

Smoke pulled a small FN Baby Browning .32 caliber pistol from his belt behind his back.

"Looking for this?" Smoke asked with a grin.

Mr. Gerald Cavatina/Blitzen Substitute's face went white. He withdrew quickly, and threw both hands high up into the air.

Smoke said, "I haven't seen one of these for a long time. It's small but efficient—I guess. Not a lot of stopping power. However, it does make a hole."

Blitzen raised his hands in surrender as Smoke leveled the pistol.

"Wait...No," pleaded the kneeling, lying, blackmailing creep.

Smoke calmly pulled the trigger and shot him through the thigh of his right leg.

Smoke was pretty sure that a single gunshot in the Lower East Side at that time of night probably wouldn't draw any attention.

Mr. Gerald Cavatina/Blitzen Substitute's mouth was wide open, but nothing was coming out. There was a lot of blood, but there was only a silent scream from the blackmailer.

Smoke stood relaxed with his arms crossed, the gun still in his right hand.

"Now—one more time—I want you to get me all the stuff you have, and I do mean everything."

Smoke kicked a T-Shirt that was lying on the floor at the creep who was still moaning with pain.

Sucking gulps of air and sobbing, he wrapped the rag around the wound.

However, to Smoke's surprise, and with a minuscule amount of admiration, he discovered that Mr. Gerald Cavatina/Blitzen Substitute had not given up the ghost.

"Listen...I get it," the creep began, "you're the muscle. You have a job to do."

Smoke waited for the inevitable.

"You're getting paid. Right? She is forking up twenty K. I mean that's a lot of money—so, you and I know that she has a lot more. I am right. Right? You know I'm right." He ended his sentence with a crooked smile.

He looked at Smoke for an opening. Seeing none, he kept going. "Man, it could be way more than twenty. The bitch is loaded, man. We could pull maybe like a hundred—even a hundred and fifty large." He grinned through a nervous sweat.

He went for a close. "I'll split it with you. You give me ten, and you keep ten." He stammered, making up a plot on the fly. "I'll send in another picture, and we grab twenty more next time."

Smoke's face had no expression.

"I know we can get a hundred and fifty—maybe two hundred." He smiled confidently like he actually had a card in his hand. "How does 70-30 sound?"

Smoke shot him in the other thigh.

The creep screamed, then passed out before the sound of the shot faded.

Smoke sat down in a chair, waiting for the pain to wake him up.

The eyes opened first, then the mouth. "You shot me again—what the fuck?"

Smoke grabbed another rag and tossed it at him. "Okay. One more time. Just once more. I want every picture, video, or audiotape. I want everything you have." He paused, bent over, and whispered, "Right now."

Blitzen tied the other rag then began to crawl to an air conditioner that was hanging out of a window. He couldn't stand up, so he pointed to the inside cover. "In there."

Smoke yanked off the cover and tossed it to the floor. On the side of the case was a manila envelope. He balanced it in his hand and felt the weight. "Okay, here is what happens now."

Smoke pulled one white envelope out and dropped it on the bed. "This is five grand. It will cover fixing those little holes. I know that you are a lying piece of shit."

"No man," he pleaded immediately. "That's everything. I swear."

Smoke grinned. He didn't want to; he couldn't help it. He leaned in close, making sure he looked straight into the creep's eyes. "I know you have more—and to tell the truth—I kind of hope you try to use it."

He slid the action back on the pistol and checked the next round in the chamber. Smoke got closer. "If she sees you on the street or near her apartment; if anything shows up at the office; if something finds its way to the Internet. Anything; anything at all."

He grabbed his hair and yanked the man's head up. "I will be back, and I will fuck you up, permanently."

Smoke let go, and the creep hit the floor hard. Smoke pulled the magazine from the handle, thumbed the bullets on the floor, and then racked the slide, ejecting the round in the chamber onto the floor. He pulled his t-shirt loose, wiped the gun and magazine, and dropped the gun on the floor.

20

"I don't understand," said Dr. O, confused.

"What part?"

"All of it. The fact that you shot a man and left him bleeding on the floor kind of upsets me. However, let's start with why you gave that piece of shit five thousand dollars."

"First, we both agree. He is a piece of shit. But not to be picky, it was twice."

"What do you mean—twice?"

"Twice—I shot him two times—one shot in each thigh."

She stared at him, speechless.

Smoke shrugged sheepishly. "Interrogation technique."

"Noted." The boyish grin helped her recover. "Let's circle back to that, but what about the money? Why give him anything?"

"Good question. We know he is a blackmailer. I got his yellow sheet— sorry—arrest report, which said he was strictly small-time. That said, again, he is a piece of shit, so he might get pissed and do something stupid like try to hurt Märta instead of blackmailing. I can't be around for her 24/7."

"Okay," she said curtly.

"If he were smart and cooperated, he would have accepted my first offer."

"But he wasn't smart and didn't cooperate."

Smoke nodded.

"Piece of shit," she said.

"Correct."

"Okay, but why five thousand?"

"I shot him..."

"Twice." She smiled.

"Twice." He smiled. "So, he needed to get fixed up. He had an outstanding warrant, so I knew he couldn't go to an ER. That would mean police and his arrest on the warrant. However, with cash in hand, he could go locally, a veterinarian, or maybe he knows a nurse who would help. The bullets were flesh wounds, through and through, painful but not life threatening."

"And why do we care?"

"Desperate people get pissed off. He only had one assault charge, so that tells me he was small-time but capable of more. The money made him less desperate. Think of it as insurance."

"So Märta is safe, then?"

"You could say I am...certain...he understands that a further intrusion into your client's life would be injurious to his welfare."

She laughed. "Is that what you told him, injurious?"

"Ah—not exactly." He withdrew three white envelopes and dropped them on her desk.

"Hmmm, curious'er, and curious'er."

He picked up a carafe of coffee and poured a cup while motioning to her. She nodded, and he poured her a cup.

There was quiet in the office.

Lo had left hours ago for rehab.

Dr. O had stayed behind to transcribe her notes from the day's sessions and to wait for an update from Smoke on the Märta problem. He had also been assigned to escort her home.

Smoke walked to the couch and sat across from her.

163

Neither spoke, but both were smiling.

She looked up at him. "I would like to buy you a drink."

"Where, someplace dangerous no doubt?"

"There is a place I go to relax and remain out of the public eye. It is difficult for me to have a personal life, which is really—private."

"I've noticed."

"No one there looks at me in any other way than as just another human being."

"Where is that—Church?"

"No, not church," she laughed, "definitely not Church."

She stood up, looked in the long mirror, smoothed her skirt with both hands, and then walked to the door.

He was still sitting in the chair watching her walk.

"You coming?"

"Absolutely," he stammered, jumping to his feet.

21

The driver turned in the seat and faced them. "Where to?"

"Henrietta's on Hudson, please."

"No problem." The car lurched forward, taking advantage of a small hole in the flow of traffic, and headed west, toward Hudson Avenue.

Dr. O sat on the driver's side, a mile away from him. He was against the passenger door, pretending he wasn't looking at her.

She was wearing what she wore to work, a grey skirt and jacket over a red blouse fastened with matching embroidered buttons.

He felt uncomfortable even in the new jacket. The black t-shirt under it made him feel a little rebellious. He had remembered to comb his hair.

He snuck a glance and noticed that she had undone an additional button on her blouse. The unfastened third button somehow, for him, retooled her outfit from office appropriate to evening provocative.

He was not the same man he was a few weeks ago. He had been that man before—a long time ago.

She was quiet.

He was quiet.

There wasn't a need to talk.

The hum of the tires produced white noise.

She was gazing out the window. "When was the last time you made love?"

He was shocked by the frankness of her question and stammered out a weak, "Ah—I don't think that's any of your business."

He immediately regretted saying it. "Sorry."

She did not look at him. A minute or two went by.

"Why did you ask me that?"

She turned her body, squared her shoulders, and slid a knee up onto the wide leather seat. She was face to face, commanding Smoke's attention.

He had no place to hide.

"I have noticed something about you. It is apparent you have an unresolved past. Something you are repressing. Something keeps you detached and distant."

He tried for no expression, but he knew he failed.

She put her hand on top of his. "I am sorry if I was abrupt with my question. I was attempting to reach out."

She sighed and cast her eyes innocently downward. "Perhaps, I was mistaken. I don't know you that well. I was out of line, asking."

She put her other hand on his. "I wasn't asking as a doctor."

He gulped and feeling a bit like a schoolboy said, "Three years ago more or less."

She didn't break her gaze. "Thank you."

"For what?"

"Honesty."

"You're welcome, I guess." He felt like he was coming up for air in a new pool.

"Was it with a lover—a friend—a casual acquaintance—or a sexual release with a professional?"

He thought back, giving the incident its due consideration. "Not a pro."

She tilted her head and smiled. "Remember who I am, please. There is nothing wrong with sex as a human function."

"She was more than a casual acquaintance—a friend, but not a lover."

"Again, thank you for your trust."

She smiled at him, but it didn't help. He was too far from his center.

Those eyes.

The car jolted as it stopped which, to his relief, ended the conversation.

Side by side, they entered the nightclub.

Smoke could see that Henrietta's was an LGTB bar, and it was also immediately apparent why the doctor had chosen this place.

Wherever she went, curious eyes followed her from the moment she walked into a room. Usually, recognition brought stares, whispering, and finger-pointing, and then the bold would step up asking for autographs or a selfie. She was famous—a personality—a genuine celebrity. However, at Henrietta's, she was like anyone else. It was a retreat from the press-covered world where anonymity and privacy were mandates.

A young woman bearing a smile pushed past a score of people waiting for entry. She greeted Dr. O with a cheek kiss, then led them into the club's inner sanctum. The blonde took the point, Smoke the rear position, and they single-filed into a dark, cavernous chamber that was pulsating with people and sound. The woman deposited them at a small, VIP table facing the dance floor. The table sat two.

A waitress parted the bodies.

Doctor O leaned close so Smoke could hear over the beat. "What do you drink?"

He leaned to her ear. "I'll have whatever you're having."

Dr. O beckoned the waitress. "Four French 75s, please."

Smoke, puzzled asked, "What is a French 75?"

"Gin, lemon juice, and brandy. I used to drink it in Paris years ago. I haven't had one in a very long time. I have to warn you they have quite a kick." She pulled back, winked, and turned to watch the dancing bodies.

He watched her as she surveyed the room. He had seen that look before, at the auction. Even here, a place she went seeking anonymity, she was wary of the attention that followed her everywhere she went.

He saw something else, too—fear.

The room was a long rectangle with a chrome and granite bar splitting the expanse in its center. A DJ was pounding the crowd with a thunderous base beat mixed with Jamaican reggae. The rhythm was tropical, erotic, and sensual. Bodies of every possible physical description filled the floor. Some were dancing on a parquet floor under a silver 70s disco ball and strobing blue spotlights. Some were strutting to the hard-thumping beat with drinks held high in the air wandering from group to group swaying, laughing, yelling—groping. Some were watching, and some were in a world of their own.

Dr. O and Smoke watched from their table on a small couch that was about the size of a doublewide chair. It was well worn, sloped into the center, and forced them tight to each other—thigh to thigh.

"Do you dance?" she asked.

"What?" he yelled, having trouble hearing again.

She leaned close to his ear.

Smoke could feel her breath. "Do you dance?"

He was about to be pulled out of his comfort zone by a gorgeous tow truck.

"Not for a very long time."

"Would you dance if I asked you to?"

All of his power to resist disappeared. "Yes."

"Good." She finished her drink. She rose, stood in front of him with legs slightly apart, causing the material on her skirt to go taught. She shrugged her shoulders, and her jacket slid off her shoulders.

She held her arms straight out, wiggling her fingers.

He finished his drink with a mighty gulp and accepted the hand.

She led—him an arms-length behind. He held her delicate hand, feeling awkward, out of place, and definitely out of his comfort zone.

Dr. O stopped at an open space and began to move her hips slowly, at half time to the beat, smiling, drawing him into her comfort zone.

The DJ was sampling a reggae beat. A Rasta voice sang lyrics with a heavy accent that had a clear message. His band was a steel slide guitar—then horns—a kettledrum, like they were flowers on the same vine.

The bodies on the floor were close and moving to the beat.

The DJ increased the base—each thump vibrating in a dancer's chest like another heartbeat.

Then a sound spun down from the ceiling. It was a soprano's voice, like a single clarinet amidst a vast orchestra. It floated above the dancer's heads raising and lowering the crowd movements with its pure, perfect tenor.

Dr. O pulled Smoke to the center of the floor where dozens of people surrounded them, all pulsating to the rhythm.

Smoke's feet began to move in spite of his previously well-anchored resistance.

He put his arm around her waist and tried to hold her politely, but the moving bodies around them pushed them together, chest-to-chest—hip-to-hip—moving to each other beat to beat.

A dark-haired woman spinning in a slow circle bumped into Dr. O. She was a veteran disco-ite, most likely in her forties and be-speckled in gold sequins. The woman spun around and around and drifted directly behind Dr. O. Suddenly, the woman dropped her arms down on Dr. O's shoulders—her head swaying side to side. She started swaying in the rhythm of her new partner.

Dr. O let her head fall forward. She moved away from Smoke backing up to the new partner. With eyes focused on Smoke, she synced with the new partner. Slowly she raised her arm, reaching out, then pulling Smoke to her. She guided him back and forth until three moved in unison.

Dr. O. then pushed her hands forward, holding him stiff-armed at arm's length. She lifted her head, gaining his eyes.

The woman behind the doctor moved her hands from Dr. O's shoulders to her hips.

The beat of the bass thumped louder and more profound.

The dark-haired woman slid her hands up from the doctor's hips to her waist. She ran her hands up and down.

The doctor raised her hands and placed them on Smoke's shoulders. The woman then raised her hands, covering the doctor's breasts with her open palms.

Dr. O flowed with the music and swayed with her two partners without objection.

She continued to gaze into the eyes of Smoke, concentrating only on him, her hips moving to the beat.

The beat changed again, and suddenly, the hands and the woman were gone.

Dr. O was still gazing straight at him, her arms bending, lowering them along his arms, moving slowly down to his hands. She gripped them, pushed her body forward, her head was on his chest. She was not the doctor. She was O.

The beat changed.

O took his hand and led him off the floor. Another French 75 awaited their return.

She swung back into her seat and raised her glass.

He noticed a thin bead of sweat on her upper lip. "That was interesting."

"That is Henrietta's." Her eyes were sparkling.

She leaned over close to his ear. "Was it making love or fucking?"

"What...what?" he stammered, caught off guard again.

She patted his arm and leaned her body into his. "In the car, you said the last time you had sex was three years ago. I am now asking if it was making love or fucking?"

He took a sip of his drink. "You are persistent. I'll give you that."

Her expression changed, becoming more serious. "It was wrong to ask in the car and way wrong now. I apologize—again."

He nodded, picked up his drink, and gulped some courage. "It was fucking—unsatisfying and a complete waste of time."

"Would you be open to a doctor's opinion?"

"Okay," he took another sip, preparing for the worst.

"My impression is that a great tragedy has affected your life. It is as yet—unresolved."

He stared at her. He was feeling exposed.

She looked a little surprised that he didn't respond.

"I'm not wrong—am I?"

The silence continued.

Undaunted, she pressed on, trying a different approach. "Although, I don't completely understand why—I think it is fairly obvious that I am attracted to you. It is also apparent that I would very much like to take you to bed."

There was an awkward pause, and she flicked something off her skirt, trying to act nonchalant.

Heart pounding but still speechless, he added wide eyes to his look.

"But..."

His heart sank.

"I don't want to fuck you—well—actually that's not true," she tilted her head. "Actually, I would enjoy being properly rodgered. I haven't had a sexual release for a while now, and I am a little frustrated by the lack of intimacy. Wait." She regrouped. "I am drifting away from the subject."

She used a finger to straighten the seam of her blouse just above her breast.

"Back to my point," she continued. "It is apparent to me that you are not ready to make love yet." She followed quickly with an academic conclusion, "I think you need to fun-fuck for a while and get some cobwebs removed. However, making love..." she just shook her head, "...not yet."

He looked at her with a blank stare. "You are not well."

She smiled. "I don't disagree with that diagnosis. I could use some counseling—that's for sure."

She took his hand. "I'm not well. I have an attraction for a man that I barely know and whom I suspect is a whole lot of trouble, but I can't resist."

He was rarely out of control. When a situation did become out of control, he either punched it or shot it. However, he was now helpless and worse, wordless.

She broke the tension, pulling his hands and smiling. "Come with me."

They rose up, and she led him down a long hallway, through and around people who were in close conversation or making out or just standing and drinking, but all of them were side by side.

She pushed open the door to what appeared to be a lounge, which had dark paneled walls and several modern tall-top tables with metal chairs. Arranged in small groups around the room were upholstered chairs and matching couches. The occupants were predominately lesbian with few gay men paired off to one side, but they were the only man-woman couple.

A woman whose head was shaved on one side had an almost life-size tattoo of a leopard adoring her naked body. She was dancing on a tabletop in the center of the room. An adoring audience stood around her, looking up in awe.

O pulled on his hand until they arrived at an unoccupied couch. She pulled him down next to her.

The bass beat was reverberating through the floor and walls.

"Smoke...I realize this is not the place to talk about the past, but it might be a place to begin to re-start your future."

She retook his hand.

"I have sex regularly." She wagged her head slightly. "More than regularly actually—often—would be more precise, but that is usually sex for gratification, with my goal limited to my own satisfaction."

She paused then continued sincerely, "I am confessing I have feelings for you." She looked into his eyes. "But—I know you're not ready for a relationship. Full disclosure, I am not ready for a relationship either. It is possible that I'm just being a big coward myself, afraid of rejection or hurt or I'm trying to control a situation." She shook her head. "So—basically, I'm not sure. However, I believe it's not the right time for us to have sex. Yet."

She ducked her head behind the cover of the hair that fell in front of her face.

"You're right," he said, surprising himself. "I'm not ready."

She looked up, brushing her hair away. "I have a deep dark issue hidden away as well."

"I will tell you mine when you tell me yours," he said with a chuckle.

She gripped his hand and smiled. "We need to release the past and give ourselves permission to live again."

She let her hand drop to his leg. It was a giving touch that communicated a closeness he was willing to accept.

"Another drink before we leave?"

"No thanks, I'm good."

They walked back down the hallway and out the door into the warm city night.

They climbed into the backseat. Instead of taking a position at either window, they sat close together. O pulled her legs up on the seat then lay down, lowering her head to his leg and curling up, stroking his thigh.

He was out of body again—the doctor that was such a formidable character was laying on his leg inches away from a spot that would not be able to disguise his feelings.

She stroked his leg with her fingertips running them up to his inner thigh. She rolled over, face up, resting her head on his thigh. Her hair flowed back like a shampoo commercial. She reached up and ran her fingers through his hair.

They came together.

They kissed.

Smoke drew her close.

She reached up, wrapping her arm behind his head.

Suddenly, she pulled back. She looked down. Then Up. Then down again. Then with her best Madelyn Kahn, Young Frankenstein impression exclaimed, "Whooooofh."

Embarrassed, he feigned ignorance. "What?"

"Ahh," she dropped her free hand and blatantly grabbed his manhood.

"Uhhh," was the guttural sound indicating the subject of his embarrassment was fully erect.

She squeezed him like she was checking fruit in a supermarket.

"Ah....you are very...aahh...large."

"I'm proportional to my height."

"Really, so then you're—like—seven foot two." She released her grip spinning around and with large soft blue eyes stared at him. Then she laughed and put an open hand over her mouth, the little girl in her now also a little embarrassed.

One second later, he laughed.

The limo arrived at that moment, and they got out together, smiling and somehow younger.

He walked her to the front door.

She turned to him and then one-handed him to arms-length.

With her head down and her free hand, she smoothed her skirt and pulled her jacket closed. Then she leaned back against the door and looked up, gaining his eyes with hers.

"As much as my sexual being wants to—and believe me—it wants to. I'm not going to make love to you tonight."

He couldn't have said anything even if he wanted to.

"We both know we are not ready yet."

He remained silent.

She leaned forward and kissed him. This kiss was different from the club kiss. She separated her lips and lightly licked his tongue with hers.

She whispered, "I could fuck you. My body wants to fuck you—

and I want your body to fuck me." She pulled back and looked at him with soft eyes, "but my heart wants to make love."

Then breaking the tension of that moment, she pushed back a little and laughed. "Not that just fucking wouldn't be fun." She gripped his arms hard with both hands.

"It definitely would be fun—also, erotic—however, I think making love with you first—before the fun fucking starts—would be better for a relationship."

She was looking for a response—any response.

"Well. What do you think?" she said over the silence.

Somewhere in his mind, a stonewall fell over.

She read the look in his eyes. "Goodnight, Smoke." She kissed him again, lightly, softly...a delicate lingering touch. "Sleep tight."

She patted his cheek then disappeared inside.

He was alone on a doorstep with red lipstick on his mouth and a new lease on life.

22

A tree protruded from the sidewalk outside her building. It was a New York street tree encased by concrete. It had enough earth surrounding it to fill a good-sized coffee cup, and a black iron grate allowed the flow of fluids to its roots. There was rain, but also there was the ooze: the hydrants backwashing gutters, and the residue flowing from the street sweepers. The asphalt cocktail contained contaminants that would prove fatal to almost anything living. This tree had survived in the face of unbeatable odds—and flourished—a real New York sidewalk tree.

Smoke was sitting on a bench, drinking excellent coffee from a paper cup. He preferred his plasma black and strong since Iraq, and the quality of coffee in this cup surprised him. He had little hope that coffee from a street vendor would be drinkable much less good, but it was. He bought his first cup the morning he arrived on his first day of recon—weeks ago.

He looked at his watch—5:30 a.m. Dawn's first light had turned off most of the streetlights. The city was yawning, not wholly awake.

He blew into the top of the open cup. He shook the paper and folded the Times lengthwise as he had seen the professional riders do on the subway. He read the top right; the big story first.

Nothing grabbed his attention. It wasn't a slow news day; he couldn't concentrate.

His mind drifted. She was at his shoulder— a whiff of her perfume drifted from her hair.

Then there was the kiss.

He made himself shiver, convulsing his body, trying to recover. It wasn't possible. Not to him.

"Stop it." He yelled, louder than he intended and entirely out of character. He looked around. Nobody noticed his outburst. The use of cellphones made talking to oneself normal.

He refocused on the door across the street.

The watcher arrived every day by 7:30 a.m. and left a half-hour after lights out in the doctor's office.

He hadn't figured out why Little Round Man was watching—yet.

On his first day in New York, he sat at her office watching the comings and goings. He spent a lot of time doing recon—both sides of the street—every face—everything that moved. When he had the pattern, the constant, he could see what didn't fit.

Smoke made a habit of doing as much background as he could before walking into something.

He used deductive reasoning, adhering to the journalist's standard reporting guide. Who, what, why, where, and when were the keys to a good story. They were also necessary to develop the evidence required to prove a hypothesis. After a few days, he had a part of who and the how, which was a good starting point.

He got up and stretched out, then got another coffee.

He had begun his recon by exploring the doctor's office building. He discovered the plus and minus security issues. The concierge in the lobby provided some defense but with a diversion could be bypassed. On the plus side, the building was not a high-rise complex, so the people going in and out were easier to identify. There were offices up to floor seven. The apartments above had a separate lobby and elevators. The other offices in the building opened at nine and closed at five. The doctor opened at ten and had hours until seven in the evening.

Next, he looked for the most likely place to watch. He found that only one building had recently rented a space that fit the bill. It was across the street, on the same floor as the doctor. For twenty bucks, the doorman shared that no one installed phones or the Internet in the office. The only information he couldn't get, so far, was who rented it.

On day three, the Little Round Man became part of the who. He appeared to Smoke to be a cog, not a wheel, in what was happening. Someone was spending money to determine a routine—a schedule.

Some threats are unpredictable and usually spontaneous—a crime of opportunity or passion. Bodyguards—big men in black suits, sunglasses, and cold stares—handle those problems. Professionals execute premeditated attacks, crimes with motive. Smoke knew this was the latter. He also knew he was the monkey wrench in their best-laid plan.

He flipped the paper over; the second featured story wasn't big either. He put his coffee down and refolded to the Sports Section. Being forced to read about the Mets wasn't a good thing. The Phillies won but were still trailing the Braves seven games behind.

He looked over the top of the fold and saw The Round Man approaching the building. He had his head down, shoulders hunched over. He carried a black briefcase, a vintage model with a chrome fastener. It, like him, looked old and worn.

Smoke perked up. His object varied from his daily routine. Every other day The Round Man had gone inside to the elevator without delay—but not today. Instead, he passed the front door, stopping at the alley next to the building.

Smoke refolded the paper. The Little Round Man had no idea that Smoke was watching. Neither did the man hiding in the shadows of the ally.

A head poked out of the darkness and swiveled around, looking up and down the street for a tail.

Smoke watched as the body of a well-built man with thick shoulders emerged. He came up from behind Little Round Man, said something, then stepped back into the shadow.

The Little Round man whipped around, surprised, and then followed the man into the ally.

A few minutes later, the Little Round Man came out, turned, and walked into the building. He took the elevator to his day job, watching the comings and goings of Dr. Olivia Bennet's office.

Smoke sipped his coffee, peeking over pictures of the perennial underachieving Mets.

The other man was a professional. Smoke decided on a name for the new character in the play. He would call him The Bull because his head and shoulders were too large for his body. Ten minutes passed before The Bull emerged from the shadow. He came out of the alley fast, turned north, and joined the pedestrian traffic.

Smoke stood up and followed on the opposite sidewalk—fifty feet behind.

The Bull went four blocks, stopping twice to check shop windows for the reflections of a tail. On block five, he caught a cab.

Smoke bolted across the street, flagged a cab, and said the words he had always longed to say. "Follow that cab."

"Hasananaan," was the response.

Smoke recognized the Arabic word for okay.

"Shukraan." The driver looked in the rearview and nodded appreciatively.

The Bull's cab pulled up to an extended-stay hotel.

"Pull past," said Smoke quickly.

"Okay, boss."

"As-salamu Alaykum." Smoke dropped a twenty over the seat.

"Wa alaykum al-salām,"

Through a plate-glass window, Smoke watched The Bull get into the elevator alone.

The lift stopped on the fifth floor.

Smoke walked up to the front door and nonchalantly looked inside.

There was nothing special about this place, just another businessman's special. He pulled his phone out and took a picture of the business register posted on the wall. He made sure the four names on floor five were in focus.

"Curios-er and curios-er."

He needed more information—who, what, where, when, and most importantly, Why?

He looked up and down the street. There wasn't a good place to stake out and wait for a re-appearance of The Bull. He would come back later and run down the companies.

He checked his watch.

She had appointments till two. He didn't need to be there. She was safe under Lo's watch in the office, but he was hesitating—it was not his usual behavior. He was lost in indecision. He knew he should wait there, but he was convincing himself that he needed to check on her security.

He wanted to see her. He had doubts about what she said last night. Did she mean it? Did this unbelievable woman mean what she said? Did she use the word relationship?

The darkness that had been overshadowing his life was fighting for existence.

His desire lost this battle. He decided to do his job and stood outside, waiting for The Bull.

23

L o walked past her boss and looked at her curiously.

"I haven't seen you with that look before."

Dr. O continued writing, knowing Lo wasn't done analyzing.

"I mean...I have seen you with the JFL before, but this one is something different."

"JFL?"

"Come on, Doc—JFL. The Just Fucked Look. You have that dewy-eyed and relaxed vacant stare." Lo drew out reeelaaaxeeed into a three-syllable word.

Trying hard to look at her with disdain, Dr. O said, "Does it look like I'm staring vacuously?"

"Yes. That's why I said it...and those are your notes on Travis, correct?"

"Yes," said the doctor, indignantly.

"Well you're noting them in Mary Reniut's file." Lo pointed to large black letters on the top of the file.

"Fuck me."

"Exactly." Lo smiled.

Dr. O pushed the mouse across the desktop.

"That's a new wrinkle though...a JFL plus a...Hmmm?" Lo put a finger to her lips and pointed her eyes to the ceiling.

"Holy Fuck," she exclaimed loudly, "Smoke—you did the nasty with Smoke."

For the first time in the seven years they had been together, Lo saw Dr. O blush.

"Oh, dear God." Lo was stunned.

Lo then smiled, put both arms on the desk, and leaned in for the girl-to-girl, woman-to-woman, friend-to-friend secrets.

She got nothing. For an instant, hurt registered on her face. She was in an awkward position like a handshake that wasn't returned. She pushed herself up, pointed her eyes to the floor, and tried, as well as an X-MP could, to mimic a teenager -toe in the sand- routine.

"Okay. You'll tell me when you're ready."

With a sigh of disingenuous exasperation Dr. O explained. "Okay, okay...I went out with him last night to celebrate."

She then attempted to derail the train by ramping up her tone on a new explanation rather than an excuse. "He stopped that blackmailer from hassling Märta. It's a pretty great story. First, he gets the number for..."

Lo interrupted, "Later—that's not important, and you are trying to divert my attention." She waved off the story. "Skip to the chase, please."

Lo pulled up a chair and sat hard with arms crossed, thereby committing the Doc to the truth and nothing but the truth.

The doctor weighed her options and decided that telling Lo might be good talk therapy.

She also wanted to tell somebody—she was bursting to tell Lo all day but held back, but now she couldn't remember why.

The Doc started slow, "Okay, I'll skip the details, but we talked for a while here in the office, and I enjoyed it. It was exciting to hear him talk, and before I realized what I had done, I asked him out. We went up to Henrietta Hudson for drinks."

SMOKE

"Good choice," interrupted Lo.

"Hmmm," was the grim response to the interruption. "We tried to continue a conversation at the Club, as much as we could in that place. It was deafening."

The doctor looked down at the desk, coyly finger trailing along before the next secret was disclosed.

"We had a few drinks." As if that was an excuse for what was next. "Then I asked him to dance with me."

Lo smiled and shifted around in the chair. "Details."

"Lo," she confessed softly, "I have feelings for him."

Lo's expression got grave very fast.

"We danced a little and talked some more then we left and when we got back to SoHo." She blushed.

Lo waited as her friend gathered her emotions.

"I kissed him." She closed her eyes and continued with a certain amount of surprise. "And...I meant it."

"Wow."

"I know—I didn't think it was possible for me. I guess I am having a breakthrough"

"I guueess." She made two syllables from one.

Then they both were quiet.

"Did you...I mean did he...I mean...I don't know what I mean," said Lo.

"This is ridiculous. I am a sex doctor. I consult on other people's sex issues. I have sex all the time, and now...now...I feel like a ninth grader. This is ridiculous."

Lo pushed back in the chair. "Ohh, you got it bad, Doc."

Dr. O looked up and smiled suddenly. "Yep...I guess I do."

Lo stood up, smiled back, and returned to the outer office.

Somehow accepting that she still had the same "feelings" for him the day after made the cloud lift a little. The doctor straightened her back, picked up her pen, and went back to work reviewing the notes of the file for her next patient.

24

D r. O turned the plastic handle, closing the shade that protected her from the world outside. She spun around, pressed her back to the wall, and raised her eyes to the ceiling. The tension she held in all day exited her body with a breath that emptied her lungs.

She bent a couple of slats and peeked out into a darkening sky. She drew a new long breath and tried to determine which piece of tinted glass concealed the watcher.

Smoke had at first suggested, then demanded, the blinds remained closed. It wasn't that she didn't take him seriously. He showed her pictures of the men. She didn't recognize them, but she was confident it wasn't—him.

Opening the blinds was defiance in the face of her fear, a statement of bravery. She refused to be weak or vulnerable.

"Doctor," Lo's voice sounded over the intercom, "Father Mark Moreno is here for his appointment."

She walked back to her desk. "Send him in, please."

He was fairly tall, about six feet, and appeared to be in his middle sixties. Thinning brown hair, boney cheeks, and a long thin nose brought her to mind of an old English actor. His most distinguishing feature, however, was not the stuff of a leading man. Two boney hands protruded from the sleeves of an ill-fitted, black suit that had shine marks at the elbows and knees.

Dr. O stepped around the desk, smiled politely, and silently directed him to the two chairs in the middle of the room.

He followed her direction taking long strides that portrayed a certain amount of confidence. His eyes darted about, which struck the doctor as odd.

Sitting down opposite him, she crossed her legs and put her hands on her lap.

There was silence for a few seconds.

Dr. O began, "Should I address you as Father Mark?"

"If you like, or Mark if you prefer." He cleared his throat.

"Okay, Father did you fill out the office forms when you came in?"

"Yes, just name and current address. I don't have insurance, but if payment is the issue, my friend agreed to pay for this session."

She shook her head. "No. Not about money, Father. There are procedures."

"Of course, and thank you for seeing me. Our mutual friend told me you are not taking new patients, but he would arrange one." He cleared his throat again. "Maybe a friend isn't correct—more of a business associate. In either case, I'm glad he is in such high standing with you." An expression vaguely resembling a smile appeared.

"Yes...high standing."

Her publisher, Phillip Dubroff, called Lo to arrange an appointment. He was emphatic and insistent the doctor see Father Moreno.

He clasped his hands together. "I require help, but to understand why, I have to start from the very beginning."

Doctor O nodded once.

"As a child I was..." he diverted his eyes to the floor, "...different from other boys. I had no friends; I played no sports, belonged to no clubs or organizations, and I was very, very unhappy."

Dr. O remained motionless.

"My mother—who was a Saint by the way..." he lifted his eyes fervently to the ceiling, "was devout Catholic—a good, saintly, person."

"A saint. Got it." She wasn't sure why he was making her uncomfortable, but he was.

"In my senior year in high school, my mother arranged a meeting with our parish pastor. He suggested that I look into my heart and see if there was an opportunity for God to play a role in my life at St. Charles Borromeo Seminary."

"You were religious like your mother?"

"No, the thought had never crossed my mind. Sure, I went to church, but I had no calling. What I had was a limited future. I was a decent student but not good enough for a scholarship, and there was no money for college."

Father Mark reached into his pocket and removed a used tissue, wiped his nose, and replaced it. It struck Dr. O as a grandmotherly thing to do.

"What the pastor suggested sounded a lot better than delivering mail or pushing shopping carts, so I agreed."

He leaned forward, engaged in his life story.

She thought he had been truthful—so far.

"I visited the seminary with a letter from the pastor stating that I was a devout Catholic and wanted to be a priest. The vocation director talked to me about an hour, mostly about life there. Two weeks later, I got a letter telling me I was accepted—my mother was in heaven." He raised his eyes to the ceiling again and added a two-handed, thank you Jesus, hand gesture.

"They gave me a room, new clothes, and three meals a day. I felt comfortable there because my classmates were mostly just like me."

Dr. O looked quizzical. "Explain, please."

He brightened at her curiosity. "Most of the boys at the seminary had similar stories to mine; introverted, few friends, and shunned." He added finger quotes.

She hated finger quotes.

He paused, looked down, hesitating to go on.

In almost every session, this was where the patient got to what brought them there.

His voice changed slightly, lower but firm. "They were like me." He hesitated. "Let's just say...none of us went to the senior prom."

She perceived him now to be disingenuous but remained silent.

Father Mark pushed one shoulder back and lifted his chin. "I'm gay."

Her expression didn't change.

"It was then that I embraced my sexual orientation."

"Ah, uh."

"I no longer felt different because I was not alone. For the first time, I was feeling good about being in a place where I didn't have to hide."

"You began having sex with your classmates?"

"Yes."

"Wasn't celibacy a part of your vows?"

A laugh burst out. "Oh my God, no. Don't misunderstand. There were seminarians and faculty who obeyed vows. But there were a lot who didn't, but I will explain more about that later."

She nodded.

"Seminary wasn't a cakewalk; five a.m. mass, the classroom schedule ended at four, followed by an hour of prayer. We were like any other college dormitory, study, sleep, repeat."

He paused and took a breath as if he were about to begin a sprint. "But Saturdays were party time. We began in small groups, but eventually, we were invited into the upperclassman's parties, sometimes, some of the faculty attended."

He leaned forward to share a secret.

She remained straight up in her seat.

"Homosexuality in the seminary has never had a lot of exposure, some, but not a lot." He paused like an attorney in court ready to present evidence. "For example, the Miami Herald reported Archbishop Favalora was known as the Godfather of The Lavender Mob. He encouraged hedonism and railroaded the seminarians that complained. That was not the only report. St. John's in Minnesota was called Gay Hogwarts, and Mundelein in Chicago was the Pink Palace."

He stopped to catch his breath. "My seminary had its own story. "Again, he used finger quotes.

She hated finger quotes.

He went for the tissue again.

"On special occasions, higher-ups from downtown attended along with guests from the outside world." He clucked when he finished.

"It was at one of those parties I met Monsignor Michael H. O'Hanrand."

"Whom might that be?"

"He's the Auxiliary Bishop of Philadelphia and, until recently, the man I worked for."

She wasn't impressed with the name or the rank but did catch a word difference.

"Worked—past tense?"

"Yes, I left two weeks ago."

"Okay, go on, please."

"I found accounting to be my strength at the seminary, and after I was ordained, O'Hanrand offered me a position at the Dioceses Main Office. I worked there for almost twenty-three years."

She was listening to his resume and becoming impatient. "Okay." She raised her hand to get his attention. "That brings us current. Now, what brings you here?"

"I am gay. My sexuality was known, accepted, and protected for more than thirty years. I worked for one of the most powerful men in the diocese." He sat up straight. "I had sex with him often. We had an understanding." Then with contempt added, "Until the Monsignor from Rome showed up."

It was beginning to feel like a Jerry Springer Show episode. "Again, why exactly are you here?"

"Okay. Okay." He leaned forward and bowed his head slightly, in the confession pose.

"The diocese is selling assets, mostly real estate, to help shore up the bottom line. We haven't been doing well financially since the Grand Jury reports on child sex abuse. Hundreds of priests and thousands of incidents were investigated, but very few have made it to court because we have spent a fortune on attorneys."

She impatiently shifted in her seat.

He pushed his lips together. "The Holy See brought in a new Archbishop, Chaput, from Denver. He is cutting back everything, personnel, overhead, and new expenditures. He has stepped up debt collections and began liquidating assets. And now," he raised his voice, "He is instituting cutbacks to priest's allowances and pensions. We are living below poverty, and there is no sign of that changing any time soon."

He pointed a white, boney finger at her. "You have to understand that we don't get Social Security, and there are no IRAs. The goodwill of the church and a small church pension is the only thing that keeps us from a metal bed at a shelter. As a group, we are reliant on the generosity of the church."

She had almost reached a limit of finger quotes and just got double banged on pension and generosity. "What's the point here, Mark? So, for the last time, why are you here?"

"Of course. I am sorry. Professional habit," he said contritely. "Sometimes, I get preachy." He waited three seconds for a chuckle that failed to arrive.

He continued undaunted. "As I said, I was working in the Chancery for O'Hanrand. When Chaput gave the direction to start selling assets, O'Hanrand put me in charge of his projects. I handled coordination, agreements, massing the individual titles, etcetera,

etcetera. He directed me to work with a company to prefect the parcel for high-rise condos and retail stores. Once the re-zoning is approved, all the properties will be sold as one large development plan."

He tried a sincere look. "There are some pretty shady things going on, and I have been in the middle of them."

It wasn't psychology, but she had become curious. "Go on."

"Right, now to the reason I'm here. I have a sister who needs help."

She blinked, not seeing that one coming.

"She has three children, one of whom is special needs and her husband recently died," He ducked his confession head again. "I went to O'Hanrand and asked for help—perhaps funds from Catholic Charities. He slapped the arm of his chair and laughed. He told me the charities only work with uneducated and underprivileged people, not priests with sob stories."

Father Mark stared at her waiting for a reaction of outrage.

"That does not explain why you are here"." She raised her voice, losing patience.

"Phillip Dubroff."

She cocked her head, again surprised. "What...wait. I don't understand"."

"I want to write a book."

She was speechless.

"Actually, he wants you to write a book about me. He thought you would take me on once you heard my story in person."

The priest grinned the big toothy smile.

She was stunned.

He plowed on. "He said it would be your next best-seller. There's my story, and there's homosexuality in the seminary. But the one I think you'll be most interested in is this." He started reaching into pockets, looking for something. "I have been copying secret, confidential documents and memos for months." He found what he was looking for and held up a thumb drive. "I was amazed at how much info can be stored in one little piece of metal."

He waved it around and continued. "I have it all—the whole story behind the sexual abuse. All of the files the Grand Jury never saw."

"Wait. Wait." She held up both hands. "I don't know what you and Phillip were thinking. I'm not a biographer, nor am I a crime reporter. I am a Doctor of Psychology."

"Right, he said you would say that."

"Who said?"

"Your publisher."

"He's wrong."

He rose from the chair and started to walk around the office. He took her book from the bookcase. He turned to say something but didn't and replaced it. He walked over to the window and twirled the wand opening the blinds.

Doctor O pushed a button on the table next to her chair, alerting Lo to come into the session.

The door open and Lo came in, taking a seat in a chair near the door.

O stood up, crossed the floor, took the wand from him, and twirled the slats closed.

They stood there at the window.

"A book would set the church back a generation, maybe more. At the moment, in the minds of most people, the villains in the incidents of sex abuse are individual priests. However, if the depth of this scandal is ever really understood, the real monsters will be identified as the ones who knew and continued to put children in harm's way."

Her cheeks had color, and her voice sarcasm. "So, now you want to expose the truth."

"That's correct. I have it all, pictures, dates, times, places, the documents the grand juries never saw—everything."

"Stop." Her open palm rose to the ceiling.

"You have to admit; it's a story that needs to be told."

"Not by me." She returned to her chair. "If you have what you say you have, it is a crime, a criminal conspiracy, not a book. Go to the police."

He hesitated but then tried one more avenue. "Your publisher said this would be your next best-seller. "

She was now angry. "So, you want me to write a book about how for the past thirty years, you knew of your organization's cover-up of the sexual abuse of hundreds of children by priests, a book that will also disrupt the business plans of a man who was your former lover."

He started to object.

"And, you came to me because Dr. Bennet the FBI profiler has creditability, and Dr. O the best-selling author will make you rich."

"Well, there's that too."

"Fuck you." She said it slow and cold.

Lo was white-knuckling the chair arms.

He walked to a spot behind his chair. "I get this is a lot to digest, so I'll give you a day or two to change your mind. However, if you choose not to accept, can I be assured that ethics will prohibit you from repeating anything said in this session to the Archdiocese, law enforcement, or the press?"

"Lo, could you please show...Mark...to the door."

"My pleasure." Lo stood and pointed to the door.

Moreno stepped towards O. "When you change your mind, I'll get this thumb drive to you. Even if they manage to get this one, they will never find the copy I have hidden."

He bent over, coming close to the doctor's ear, and whispered.

Lo moved the instant he started leaning.

Lo grabbed his arm with her good hand and yanked him back.

Doctor O pushed him with an open palm. "You need to leave now."

"Thanks for your time, Doctor Bennet, and God bless you."

She almost threw up.

After leading him out, Lo returned to O's office. The doctor was still sitting in her chair.

"Is he gone?"

Lo nodded.

"Phillip set me up." She shook her head, showing equal parts of disgust and disappointment. "

"You're going to need a new publisher."

The doctor walked back to the window and peeked out between the slats. It was night, but it was never dark in New York City.

There were three men behind the glass across the street.

The Bull stepped back from the window. "The office is dark. You're certain it was him?"

"Yes." The Little Round Man smiled with confidence. "Look." He held out his camera. A picture of a man coming out of the lobby door appeared on the screen. "See."

The Thin Man scrutinized the picture. "It's him." He turned to the Round Man. "What time did the office lights go off?"

Off guard at first, the Round Man stumbled on his words. "I don't know exactly. Ah, maybe twenty minutes or so."

The Thin Man stood for a moment. "Okay. We are going in."

The Bull nodded slightly.

The Little Round Man seemed relieved and started packing up. "Good luck."

"You're not going anywhere." The Thin Man put his hand on the camera case. "We still need you."

The Little Round Man's face went from relief to primal fear. "What for?"

"You're going to help us get into that office."

The Round Man's cheeks flushed, and sweat formed on his forehead. His voice cracked. "How can I help?"

"You are going to provide a diversion."

25

The Little Round Man, mouth open and belly out, was squeezed between his cohorts. He had trouble keeping up with the pace of pedestrian traffic on a good day but stuck between these two heavies pushed his limited physical abilities with every step he took. He was gulping air as the task ahead troubled him more than his pulse throbbing in his ears from his overtaxed heart.

The Thin Man looked at him sideways with cold black eyes. "You better make this work."

Two words squeaked out of the man in the middle. "I'll try."

"Don't try—do." The Thin Man bumped him hard into The Bull. "It's simple, even for a twit like you." He started the script again. "You go up to the counter and ask if there is someone in the doctor's office. If they say you can go up, that means—someone is still there. If they say you can't—then there isn't anyone in the office. Either way, you leave."

Again, the weak voice squeaked. "Why don't you just ring the phone?"

"Because not everyone answers the phone after office hours."

The Thin Man, frustrated, added, "Just do what I tell you, asshole."

The Little Round Man gulped with fear.

Ten paces short of the glass door leading into the office building, the two men vacated their shoulder-to-shoulder positions. They separated, taking up new posts with their backs to the wall near the door.

The Little Round Man, guard-less, reduced his speed to recover his breath. His slow movement left him pin-balling against the fast-moving crowd of people.

The Bull grunted loudly, gave him an angry look, then nodded his head toward the door.

The Little Round Man took a step—then another—putting his hands on the eight-foot-tall door into the lobby. He pushed expecting heavy resistance, but it opened easily, and he stumbled forward. The Round Man took short, quick steps to regain his balance. Righting himself, he staggered toward the front desk to where a man in a grey suit with red lapels and a gold-plated ID badge presided.

The Little Round Man tried to speak. He opened his mouth, but nothing came out at first. Panic set in. He went off-script. "I...I...I have an appointment with Dr. Bennet." His voice was weak and breathless.

The concierge, whose badge read Gus, looked quizzically at the man. "I believe they have gone for the day, sir. However, I can check." He went to pick up the phone, but his eyes remained fixed on the grey-faced man. "Are you okay, man? You look pale."

The Thin Man was watching intently. He needed the guard to become distracted so that they could walk through the lobby to the elevator.

All the fucker had to do was distract him for a few seconds then leave.

But—shit happens—and plans change, and plots thicken.

Suddenly, the Little Round Man grabbed his chest and moaned.

His heart was beating so fast he thought the concierge might have heard it.

He put an arm on the counter and tried to stay on his feet, but his legs refused to hold him up. Slowly he sank to the floor.

"Hey, Mister?" The concierge jumped up from the chair and rushed around the counter.

The Thin Man and The Bull skated to the bank of elevators, unnoticed.

The Thin Man pushed the UP button then looked back to see the guard pushing down on the Round Man's chest.

The Bull said, "Is that little fucker having a heart attack?"

"Looks real to me." The Thin Man paused a second, contemplating. He smiled a bit. "Hopefully, it will save us some additional time and effort."

They exited on seven and walked down the hall to its end; passing the door marked Dr. Olivia Bennet. All the other offices were unoccupied. They walked back, looking and listening, making sure they were alone on the floor.

Satisfied, The Thin Man took a series of picks from his pocket and popped the lock. Seconds later, they were inside. The Thin Man turned on the light, and they went to work.

Bull's task was to find the recording machine and its tapes. They knew their guy was the last session of the day, and they knew that every shrink recorded their sessions. They assumed the tape would, most likely, still be in the machine.

The Thin Man had a more challenging mission. He had to find a flash drive that their quarry might have passed on to the doctor. He was told the priest stole information on a portable metal drive. His employers were confident he would bring it with him and give it to the doctor.

He stood in the center of the office—looking—assessing —searching.

The Bull's search of Lo's office began, and he was not neat.

Suddenly, the phone rang.

They continued searching without interruption.

It rang eight times, then stopped.

Lo was three blocks away and waiting on the subway platform when her cell rang. "Lo...Lo. Hello. Are you there?"

The connection was weak, but she heard Gus's voice over the static. "Yes, what is it, Gus?" Lo was a little mystified.

"Hey, you guys had another appointment today. I tried your office, but no one answered. So, I called your cell."

"What? There weren't any other appointments." She pondered a second. "Are they still there? Is there a name?"

"Yes and No. No, I don't know the man's name. And, yes, he's still here. He's on the floor in front of the desk. I think he had a heart attack."

"What?"

"He's not dead or anything. He went down, and I called 911 immediately. They're on the way."

"So am I. I'll be right there." She disconnected.

The subway platform was noisy and crowded with the homeward bound work-pack. Lo pushed her way back through the mass of waiting crowd and then took the stairs two at a time.

Ten minutes after the phone call, she saw the red flashing light on the EMT truck. It was double-parked and jammed traffic in front of the building. Breathing hard from double-time, she pushed the door open.

Gus was standing near the desk, hands in his pockets.

A gurney pushed past her, an oxygen mask concealing the face of its occupant.

Gus came on her shoulder. "I thought he was going to be okay, but right after I called you, he slumped over. The EMT said he was in cardiac arrest and they're rushing him to Mt. Sinai."

A big man in blue coveralls carrying a large red plastic EMT case was trailing behind.

She came up close to the gurney and the EMT. "Did you get a name?"

"Lady, we were lucky to get a freakin' pulse."

She turned to Gus. "Start from the beginning. Tell me exactly what happened."

"The guy came here about twenty minutes ago. He was stumbling a bit. At first, I thought he was drunk or something. He comes up to me and says he had an appointment with the Doc. I said I thought you guys left. Then he grabbed his chest and fell on the floor. I called 911. I called you."

The ambulance siren overpowered their conversation.

Lo slapped the counter, gaining Gus' attention. "Did the guy specifically asked for Doctor Bennet?"

Gus scratched his chin, thinking. "Yes—without a doubt, Dr. Bennet. That's what he said, Dr. Bennet."

"What did you say?"

"As I said, I told him I thought you guys were gone."

Her face puzzled; she said, "Very weird."

"Thanks, Gus" She smiled a little, turned, and started to leave. Halfway to the door, she stopped and turned around. Lo stood there, thinking. She started for the door again—then stopped. She turned quickly, headed for the elevator, and shouted at Gus. "Did anybody check the floors?"

"No way, can't. I'm here by myself."

Lo nodded. "I'm going up to check our office. You should call somebody to check the rest of the building."

Lo reached for her phone and punched the automatic dial for Smoke. He answered on the second ring.

"A man just had a heart attack in the lobby of our building."

"And?" said Smoke.

"The man said he had an appointment with the Doc—but he didn't."

"Is she still in the office?"

"No, she left before I did." Lo checked her watch. "Almost forty-five minutes ago."

"Where are you now?"

"Headed up to seven to check the office."

"Don't go in the door." Smoke was yelling, and she pulled the phone from her ear. "Wait for me and call the cops."

She yelled back. "Really? The cops—you're kidding, right?"

With less volume but equal intensity, Smoke insisted. "Listen to me. It doesn't feel right. Call the cops or wait for me. But don't go up there without me. I'm ten minutes out—fifteen max."

She hit the up button on the elevator call panel. "Did you forget I'm a Marine?"

"A one-handed Marine," he countered.

"Smoke. Smoke, you there?" The phone call dropped off.

She gave a thought to waiting for him in the hallway. She certainly wasn't going to wait in the lobby for the cavalry.

The door slid open on seven. Lo peeked out and down the empty hall.

She stepped out and removed the Glock from under her shirt. Lo held it gingerly in the bad hand and racked it with her good hand. The safety clicked when pushed to the off position. The elevator door closed, and she heard it start down.

Maybe that's Smoke coming up.

Lo began pacing like a zoo cat in a cage. So many thoughts were going through her head. She hadn't been in a go situation for years.

She looked at her gun hand. It wasn't her shooting hand, and the weight felt odd in the offhand. However, this was not the gunfight at the O.K. Corral.

Chill out, girl. Wait for back up.

She inched down the hall and saw the light coming from under the door.

I know I turned them off.

She pinned the Glock between the cast and her chest, pulled out her phone and hit redial.

Smoke answered on the first ring.

Lo whispered, "The lights are on in the office. I turned them off before I left."

"Dammit Lo, I asked you to stay in the lobby."

She didn't respond.

He broke the silence. "You sure you turned them off?"

"Yes. Positive."

"I'm coming up the block. Wait for me."

She pushed the end call button and got the pistol back into her good hand. Her back to the wall, she approached the light under the door.

Lo moved slowly—listening hard. She heard drawers opening and closing. Somebody was inside. The door wasn't completely closed. There was no damage to the lock. So, they either picked the lock or had a key.

Her wristwatch was on the wrong hand. She turned her arm awkwardly to see how much more time she had to wait for Smoke to arrive. For a moment, it was like back in the day when she wore a badge and came through a door hard and fast.

The minutes were becoming longer and longer.

The Thin Man was standing behind the doctor's desk, carefully surveying the room, looking for the file. It had to be new and most likely was still in a to-be-filed tray. The office was neat and clean. No random paper or mail. He ran a finger on the desk then sat in the chair. There were three drawers on the right side and three on the left.

He was patiently tapping his fingertips together, thinking.

Which one?

His choice was top left. The drawer slid open, and a new, brown folder lay on top. He flipped it open.

Name Mark Moreno Address: 110 Avenue M Brooklyn, NY. Phone: none

The rest of the form was blank. The Thin Man smiled, took a picture with his phone, and replaced the file.

The Bull became impatient with his search of Lo's office. Frustrated, he pushed the desk chair out of his way. It flew across the room, slamming into a table and sending a lamp crashing to the floor.

The sound of breaking glass echoed into the hallway.

Anger filled Lo's face with blood. Her beautiful office was getting trashed.

Motherfucker.

Her anger overcame her training. She spun off the wall and hit the door with her shoulder. The impact and the weight of her cast caused her balance to be off. She shifted her weight and feet getting into a ready position.

"What the fuck are you doing to my office?"

She saw The Bull—caught in the light behind the desk. His hands hung at his sides with his mouth open in surprise.

Lo swung the Glock to center mass of the man with spiked grey hair. "Freeze."

The Thin Man appeared in the corner of her eye.

The next two seconds seemed to take a lifetime.

In the first second, she knew what was coming.

In the last second, she saw her mother.

The Thin Man shot her in the head. She fell on her back under the portrait of the confident, beautiful, Olympia.

The Thin Man leaned sideways, resting his shoulder against the doorjamb.

He lifted the barrel of the gun to his lips and blew the smoke away from the silencer. "Did you find it?" he said calmly to The Bull.

The Bull looked at the Thin Man, his mouth still open. "No, I haven't found the tape machine yet."

The Thin Man walked over and pushed past his partner. He spotted a small remote control on the desk and picked it up.

"What's that?"

The Thin Man put a finger to his lips. "Sshhh." He pushed the green button on the remote.

They heard a soft mechanical click emanate from a box that was lying flat on the bottom shelf of the bookcase behind the desk.

He flipped the lid; the tape deck was inside.

He pushed rewind on the remote. He let it spin for a few seconds then pushed play.

Dr. O's voice came out of the small speaker first.

"You mean Dr. Bennet, the FBI profiler has the credibility, but Dr. O, the author, will make both of you rich."

"Well, that, too."

"Fuck you."

"Philip said you would say that. But he also said if you do decide not to cooperate, your professional ethics will prohibit repeating anything I said to law enforcement or the press."

"You need to leave. And I mean now."

He pushed the eject button and looked triumphantly at his partner. "Did you find a flash drive?"

The Bull shook his head.

"Well, it sounds like their meeting didn't end well, so he probably didn't give it to her. We have the tape, so we'll listen and confirm. Let's get out of here before any other heroes show up."

They closed the door behind them and took the stairwell down to the garage. The camera above the garage exit door was looking at people coming in, not going out, so a piece of duct tape covered their retreat. They walked up two levels of the parking garage and disappeared into the sidewalk crowd.

The elevator took forever and opened to an empty hallway.

Where is she?

Smoke walked fast; gun drawn. The office door wasn't closed completely. He stood to one side and pushed it open.

He saw her on the floor.

His heart beat hard. His gun at ready. His eyes darted to each corner of the room. He opened the doctor's office door and cleared that room then ran to her motionless body. He lowered his gun to his side.

A small amount of air escaped from his lips as he knelt. "No."

The only color on her pure white face was a small red circle, the size of a cherry, in the center of her forehead.

Her gaze was fixed on her final destination.

Smoke brushed her cheek with his fingers, then closed her eyes.

He glanced at the wound. It told him that death was instantaneous, and the gun was a small-caliber pistol. A low-load, fragmentation bullet explained the lack of blood. It also told him the shooter was a professional.

He brushed her hair and straightened her collar. He noticed a familiar-looking chain around her neck. Slowly, he drew it out from under her blouse. The chain held her dog tags.

He gripped them tightly in his hand and lowered his head. From the depths of his being, his body filled with steel-eyed determination.

"I will kill whoever did this."

END OF PART ONE

II

REDEMPTION

26

The airplane was lit by the yellow haze of the aisle lights. The pilot clicked off the overheads after the plane reached 10,000 feet. Aside from the low drone of the engines, it was church quiet. The few passengers that were not sleeping spoke in low tones or stared out the portals at the starry, starry night.

Smoke, although exhausted, was not asleep. It wasn't like he didn't try. He spent many, many hours trying to learn how to accomplish what for others seemed to be a natural task. His attempts at mastering inflight sleep were in a C-17 Globemaster troop transport. It stacked and racked more than a hundred soldiers, along with tons of ammo and supplies. Some of his buddies could fall asleep on a fence and cut a long flight in half—but not him.

Even the expensive first-class ticket was not going to break the sleepless streak. Smoke had not slept in twenty-four hours. This flight now would add four hours and eighteen minutes to the total.

"May I get you water, coffee, or perhaps a drink? We have wine, beer, and scotch, bourbon, and gin."

Smoke looked up at the bright white toothy smile of a thirty-something attendant.

"Water, please."

"Coming right up."

The attendant looked over to Doctor Bennet. She had pulled her feet up on the seat, angling knees toward the window, her head resting on a half-sized pillow.

Smoke shook his head.

The attendant quietly disappeared toward the galley.

Smoke wrapped his mini-pillow in the half-sized blanket and stuck the combination behind the small of his back. Surprised, he found his invention to provide a bit of relief. It did recline further back than the half inch of the torture rack called an economy class seat. The doctor fit comfortably in her chair, but his body fit in only one direction.

A bottle of water arrived with the attendant. "Here you are, sir."

"Thank you. What's our ETA?"

"Six twenty-five a.m." The attendant checked his watch. "In about four hours."

"Humph," grumbled Smoke.

Dr. O rolled over, eyes closed, facing her flying partner. She snuggled into the seat.

He looked down at her.

Her eyes opened. She smiled ever so slightly, then closed them again.

The traveler in front turned on the reading light.

A bit of the yellow beam fell onto her face. She seemed older than she was just a few days ago. There were shadows and lines he hadn't seen before. She made no effort to conceal the dark shadows or the red puffiness around her eyes with makeup.

A different voice came from the aisle. "Is that you? You're Dr. O... right?"

Smoke looked up and saw a man in a western-style shirt complete with a bolo tie secured with a huge silver clasp. There was a chaw of tobacco bulging his cheek proportioned equally to the bulge hanging over his belt

The attendant appeared and was standing in the cowboy's path. "You should return to your seat."

The man appeared unaccustomed to being challenged, especially by the help. "Hey...Hos...hold on now. This'll only take a second."

The cowboy turned to the shadow where the doctor lay huddled. "I saw you gett'en on and I juss wanna autograph for the wife. She loves you."

"You will need to return to your seat, sir." The attendant's voice was hesitant but firm.

The cowboy didn't retreat. Instead, he put on a tough-guy face and took a half a step towards the aisle-blocking attendant.

The attendant's eyes showed a bit of fear but he stood firm.

Then, another force weighed in.

The cowboy wasn't paying much attention to the second guard on duty. Smoke reached up and gripped the western shirt's elbow.

Progress arrested; the cowboy looked down.

There is a second in time—a moment—when a look in the eyes speaks with a voice that is louder and clearer than any spoken word.

The attendant breathed out.

A hand reached across Smoke's body, and Dr. O wiggled her fingers without raising her head or opening her eyes. "It's okay," she said weakly, "Have you a pen and paper?"

"Ah...Yeah, I mean yes... sure thing, ma'am, ri...right here."

She took the pen and scribbled quickly.

The attendant took back the half step he lost to the cowboy and with authority said, "You may return to your seat—now."

Looking down at his paper, his quest complete, the cowboy left quickly.

The attendant said softly, "I apologize for that interruption. It will not happen again."

Smoke nodded at him with respect.

The attendant, head up, proudly disappeared forward again.

"I am a little surprised you didn't punch him in his nuts." Her voice cracked from its lack of use.

"A joke...that was an actual joke." Smoke acted stunned.

The corners of her mouth could not restrain a grin.

Somehow, he felt reborn.

She wriggled her head into the pillow and closed her eyes.

He reached over and pulled the blanket up to her chin.

He continued to stare at her. It made him feel a little pervy, but he couldn't help himself. He had never met anyone like her before.

His mind drifted back to when he told her what happened to Lo. The shock was devastating, and she immediately collapsed into his arms. But within minutes, she recovered, and in short order, pulled herself together.

First, she made the call to Lo's mother. That was hard, but she hung on and volunteered to assist with the arrangements. Using her influence with the NYPD, she made getting Lo home a first priority. She put her practice on hold and contacted all her patients referring them to a colleague.

The doctor informed American Express of a new administrator on her account. A new card was hand-delivered to her New York apartment within four hours of her phone call. Henry Smokehouse appeared in silver letters on a black-titanium card.

He was amazed at how the card seemed to move mountains. The heavy black metal rectangle could magically convert apathy to enthusiasm.

Lo's remains were released within forty-eight hours, and Smoke had her body on a plane to Idaho on the fifty-hour mark. He also made the transportation arrangements for them, securing flights and a car. Travel was first-class tickets from Newark to Salt Lake City International Airport. A vehicle suitable for the three-hour drive to Twin Falls, Idaho, needed to be fast and maneuverable, just in case.

Accommodations were a little challenging. Her choice would have been a five-star hotel. Cactus Pete's Resort and Casino was the only choice, which he deemed inappropriate. He chose instead, the Red Lion Hotel because there was an online picture of their lobby featuring a massive stone fireplace and a couple of comfortable chairs.

They flew from Newark the morning after Lo made her trip.

Dr. O held her emotions in check. She was strong when she met Lo's mother and sister. She also maintained control through the church and the graveside service. During the hour drive back to the hotel, she stared in silence at the endless rows of corn flying by.

When they arrived back at the hotel, Smoke opened the door to the room and escorted her inside.

She politely excused herself and closed the bathroom door.

He wanted to stay close.

She didn't break down in public or in front of him. But even with a closed bathroom door and a faucet running full blast, he could hear her crying hard tears. It was a torrent of emotion.

He just stood there waiting for her—silent—like he was standing a post.

He saw the horror in her eyes when he told her what happened. He saw the disbelief, the denial, the guilt, then the welling of deep sorrow and pain. He watched her pull it back and gain control.

In public, she was a rock. Her face filled with remorse and grief but always remained in control. He saw a single tear falling slowly on her cheek in the church when she gave Lo's eulogy. She held back again when a lone Honor Guard bugler played Taps.

The mournful tune made him camouflage his own emotion. He ran his fingers through his hair while wiping his tear. Rangers don't cry—even during Taps.

27

There was peace. It was sleep, dark and deep. It arrived reluctantly and left suddenly.

"This is Captain Campos. We are flying at 25,000 feet, and we are anticipating a smooth ride into Philadelphia International Airport."

Smoke's eyes blinked open. His ears disregarded the rest of the announcement.

"Would you like something before we land?" They were the attendant's first stop.

"Two coffees—extra black."

The attendant nodded.

O's eyes flickered open. She rolled her head and gazed at her partner, giving him a once-over inspection. "You look like..." a small grin formed, "...shit."

"Thanks, I needed that." His sarcasm was as thick as his stubble.

"Ummm," she mused, "You should go to the head...that's what you call it...correct? You could use a shave."

"I don't have a razor, and it is a latrine, not the head."

"What...oh ...it's not head?"

"Nope, the head is Navy. In the Army, it's a latrine."

"Right." She looked up at him. Her eyes welled.

He understood the cause and squeezed her hand.

"Lo would have corrected me, too." The tear stayed put.

The attendant returned, placing two cups with saucers down on their trays.

"Can I get you anything else?"

Dr. O summoned all of her star power. "My associate needs soap, a towel, a razor, and crème. Can you assist me...or rather him...with that?"

Smoke knew if she had asked for a four-course steak dinner with a chocolate soufflé, this attendant would somehow make it happen.

"Certainly, give me a moment." He disappeared in a cloud of Lone Ranger dust.

"Geez," said Smoke, "I thought a right hook was powerful."

She smiled and patted his arm.

He never expected to feel this way—again. He was somehow younger and ready to—climb a mountain—slay a dragon—swim a river—or however the fuck fairy tales test the hero.

The attendant beckoned, and Smoke rose to freshen up as requested.

He felt the plane begin the slow descent on his return and plopped into his seat a new man.

Dr. O was finishing a second cup of coffee. "There is something I don't completely understand."

"What's that?"

"Why are we going to Philadelphia? You want me to disappear for a while, okay, but why not Paris or Hong Kong?"

Smoke hesitated to divulge his real motive.

She frowned and tilted her head. Her face bore a—I can handle it —look.

"Okay, but I'll need to start with what we know before I get to where we are going." He changed his tone to somber. "Some of this might be tough to hear."

She gave him a repeat of the look and added a—I'm getting pissed —frown.

"What we know is, there was a break-in and a murder."

She winced.

"The motive and the perpetrators are unknown."

"More than one? How do you know that?"

"The surveillance camera in the lobby focused on the desk, not on the door or the elevator. They covered the camera above the garage with a piece of tape. The camera at the street exit of the garage showed two men walking out. No faces, just their backs. The shorter guy has the same build as the man I saw talking to the man who was watching your office."

"So, there are three in the...crew?"

"Yes, there is the Little Round Man, the short, stocky guy, and now...from the tape...a tall thin man."

"Conclusions?"

"They planned the break-in. They knew how to avoid detection. They used a diversion. That plus the gun used to kil..." He stopped abruptly. "... used...indicates a professional crew."

"What about the police? Can't they help?"

"Their primary focus will be on the criminals you helped put away. I've seen a list of the case files you worked with the FBI, and there are potential candidates. Their investigation will be by the book. That would be the obvious starting point, but I believe it is a waste of time."

She considered his hypothesis for a moment and then nodded, agreeing with him.

He scratched where his scruffy beard used to be. "So, from the beginning, it is probable that two men broke into the office, using the man we know was watching your office as a diversion to get past the concierge. They didn't ransack it, but it's clear they were looking for something."

"Yes, I understand, but I don't know what that could be."

He looked at her with confidence in his eyes. "Something you are unaware of motivated the surveillance, a break-in, and a murder. We will figure it out. It will just take some time."

She turned away and looked out the window. "That is a beautiful city. What a magnificent skyline."

Two tones rang out, indicating the plane had descended to 10,000 feet.

She turned and looked at him. "What happened to Lo...was that meant for me? Did I get her killed?"

"No...absolutely not. They were not there for you. She surprised them. They reacted to the unexpected."

She nodded acceptance. "There seems to be a lot of the...unexpected."

"You're correct. The decoy had a heart attack instead of disappearing into the night. He is rushed to the hospital where he can talk and identify his partners. Unexpected. The concierge called Lo who was close enough to return and catch them in the act. Unexpected."

"Won't the man in the hospital give up the other two?"

Smoke shook his head. "I called New York yesterday and checked with Detective Dolan. I wanted to know if they interviewed him. The man went into ICU and was critical but stable. Two hours after admission, he was dead. Nobody saw anything suspicious, but they will do an autopsy. No interview, no last words."

"What's next?"

Smoke took a beat and started slowly.

"The mystery we have to solve is what they were looking for. That is the key."

"How do we do that?"

"If we can narrow the possibilities, perhaps it will spark a memory that will help."

"Okay, let's try."

"They didn't take anything that you know of...correct?"

He watched her rebuilding the images in her mind's eye.

"I walked through the office with Detective Dolan. I thought I was pretty careful in doing an inventory. All the equipment was still there. My files looked right... my notebooks. I just don't think anything was missing."

"Ladies and Gentlemen, we are now in our landing approach to Philadelphia International Airport. We will be arriving at gate C 24."

The undercarriage of the plane thumped when the hydraulics locked the wheels in place.

Smoke cut to the chase. "We know they are coming, and we have changed the playing field. That will force them into the open. If we prepare properly, we will win the battle and then perhaps the war. Remember they are hired help. The key to end this is still what they were looking for in the office. That will tell us the why."

He saw the light go on when she suddenly understood what he was reluctant to tell her in the beginning. "So...you're using me as bait. That is why I'm here on your turf rather than in the penthouse at Hotel Ritz in Paris."

"Yes. That's my plan. I want them to come on my terms. You're the target but I can protect you if I have the reins. Understand?"

"You're sure?"

"The perps know all about your movements in New York. They probably have picked out and cased several ambush sites already. Sooner or later, you will be vulnerable and unprotected. So, we move the battlefield. Philadelphia is new to them, but not to me."

"Okay, I get Philadelphia now. Your turf. However, we still have not established why are they coming after me?"

"Actually...I'm pretty sure about that. They were executing a plan in the order of importance. First, they were looking for something in your office, which we have to assume they got. Then, they come for you."

"Why the break-in first?"

"Because if they had come after you first...shot you in your apartment, or pushed you in front of a train, or even if you're struck by lightning...your office would be sealed tight and guarded. They would not be able to break in and recover what they were looking for. They needed to get that before they came for you."

"Maybe they got what they wanted and will go away."

"Maybe, but I don't think so. You are a doctor that hears all the deep dark secrets. They came for something you have that is important to somebody. And they will come for you because you know about whatever that thing is."

"But I don't remember having anything like that in my possession. A lot of my clients have secrets, but no one has given me anything."

They felt the plane's speed change. It was that moment when flight speed quelled just before the wheels hit the tarmac, and the engines started screaming in reverse.

She placed her hand over his. It was like silk over a baseball mitt. "I am with you. I trust your knowledge and instinct."

He nodded in anticipation of a reservation. "But...?"

"Not a but...a so. So, there are no police to help, and we are alone. How is it possible that I am safe?"

"It will be okay. I have someplace to go, and more than that, we are not all alone. There are reinforcements available."

Before she could ask who, he continued. "In a battle, when you know who, where, and how many of the enemy there are, the worst place to be is in a fixed position. One establishes a front and discovers their flaws. Then one develops a battle plan to surprise and outwit the opponent...to make them vulnerable to an attack. Follow?"

She nodded.

"But the exact opposite is true when you don't know the who or the when. When you don't know how many, or from what direction, one must put oneself someplace with the greatest field of vision. That is usually in a fortification that will stand up to an attack. In short, make them come to you. We don't know who or how many. What we know is, they are ruthless, and they are coming."

The plane taxied off the runway towards the gate.

"I think we have four or five days before they figure out where you are. That's about how long it would take me, so I figure that would be about right for them."

He turned to her for his summation as the plane pulled into the gate.

"We need to get to a fortified position. We need to figure out what you had that they wanted. And we need to develop a plan to make this thing end." Smoke stopped short.

She said nothing.

His face became taut, and his eyes narrowed.

He hissed through gritted teeth. "And...I kill the motherfucker who shot our Marine."

She stared straight back into his eyes, leaned close to his ear, and whispered, "Oorah."

2 8

It was late and the office was deserted except for Nancy Ferris and the odd-looking man in Lawrence Campbell's office. Nancy watched him sitting at the conference table from her desk because she was uncomfortable being alone with him but unwilling to leave him unguarded.

The Thin Man had pale skin on a narrow face anchored with a long thin nose. He cut his hair close on the sides but left it longer on top. It stuck up like spikes of grass on a lawn. Younger men wore that style trying to make a fashion statement, but to her, he looked like an unkempt Q-tip. His legs, sporting perfectly creased pants, were crossed. He seemed calm and relaxed as he rolled the fingertips of both hands on the conference table like an accomplished pianist.

She also saw a man who looked like he could kill with no remorse.

She heard her boss coming down the hallway to her reception area.

"He's waiting in your office, Sir."

He blew past her desk, "No shit," slamming the door closed behind him.

Campbell stopped a step inside and put both hands on his hips. It was a calculated power pose—a move he performed many times. Breathing heavy and not in complete control, he needed a second to recover.

The man responsible for his condition sat with his head down, watching his fingers.

The Thin Man had not looked up.

Neither the door slamming nor the dynamic CEO personality stance had any effect. Eyes fixed on the nemesis, Campbell walked slowly to the captain's chair at the end of the conference table. He sat, his back to windows and the wall-to-wall view of the New York skyline. He pointed at the man obstructing his future, trying to command his attention. "Explain yourself."

The Thin Man finally raised his eyes and looked like he was about to speak. Instead, he pointed his finger, letting it linger in the air. A long moment passed, then he spoke. "I would like coffee."

Campbell hesitated, the request and attitude caught him off guard. He stood fixed. His breathing back to normal, but his blood pressure was still surging. He wasn't sure what to do next. The power of position hadn't worked; neither had anger. Keeping a hard stare, he pressed the well-worn intercom button. "Coffee."

The CEO changed his tone and tactic to business-like. "I need an explanation. What happened?"

The Thin Man stopped drumming and responded in a low, squeaky voice. "The unexpected."

"No shit. And again..." Campbell's voice rose from low to medium. "Explain."

The Thin Man leaned back slightly in recall mode. "In the beginning, I was engaged by and received instructions from—our mutual friend—the man in red."

Campbell struggled to keep his building frustration checked.

"They were simple. Find Father Moreno and recover the

documents he took. The best outcome being to locate him before he divulged any information. We began looking and made some progress, but real-life is not a TV detective show. The bad guy isn't found with a couple of computer keystrokes before the next commercial."

Campbell listened stone-faced.

"While we searched, we developed an intercept plan based on the lead the red man and the monsignor gave us. They told me the priest was to meet Doctor Oliva Bennet in New York to pass the information so she could write a book. Knowing this, I put a watcher on the office—the man our friend insisted we use to keep the cost down." The Thin Man shrugged his shoulders and made a disapproving face. "He did spot the priest in the doctor's office and called me immediately as instructed. We hoped to catch Father Moreno when he left, but we missed him."

"You missed him." Campbell slapped the table.

"Like I said—an interception would have been the best outcome, but—it wasn't the most likely."

"How was failing to pick up this guy not the most likely outcome?"

The Thin Man went from recall to lecture mode. "The best outcome was to confront the missing priest before he got to the doctor." He tapped the table. "However, confronting him in public— on the sidewalk—or especially in the doctor's office, was never the plan. We needed him alone, with no witnesses. That was the only way."

"So, you lost him and killed a woman in the process."

"First off, we didn't lose him. In fact, that is when we found him."

Campbell scratched his head, confused.

"And as far as the girl goes..." The Thin Man smiled a crooked smile. "Yeah, that was a bonus. You can rest easy. She was on the house—no charge."

Campbell sucked a little air through tight lips.

Nancy came through the door with the coffee and placed a cup gently in front of Campbell, careful to lean forward to expose her breasts as required.

Campbell didn't look at her. He was still processing the ice-cold attitude of the man in the chair.

Nancy walked around the table, sliding a cup in front of the Thin Man and spilling some into the saucer. She walked to the door then stood to wait for her boss's permission to leave.

Campbell gave her no attention and addressed the Thin Man. "Please explain why there is a dead secretary."

Nancy's eyes widened.

The Thin Man looked at Nancy, then Campbell.

Campbell made a keep going gesture with his hands. "Why?"

The Thin Man shrugged. "Okay, yeah—the woman. Like I was saying. We waited till the office closed then went in. We were looking for three things: the thumb drive, an address for the priest, and the tape."

"What tape?"

"Every shrink records their sessions. So, we looked for one and found it."

"Okay. Did you get an address?"

"Yep, upper left-hand desk drawer—a new file with the address." He seemed very proud of his accomplishment.

"How about the thumb drive?"

There was a hesitation. "No."

"Why?"

"The secretary came busting in while we were looking and..."

"You killed her."

"Yeah...unavoidable. This doc is high profile, and the police would be all over it. She would have identified us, and if I get picked up, they might ask me to make a deal to stay out of jail. I would have to identify you and the guy in red. Not good for you. I don't do time, but no one ever hires me again." The Thin Man shook his head slowly. "Leave a witness...yeah...that's a non-starter for anybody."

Campbell digested the cold fact then moved on. "But no thumb drive."

"Wasn't there."

"How do you know that?"

"The tape." He smiled a pleased-with-himself smile. "I listened to it carefully. The priest babbled about all the dirt that was on it. But get this...she didn't take it."

"Take the thumb drive?"

"Right. He tried to give it to her, but she wouldn't take it. And... I don't know if you guys were worried about this or not, but get this, she refused to write the book. The doctor threw him out."

Somehow, Campbell knew there was more. "And?"

The Thin Man now seemed a little nervous. "I got the address... so, no worries there. I will get the drive—probably tonight."

"And?" Campbell repeated.

"There may be a copy."

"What?" Campbell felt his face go red again.

"I listened to the tape. The priest's voice was low, but I am certain that he told her where he hid a copy."

"Fuck me." Campbell spun around in the chair and looked at the black night and white lights.

"He told her what was on the thumb drive. We would've had to deal with her no matter what. As far as the copy goes—"

"You need to find the doctor," Campbell said to the window.

"No...not her."

Campbell spun around. "What do you mean?"

"Not her...him. The bodyguard...we find him, and we find her."

"I don't understand. She is rich. They could be anywhere."

"People Looker.com"

"What the fuck?" Campbell was ready to stroke-out. "This is ridiculous."

The Thin Man raised a stop sign hand. "He's protecting her. That's his job. His picture and name showed up in a Page 6 photo. It isn't like finding the missing priest. This guy isn't hiding."

"What the fuck are you talking about?"

"I found him on that website. There wasn't a lot, but he is a professional, and he's good. So... that tells me he knows the break-in was also professional. Therefore, he will do exactly what I would do."

"Which is?"

"Hole up in a place he knows and wait for us to come to him. Like I said, I find him—I find her. End of problem."

Campbell's rollercoaster blood pressure eased.

The Thin Man returned to examining his fingernails. "We will deal with the bodyguard and the doctor right after we clean-up here."

Campbell thought he knew what that meant. "The heart attack guy?"

The crooked smile appeared again. "Na...dealt with him already. The monsignor said he was expendable...so...he's not an issue anymore."

Nancy let out half of a gasp.

Campbell's eyes flickered toward the noise then back to the man across the table. "What's next?"

The Thin Man held his manicure to the light. "If you're asking me, I guess that means you want to know."

"Yes." The CEO demanded an answer. "I want to know. More importantly, is there anything else that ties us to the break-in?"

"Father Moreno is still a connection, but we handle that tonight. There's the doctor, and it is clear from the tape—she knows. The police will make the patient connection soon enough but without the tape, and no witnesses...they got nothing."

"The doctor?"

The Thin Man shrugged. His intent was clear.

Campbell paused, knowing his silence was agreement.

"What if the doctor tells somebody else?"

"If she isn't around to back it up—anything she says to someone else is hearsay and inadmissible in court. They still got nothing."

Campbell coughed and was feeling the floor coming out from

beneath his feet. "She's pretty famous...got that book...and there is the noise the press will make."

"Without evidence—who's going to print? Not the Times...maybe the rags next to a story about Aliens, but the story would not have any wheels."

Nancy coughed loudly.

The CEO turned around and glowered at her.

She didn't back off and beckoned him outside, leaving the door open when she left.

Reluctantly, he stood. "I'll be back." He followed Nancy.

"What?" He did the hands-on-hips power thing. O for two.

"Are you forgetting about the copy? He said there is a copy."

Campbell realized he had and almost gave her credit.

She looked up at him. "Every time that monster shrugs his shoulders and you don't respond, he has permission to kill somebody. You do realize that, right?"

He stared at her, his batting average combined with pointing out something he missed made him angrier. "When this meeting ends, get that faggot monsignor in here."

He turned and started back inside.

She put her hand on his shoulder. "Larry..." she didn't get to finish.

He whipped around and gritted out all the anger he couldn't use on the Thin Man. "Don't you ever call me Larry again. Understand?"

"Get on the phone and get him here...now."

He pulled the door closed on his secretary...and two more lives.

29

A four-wheel-drive Jeep Cherokee was parked in slot A38 in the airport garage. It had standard tires and a few too many luxury features for Smoke, but it was a rough and tumble vehicle. Before they left the Hertz airport counter, he confirmed that the contract contained the maximum amount of insurance.

O settled in and fastened her seatbelt. "You do live near here, don't you? Are we going there?"

"Yes and no. No, we aren't staying in the city. Yes, we're headed to my cabin. It's north—in upper Bucks County. A couple of hours from here."

"Two houses?" she mocked. "I only have one."

He countered. "Not two houses, princess. I rent a one-bedroom apartment in the Northeast. It suits me when I'm working. When I'm not, I stay at a cabin I built in the woods." He pondered his description. "Actually... it's not so much in the woods. It's more like, in a clearing—on a steep mountain slope. So, in response to your sarcasm, I own—one house."

"A cabin, in the woods...hmmm. Is it safe to assume electricity, heat—all the essentials?"

226

"All the comforts of home. Not your home... of course." He tried matching sarcasm which almost worked.

"So, candles and outdoor plumbing?" She made herself laugh.

"Very funny." He laughed too. Her's was better.

She turned to look out the window where the structures they passed on I-95 north piqued her interest. Like New York or any old residential city, one could see Philadelphia's evolution, if one took the time to look. Old becomes new block by block. Boarded up windows and abandoned becomes clean glass and recolonized. On the river side of the highway, old brick factories were metamorphing into new condo buildings. On the other side, neighborhoods of row houses wore history on their walls.

"Did you grow up near here?"

"Yes. We just passed the exit to my old neighborhood."

"You should have taken me there. I would have liked to have seen where you came from."

He looked at her curiously. "Why? There are only old row houses, a park, and mom and pop stores. There is nothing there that would interest you."

"Wow." Her expression first read surprise then changed to hurt. "You couldn't be more wrong."

"I don't understand what I did, but I'm sorry."

"Where did you think I came from—a solid gold vagina?"

That shocked him.

"I have humble beginnings—like yours. A much smaller town than your Northeast Philly granted, but still very blue-collar." She pointed a finger at him. "Just because I managed to get lucky doesn't mean I forgot where I came from."

"My bad...really. I apologize."

She nodded but remained silent.

A couple of minutes went by. He started slow. "I...I guess I was embarrassed. Which is weird for me." He took his eyes off the road. "I guess I didn't care what people thought of me before."

"Before what?" she snapped.

"Before you."

The tires tapped a beat on the concrete drum beneath.

She cracked her window. The air rushing in wasn't exactly Iowa clean, but it was way better than United Airlines recycled.

With her head turned and watching the scenery she reached over and felt for his hand.

The awkward moment ended. "Do we need supplies—food, paper towels—perhaps a hairdryer."

"There's a market on the way where we can stop and stock up. We definitely need food and...a hairdryer. "

She patted his hand affectionately. "Thanks."

He tried to say something witty but, "You're welcome," was all that came out.

A half-hour after the market, Smoke slowed on the quiet two-lane road outside of the town of Elephant, Pa. He slid the transmission into four-wheel drive. They rolled forward about fifty feet, then Smoke turned the Jeep across the macadam at a break in the tree line. To someone driving by, the opening appeared to be a washed-out stream bed covered by low hanging tree branches.

The truck's transmission was tested as it pushed under the green canopy and fought its way up an eroded embankment.

O held on tight to the overhead strap. "Where are you going?"

About ten yards off the road, the rocky path became an almost recognizable driveway.

Smoke looked at her and grinned. "Almost home."

He maneuvered over roots and around large boulders. It was slow going, but the truck was up to the challenge. After a hundred yards of a steep climb, the Jeep emerged from the woods into a flat clearing.

In a life filled with first impressions, this moment was memorable.

A green, tin-roofed cabin sat centered in the meadow surrounded by tall pines. Sunlight flashed red and orange and yellow on cotton clouds hanging above the treetops. Built on a stone foundation, it had weathered grey cedar siding and a long porch. A swing made from pine trees hung from the rafters.

She breathed out a soft word. "Beautiful."

"It's the lighting."

"No, it isn't." She laid a hand on his thigh. "This is something special."

The truck made a new path, neat and narrow, through waist-high meadow grass. He pulled up to the front steps, got out, and started stretching.

She jumped out, came around the front of the Jeep and headed for the door. Whiffs of cedar, pine, and the meadow grass smelled like Barney's best perfume.

He joined her on the steps. "Why don't you take a walkabout while I bring in the supplies and straighten up."

She pushed past him and with mock disapproval said, "Not a chance."

The curiosity train was unstoppable. He gestured to the door. "If you insist... it's open."

O turned the knob and pushed. A small amount of dust rose from the floor and danced in the sunbeams pouring through the windows. She stood motionless, drinking in the craftmanship. A leather couch and chair faced a fieldstone two-sided fireplace, centered in the cabin. On the left was the kitchen. On one end of the counter was a farmhouse hutch complete with neatly stacked plates and cups. Next was a black, cast-iron stove. At counter's end sat an old refrigerator, door open and empty. On the right of the fireplace was a pine table and chairs. On the right wall, a door leading to a bedroom stood open. Next to the bedroom door was a wooden ladder leading up to a loft that filled the peak of the open beamed roof.

He stood behind her, carrying bags of groceries.

"You built this?"

"I had some help occasionally. It took a while...but I had the time."

She turned and looked up at him.

He looked at her, puzzled.

He put two large bags on the table and started back outside.

O came off the wall like a shot. She threw her arms up around his neck and kissed him.

She pulled back and smiled a gleeful smile.

His hand went flat on O's back. He pulled her closer.

Suddenly, he pushed her shoulders back, turning his head and his ear to the door.

"What? What's wrong?"

"Wait one."

She cocked her head toward the door. Then she heard it. It was getting louder.

He pointed to the ladder. "Climb up to the loft. Stay out of sight."

Smoke went to the hutch and popped open the side panel. He removed a Winchester lever-action rifle and a box of 30-30 shells. He turned the gun sideways and shoved eight cartridges into the magazine, racking the last one into the chamber.

Gun at the ready, he peered through the open door. He cleared the right and left flank. Smoke determined it was a single vehicle not trying for a clandestine approach. Satisfied, he walked out and sat on the swing. With the rifle across his lap, he focused on the edge of the woods, looking down the path the Jeep made through the meadow grass.

Smoke heard the sounds made by branches sliding across metal getting closer.

A white Land Rover emerged from the woods exposing its underbelly as it rose up and over a boulder. It fell back to earth with a thump, and a familiar voice yelled obscenities.

"Mother fucker."

Smoke smiled and leaned the rifle against the wall.

The—used to be spotless—luxury sports vehicle came to an uneasy stop behind his Jeep.

Felix Upton Grant emerged from the driver's side. "I truly don't know why, on God's green earth, I'm your friend." He smoothed the hood of the SUV with a loving hand. "I should never have put my honey through that abuse for you, Bucko."

"You didn't do it for me, Ranger," he reminded his friend.

Felix sobered up immediately. "Right...where is she?"

"Here I am." Dr. O stood, hands on hips, at the top of the porch stairs.

"Oh, honey." Felix's arms were flying in the air as he rushed to her. "I am so sorry about our girl."

Dr. O disappeared in a massive bear hug.

The sound of another door closing turned heads.

Smoke saw Gia who also was sporting a concerned look.

"Hi," Smoke said, surprised.

"Hi back."

Felix disengaged, letting Dr. O reappear. "Smoke, you remember Gia—from the club. She's a friend... and she volunteered for this mission."

"Insisted." Gia went up the stair towards Dr. O.

Felix continued the introduction. "She's here for moral support for our girl. She can also stand watch when we need a breather... and most importantly—she is a damn fine chef. Now listen here, you can't bring a man like me out to the boonies and expect me to eat moose burgers. I require fine wine and..." His eyes went wide and hands went up. "Oh, my God... the wine."

Felix sprinted to the back of the SUV, hitting the button to open the rear hatch. "We're good." He smiled, relieved. "No casualties."

Smoke laughed. The man who seemed focused on the ridiculous and silly was an absolute monster in a fight. Smoke could not think of another soul on earth that he trusted more to have his back—and now hers.

"Okay, then." Dr. O gave orders from the porch. "Let's get settled in, make some dinner, and drink some of that wine."

"Now that's a plan." Gia nodded and followed O into the cabin.

Alone, Felix got serious. "I headed down here when I got your message. I take it you're expecting trouble."

"Yea. I know it's a professional crew and I'm certain they'll be coming for O. I think there are two, but they will hire on hands to come up here. I figure a minimum of six."

"That makes us a couple of hands short. Do you have gear?"

"I can make a couple of calls for the equipment but the guy I'm thinking of to help may not be available. He'd be conflicted— being he's a cop."

"Yeah, that's a problem. I might be able to help on both fronts. How long before jump off?"

Smoke paused a beat. "I think two maybe three days. They might get lucky and find this place sooner...I can't rule that out. They are serious professionals who killed once and won't stop till they clean the scene."

"Which is her, of course?"

"Correct."

Félix grimaced, then put his arm around his friend. "I just want you to know and I mean this from the bottom of my heart...I would have never driven my baby up here just for you."

"I know... nor I for you." Smoke slapped the Jeep. "This is a rental."

30

The Montgomeryville Mall is a typical, suburban, middle-class shopping experience. Big box department stores anchored each end of a long commercial corridor filled with busy people who didn't see a face or remember a who.

Dressed as a civilian, Monsignor Giuseppe DeFrancisco felt safe here, hiding in plain sight. He sat at a Starbucks kiosk drinking what passed for Espresso from a paper cup. Small ceramic cups filled with foaming Italian coffee was only one of the many luxuries he missed from his homeland.

He placed the cup on the table and re-crossed his legs. Lawrence Campbell was late.

The monsignor refused to meet Campbell in New York. He had concerns about Campbell's explosive personality. When the secretary demanded he come to the office in Manhattan, he hung up.

The monsignor's phone rang within minutes of the hang-up.

Campbell immediately called Archbishop O'Hanrand, and with the partnership at a turning point, the archbishop interceded. He instructed the monsignor to comply with their business partner's request, suggesting the meeting take place on neutral grounds—

someplace public. He also told DeFrancisco he needed to convince Campbell it was too late to get out of the deal.

He picked up the coffee and swirled the last drops. His mind drifted to his favorite cafe in the piazza, Campo de'Fiori. He ate and drank there, sitting for hours amongst the pigeons and the tourists. It was where he first met the Auxiliary Bishop of Philadelphia. It was also where O'Hanrand offered him a job.

The archbishop DeFrancisco had been working for in Rome made the grade and was elevated to Cardinal. The then Father DeFrancisco had played an essential role. He was a fixer, working behind the scenes to keep all the doors meant to be closed, shut tight. When the new Cardinal got his red galero placed on his head, Father DeFrancisco's services were no longer required.

O'Hanrand was happy to take the priest to Philadelphia because he also wanted to move up the food chain. He needed a fixer to handle his faulty locks.

To Father DeFrancisco, the new position meant thin red piping appeared on his cassock along with the title, monsignor. In Philadelphia, instead of being one of the staff, he became the Vicar General or using a more familiar Mafia term, the Archbishop's Consigliere.

The monsignor took to his position immediately and managed to put out several fires, but the priest who disappeared with a pocket full of goodies became a difficult task. He would be tested because it involved the world outside the walls of their domain.

His plan involved a lot of moving parts. The stolen documents and anyone leading back to him or the archbishop needed to be eliminated. He could have hidden the cost in-house, but every dollar was being watched. The money had to come from the outside. His plan called for a wealthy, egotistical, narcissist with delusions of grandeur, and Lawrence Campbell was a perfect fit.

"I'm here, let's go." Campbell arrived fast and spoke faster. "Let's go... let's go." Campbell waved his hand and started walking ahead. He took a few steps then stopped, waiting for the priest to catch up.

The monsignor stood up and slowly replaced the chair under the table. He shot a glance left and right, making sure Campbell was alone.

Standing six feet away, Campbell began to rant. "You and your boss have really fucked up my life."

The monsignor took slow steps and put his hands together like he was beginning a Sunday sermon. "We have a choice on how to handle this situation."

"Choice," Campbell bellowed. "What choice do I have?"

The monsignor in a softer tone used the exact same words. "We have a choice on how to handle this situation."

Campbell cocked his head, impatient but silent.

"I will feed you information that will lead you to the objective— all of the objectives. You can instruct your people on how to best handle the problem."

Campbell got loud again. "Handle the problem—that's cute."

A couple approaching gave them a wide berth.

Campbell recognized he was loud and lowered his voice. "When all this started, O'Hanrand told me this would be a quick, simple operation. You both swore the people you hired—then dumped on me—were experienced professionals. You were both wrong. Now, instead of an approved project, which you promised, we have a dead secretary and three more—problems—to handle."

The monsignor sniffed and pinched his nostrils. "The action taken in the doctor's office was regrettable—but reasonable—given the circumstances. It was necessary to protect everyone—including you, but..."

"Yeah...here it comes...the big but."

Undaunted, the monsignor continued. "But...the plan did, to use an American colloquium, go off the rail. So, given our circumstances, you have a decision to make. You can take the action necessary to put it back on track or..." he paused for dramatic effect... "don't."

The monsignor stopped walking.

Campbell did as well.

He looked straight at Campbell, pointed a long finger at him. He changed his approach.

"I cannot believe that you are this surprised by a sudden unexpected turn of events. You came to us representing you were a land developer. We thought you were more experienced. Now, I realize you were thinking you were dealing with an unschooled religious order who didn't know what to do with an old, overlooked, undervalued property but, my friend, the truth is you, sir, are an absolute amateur in the field."

Campbell sputtered an unintelligible sound.

The monsignor began a lecture in church business 101. "Imagine yourself arriving in a foreign land, and the people give you property in prime locations. They pay for the buildings you build. You staff those buildings with people that are completely under your control and reduced to indentured servants. Then...the people who gave you the land and the buildings show up every week and buy what you sell...which is...an idea."

The monsignor paused to gauge his audience.

Campbell was riveted.

"Imagine you perfect the business model over two thousand years. Imagine your entire business plan has no manufacturing cost and minimal operating expenses. And—bonus—no taxes. You get to invest in anything—own everything, and all of it is—tax-free."

Campbell was getting schooled.

"You're an amateur. You don't have any idea what you're dealing with—but in fairness—you're not alone. The Catholic Church is one of the biggest corporations in the world with branch offices in almost every neighborhood. Our global assets exceed those of Microsoft, Amazon, and Apple combined, and in spite of—our recent embarrassments—our worldwide collections and donations are still second only to the collections of the IRS."

His victim was paying close attention.

"Americans think their church is theirs, that it is American, and they are delusional. The Vatican is an independent nation. It is a government operating freely within foreign countries. Not one other organization in the world even comes close to that business plan."

He looked straight at Campbell. "You need to understand no matter what decision you make, the only one who loses is—you."

The monsignor, seeing his reflection in a store window, reached up and stroked his black hair flat against his head.

Campbell was quiet—his face blank.

The monsignor suddenly whipped around. "If you walk away, the deal would fall apart, and I would get to go back to Rome." A toothy grin appeared. "You know...you people really cannot make a good cup of coffee."

The developer's head slowly shook side to side.

They started walking again.

The monsignor was pleased with himself and expected a favorable decision.

Campbell seemed deep in thought.

Past Cinnabon. Past the Le Sur. Past the Victoria's Secret.

Campbell came to a jerking halt.

The monsignor had taken several steps forward, not realizing that his companion had stopped. He turned around to see that Campbell's face had gone white, and his eyes were wide.

"What you just said was all bullshit." Campbell looked like he had been hit with a bolt of electricity.

The monsignor looked down. He had underestimated this man.

Campbell stepped forward and yelled straight into his face. "This isn't about the power of the church. It is about how you and that rat bastard boss of yours are just fucking criminals. You're both—just turned-around collar criminals."

A mother holding her young daughter's hand eyed him with disgust, turned around and quickly walked away.

Campbell stepped forward and pointed his finger into Monsignor Giuseppe's chest. "You awarded me the contract for development, then purposely held up all the documentation, the deeds, and title reports, the city reviews, and the approvals. You knew the delays would stretch my financial resources to the breaking point. Then when it seemed hopeless—you dangled a solution in my face. A guarantee that will resolve all my problems...if...wait for it...a whistleblower priest disappears."

The monsignor reached out, placing one hand on top and one hand below Campbell's arm, then guided him to a less-trafficked area.

Campbell followed but was on a roll and unstoppable.

"You made me believe the project and my money would vanish into thin air. Then right when I'm ready to jump off a bridge, you reel me back." Campbell mocked the monsignor's voice. "Don't worry, Larry—you say—we have a plan that will fix everything."

Mad spit followed every word leaving Campbell's mouth. "You tell me you have already put a team in place, but you need me to take over supervision—and pay for the problem solvers you had hired."

Campbell's arms were flailing in all directions.

The monsignor tried to interrupt. "Mister Campb..."

"Goddamn it...and goddamn you." His fingers were now poking in the priest's chest. "You knew about this defector all along, and you manipulated me, so I had to pay for your problem—and so you had plausible deniability in case something went wrong."

The corners of the monsignor's mouth lifted into a little smirk. "You may think you are right, and you might even be correct."

"I'm right. You two bastards set me up."

The monsignor waved his hand dismissively. "It doesn't matter if we did or didn't. This kind of speculation is unproductive and a waste of your time."

The mall shoppers heard only a few words, but they were loud, and they hurried past them.

They were standing toe to toe. It was the showdown. The question was who would break?

The monsignor went first and started strong. "We are in this situation because your money and our project are at risk. If those documents are published or if a witness testifies, the project is as dead as the secretary." He lowered his voice. "What happened in the doctor's office was unfortunate, but the die is cast. Mr. Campbell, there are two paths, and you must choose one."

"I hate..."

The monsignor overrode Campbell's objection with an open palm. "It doesn't matter how you got here—you're here. Now, you must choose."

Campbell said nothing. His face was red, but he was silent.

The monsignor retook Campbell's arm and began walking. "If you choose to protect your investment, additional funding will be required. You need to wire $100,000 to the account."

The monsignor let go of Campbell's arm, turned, and walked away, disappearing into a crowd of shoppers.

Campbell ducked his head in defeat. "Sons of bitches."

31

The stiffness in his back was a wake-up alarm to which he responded slowly. The sleeping bag hadn't provided much padding between him and wide planks of the loft. He yawned, rolled over, and saw Felix. A short blanket covered only part of the other body on the floor. A bearded head and almost equally hairy legs poked out of both ends. The blanket swelled then ebbed with each gulp of mountain air. The hard floor didn't seem to bother Felix.

What brought Smoke to consciousness wasn't the indescribable guttural blasts of his friend nor the pain in his back. It was the aroma of bacon. It drifted up to the loft, summoning him like the mythological Greek sirens luring sailors to a shipwreck. Pangs of hunger commanded him to rise—and rise he did.

He pulled on his jeans, grabbed a clean t-shirt, and climbed down to what he hoped was ample supply of the mystical meat. At the bottom of the ladder, he spied Gia in the kitchen. The popping and hissing coming from the stove drew him toward perhaps the unhealthiest delight on the earth.

Gia cocked her head and smiled as he entered. "Morning, Mr. Smoke. I hope you're hungry."

He smiled back. "Please—just Smoke."

She saluted with a spatula.

The scent of the sirens fought for dominance over the coffee Gia began pouring for him. She was wearing a full white apron, which sported *Will Cook for Wine* embroidered in pink letters across the front. The garment had to be hers because it wasn't his. Her frizzed hair stood out from her head in every direction. She had no makeup, no shoes, and apparently, no clothes under the apron. When she turned around to open the refrigerator, the apron parted in back, and two delightfully round, perfectly formed cheeks greeted him with their own smile.

"Good Morning." O came into the kitchen, yawning.

"Uh... yep... uh... morning." He spilled his coffee when he jumped up with a case of the guilts. "You want some coffee?"

"Sure." She turned toward Gia and saw why he was behaving un-Smoke-like.

Suddenly, a roar erupted from the loft. It took precedence over Smoke's embarrassment. Grunts, snorts, and groans preceded stern words. "There had better be plenty of food left for me."

The diversion allowed Smoke to recover gracefully and, now composed, finished filling a mug for O. He handed her the cup. "It... is... alive."

"Indeed."

They all listened as the grumbling beast climbed down from his perch.

Felix jumped into the kitchen like Superman. He landed with feet apart and hands-on-hips.

It took a second for the group to take in the sight of Felix's fashion choices. He sported a pair of 3X Mickey and Minnie Mouse gold and black pajama bottoms. The legs were hand-cut to Capri length because they wouldn't fit over his tree trunk calves. He topped the ensemble with a Green Bay Packers Jersey sporting the number 43.

The jersey once belonged to Dave Koplay, who was the first NFL player to come out. It was a gift from Smoke and one of Felix's most valued possessions.

The beast carefully inspected the array of breakfast delights, eggs, pancakes, coffee, bacon, and a plate of white powdered pastries with red raspberry filling oozing out from the middle.

With a sweeping gesture mimicking a Medieval Knight, "I have judged this feast—is sufficient. I shall spare your lives."

The performance began a meal filled with laughter. The back and forth between Smoke and Felix might, with some editing for language, make a good TV sitcom sketch.

It was the first break from reality the Doctor and Smoke had in a week. Their troubles went on hold, and the humanity of love and friendship overpowered the sorrow and the fear.

"I really like your place," said Gia, finishing up a pancake.

"Thank you. It's taken a long time to get it to this level of finish. It isn't finished, but it's getting there."

"I like it, too." Felix ragged on him a bit. "There—my gift for inviting me— an unsolicited compliment."

"Gee, thanks, I think."

"However..."

"I knew this was coming."

"In my opinion—the bathroom needs a lot of help. The shower is too small, and the hot water runs out pretty quick."

"That, oh giant one, is an unanticipated issue. It is sized for one— or two—even three average-sized guests. I didn't anticipate storing enough hot water to wash your fat ass."

Disregarding the fat ass comment, Felix announced, "Guest— guest—Did I just hear him say we are guests? It's official, my friends. Smoke has rejoined the human race. He has guests in his house."

Smoke pointed to O and Gia. "They are guests—you are an occupant. Besides, if you need more hot water, you should head up to the hot spring. There's plenty there."

There was a pause. Smoke looked around, and they all had puzzled looks on their faces.

Felix broke the silence. "Did you say there's a hot spring here?"

"Yes—a real, honest to goodness, 100-degree, all day, every day hot spring."

More silence.

Felix spoke for everyone. "Where is it, and when can we go?"

Smoke pointed up the mountain. "Not far, as the crow flies, but it's a bit of a hike."

They all just stared at him in amazement.

"If you want to go, it's best to be there around noon—when the sun is straight up."

His guests were silent and sitting still.

"The locals call this ridge behind the cabin a mountain, but it's really a foothill. If you're going, we should pack lunch." He looked at his watch. "To be there by noon we should leave in about an hour or so."

O stood up and brushed off her Khaki shorts. "Sounds like fun. Why don't we clean up the kitchen, change, and head out? I could use some cardio."

Smoke started for the door. "I have a call to make first."

"Sure, you do." Felix looked around at the breakfast aftermath. "You have KP at dinner."

Smoke stepped down off the porch and walked across the field. He brushed through the tall grasses and sat on an outcropping of boulders near the woods, far enough away from the house so he couldn't be overheard.

He pulled out a cell phone and dialed the Philadelphia Police's 15th District.

A deep voice with a matter of fact tone answered. "15th Police."

"Lt. Aimer."

"Who's calling?"

"Lee Harvey Oswald."

"Hold on."

There was a pause and then a click, then a ring. Lt. Robert Aimer answered. "Lee Harvey...how's it going, buddy."

"Hey. I can't believe the Sergeant didn't break. He just put me right through."

"He's young, probably thinks you're a three-name lawyer from Rittenhouse Square. Listen, Smoke, and no kidding around; the New York PD is pissed. Half of the detectives involved in this case want to detain you as a material witness, and the other half want you arrested for impeding an ongoing investigation."

"Nice to be wanted."

"Come on, Smoke, I'm telling you this is serious. You disappeared with a celebrity, a best-selling author whose secretary slash bodyguard was murdered in a B&E of her office. Some questions need to be answered."

"Like?"

"Like, was it a patient or an angry spouse—was it somebody after the secretary? They also want to know if the doctor got hate mail or recent threats. You know, like cop questions."

"I'm sorry if this puts you in a tough spot."

There was a long pause on the phone.

"Is this Henry Smokehouse—did you just apologize?"

"I'll let that proper name thing go this time, but don't let it happen again."

"Will you be serious, please."

Smoke dropped the cover and gave Aimer what he needed. "Whoever did this is a professional, but you know that already and so does NYPD. So, we know it's more than just breaking and entering. I'm ninety nine percent sure it's not any of the usual suspects. This is bigger and darker than that. They may not know, but you know she is not safe in New York. If I hadn't gotten her out, she'd probably be dead by now."

He waited a second for an objection and heard none.

"I took a calculated risk in going to Twin Falls for the funeral. It was in a small town in Iowa. Anybody and everybody who shows up there would be recognized. Besides, if I didn't take her, she would have gone anyway."

"Sounds like your kind of girl. Where are you now?"

The old familiar Smoke silence was back.

After another long pause, the lieutenant got the meaning. "Oh... okay—okay—I get it. You can't tell me cause if ask I would have to report it. I get it. So, tell me, oh wise one, why did you grace me with this call?"

"I need some information. I gave the NYPD a photo of a guy who was watching the doctor. Did they ID him?"

"Actually, no, but he is the same guy who had the heart attack in the lobby. He's in a medically induced coma in intensive care. He had no wallet and no ID. They took fingerprints, but there were no matches in any system."

"FBI too?"

"Yes."

"Bobby, he isn't a player; he's a pawn. But—somehow, he is connected to who hired these guys. Give them the heads up if you can—they better guard him tight."

Now Aimer was quiet. "I'll tell them about your concerns."

"Will they listen?"

"Maybe. You got something to keep them occupied?"

"The heart attack guy is one of three. There is a tall, thin guy about thirty and a medium height man about fifty with short grey hair."

"Are you sure this was a professional crew?"

"Positive."

Again, there was a silence that Smoke did not interrupt.

The detective was detecting. "Okay, assuming professionals got in using the heart attack as a diversion, how did they get out unseen?"

"The emergency exit door in the garage only opens out—no camera. PD already has the tape. Tell them to look for two men fitting that description, leaving about fifteen minutes after the heart attack. There will be time stamps on the lobby and the garage camera."

A long pause followed.

"Okay, Smoke, I'll give NYPD a call and tell them you phoned in. No problem. What do you want me to tell them about the doc?"

"Tell them—she's in protective custody."

"You need me to do anything?"

"I'll call you when I figure this out, but—yes—I will need your help."

"Anytime, Smoke, anytime."

Smoke pushed the disconnect button.

Felix appeared on the porch. "Hey, mountain man. Are you ready to go or what?"

Smoke pushed himself off the boulder and walked back across the field. When he walked through the door, he saw a pure city audience lined up and waiting.

Gia was barely wearing a bikini and sandals on her feet.

The doctor changed into a pair of short-shorts and a halter-top. The outfit exposed her legs, arms, and midriff to the elements.

Felix was wearing shorts that were just wrong in so many ways and a tank top.

Smoke broke into a knowing laugh. "We will be walking through heavy brush, and unless you like the pain of open wounds, you'll put on long pants, long sleeves, and socks."

Gia looked disappointed, and Felix grunted like a chastised bull. They both shuffled off.

O hung back. "Who were you talking to?"

"I was calling my doctor."

"Oh, is there a problem?" She notched an eyebrow.

"Yes, and the remedy is a day off. No pressure, no worries, just sun, and fun."

O smiled. "As the consulting physician, I concur."

3 2

They struggled up a rocky path that had almost given its purpose back to the mountain. Smoke led the now properly attired troop up the steep trail. He was a bit surprised the trek had not dampened the group's spirit of adventure.

"Not that I'm complaining—but how much further?" O wiped her brow and drew air.

"Actually, we are almost there." He welcomed the break, although he didn't show it.

She smiled. "Cool."

They were in a deep, dense forest. Towering evergreens, branchless up to where the sun reached down to their bright green tops. Nestled tight, leaning close, they supported each other against the wind and sheltered all that chose to live below. Amongst the pines were occasional stands of shorter denser hardwood trees, adding darker shades of green and brown to the forest backdrop.

They continued the assent until Smoke announced. "Just a little further."

His three companions seemed puzzled.

Felix scratched his beard. "I don't see a hot spring, just more freekin' trees."

Smoke pointed to two trees that were twisted around each other and bonded at the trunk like a heavy rope. "It's past that tree and near the cliff behind it."

Smoke stepped onto a mossy embankment, pushing away some brush. "This way."

They formed a single line and followed. Smoke moved sideways past the twisted tree, up and over a windfall, and then maneuvered around a gigantic boulder. Their forward progress halted at a cliff of stone that seemed impassable. The slope rose higher than the treetops and outcroppings of jagged rock jutted out like free-formed bollards preventing anything from passing up, over, or around.

"What now?" Felix voiced what seemed to be a group question.

"This way." Smoke walked toward an arch-shaped shadow off to their right. He stopped, beckoned to them, then stepped into the shadow. It was a cave—narrow, dark, and a little scary. Water dripped from a low ceiling, but a small circle of light ahead indicated hope to the journey's end. As they got closer, they heard a soft sound—like a sleep machine's version of a babbling brook.

They emerged into Smoke's secret place and were overwhelmed by unobstructed sunlight. Through blurry eyes, they saw an oblong, treeless crater that looked like it was created by the foot of a giant ancient god. Mounds of grey rock rose more than a hundred feet all around. The flat bottom was a stone's throw from one end to the other and half a throw wide.

Their quest was at the far end. A funnel of gray steam emerged from a fissure on the face of a sheer rock wall. The mist accompanied a stream of sparkling water that fell to a pond beneath.

It was something from a Sci-Fi movie set, a screenwriter's dream —a place that existed only in the mind of an author with a tilted sense of reality. Yet here it was, a paradise, hidden until now from all but one.

Gia broke the church-like silence and yelled out. "This is

tremendous." Her voice echoed off the walls amplifying her enthusiasm. She dropped her pack and pulled off her clothes as she ran for the pond. Naked, hands stretched up to the heavens, she waded into hip-deep water.

Felix followed behind. He stripped as well, all except for fire-engine red and neon yellow socks, the sight of which caused Smoke to laugh out loud.

The two stood side-by-side, hot water falling down over their heads.

O turned to Smoke. "Are you coming in?"

He didn't say anything. He just stood there.

Keeping eye contact, she stepped back and unbuttoned her blouse. She left it hang open. She unzipped her shorts—wiggled—and they fell to the ground. She shrugged her shoulders, and her blouse followed.

He was spellbound.

Her breasts were trapped in a sports bra that was binding them to her unnaturally. In a flash, it also fell to the ground.

The sunlight surrounded her—backlighting her hair and caressing her body.

Afterward, in a dream, he remembered she had worn purple panties that had wound up on a rock as she walked away toward the hot spring.

Felix cupped his hands and bellowed. "Are you coming in or what?"

"What."

Smoke walked away and climbed the far slope to the top of the ridge. He found a flat spot on the rock ledge and leaned into it like it was a lounge chair. He closed his eyes to the sun.

A treetop high breeze touched his face. Voices of pure joy floated up with the grey mist. As sounds intermingled, he drifted away.

Time stopped. The past swelled within him.

"It's time." Her voice became a soloist.

She was there but only for a moment.

The voices below were gaining clarity.

"Smoke."

Light broke into his darkness.

"Live." Her voice ebbed as it floated away.

Smoke sat up, rubbing his eyes.

He looked out over the top of the crater. He could see forever.

Felix held up a bottle of wine and a sandwich and shouted up to Smoke.

"If you don't come down, I'll eat half of your sandwich and drink all your wine."

Smoke waved and started down.

Felix had dressed and started organizing the food and wine for lunch.

O was off drying her hair with a towel.

Gia was sun worshiping on a flat rock. She was what *PLAYBOY* tried to photograph but never achieved.

"What's up with you?" Felix began chastising Smoke immediately on his arrival. "Beautiful, naked women—the best hot tub...like ever—and you're up on a rock like a mountain goat." He stepped back and put on an exaggerated shock face. "Wait...are you coming over to my team?"

Smoke answered quietly. "I needed some space. There was only one other person that knew about this place."

Felix immediately looked down and kicked the dirt. "Fuck me. I'm sorry, buddy. I wasn't thinking."

Smoke interrupted, "No, there was no way for you to know. It just came on me all at once, and actually, something happened. I'm okay with..."

"Is this a private meeting, or can anyone join in?" O held out cups filled with wine.

"Smoke and I were just talking strategy." Felix went with a diversionary tactic.

"Really?" Her expression suggested disbelief.

Smoke doubled down. "Felix and I were talking about what's necessary to secure the cabin. A Winchester and a box of 30/30 shells won't cut it."

Felix stepped up with more information. "I'm going to get what we need in the city. I'll head in tonight and be back first thing in the morning."

She crossed her arms, her face drawn with concern. "Are you sure this is necessary?"

Smoke took O's hand and guided her to where Felix had laid out lunch. "We are sure of two things. First, the men that broke in were professionals. Second, somebody hired them. That's what we know. What we don't know is why. We can assume that they broke in to recover some physical evidence. We must also assume they consider you a witness."

"What, a witness? I don't understand."

"Your job is to listen to people's problems and confessions. That is what you do. Somebody you talked to—is somebody who is connected to the break-in. They will come after you to silence the witness."

"Oh, my god."

Felix patted her shoulder. "That's why we have to prepare."

O folded her arms and lowered her head.

Smoke lifted her chin. "The police will never be able to protect you, especially in New York. But here...we'll see them coming. You will be safe."

Tears welled in her eyes. "I understand, but I can't live with the thought that either one of you will get hurt."

Felix blustered. "Listen, doll face, Smoke and I have been down tougher roads than this—believe me. We'll be fine and so will you."

Smoke nodded.

O shrugged a reluctant acceptance.

Smoke plowed on. "We need to find out who hired these guys. A starting point is who was the Little Round Man. We know he was watching the building and involved in the break-in. It is also obvious that his heart attack was bad luck for the crew."

O looked up at the sky and held up her hand. "Stop. Can we pick this up later? It's a beautiful day, and this was supposed to be a day off, remember?"

"Absolutely." Smoke immediately backed off.

O shook her empty cup at Felix. "Can I have some more wine?"

"Certainly, darling." Felix grabbed her cup and poured. He then shouted at Gia. "Hey, naked girl—you want some more booze?"

Gia lifted her head and shouted. "Fuck, yes."

Felix, cup in hand, walked towards the pond. Halfway there, he apparently changed his mind. He gulped down the wine, pulled off his clothes, and ran into the pond—again with his socks on.

O and Smoke laughed at the sight. Gia jumped up from her rock and dove in behind Felix.

Smoke saw something rise in O's eyes. "What's up?"

"Will we be okay without Felix tonight? I mean, you with no backup?"

"Don't worry, we still have a couple of days. But just in case, Gia can take a shift this evening, and I'll stand watch till morning."

O's focus was drawn back to the pair frolicking in the pond. "This is an extraordinary place. Thank you for bringing me...I mean us...here."

"You're welcome. I hope it helped ease...I mean, helped to—"

She reached out and put her hand on top of his. "More than you know."

She leaned over and kissed his cheek. "How did you find this place?"

"On an unbelievably cold day, I saw what I thought was smoke up on the ridge. I poked around but finding the cave entrance to this place was just dumb luck. So, what I thought was smoke turned out to be steam. On most days, it dissipates before it gets to the top of the ridge, but on that day, I saw it and found all this."

"It seems so natural."

"Maybe and maybe not. Back in the day, streets in Philadelphia were lined with curbs made of stone. The slabs were cut from rock formations just like this then hauled, in barges, down the Delaware River."

"And the hot spring?"

"It's possible they used dynamite. I think it's possible a blast ruptured a vein in the rock. The vacuum it created continues to draw water up from the deep and dark."

"Does anybody else know about this place?"

"No." He said it quickly then took a beat. "One other person knew... once."

She reached up with both hands and kissed him gently on the lips.

"Thank you."

He knew that she knew.

"You're welcome."

He stood up and put his hand out.

O took it.

They walked together toward the pond.

The sun was directly overhead when they first emerged from the cave. It was three o'clock and the sun was about to disappear behind the high rock ridge.

Smoke and O were sitting next to each other, enjoying the last moments of their adventure.

Felix was policing the area, leaving no trace of their intrusion on the secret hideaway.

Gia was still naked. Smoke thought that she would have been the model Michelangelo would have chosen if he ever chipped marble to represent the David of womankind.

"Beautiful, isn't she?"

"Very." Smoke said it easy, with no reservation.

"Have you had any conversations with her?"

"Not really."

"She is a lot of fun. Aside from her obvious talent, she speaks six languages. So, I get to practice my French, and she challenges me with conversations in Spanish and Italian. She likes philosophy, cooking, and is totally committed to becoming a dancer."

"But that's not all she is about—is it? I mean, her job is to have sex with people."

"True, but if you think about it—I could say she and I have the same job. Only instead of—physically—helping someone reach a new level of sexual understanding—I just talk about it. Gia's job is actually a lot more rewarding than mine. She gets to enjoy the fruits of her labors—I just hear about it after the fact."

He grinned. "That's a unique way of looking at it."

They walked to the water.

She picked up a stone and threw it into the pond then turned to him. "I'm scared."

He picked up a stone, flipped it up and down, then skipped it on the water.

"I could say, don't be, but that would be bullshit."

"Are you scared?"

"You were just talking about your job. So... if you think about it... I could say...you and I have the same job."

"Okay... using my own words. Now, this will be interesting."

"You advise people about how to do things they have never done before. Sometimes, they are afraid, correct?"

"Actually, always."

"Are you afraid?"

"No...why do you ask. Oh—I get it."

"You're not afraid because you have the knowledge and the skill to use it."

She nodded. "Correct."

"I have the necessary knowledge and skill. As your patients trust you, you need to trust me."

"My patients don't have guns."

"Ah... think about that."

"Okay, point taken."

She tried to skip a stone. It hit the water and sunk immediately.

He picked out a flat rock and threw it. It bounced across the pond, landing on the opposite bank.

"Showoff."

She looped his arm. "Am I right to assume whoever hired these guys are powerful?"

"Yes, very."

"And yet you're still not afraid."

"When the heart is fearless, the power is unstoppable."

"Hmmm...I don't think I mentioned that my father was a minister."

"You have not." He was surprised.

"I think I have heard that quote before. It seems very appropriate in this situation—David and Goliath—the book of Samuel, 1-48. Am I right?"

"Actually, It's the Book of Smoke, 3:12 p.m. Time to go."

She laughed out loud, slid her arm inside his, then pressed against his side.

From across the pond, Felix yelled out, "Hey, we need to get going if I'm going to be back by morning."

Gia appeared, casting a shadow on them and pouting like a child. "Do we have to go?"

Smoke didn't fidget or look away. It was like he had permission to appreciate her beauty.

Dr. O answered. "I think—sadly—we must."

"Okay." Gia bounded away, tiptoeing over the rocks.

O pulled on Smoke's shirttail, grabbing his attention. "I have known you for only a short time, and—a lot has happened. Being in your house—and now, here in this place—somehow I feel as if I have had a crash course in Mr. Henry Smokehouse."

He felt lighter and heavier simultaneously.

She took his hand and held it as they walked.

He was tempted but he didn't say anything, not wanting to damage the memory of this moment by saying something incredibly stupid.

They left the enchanted hideaway, down through the forest, to the cabin below, and back to reality.

33

As a young street cop, Sergeant Angelo Franco was tall, trim, and had curly black hair. The accessible and popular beat-cop was the law on Levick Avenue. Two years, eight months, and seventeen days from retirement, the only thing thin on him was his hair. The duty desk was his domain. It was where he lost his good nature but held onto respect. In spite of his now caustic attitude, the rank and file had a high opinion of his efficiency. They often defended him to those who mocked his button stretching uniform and semi-reflective head.

He was the best desk Sergeant the Northeast 15th Police Division ever had. Every phone call was documented, every arrest form complete, and every watch accounted for in detail. The Sergeant knew the 'Bars in Charge' loved clean paper, and the silver bar standing in front of him was no exception.

Lieutenant Robert Aimer read a FAX and frowned. "What time did this come in?" When Aimer looked up, he saw a 'what the fuck look' on Franco's face and immediately recognized his mistake.

"Just how long have you worked here?" The Sergeant pointed to the time stamp on the NYPD Police Incident Report.

"Right." Aimer, embarrassed, read out loud. "09:38 a.m. Thank you, Sergeant."

"Grummph."

"Wait one." Aimer studied the incoming stamp. "This came from the hospital, not the precinct."

"Read the cover sheet, Lieutenant."

He turned to the first page. "From...Doctor Brightman."

Aimer headed for the stairs as he read the Incident Report filed by two NYPD detectives who responded to a suspicious death call from Belleview Hospital.

A John Doe patient was brought into the Emergency Care Unit suffering from a STEMI myocardial infarction. The patient was placed in a medical coma until the patient could be stabilized. He remained in a comatose state for four days. Sometime after 3:00 a.m. this morning, he coded and died. Doctor Robert Brightman recorded the time of death. He noted death could have been caused by an embolism from a brain, a lung, or a deep vein thrombosis. Death could have also been caused by a needle of full air injected into the bloodstream. Upon observing a needle mark on the patient's neck, the police were called to investigate a suspicious death. An autopsy to determine the exact cause of death is scheduled.

Aimer reached the squad's office and picked up the phone nearest him. He dialed the NYPD detective in charge of the break-in at Doctor Bennet's office.

A low, deep voice answered. "Casey."

"Lt. Aimer, Philadelphia PD—you called about Smoke—I mean Henry Smokehouse."

"Right—yes. You're calling me to tell me he's on his way in, I hope."

"No." Aimer changed subjects. "Did you know your John Doe is dead?"

"Wait...What?"

"The heart attack that transported to Belleview from the crime scene.... He's dead."

"Fuck—we never got to do the interview. No access—he was in a coma—Hey, how did you get this before me?"

"I called the nurse's desk early this morning for a status. They said they would get to the doctor on rounds. We received a FAX. It was the IR and a cover sheet from a nurse who said they got it from the detectives for their records. I guess that was the doctor's response."

"Who caught the case for the NYPD?"

"Detectives...aaah..." Aimer flipped the fax around to read the names, "Mahoney and Kelly wrote it up. Just out of curiosity, Casey —you got anybody working there who isn't Irish?"

Casey didn't laugh. "Listen, Detective..."

"Detective is for perps and my in-laws. It's Bob or Aimer or Shithead."

"Aimer, we are looking into the names in the doctor's appointment book."

"And?"

"And...the last notation in her calendar on the day of the break-in..."

Aimer heard paper rustling.

Casey came back. "...was Father Mark Moreno."

"A priest? What about him?" Aimer was puzzled.

"He was found beaten to death this morning in St Nicolas Park, near Harlem."

It was Aimer's turn to be surprised. "Fuck."

The pause was longer this time.

"Also—your Archdiocese sent out a press release.

" *'Father Mark Moreno, a priest in the service of the Archdiocese of Philadelphia, was killed in New York City as a result of a possible Hate Crime. Father Moreno was a valued member of our Church and served faithfully in his duties as a priest. His life and service to Mother*

Church will be celebrated with a Mass and prayers will be offered for his soul and the souls of those who took his life. Auxiliary Bishop O'Hanrand will celebrate the Mass when Father Moreno's remains are returned to Philadelphia.' "

"First off, I'm in Philadelphia, and we didn't see any press release...and second...was hate crime part of the Incident Report?"

"First, the release only had New York press emails on it. And... the second answer is...no. Hate crime was not in the IR."

"So, who said it was a hate crime?"

Casey lost the lilt. "They did."

Aimer started from the beginning. "What time did the release go out?"

"Timestamp reads 7:38 a.m."

"When was Archdiocese notified?"

"Ahhh...My file says 7:17 a.m."

"What? Twenty-one minutes to react, draft, approve, and send a press release?"

"Maybe they wanted to be out in front of the morning news."

"Or...?" Aimer knew the dead air that followed meant two cops were working on the new info.

Casey regained his lilt. "Or...they already knew."

"I agree—possible. "

"What about Doctor Bennet and your guy, Smokehouse? I take it we'll be seeing them soon?"

"Listen, Casey, you have absolutely no reason to trust what I am saying, but this guy knows what he is doing. I'm also telling you he is acting in her best interest."

There was a pause, and then the voice said, "Is that you as a cop or you as a friend?"

Without hesitation, Aimer answered. "Both."

"I asked around about you, and the word is you're a good detective."

"Don't believe everything you hear."

"The question is, how good a friend is he?"

"Do you have a friend you would take a bullet for?"

Casey responded quickly. "Just one."

"Same guy."

"Okay...got it. Wait one." The phone rattled, and Aimer heard footsteps then a door close."

"Okay...I apologize for not doing this sooner."

"What' ja got?"

Casey said, "We have an ID on the heart attack, the John Doe. His name is Father John J Wallace. He is also—a priest from Philadelphia."

"No fucking shit."

"No fucking shit." Casey then took the next obvious step. "Two dead priests in New York both out of Philly—cross-jurisdictional cooperation?"

"Absolutely. I'll get into both priest's backgrounds and get back to you."

Casey waited half a second. "Black and Hispanic."

"What?"

"The two cops that reported the heart attack...Mahoney and Kelly. Mahoney is black and married to a hose-jockey. Kelly is the wife of an ADA in Brooklyn."

Aimer laughed. "So, one only needs an Irish name to be a cop in New York."

"I can see why some call you Shithead. Listen, Aimer, I'll call the dogs off your boy and the doc... and... I'll do what I can to keep my command's bullshit about cooperating with Philly cops uphill."

"Thanks, Casey. You're the first call when I get something."

Aimer hung up and dialed Smoke's cell. The call went unanswered, so he left a detailed update on voice mail.

3 4

M onsignor DeFrancisco pushed the glass entrance doors at 222 North Seventh Street. There wasn't anyone walking near the entrance to the Archdiocese Chancellery Office and he was grateful for that. His steps were quick, and he was in a hurry.

He turned right and then right again, cutting through the alley leading to the Basilica of Saint Peter and Paul on Race Street. He could see his objective; it was only a block away. He had always looked at the structure as a cheap knock off of the magnificent cathedrals of Rome. However, compared to the cattle shelters they called churches in the rest of the city; this was the gold standard. He turned around the corner of 19th and ran past the brownstone walls to the black and gold bronze doors. DeFrancisco genuflected when he reached the center aisle then skirted around to the side, past the seven stations of the cross, walking toward the sacristy.

A small crowd of the faithful had begun to trickle in for the Tuesday 12:05 Mass in the Chapel. It was the Auxiliary Bishop of Philadelphia O'Hanrand's weekly duty mass and the one that least conflicted with his schedule. He had gotten used to eating lunch late one day a week.

The Monsignor went through the altar gate and strolled across the green and white tile floor and into the sacristy. His boss was sitting on a black iron stool waiting on the seminarians who were readying his vestments.

"I need a moment." The monsignor nodded towards the two helpers indicating privacy was needed.

O'Hanrand understood and gestured to the seminarians. "Please leave. Come back in—"

"Ten minutes."

O'Hanrand winced. "Five minutes. Come back in five minutes. I don't want to be late for lunch."

DeFrancisco waited until the door clicked closed. "I had a call from Rome."

The Archbishop went from bored to attentive.

"I have spoken to you about Marcello. We went to seminary together."

O'Hanrand nodded, losing patience already.

"There has been a decision to move..." The Monsignor whispered... "Chaput."

"What?" O'Hanrand came off his chair laughing. "That's terrific. Anything else? Did they decide who..."

"No—I mean no he doesn't know who."

"Really, he doesn't know? I don't believe that. Call him back and find out."

"He promised he would call as soon as he knows."

The Archbishop laughed again. "It's happening. It's finally happening. Thank God."

"I would think... thanking Giuseppe DeFrancisco would be more in order, don't you?"

O'Hanrand winced then smiled. "Yes—of course."

The Monsignor waited for it but he heard something other than thank you.

"Are you sure our problem is handled? I don't want anything to happen now that would hamper my ascension."

"Yes. I'm sure. We have a location and the problem will be handled tomorrow."

The Archbishop looked pensive. "Giuseppe, I have personal business associated with this real estate."

"I'm aware."

"I know you are. I have to make the final payments on the Lake George property in ninety days."

"I am aware."

"This needs to settle...soon."

"I am aware."

The Archbishop then dealt the card the Monsignor was waiting to hear. "You will benefit as well. The day I am elevated, you will become Bishop. The appointment will need to be ratified in Rome eventually, but it will. I will see to it."

"Thank you, your eminence."

O'Hanrand held out his hand.

The Monsignor looked down at the ring he had to kiss. He bent from the waist dramatically and puckered.

It's better than his ass.

35

"You sure you don't want me to take Gia back with me?"

"I'm sure, Felix. The guys looking for the doc will look at all known associates. That includes you, and both of you were missing for a couple of days. So, if she suddenly reappeared, they might assume she might have info on our location."

"Right." Felix frowned. "I shouldn't have brought her here."

"No harm...besides I didn't feel like cooking tonight anyway. I'll get her out of here tomorrow."

Felix bro-hugged Smoke then jumped into his SUV and headed out.

Smoke pulled out his cell phone to check his messages.

Aimer's voicemail gave him a significant piece in the jigsaw puzzle.

The scent from the pine forest mixed with the honeysuckle vines drifted across the meadow.

O looked peaceful, standing in the last rays of sunshine. She leaned on a porch post, watching as he walked to her.

He was about to drastically change her mood.

"You okay? You look worried." She unfolded her arms and moved to the steps.

"Let's take a walk."

They crossed the field, and he lifted her onto one of the boulders at the meadow's end.

"I got a voicemail from my contact in the Philadelphia Police. He's been checking in with the NYPD."

"What did he say?"

"I'd rather ask you some questions first. If that's okay."

"Sure, anything."

"You told me you had four patients the day of the break-in."

"Yes, two in the morning and two in the afternoon."

"No others?"

"No patients, but...well, there was somebody, but he wasn't a patient." Her tone changed. "Philip—who published my book—asked me for a favor. Philip wanted me to meet a priest. He said the priest had a story that would make a great book."

She put a hand on his shoulder. "I didn't think about that before. It just didn't seem relevant."

He nodded. "Tell me about him."

"He was arrogant and rude. It was the last appointment of the day, and I asked him to leave when he told me what he wanted me to do."

"What did he want you to do?"

"He said he left the priesthood because he was getting screwed by the Church on retirement. He said he had a thumb drive filled with dirt, and he wanted me to write a book about his life. He wanted to cash in."

"Was his name Father Mark Moreno?"

Her eyes showed surprise. "That's him. How did you know his name? Your police friend?"

"Yes...but let's put that on hold for a minute." He leaned forward, taking her hands in his. "I want you to think hard about this. You told me you record all your sessions."

"Correct."

"Did you record him too?"

"I didn't know what he wanted, so I did what I usually do, I recorded it."

"Would everything be recorded clearly?"

"Yes. It's a good system."

"Good—okay. Next question, after the break-in, when you walked through the office with the detectives, did you account for every tape? Were all the tapes there?"

"I believe so." She looked up. "Wait...I went in to look over the office...I checked the files...I checked the petty cash box...I checked the tape storage box and the.... Wait—damn it. I left the day's tape in the machine."

Smoke looked at her. "It was gone?"

"I remember now...the machine was empty."

"Next question. What was the meeting with the priest about?"

She took a breath and began. "The priest said he worked in Philadelphia for an Auxiliary Archbishop. He said his boss was a crook involved in blackmail, extortion, and theft. He also said he had evidence of a cover-up in the child abuse scandal in his diocese."

"Did he show you anything?'

"Not really—he just showed me a thumb drive."

"Did you take it?"

"Absolutely not."

"The crew that broke in must have been looking for the drive. I think they would also look for a recording."

She raised her voice in frustration and anger. "But he didn't give me anything. He tried to give it to me, but I wouldn't take it."

He squeezed her hands. "They have the tape. They heard him tell you what was on it. You are a material witness."

A tear welled then slowly ran down her cheek.

She turned away, used the back of her hand to wipe her face then spun around. "I'm okay. Keep going."

One tough lady.

"Good. Let's rerun the scene. Stop me if I get it wrong."

"Go."

"He had an appointment. He told you his story and offered you proof. You declined, sending him on his way. Correct so far?"

"Yes."

"We know he had an appointment." He stopped and considered his next logical conclusion.

Curiously, she looked at him. "What? You have something, don't you?"

"If you had accepted his offer, he would have given you the thumb drive, correct?"

"Yes. This tells you something. What is it?"

He spoke quickly. "If you took the drive, he would've had a—"

"A copy." She finished his sentence. "He told me there was a copy."

"Okay, good. So, did he have it with him?"

"No." She looked up thoughtfully. "Towards the end, he leaned over and got close to me. I remember him doing that because I was sitting and had no place to go. It was creepy and weird."

"What did he say...exactly."

"He said...The O in Indiana's love holds the secrets."

Smoke stood up, shock on his face.

Indiana's love. Son of a bitch.

He started pacing again, holding back his realization.

She studied Smoke's tennis-match pacing.

Turned to her, he stopped. "Is it possible the tape would have recorded what he whispered?"

"He did whisper...so no... it would not have been recorded."

Smoke gripped her hands again. "I'm more certain than ever that you are in harm's way."

Her courage ebbed.

268

Smoke decided to put it all on the table. "I had a message on my phone from my police contact. Your appointment, Father Mark Moreno... he is dead."

She gasped.

"The NYPD found him last night in a park in Harlem. It was a homicide. How he was killed tells me it happened after they got what they wanted. Not before. Now, we know he told you where a copy was hidden. In court, if documents are backing up what he told you in your office...their employers...are dead men walking."

Smoke hesitated.

She scrunched her shoulders. "What? Is there something else?"

"The watcher, the Little Round Man that had the heart attack."

"Yes...what about him?"

"He was a priest too."

"Was?" Her voice was low and slow.

"He died in the hospital this morning."

She shook her head in disbelief.

"Your appointment was with a whistleblower. The Little Round Man was sent to spot Moreno when he showed up."

O lifted her hands and held her head. "This is crazy. They are priests. Do you really think the Catholic Church is involved in this?"

He took her hands down and held them to his chest. He looked into her eyes and said. "What I know for certain—bad people do bad things."

She relaxed under his touch. "What can we do?"

"The real enemies are the ones who hired the crew, but finding out who they are will have to wait. First, we have to handle the people already in motion. We can't prevent that battle, but you need to know...Felix and I will handle it."

She took a deep breath.

He helped her down from the rock and they started back to the cabin. "We will need more information to identify who is at the root of all this, and the thumb drive the priest hid will get us there."

"How...I mean... what is the Indiana thing?"

"It's not a what, it's a where...the O in Indiana's love."
"I'll really be impressed if you've figured that out."
"Prepare to be dazzled."

It was clear and calm when nature's color wheel began its slow spin into the dark of night. The glare of the afternoon gave way to the softness of dusk, painting the sky with colors that have inspired masterpieces. Slowly the horizon, once blazing with red and orange, gave way to the passionless depth of night. Then, as the last of the light disappeared, brilliant specks of light began to appear. The tiny beacons, flashing and pulsating, filled the sky, giving direction to the next horizon and the next ray of sunshine.

The evening was also signaling an end to the day-off atmosphere. Only a few more hours left, so the front door was shut tight against the world outside, and the fireplace gave warmth to a feast fit for a king.

Gia's efforts to prepare the meal were extraordinary. It was seven courses with wine accompanying each and the pauses in between.

A gender alliance of Gia and O formed quickly, leaving Smoke basically defenseless. He was the victim and became the main course during the main course.

"Don't stop." O pleaded while simultaneously suppressing a laugh. "Try one more time...please."

Smoke nodded, but French was getting stuck in his Philadelphia mouth.

O pointed a schoolteacher's finger. "Say...born."
"Born."
"Now ...ghin."
"Ghin."
"Good. Now...yawn."

270

Smoke stretched out both arms, reaching for the sky. "YAAAAWAN."

O laughed and punched him in the arm.

Gia broke up.

He winced for effect. "Wait. I got it. Born...ghin...yawn." He waggled his head at his success but then pushed his luck. "Beef Boreunion."

Laughter erupted from all three.

O wiped her eyes and looked at Gia. "Il est vraiment très intelligent."

"Je sais... et... beau aussi."

O blushed.

"There's a penalty flag on the play. Fifteen yards, illegal use of words."

"Don't be so sensitive." O threw another punch but missed. "I just said...you were brilliant in spite of your language skills."

Gia smiled and ladled another helping of the Beef Bourguignon onto Smoke's plate.

Smoke tried recouping dignity. "Gia, thank you for cooking dinner, it's delicious."

"Merci et bienvenue."

Smoke looked to O for a translation.

"It means—thank you and you're welcome."

He shook his head. "Outnumbered and outmatched."

At dinner's end, O cleared the table, and Smoke took KP.

He sent Gia to stand watch at the window. He wanted time alone with O.

He took a dirty plate handoff. "You okay?"

"Doing alright. That helped—the fooling around." O watched him dunk and wipe.

"You blushed the first time she answered in French. How come?"

"I told you, she said you were smart."

She blushed again.

"And?"

"Smart and... good looking."

His hands were handcuffed in a sink of hot soapy water. "That's embarrassing. Sorry I asked."

She took advantage. "I think so too." She lifted herself on tiptoes and slowly kissed his lips.

272

3 6

Glowing red embers exploded in the fireplace when a log broke in half and plunged into the flame.

Gia, relieved from her post, sat next to O facing the fire.

Smoke, seated near the window, scanned the shadows outside. Standing post tonight was more caution than expectation. The crew in New York had finished up their clean-up last night. It would take at least two days to mobilize, recon, and prepare. They will come, day after tomorrow at dawn, given the terrain too difficult to navigate in the dark.

He stood and grabbed another split of oak for the fire. Fireworks erupted when the wood was placed on top.

"You have any music?" Gia broke the silence.

Smoke pondered a moment. "I have an FM radio somewhere. It might still work."

O reinforced Gia's request. "Music sounds good. I could use a little entertainment."

Smoke found the old Motorola radio in the hutch, plugged it in, and turned the dial. To his surprise, Roberta Flack's voice came from the speaker as clear as a bell on the morning breeze.

"The first time ever I saw your face..."

"I love this song," came the voice from the hearth.

"You're not old enough to know that song." Smoke mocked.

"Leave her alone. You bully."

He walked to the couch. "You're not old enough, either." He held out a hand. She took it, and he pulled her red fingernails off the couch.

She had made him dance at the club. For years, a gun to his head wouldn't have made him dance but she changed that. Now, he wanted to dance.

His hand found the small of her back. He pulled her close and discovered her body fit perfectly to his.

"And the moon and the stars were the gifts you gave
To the dark and endless skies, my love."

She laid her head on his shoulder and lifted his hand close to her chest.

A loud yawn was heard over the music. "I'm turning in."

They kept dancing.

"Okay—then—good night."

They kept dancing.

Gia shrugged and walked to the ladder leading to the loft. She gave it one more try. "Night."

They kept dancing.

The fireplace supplied soft, yellow light. It flickered brightly then dimmed, casting muted shadows across the floor.

The FM station played another song. They heard the beat and the melody, but their concentration was elsewhere.

Smoke, still holding on to her as they danced to their own song, dragged the blanket from the couch. He swung it out, and it fell near the hearth.

She sat down, looked up, raised her hand, and pulled him to her side and her lips.

It was a long, slow, deep, loving kiss.

They lay down. She rested her head on his arm. Her body pressed to him, side by side.

His hand went to her stomach, his face inches from hers.

They were speaking without words, feeling without touching, releasing the old, and accepting the new.

She turned and kissed him again, brushing her tongue against his. Her mouth continued to explore his. Her eyes were open and searching.

Their bodies pressed together, gripping and regripping, close but not close enough. Cloth and buttons were in the way—her blouse then his shirt, her pants, then his.

O rolled over and stretched her arms up over her head. Firelight glistened on her breasts. Flickering shadows became dancers on a moving stage. She pressed her shoulders flat on the blanket—black hair spread out like a feathered crown. Her eyes were closed. Her lips blushed red with passion.

He lay still, staring, overwhelmed, and not wanting the moment to end.

She turned back, reached out, and gently touched the scars on his arms and legs. His wounds became hers. She ran her fingers on his cheek and neck then on his belly. She looped a finger into his underwear and slipped her hand inside.

He gasped.

She arched her back and lunged forward, kissing him hard.

The momentum changed.

She released her grip on him, removed her hand, and rolled over. She pulled down her panties and flicked them into the air with a painted toe. She grabbed the seam of his boxers and yanked them down to his ankles. He rolled over, kicked a leg, and his underwear went flying high.

They lay naked, exposed, and secure in each other's eyes.

O slid onto his chest. Snuggled tight, caressed his cheek with the palm of her hand. She touched his lips with hers. Laying her cheek on his, she raised her mouth to his ear. She kissed it and whispered, "I'm in love with you."

He put both hands on her arms and pressed her up into the air like a barbell. He held her ridged, her toes touching his legs, her shoulders at arm's length from him. Slowly he lowered her, stopping an inch away from his face.

"I'm in love with you."

The inch vanished, and they kissed.

Her body lay flat on top of his. His arms enveloped her, sliding down her back and over the curve of her bottom. He slowly shifted his weight back side to side, guiding her legs apart ever so slightly.

She took a breath of anticipation.

He pushed into the space between her legs.

She lifted her hips and opened her body to his.

Slowly, naturally, almost without effort, they joined together, filling the voids, body to body, breath to breath.

They lay motionless, as close as two bodies could be.

He didn't move. He held her—fulfilled without an ending.

They relaxed, hands roamed, lips touched. Their bodies began moving—slowly, up and down, right then left, always together, in motion and in sync.

The rhythm increased—probing, prodding, caressing, embracing.

O's head and shoulders fell back. Her hips pushed into his.

She gasped.

Her sound matched his breath.

Their rhythm was fueled by their heat.

Suddenly. Uncontrollably. Together. They were freed.

Their bodies tightened as spasms of energy surged through them. Volumes of air flowed out from the bottom of their lungs.

The intensity of their embrace gradually diminished as their bodies absorbed the energy. Warm sweat teased their skin as it trickled down.

Pure joy became smiles. Then laughter. They lay naked in the light of the fire and the afterglow of love.

O played with the hair on his chest. "Well, that was fun."

"It was more than that."

She kissed him. "I know. It was more. I don't know what to say or how to feel. I can't ever remember when—"

"Let's not do that. I don't want to compare you, or us, to anyone, ever. We are who we are to each other and no one else."

"You're right." A joyful look came over her. "The student becomes the teacher."

O laid her head down, gently playing with curls of hair on his chest.

They were quiet together for a long moment.

She looked at him with a wry grin. "There is something I need to tell you."

Propping herself up on her one elbow, "There is one thing I can share with you...it's kind of a secret woman thing."

"Okay." He was hesitant but trusting.

She slid on top of him, kissed him, wiggled around, and smiled broadly. "The rumor is definitely not true...size absolutely matters."

She pulled the blanket over them.

They stayed under the covers in their comic book and flashlight fortress of solitude, making love until morning. Pretending it would last a lifetime.

S moke heard the truck coming up the hill and went outside to await Felix's arrival.

Felix arrived just before noon. The usually snow-white Range Rover was filthy; each wheel-well marked with streaks of black mud. Amongst other debris stuck here and there, a long pine bough was trapped under the roof rack keeping time with the ups and downs. The Lone Ranger, riding his faithful Silver, burst into the clearing, sped up to him, coming to rest in a cloud of dust. The long limb continued to wave hello well after his vehicle came to a stop.

Felix exited quickly. He had on army camo's and a matching army patrol cap. Without a word, Felix beckoned Smoke to follow him to the back of the truck. Felix pushed the remote door release then pulled back a blanket like he was unveiling Door Number 3. He stepped back, bowed slightly, and with a long-exaggerated Ring Master's gesture, exclaimed, "Ta-Dah."

Smoke looked a little stunned. "Impressive."

There were two M-16s lying side-by-side. Next to them were a 12-gauge shotgun and two 9-millimeter automatic pistols. Next to the armament were stacks of yellow and black boxes containing the ammunition needed for each weapon. In addition to the firepower, Felix acquired two pair of binoculars and four handheld radios complete with Bluetooth headsets. Topping off the haul was four smoke grenades and two stun grenades.

"Jesus," said Smoke. "Where did you—?"

"If you make me tell you where I got this, I'll have to kill you."

The passenger door opened, and David emerged in matching army attire. He had a military fade haircut, a close shaved face, and a determined stare. He looked battle-ready.

"You remember David?" Felix used an abbreviated gesture to introduce his partner.

"Yes, of course." Smoke reached out his hand. "Thanks for this. I trust that Felix filled you in, but I need to say this to you myself. Whoever is coming up that hill will take no quarter. They will come hard. They intend to kill her, and anything in their way. Understood?" Smoke continued to grip his hand.

"Hoorah." David smiled a soldier's smile. "I earn a living as an accountant, but I was Special Forces in Afghanistan for two tours. I appreciate the briefing, but you should have no worries about me. I understand the sitrep, and I'm all in." David squeezed a little harder. "She's my friend too."

Felix interrupted the testosterone moment. "He also brought an amazing carrot cake."

David rolled his eyes. "Really, Felix—a cake."

Ignoring Felix, Smoke put his hand on David's shoulder. "Thanks, I—

I mean we—appreciate this."

After the equipment and the carrot cake were unloaded and stored, Felix and Smoke walked to the boulders.

Smoke gave him an approving once over. "I know this is hard for you...so thanks for dressing appropriately, but," he pointed to Felix's

279

head, "I would still put the silver hair thing you have going on under a knit cap, Bucko. Kinda makes for a good target."

"Very funny. I suppose you want me to put camo paint on my face too."

"I hadn't considered that, but now that you mention it..."

"Stop it." Felix changed the direction of the conversation. "What's the plan?"

"Let's get David involved in the strategy when we go back inside."

"Any news from your Philly cop friend?"

"I had a message from him last night."

Smoke updated Felix on the Little Round Man, and O's last visitor. Then included details he didn't mention to O.

"The priest was beaten to inflict pain not death. There were bruises on each temple, several broken ribs, bruising on the stomach and lower chest, also strike marks on the upper thighs and testicles. The medical examiner confirms he was tortured by somebody who knew where and how hard to hit. The deathblow was most likely a Karate knife-hand to the throat."

Felix leaned back on the truck.

Smoke scratched his beard, verbalizing, helping him understand the facts. "It was the way they beat him. I believe they tortured him until he gave up everything, including the thumb drive and what he told O in her office."

Felix looked confused. "What does that mean? I don't understand."

"It means we need to move faster than I anticipated. I need to get the thumb drive first—like today."

"I'm still a little fuzzy. How does that impact our girl?"

"Okay, listen up. O is a material witness. The priest told her he had evidence and then went on to describe it. She can testify to that. These pros are in motion and on the move."

"You seem certain. Are you sure?"

"There is an on-going triple homicide investigation in New York.

Philly cops are cooperating. The only connect-the-dots witness to all three is O. The pros got the tape of the session when they broke in, so, no doubt, that's already destroyed. If there is no thumb drive of evidence and O is dead—"

"There is no case."

"Exactly." Smoke put his hand on Felix's shoulder. "I know where the copy is, and now because of the way the priest was tortured, I think they do too."

"Okay and why do we need this so bad?"

"Stay with me...The priest tells O about what's on it. Somebody hires pros, who have now killed three people, to retrieve and/or destroy all links to them. A copy of the evidence exists but is hidden. Its contents would expose who is most injured and therefore is the most likely suspect."

"This thing is hidden, and you know where."

"Yes, I believe I do." They started walking. "Killing her first is the smart thing to do. If she is dead, they can take their time retrieving it or could just leave it there till it rusts away."

"When will you go for it?"

"Tonight, although retrieving it might be a little tricky. It needs to be done at night and it'll take two people."

"Who are you taking?"

"I'm taking Gia to the train station. You and David need to prepare, which leaves O."

"Isn't that a little risky?"

"Maybe, but if I leave her here and I'm wrong it leaves just two of you to protect her. If, on the other hand, they come when I'm gone you two just hide in the woods. No worries. They're after her not you. We'll be back by 23:00, latest."

"Just how in the world do you know all this?"

Smoke smiled. "Magic."

Felix smiled knowingly, "And, of course—"

"—I have a plan."

About an hour went by without much conversation. Everyone was busy prepping either for a meal or a battle.

David and Felix broke down, cleaned, and reassembled every weapon.

O assisted Gia in the kitchen, making lunch. Their attention divided between making soup and sandwiches and watching men in uniform preparing for war.

Smoke stood at the window, looking out—planning.

He changed post assignments with David.

He walked to the kitchen, coming up behind O.

She welcomed his arms when they wrapped around, pulling her close.

He got close to her ear. "You're going to be fine. I promise."

"I know." She spun, now confident in his arms, and kissed him.

He kissed her, then pulled back and looked down at her. He didn't speak, but he communicated.

She quick kissed him. "I know, me too."

Felix, predictably, broke the moment.

"Okay, enough—lovebirds. What the fuck is the plan, Smokeman?"

The group gathered around the table.

Smoke began the briefing after the last soup spoon hit the table. "The thing we need to wrap this up is the thumb drive. I think what's on it will identify who is behind the crew."

Smoke looked at O.

"We talked about what Moreno told you about the thumb drive."

"Yes. Moreno whispered it low, but I heard what he said."

Everyone stopped eating, eager to hear the big clue.

O looked around. "He said, 'It's hidden in the O of Indiana's love.'"

No one spoke at first. There were a lot of blank expressions.

Felix jumped first. "What the f does that mean?"

O smiled. "Smoke knows."

David spoke first, this time. "That is one cryptic clue. I, for one, will be very impressed."

"Me too." Gia chimed in.

Smoke put up a hand. "Let's come back to that. Gia, do you have relatives near here?"

She responded but was confused. "I have an aunt in Baltimore."

"Perfect. Pack up. You're coming with us. You've been a huge help, but this is going to get a little dangerous, and you're a lover, not a soldier."

He turned back to the guys. "While we're gone you need to do some recon. Find a post at the bottom of the driveway you can get in and out of quickly. One of you should be close enough to the road so you can count how many show up. The other position should provide cover for a move uphill."

David and Felix nodded.

"Then find a spot halfway up the driveway where you can pinch them off as they advance and divide the force. Okay?"

"Roger that."

"My guess for timing is still in order. The assault should start at sunup tomorrow. They won't come at night—the terrain is unfamiliar and too difficult to navigate in the dark. They finished cleaning up their mess in New York last night, so I still think tomorrow morning is jump off."

"Hoorah."

O chimed in. "Where am I in this?"

"You should dress for an informal dinner."

She tilted her head.

"We're headed to Philadelphia to drop Gia at the 30th Street Train Station. After that, we'll have dinner at my favorite restaurant."

"Sounds nice...do I wear a vest?"

"Nope...your health will only be in jeopardy from overeating. Mussels red and the best bread you have ever had in your life."

"Hmmm."

"Oh, and one more thing..."

"What's that?"

"We are going to pick up Moreno's thumb drive on the way back."

"You really know where it is?"

"I know exactly where it is."

Four faces looked at him.

O spoke. "How?"

Smoke raised a finger. "Ahh. The answer to that question is really the biggest mystery."

38

L awrence Campbell arrived at the office at six in the morning after a fitful night's sleep. After pacing for an hour, back and forth like a caged lion, he had a revelation. He needed to stop being angry about being suckered in by the two bible waving crooks.

It came to him like a vision. The end was in sight. Forget about what happened and look forward. The new plan was simple.

He stopped pacing, plopped into his chair, and stared at the skyline.

It will work.

He fought off the demon in his brain. The voice was whispering; it was an all-in bet. He was pushing his chips to the middle of the table. If he got the cards, he would win the pot. If he didn't, he would walk away broke.

It has to work.

The sun peaked above the skyline, its beams of light warming the front of his pants.

He spun around and hit the intercom, buzzing Nancy's desk. He then picked up the receiver and called the accountant to move money. He was pushing all-in.

Nancy came through the door with a pad, pen, and a smile.

Without a word to her, he pushed the chair back and spread his legs.

She walked forward—her head lowered—placing the pad and pen on the edge of the desk. She unfastened her skirt and dropped it to the floor. She removed her panties then got on her knees.

"I don't care what they say. You get me an extension on that loan." His voice was raspy. "They fucking owe me. Get this done."

He pushed the chair toward her, and she inched forward, unbuttoning her blouse, her hair hanging down in front of her face.

As the blouse slipped to the floor, he suddenly reached over her back and yanked her bra up violently, breaking the clasp.

The aggressive act was new to her. Usually, Campbell just sat still, but today was different. He had become more assertive lately, and she became almost paranoid thinking that it was she and not business making him so aggressive. She thought maybe he was getting bored with her, and the more she tried to be better at everything, the worse it seemed to become.

He didn't take too long to finish.

She looked up, but he didn't look down. He was waving his arm as he yelled into the phone.

She bent down in front of the chair to retrieve her bra. She picked up her blouse with her other hand.

Campbell reached out, grabbed the blouse, and wiped his hand on it. Something inside of her snapped.

She mindlessly picked up the rest of her clothes and walked out.

Nancy Ferris had entered the office as an Executive Assistant to a man who was her destiny. She left an empty hull with no rudder, no wind, and no future.

Nancy was having trouble re-hooking her bra. She didn't realize it broke when he ripped it off her.

She was staring straight ahead, eyes wide, jaw slacked, and a small amount of drool oozing from the corner of her mouth. She was repeating the same motion over and over again and each time failing to fasten the broken clasp. After twenty or so almost mindless attempts, she brought the end up to her face, finally grasping that it was not going to hook. She turned slowly toward her desk for a safety pin.

Nancy started redressing. She found and put on her panties. She pulled on her skirt, but it was hanging crooked on her hips. She was still naked from the waist up.

He always made her get entirely naked when she serviced him even though he never touched her or did more than unzip his fly.

She opened the drawer and stared into it, forgetting why she opened it in the first place. Her hand moved to brush the hair off her forehead. It wouldn't come loose. Some of his ejaculate had dried, sticking her hair to her skin.

He had always been cold to her even when she was touching him with her mouth. Despite it all, she still believed one day he would see she was a true believer in Lawrence Campbell.

He was her way. He was her only way.

Her boss had a tough day and still had an urgent call to make. He needed to be relieved. Nancy was always there to do whatever he needed to be done.

A noise behind her caused her to turn.

Campbell emerged from his office with a handful of documents clutched in one hand and a pen in the other.

She didn't raise a hand to cover up. She just stood there looking in Campbell's direction. Her eyes were wide, her skin pale white. She was disoriented, confused. There was a ringing in her ears that made it difficult to hear what he was saying.

He shook the papers in her face. "I have signed all but one of these letters. This one..." he separated one with a gold letterhead from the stack. "This is a joke—three misspellings and the margins are all off. What the fuck."

He dropped all the signed papers on the desk, crumpled the odd one, and threw it on the floor. He spun around and walked back into his office without another word.

She stood, hands at her side, tears now running down her face and falling on her naked breasts.

He slammed the door for effect. He was pleased with his performance as a preliminary to justify his decision to get rid of her.

He had spent so much time blinded by anger and did not see the Thin Man could be a tremendous asset. Looking back, the money he spent was petty cash compared to the money he wasted solving problems through legal channels. His assistant was too close; she knew too much, and she was showing her age.

He didn't notice that Nancy Ferris had followed him into his office.

She took a few steps then stopped, hands at her side, naked from the waist up.

The site of her shocked his reality. Her appearance left him speechless.

For the briefest moment, somewhere deep inside, he was moved.

He stammered out cautiously, "Ah...are you okay?"

There wasn't enough humanity in what he said to save him.

A voice much deeper than he had ever heard before emerged from her. "You hate me."

He wasn't in control of her; it was odd, unusual, and unsettling. "I don't hate you."

The same voice came back a little deeper. "You use me."

Again, he stumbled. "You have many fine attributes—and you are

—very useful. Yes—that's right, you are extremely useful." He smiled a plastic smile.

"You made me worthless."

The attempt at being nice failing, he reverted to his natural self. "No—I didn't make you worthless—you were always worthless."

Her eyes were vacant and distant. Her face was pale and streaked with black.

He was scrambling for something to say.

There was a deafening silence.

Lawrence Campbell looked at her, standing there frozen in the center of his office. He didn't understand the expression on her face and backed up a step, a little scared.

Then, he made his last mistake. "Look, you may have some typing issues...but...your tits are very nice."

A low roar came up from the bottom of her lungs, exploding from her mouth. She sprang across the room with both hands stretched out, now screaming. "Ahhhhhhhhh."

"Wait...Wait..." He retreated to his desk and fell into his chair. "What are you doing?"

He raised both hands in defense. His mouth was open, but nothing came out.

Like a comic book supervillain, she leaped into the air. Nancy hit the desk with one foot, grabbing his custom-made gold-plated letter opener with a single motion. Her body lunged forward, landing on him with both knees on his arms, pinning him into his chair.

The power generated by his fear was overwhelmed by the strength of her rage.

She raised both hands above her head.

"Nooooo."

She plunged the opener down, straight into his chest. She pulled it out, then stabbed him again, and again, and again.

She got up, breathless, covered in blood, watching him as dark black ooze gurgled from his filthy mouth.

The weapon fell to the floor. It clattered when it hit the hardwood.

She never heard it.

Nancy was dead inside.

S moke wanted O to see Philadelphia the way he saw it. One of many scenic views appeared when driving south on the expressway connecting the city to the suburbs. Just past Strawberry Mansion Bridge, fifteen mansions comprising the historic Boat House Row lit the night, their reflections glimmering off the river. A mile further on, the piece de résistance of Hallmark moments became visible through the windshield. The Philadelphia Museum of Art showing off all her porticos and facades dominated the city skyline. The museum is Philly's keystone structure, housing works of the world's greatest impressionists. It was also where Rocky ran up its stairs.

O and Gia were chatting away like they hadn't a care in the world. A temporary suspension of reality that ended when Smoke exited the expressway onto the crosstown bridge onto Market Street.

Smoke brought the Jeep to rest at the entrance to 30th Street Station. He checked his watch. Plenty of time to make the 4:50 to DC.

As the Jeep pulled to a stop, Gia grabbed her backpack, slid out of the backseat. She bent over, looking past Smoke at the wheel, expecting to see the doctor in the passenger seat.

O however, not accepting a passive goodbye, had bolted out and around the back of the Jeep, taking Gia by surprise. The Doc pulled her in for a hug. "Thank you so much."

Smoke, now out of the car, picked up the backpack. "I'll call you as soon as this is over. Okay?"

Gia broke away from the Doc and hugged Smoke. She kissed him on the cheek, slipped on her backpack, and skipped away through the brass and glass doors, disappearing into the crowd.

It was quiet in the car as they drove away, then O reached over and laid a hand on his thigh.

"That's not very safe. I could be distracted."

She smiled. "I have every confidence in your driving under all conditions."

"You've been in Philly before, yes?"

"I have, but just for business. I've never had a guided tour."

"Well then, City Hall coming up." He pointed to William Penn and his famous hat. He turned right to circle the white granite building.

"City Hall is the epicenter from which all city blocks are square, which makes direction easy. One only needs to know a number and a name, and you're there."

"Interesting. Where are we going?"

"9th and Catharine."

"What's there?"

"A surprise."

He turned, leaving Billy Penn in the rearview and headed south on Broad, past the Academy of Music and the Art District.

"Wow, this is beautiful. When we get some time, maybe you can show me around to your favorite places."

"We're headed to one of them now."

He turned left onto Washington Avenue and left again on 9th

street, a narrow one-way street at the end of the Italian Market. It was evening, and quiet on the road made infamous by Rocky Balboa.

Smoke stopped in the middle of the block at a building with a small glass-enclosed porch and an inconspicuous sign—Ralph's Italian Restaurant. On the sidewalk, lined up at the door, were about a dozen people waiting for a table.

A valet stepped out between parked cars and quickly opened Smoke's door.

"Hey." The valet, with youthful energy, held out a ticket.

"Hey, Anthony, how youse doin'?"

"There's a line." O pointed politely.

"Uh-huh."

He walked with O on his arm, past the crowd, and opened the door. "JP."

"Yo. How youse doin'?" The Concierge, Maître d', Greeter, and Sergeant at Arms surveyed the room. "Wait one."

Smoke watched as O's mood suddenly changed to nervous and antsy. Someone would say, "Isn't that," which turned into "Look who's here." After that, the "Can I have an autograph" would start.

JR guided them to a table for two in the back of the room.

A couple of people took out cell phones and started taking pictures.

A woman got up and started for Dr. O.

A waiter wearing a non-approachable face magically appeared and wagged a finger at the intruder. "Nope."

Wine and bread came out immediately. O took his advice and let him order.

JR stopped back, "Everything okay, Smoke?"

"Yeah, no worries. Jimmy here tonight?"

"Nah, not tonight, you know. But Ronnie is back there. You need to talk to him?"

"No, I know he's busy. Tell him I said thank you."

JR turned to walk away.

"Hey, JR. Ask Anthony to keep an eye out on the street. There may be—"

"No problem." JR leaned in, "Police...Or?"

"Or."

JR nodded and walked away.

O tapped Smoke's arm and whispered. "That was odd. Are you sure that's okay, involving them in this? I mean—"

"Not an issue. A lot of the people working here have been given second chances by Jimmy and Ronnie to...work shit out. So, a lot of the people here are...seasoned."

"Really. That's impressive. Your friends must be good people."

"The best. The people have a deep understanding of what a neighborhood is and what it means. They are good at what they do and put a great deal of meaning on...respect."

They sat for the better part of an hour eating pasta and mussels and the best Picante she ever had.

Filled and satisfied, Smoke sipped a cup of black coffee, then threw his napkin on the plate. "I surrender."

JR got his eye.

"I'll be right back."

He stood up, and as he did, a camera came out from the next table.

A napkin dropped on top of the hand that held the camera. Ben, another waiter, wagging his finger. "Nope."

O looked at her protector and mouthed, "Thank you" in his direction.

Smoke walked to the podium.

"Anthony tells me there are two mooks on the corner. He's never seen them before. Looks like their waiting for somebody." He paused. "Is that somebody, youse two?"

"Possibly."

Smoke took a beat. "We're going to head out, and I need a head start...possible?"

JR smiled. "Absolutely."

Smoke turned to go, but JR stopped him. "Somebody came in the back and is waiting to talk to you." He pointed to the bar between the stairs up to the second floor and the kitchen.

Smoke started to say, "Make sure she's—"

"Like my own mother."

Aimer was seated on a stool. "Long time, no see."

"How?" Smoke was genuinely surprised.

"My new best buddy in the NYPD called me. It seems the NYPD needs to speak with you and your date, right away." He used a thumb to point to the Dining Room.

"Okay. Why?"

Aimer got serious. "The autopsy on the heart attack priest came in this morning. Somebody stuck him with a needle of air. It was a homicide."

"Hmmm."

"So, recapping...Your friend is murdered in a B&E, the Doc's last appointment is beaten to death in a park, and the man who diverted attention for said B&E is also a homicide. And...both men are priests. Then you disappear with the key witness in the center of the shitstorm. People are looking for you."

"Yeah, that would do it."

"Casey got a warrant to track her credit card. He traced the rent-a-car to your cabin in the woods."

"Fuck me...that was fucking stupid." Smoke spit out frustration. "Every rental has a GPS tracker."

"How the great have fallen." Aimer reveled in the rare moment.

Smoke moved past his mistake. "How did you find me here?"

"Casey was looking to me for help in pulling you two in, so I started looking. I followed the car GPS, which showed you parked in a lot on 12th Street. Naturally, I deduced Ralph's."

"Fair enough. That also explains my friends on the corner."

"Wait...what?" Aimer looked surprised. "You got a tail?"

"There are two guys on the corner. I think they are waiting for us."

295

"Okay...but wait...go back. I know how the cops found you and how I found you, but how did they find you?"

"Can only be one way."

"Somebody in NYPD leaked info?"

"Possible, but a couple of bucks to a car rental agent would get a tracking number. It doesn't matter how they know."

"Fuck man...who are you up against?"

"The crew after us are professionals. They're doing what I would do, except for the cold-blooded murder part."

"You want me to roust 'em?"

Smoke started pacing. He was better moving, even in a small space.

After a minute of consultation with the floor, he looked up. "No, definitively. No. Them being there tells me something I didn't know."

"What?"

"The priest hid something, and they beat him to death to find out where." Smoke ducked his head, thinking. "He must not have told them, or if he did, he gave them a false location. Hmmm. They have the GPS, so when we left the cabin, they must have thought we were going to retrieve it. That's why they sent people to follow us."

"What are they looking for? Oh, wait, I'm sorry...like always...you can't tell me."

Smoke pushed on. "There is something, though. Can you arrange for the cavalry to hit the cabin tomorrow morning?"

"Sure, but can you tell me why?"

Smoke looked at him. It was a bro moment.

Smoke put his hands-on Aimer's shoulders. "This is you and me, right? Not me and you, the cop."

The Lieutenant thought about it for a second. "Will I lose my badge?"

"Not a chance, but you can't—"

"I can't ask, correct?"

"Right, but I can give you this. The guys that are after her are good. They kill without remorse, and powerful people have hired them. I also don't know how many are coming after her, but I have enough backup. I need one more piece of this puzzle, and I can't get it if the police are involved."

"So, you need some time."

"Right. I need some time."

"Again...I still get to keep my badge, correct?"

"Yes. You'll solve a big case, and Doctor O—"

"Walks away." Aimer scratched his head. "I'll have the cavalry ready to jump in the morning."

Smoke nodded and reached out a hand.

They shook.

"Hey, Smoke, what happens if they bring a lot of bodies?"

Smoke responded, walking away. "Then, a lot won't be going home."

Smoke walked back out to where O was nervously fidgeting with the remains of her Dark Side of The Moon dessert.

Smoke looked to JR and signaled; they were ready to go.

JR caught Anthony's attention, and he left to retrieve the Jeep.

Smoke and O walked toward the door. O stood up on her toes and kissed JR on the cheek.

When they came out, the two mooks on the corner flicked their cigarettes to the ground and started towards them.

Smoke and O stood still at the curb watching them advance.

Two other men cut between parked cars and stopped in front of the advancing strangers. They were short and wide with serious looks tattooed on their faces.

The mooks moved to go around them by stepping off the curb onto 9th Street.

Two more men of similar stature came out a door behind the mooks. There were now four obstructions.

One of the shorter, wider men spoke. "So, how youse doin'?"

The mooks stood straight, assessing their position. One looked like he was thinking about where to attack first.

"You guys seem to be lost." A latecomer joined the party.

The mooks turned around and saw Ronnie coming out of the ally leading to the kitchen.

He wasn't short or wide, and he wasn't built like a brick shithouse. He was the whole fucking house.

Smoke grinned.

The mooks looked at each other, confused. This was Little Italy, and they were surrounded by the cast of Godfather 4.

Anthony turned the corner, driving Smoke's Jeep.

O looked concerned. "They won't actually—"

"Nah," Smoke opened the door for her. "They will politely ask them not to follow us."

O looked relieved. "Really?"

Smoke closed the door. "Nah."

40

Smoke drove a little too fast. He kept an eye on the rearview mirror expecting a tail, but, so far, he'd not detected one. The Jeep navigated 9th Street better than the washed-out path to his cabin, but at least the obstacles there were stationary. He swerved to miss a parked car opening a door near Pennsylvania Hospital and gunned the engine through a yellow light. When he narrowly missed a homeless man with a shopping cart of cans, he finally backed off the gas pedal.

They drove north on 9th, past the Civic Center and into Chinatown, where banners of colored ribbons draped from building-to-building became a ceiling of color.

Smoke turned left onto Race Street. Billy Penn's statue perched on City Hall came into view again.

"Are we headed back to the cabin?"

"Yes, but I need to make a stop first."

"Okay." Her tone was hesitant. "May I ask why?"

"We are going to get the thumb drive."

"Now?"

"Yes. Right now."

She looked at him with a doubtful frown. "The riddle was very cryptic. How sure are you?"

"95 percent." He hesitated then corrected his projection. "Wait...80. No, 75 percent but a positive 75 percent."

"You're not manifesting."

"Oh, brother."

"Don't you oh brother me, you big ape." She slapped him on the arm.

"That's getting to be a habit, Ms. Non-Violent Doctor Bennet."

She stared at him with a considered look on her face then punched him in the arm. "Better?"

He pointed off to her side of the car. "There it is."

"Where?" She craned her neck. The street had traffic in both directions; the buildings were still lit but not open for business, and people were walking along the Parkway. "I don't see it."

"Remember what Moreno said? *In the center of the circle of Indiana's Love.*"

"I don't. Wait...I see it." O pointed at a freakishly out of place piece of metal in the middle of a park. "You're kidding me."

"Yep."

In the center of JFK Plaza was Love Park, where, amongst other things, a water-spouting playground shot streams of water into the air. During hot summer days, it provided hours of entertainment for kids who danced with endless energy through the sporadic eruptions. Just behind the watery playground, on an aluminum metal frame that resembled a very tall kitchen table, were four painted red letters stacked two on two, spelling out the word LOVE.

"The pop sculpture *Love* by the artist, Richard Indiana." Smoke pointed to the top right and the letter O. "In the center of the circle of Indiana's Love."

"It's in the O?" She snickered. "That can't be it."

"Yep."

"Really. How on God's earth did you figure that out?"

"Somebody I knew once hated that monstrosity and constantly berated the artist and the guy who donated it to the city."

"Why would he hide something here? There are safe deposit boxes and lawyers. I mean, it just doesn't make sense."

"Maybe he didn't have time for the conventional ways. One thing I have learned for certain, it's human nature to be drawn to what's familiar. So, if he's running and acting fast, he hid it in a familiar place."

"Gotcha, but still of all the places."

"See the church with the green dome?" Smoke pointed to an enormous brownstone building. "That's the Basilica of St. Peter and Paul, the center of the Catholic Church in Philadelphia. And..." He pointed out the other window. "Right over there, next to the Hilton, is the Chancellery of the Archdiocese, where Moreno worked. That metal—Love thing— was really familiar to him."

She grabbed his arm and shook it. "This is all so weird. I'm thinking about how this all got started. You're involved because Felix knew you and because I got hurt. But now, looking back, everything that happened seemed to be anything but random. But this is the pièce de résistance, the main dish of the meal. I mean, you're not exactly an art aficionado, and you're the only one familiar with a piece of art where Moreno hid the magic beans. Which now also makes you the only one who could bring down the whole house of cards."

He thought about his response. "Maybe, but let's talk about it after we successfully retrieve it."

He brought the car to the curb, stopping the conversation. There was no parking, so he hit the emergency blinkers. The vehicles behind started to go around the Jeep.

He tried to look convincing. "Okay. This is where it gets a little hairy. You have to do something you might not like."

His expression reflected the urgency in his voice. "Okay, I'm ready for anything."

"You need to drive."

"I can do that. I haven't had to for a long time, but I can still drive." She turned her head back and forth, looking at the cars on the Parkway. "Besides, there isn't that much traffic."

"Not here—there." He pointed toward the middle of the park.

"Where?"

"We need to jump the curb, drive through the fountain, then park in front of the LOVE sculpture. I can't reach the platform from the ground. So, you have to pull up close. I jump out, get up on the hood, pull myself up, and grab the thumb-drive. Then, I jump down, you move over, and I'll drive away. Simple enough, right?"

"Really, oh, sure. I can't see anything going wrong with that plan."

He crossed his arms.

"You have a different plan—something we can pull off here in about the next five minutes? Before we get stopped by police, questioned, detained, and sent back to NYC into the arms of the unknown bad guys?"

There was a long pause.

"Well?" He added, foot tapping.

The concern turned into a smile. "Okay, I'm game. Across the pavement, through the fountain, and park in front of the statue. Let's go, Cowboy."

He jumped out and ran around to the other side of the car.

She slid across, quickly took the Jeep out of gear, and gunned it.

"Easy there, Speed Racer. Act like we are supposed to be doing this, not like we are going to crash into something."

When the Jeep drove over the fountain, streams of water noisily sprayed up, over, and under the truck.

"Closer, a little closer."

She kept moving forward, slowly stopping with the hood up close to the bright aluminum frame that held the sculpture.

"That's it, stop here."

He swung the door open, and a stream of water from the fountain hit him in the face.

302

She started laughing.

He turned around, water dripping down his face. "Not funny."

She laughed harder. "It is too."

He jumped up on the hood, grabbed the upper rail, and pulled himself up to the narrow edge of the metal base.

"Hey, what are you doing there?" A voice of protest rang out from the darkness.

Smoke, standing on the rail, wasn't tall enough to see into the dark voids between and inside the top two letters.

"You'd better get down from there, or I'll call the police."

Without turning around to see whom the objections were coming from, Smoke stood in the middle of the letter E and reached into the slanted letter O. He slapped his hand down and around feeling for something—anything.

Nothing.

He slapped it around again from edge to edge—still nothing.

Then he felt an edge. It was tape. He peeled it back, and without examining the lump, he turned and jumped down to the Jeep. The hood was wet and slippery. His feet went out from under him, and his arms flailed in the air, trying to maintain his balance. Smoke fell on his butt then rolled, none too gracefully, to the ground. He was dirty and wet when he opened the driver's side door, but he was victorious.

She was riveted to the driver's seat, laughing too hard to move over.

He butt-pushed her while handing her the sticky wet mess he pulled out of Indiana's letter O. He backed up and cautiously exited the park.

She spent a couple of minutes regaining composure while pulling the tape apart.

Smoke's eyes darted from the road to the shapeless lump of grey tape.

O grunted, struggling with the sticky mess. Then, finally, she

303

dropped her hands in her lap, and she turned to gain Smoke's attention. She frowned and shook her head.

"What? What is it?"

Her eyes brightened, dispelling the fake frown when she held up the chrome rectangular device.

He looked out the windshield.

Intervention.

41

The Thin Man had changed from his daily business wear into more appropriate garb for the occasion. He had chosen a pair of creased black dungarees and a long sleeved, zippered, black hoody over a black T-shirt. He wore calf-length socks that coordinated with his expensive Isabel Marant Black Suede hiking boots. Under the hoodie, he had a Galco Light shoulder holster, which carried a pistol low under the arm. He had chosen this brand carefully as it was a device that allowed for an unobstructed quick withdraw of a weapon. The weapon chosen was his Glock 17, which he had the standard seventeen-round capacity modified to hold nineteen cartridges. He checked its slide twice, snapped the weapon into the holster, and zipped up the jacket.

He then checked himself in the full-length mirror.

He didn't wear a flak jacket and carried just the pistol. The others, the ones hired, were to carry the heavy artillery. They were the plow. He was the blade.

He walked over to his laptop, which was open on the dresser near the motel's TV, and rolled the emails forward. A new email had arrived confirming his United Airlines first class ticket to London, leaving tomorrow at 9:37 a.m. from JFK. It was directly above the email from his Cayman Bank, confirming the deposit of $200,000.

He would be in London in the morning and Thailand the day after, a place where he could disappear and live like a king.

He flipped open the file he received from DeFrancisco and reread the doctor's bodyguard's record. It was helpful but full of gaping holes. It stated that he had a stellar military record, trained as a Ranger, had a fistful of medals, but then disappeared after discharge. The Thin Man decided to be cautious and not underestimate the combat training. He might even be dangerous.

He flipped the file closed.

When strategy fails, overcome the objective with sheer force.

He checked his watch: 4:10 a.m.—on schedule.

He packed his travel case and his computer, checked the room, and then turned off all the lights. He pushed open the door and exited quickly. It was an old habit but useful, never walk into a dark space from a well-lit background. Take no chances—leave nothing behind—including witnesses.

The Bull was standing by the rental car. "Are we ready to go?"

"Yep, ten guys are waiting in two pickups three miles up."

"Rundown."

"All bikers. A couple have some military background. All but one of them has done felony time and two are still on parole. They should be good to go." He sounded satisfied with his recruiting decisions.

"True, but if they get caught, they'll sing like Pavarotti."

The Bull ducked his head, disappointed with his boss's reaction.

The Thin Man opened his door. "Let's get going."

Three miles later, their black four-door sedan drove past two pickups that were idling on the side of the highway. The Bull slowed down, beeped, and the caravan started. They would reach the objective in forty-one minutes, 5:45 a.m. Twenty minutes before sunrise.

42

S moke was awake on the mattress lying close to O, who had finally fallen asleep about an hour before.

He could hear the night outside the open window. There was a breeze blowing through the tops of the trees, knocking the branches gently together. In the distance, he heard a deep sputtering series of five hoots and knew a Great Horned Owl was looking for breakfast.

He checked his watch: 4:30 a.m.

He carefully and slowly lifted the blanket and slid out of bed. He pulled on his jeans and walked barefooted into the cabin. The lights were off, and only the fireplace supplied the light needed for Felix and David. They were busy readying for battle.

Felix said, "Lifer juice is up."

Smoke nodded and picked up a mug and filled it with black coffee and then reached for a Kevlar vest.

Smoke watched as the two men silently and efficiently checked each piece of equipment, double-checking every weapon, and every strap.

"Did you come up with a plan, Felix?" asked Smoke.

"You bet. We recon'ed the driveway from the highway to the open field in front of the cabin. We decided that David will take a position about twenty-five yards up from the road where he can get a personnel and equipment count. The brush is deep there, and he will be able to see without being seen."

David chimed in, "From there, I will be able to report in on enemy strength then move up about 100 yards to where I'll be opposite Felix on the road coming up to the cabin."

Felix said, "Then, depending on the headcount, we will either split them in half, forcing one half forward up the hill toward you and force the other to retreat. Then once you begin your frontal attack, the ones that went up should be forced back into us, pinning them in a crossfire. The ones in retreat will most likely hear the firefight and leave or, if they return, will walk right into us in a secure position."

"We will only fire at them if necessary," said David.

Felix added, "We have a plan. If it works, we might be able to minimize casualties, including our own."

David looked at Felix and said, "You go..."

Felix looked at Smoke. "If they come alone or just one or two, then this is easy-peasy, but if they come in force... David and I... will only be able to reduce the infantry. You know as well as we do that the brains—the front men—the guys who killed Lo—there is no doubt they will get around us, and you will face them alone."

"He won't be alone," her voice came from the darkened door.

O stepped out, "I'll be there... right there."

Felix said, "Ooooh... you go, girl."

Smoke walked back and handed a cup to O. "I can handle this. Don't worry."

"Who's worried?" She looked only semi-scared.

They walked together to where the fire was slowly dying.

"I want you to stay in the cabin, in the bedroom, no matter what. I have the windows shuttered, and the door is an inch thick."

"Ah, huh."

"Is that a yes?"

"Ah huh," She raised the cup and sipped the coffee.

Felix chimed in. "We need to get started. Let's test the mics."

Each of the men clicked on the mics and headsets.

David acknowledged, "Good to go."

Smoke gathered in close, "Stay on mic one. If anything happens to me, one of you has got to get back here to protect her. You know as well as I do that—"

"No battle plan survives the first shot," said Smoke.

The soldiers in unison loudly added, "Hoorah!"

They left.

He finished getting ready. He put on the Kevlar, picked up one loaded automatic pistol, and pumped the slide of the shotgun then slung it across his chest.

He walked to the door, opened it, and was about to walk out but stopped on the threshold.

He turned around and saw O standing in front of the fireplace, dying embers behind her and the shadows hiding her tears.

"I love you," he said and disappeared into the night.

43

David carried his M-16 across his chest, minimizing contact with the brush. The night sky was clear, a quarter moon providing a dim, but adequate light helped Felix and him make their way down the rutty, backwashed driveway to their positions.

When he got to his spot, David signaled by pressing the microphone once.

A single click came back, indicating Felix heard David's signal on his headset.

Felix's post was ten yards above David's position. When David needed to retreat, Felix could provide covering fire, if necessary.

David checked his watch, 05:25.

Sunrise 06:33.

He settled in behind a boulder and checked his weapon one more time.

At 06:05, two pick-ups, driving close together, slowed, stopped for a moment, then drove past the driveway. Ten minutes later, the trucks returned, pulling onto the shoulder, short of the driveway.

David pushed the mic button. "We have company."

He heard one click then two clicks, indicating Felix and Smoke received the message.

The trucks killed their lights but left the engines running. A car approached from the opposite direction.

The car slowed, and David saw the driver of the first truck give a thumbs-up from a rolled-down window before it sped up, continuing down the road.

David focused the binoculars through the branches trying to get a headcount. Both trucks had four doors.

"I got ten heads."

The driver in the second truck opened the door. The inside light went on. When he got out, David could see the man was wearing a motorcycle jacket bearing colors. The man walked to the other driver, who opened his door and got out. Both had the same jacket. The first man pointed to the driveway.

David whispered into his mic. "I think they're going to try to drive up."

Smoke's voice came over the headset. "What kind of trucks?"

"Standard pick-ups, nothing fancy."

"The moment the first truck starts up the hill, you get out. That truck will probably get stuck. Don't get stuck behind them—move up."

"Roger that."

The rising sun lit the treetops.

The first truck revved its engine and started forward.

"Both trucks on the move." David hunched over and took off up the hill.

The trucks got about twenty yards. The lead pick-up got hung up in the first ditch. The second vehicle, following too close behind, lost momentum, also got stuck, both now unable to back-out.

When he heard doors opening, David stopped to listen.

The first driver seemed to be in charge. "Come on, grab your shit. We'll pull these out after we get this bitch."

David counted heads. Eight—nine—ten.

"Got ten. I'm in front and moving to position two."

Felix's voice came on. "Roger that."

David, careful to stay hidden in the woods, double-timed up the hill. He didn't see a pair of headlights coming back up the road.

The sun turned the black of the forest to light grey.

Felix heard a noise from below, footsteps. It wasn't David, who would already be in position straight across from him on the other side of the drive.

The clatter belonged to men who didn't care if they made noise.

Felix concentrated, looking through the brush for the first movement.

Gottem.

"They're single file...ten Haji all in a row."

Smoke answered back. "Are you in position?"

One-click, then a second came over the headphone.

Felix whispered. "I have a good sightline. Wait till they're directly in front of us."

Felix flicked the M-16 from safety to semi-automatic.

Through the brush, blue jean pant legs walked by. Felix counted bodies.

Three, four, five, six. Now.

Felix stood and fired over the heads of the line of motorcycle jackets.

David began firing from the other side of the driveway.

A voice rang out over the echo of the automatic rifle fire. "Over there."

The men began firing, their bullets striking the leaves and branches above Felix.

Felix clicked his safety on and headed uphill. He cut to his left to the edge of the driveway. Still in the cover of the trees, Felix took a beat recovering his breath. He looked up and down the driveway before stepping into the open, firing his weapon down the hill, rattling the trees and cutting off branches. He changed clips, then advanced toward the enemy.

The plan called for David to move opposite Felix, cutting off the retreating column. Felix heard David's two smoke grenades go off. Then he heard voices yelling in confusion and random pistol fire.

"Status?" Smoke's voice came in clear despite the racket.

Felix responded. "Haji's column divided. We pushed six, maybe seven down the hill. The rest are moving up to you."

Felix threw a stun grenade as far downhill as he could and smiled when he heard a panicked voice yell, "Grenade."

He followed the path of the grenade. They were easy to find. They were a group of confused, disoriented, but still armed men trapped between a rock and a hard place.

Felix smiled.

Not wanting any gunfire near the cabin, Smoke took a strategic position between it and the woods. He could see the top of the driveway and still keep an eye on the cabin.

The first head emerged from the woods and took cover in the high grass. It had a headful of long hair that sat atop a skinny body sporting a denim motorcycle cut. The gangbanger held a pistol, his eyes nervously darting from the woods to the cabin.

Another round of M-16 fire opened up from down below.

The denim vest full of colors ducked down but held the handgun above the grass in a ready position.

I could blow his hand off right now.

Smoke saw more movement at the edge of the woods. Number two emerged, wearing the same vest and colors. This one was fat and carrying a shotgun across his chest. He was breathing hard and didn't seem worried about gaining a superior position.

Two hired thugs, but no pros?

Branches moved at the tree line.

Fuck.

Two more came out, side-by-side, advancing military fashion. One held a position providing cover while the other moved forward. They had automatic rifles.

Smoke whispered into his microphone. "I got four heads."

David came back to Smoke's earphone. "We have five secured. One on the loose."

Felix chimed in. "David will stay on the MIA. I'll make sure these guys stay put, then move to you. I'll be there in ten."

"Roger that."

There was a pause, then Felix came back. "Stay alive, partner."

"I'll do my best."

Where was the Thin Man?

The first two jackets remained stationary, not posing an immediate threat. Smoke realized the other two could flank him.

Smoke pulled a stun grenade, took a breath, stood, and threw a strike. It landed at the feet of the two military bikers. It went off, and they went down—hard.

Smoke stood again and fired both barrels of his shotgun over the skinny and fat biker heads. They took off immediately, retreating the way they came—right into Felix.

"Two coming at you."

Smoke hunched over and sprinted across the field toward where the other two bikers went down. They were both still on the ground, one rolling around, holding his ears, the other down but waving a pistol in the air. The moment he saw Smoke, he began firing wild.

Smoke dodged left then right, now moving fast. Three bullets whizzed past. Then one hit his left arm. The impact spun him around, he kept his feet but lost the grip on the shotgun.

"Smoke." O yelled in horror from the porch.

He dove forward, hitting the shooter with an elbow to the middle of his face. The biker's eyes rolled back in his head, out cold.

Smoke jumped back up and saw O still standing on the porch.

"Get back."

The other biker had found his nerve and his feet. He was holding a pistol ready to shoot.

Smoke dove, hitting the ground near his shotgun. He grabbed it and rolled.

A bullet hit the ground, blowing dirt in his face.

He swung the shotgun level and fired a blast wide of his target.

A couple of the buckshot hit the biker's leg with sufficient force to buckle the knee. The man fell on his ass, holding the pistol in one hand and his leg with the other.

Smoke sprang up and caught the long haired biker with a roundhouse kick that sent the pistol and several teeth flying—the man joined his friend in unconsciousness.

Smoke ran to O. She had backed up into the cabin but was still visible in the shadow.

Ten yards. I have to get there.

Out of the corner of his eye, he saw the weeds move near the boulders. The high grass was parting, making a fast path to the cabin.

Fuck.

Smoke stood up straight and ran hard, yelling and waving, "Get back." He pulled his pistol and emptied the clip at the moving grass.

Shots came back from behind the boulder.

Two.

One hissed past his head. The next one hit him in the leg.

He went down.

The grass kept moving closer and closer.

Smoke saw O coming out to help. "No... get inside." He forced himself to stand, moving forward with blood pouring from his thigh.

He saw a head pop up from the weeds—ten yards from the porch.

It's him.

He ejected the empty clip, slid a new one into the pistol, and fired.

Another shot missed.

Ten more feet.

O stepped out from the doorway, both hands outstretched.

"No." Smoke fired the pistol at the boulder.

O backed up, just inside the door.

The steps were in front of him. He holstered his pistol just as his foot hit the first step. Smoke blocked the sightline to the door, spreading his arms, making his body as wide as he could.

A shot rang out.

The bullet hit him under the bottom of the Kevlar vest and above his belt. A half-inch higher, and it would have been stopped by high-impact plastic instead of low-impact flesh.

He fell forward, landing flat-out in front of the doorway.

O came out, bending forward, grabbing Smoke by his shoulders, pulling.

A shot exploded the door jamb.

Smoke pushed with his feet and pulled with his arms, trying to get up.

Another shot.

The impact stood her up, her feet taking quick, short steps backward through the doorway, into the cabin.

Smoke saw her fall on her back—blood on her face. He pushed up on his knees and lunged through the doorway. He rolled over and slammed the door shut with the uninjured leg.

Smoke crawled up to her.

The bullet hit her above the eye. She was unconscious and bleeding profusely.

Smoke heard the footsteps on the porch. He struggled, pulling the pistol from his holster.

The door flew open.

The Thin Man came in fast, kicking the gun out of Smoke's hand.

Smoke, still on his back, reached down to his boot for his knife.

"Nope. Don't do that." The Thin Man calmly waved his pistol back and forth.

Smoke reached up to his microphone.

The Thin Man bent over, put the barrel of the gun on Smoke's head, removed the mic, and dangled the black wire in the air. He stepped back and scanned the cabin. "I didn't have a chance to appreciate the moment when I shot the secretary in the head." He stepped further into the cabin, checking the bedroom. "She just sort of walked in. So, I had to...you know...kill her quick." His lips formed into a thin gash of a smile. "When I get to kill somebody, I try to savor the moment. The look in their eyes." He walked back to where Smoke lay on the floor. "I feel a little cheated." He slowed his words. "I didn't have time to enjoy...the thrill of the kill."

He strutted back to the front door and looked out. "It seems my hired help have accomplished their mission...keeping your hired help busy while I flanked your position."

Turning away from the door, he dropped his pistol to his side and began tapping his leg with the barrel. "I am a professional, and I was certain you were too. But now...seeing you like this; I have to tell you I'm not impressed."

He flicked the gun barrel towards O, lying motionless on the floor. "I guess I should thank you for one thing." He stroked his grey hair flat with his free hand. "I got more money, thanks to you. Hiding the doctor made my efforts much more profitable."

The pain was excruciating. Smoke's hand went to his side and came back covered in blood.

"The initial contract was 150k for the whistleblower. But when O'Hanrand and his Italian gofer gave me the Round Man with the heart attack, I got another 50k." He paused and looked at O, lying motionless on the floor. "But the big prize was 200k for the doctor... yeah...that's right, 200 large. Isn't capitalism just the best."

The Thin Man racked the slide of his automatic, checking the round in the chamber.

"You, my friend, are a freebie, like the secretary. I didn't get to appreciate that kill, but I'm really going to enjoy killing you."

His face turned stone cold as he raised his gun.

Smoke heard the shot.

So did the Thin Man, but the stone-cold face was now grey and bloodless. He dropped his pistol, both hands going to his chest, pulling at the hole in the middle of his jacket. The impact put him against the wall, and he slid slowly to the floor.

He looked at her, his eyes filled with surprise.

"Hoorah...you son of a bitch."

Smoke rolled his head to the right and saw O lying in a prone position on the floor, still pointing Smoke's gun at the Thin Man.

The Thin Man slumped over—dead.

O dropped the gun and crawled to Smoke. She propped herself up and pressed her hands down hard on his wounds.

Smoke grimaced in pain as she applied pressure.

"Help." She yelled as loud as she could. "Help."

O used the back of her hand to wipe her own blood from her face then screamed louder. "Help."

A large shadow appeared in the doorway.

Felix scanned the damage as he ran to them.

O looked up. "Help him." Her head fell forward, and she collapsed on Smoke's chest.

Felix picked her up and laid her on the couch.

Smoke was straining against the darkness. It was closing in on him, but he had to fight it off. White lights were going off as he reached into his pants pocket. He didn't recognize his own voice. It was weak and squeaky. "Felix."

Felix returned and leaned close.

"Take this." Smoke opened his hand, revealing the silver thumb drive.

Felix took it.

"Get my phone."

Felix rummaged Smoke's pockets.

"Redial the first number. It's my cop. Tell him...come now."

It all went black, Smoke's head banging on the floor as he lost consciousness.

44

The cavalry arrived with flashing lights and screaming sirens. Three black and whites, one K-9, an ambulance, and one sedan slid to a stop.

David, waiting at the cabin's driveway, was unarmed and impatient.

"They're here." David clicked his mic, alerting Felix. "Six black and whites, two unmarked and an ambulance."

David ran out, arms waving.

The troops came to a halt, and Lieutenant Aimer jumped from the passenger side of a black sedan. "Where are they?"

"They're in the cabin." David pointed up the hill. "Smoke and the doctor have been hit. The driveway's blocked."

"Felix alerted me when he called in. The medevac chopper's en route."

"Good." David continued the briefing. "There are five bikers tied up about halfway up. There are two near the top and two more in the meadow near the cabin."

"Are they alive?"

"Of course, they're a bunch of thugs, but one of them did sustain a minor bullet wound to the leg."

"Nine captured and only one minor injury? How many of you were there?"

"Three."

"Is that all?"

"Yes. Felix called you. Smoke you know, and me."

"Hmmm. Okay. All of the bad guys accounted for?"

"No. Seven disabled, one is unaccounted for, and one is dead."

Aimer's eyes widened. "Dead? Where?"

"In the cabin. Felix thinks he's the one from New York who organized this assault."

"Who killed him?"

"I don't know, but this can wait, can't it?"

"Harry," Aimer turned to a man in a suit standing nearby. "Take four units and secure the suspects and bring the K-9 unit for the runner. This man will point out the runner's last known position."

David and Aimer joined the parade of police moving up the hill. They stopped when they encountered the bad guys.

Aimer signaled for the K-9 officer, and David pointed out where the man went into the woods.

The K-9 officer scratched the head of his partner. "Rosco, hunt. Hunt." His partner barked once and ran into the woods.

The team of police then divided. A few took charge of the prisoners and escorted them to the waiting police cars. The rest double-timed up the slope. When they arrived at the meadow, chopper blades thumped in the distance.

Two of the uniforms took guard positions at the perimeter. The others rounded up the bikers, who were still where Smoke had disabled them.

Aimer and David ran across the meadow and into the cabin.

Felix was pressing one hand on Smoke's bloody leg and the other on the belly wound.

Smoke wasn't moving.

O was sitting up, her head on the back of the couch, holding a compress against the wound.

Aimer took charge. "Condition?"

Felix, still pressing hard, shook his head, looking a little panicked. "He's lost a lot of blood, and the pulse is weak. He needs a transfusion, ASAP."

The Lieutenant hit his mic, checking on the chopper. "Eight minutes out."

Aimer started towards O but stopped and turned to Felix. "Did you see what happened here?"

Felix shook his head. "No. I was—"

"Stop talking." Aimer cut him off and gave him a stern cop-like stare.

Two uniforms came in.

Aimer pointed at them. "Take positions outside, front and back. We have one on the loose."

Aimer waited for them to leave, then walked to O.

She lowered the blood-soaked compress.

The wound made Aimer wince. "David, can you get another towel for the doctor?"

He calmly asked, "Who shot that guy?"

She was shaking. Aimer grabbed a blanket and covered her. David returned with a clean towel.

O looked at the body on the floor. "I did." She choked up and looked at Aimer, eyes filled with tears. "He was about to kill Smoke. I was on the floor, and the gun was next to me." She pointed her finger. It shook like her voice. "That man had a gun in his hand. He pointed it, and I...I shot him."

Felix jumped in. "I think she should have a lawy—"

Aimer snapped around. "I told you to stop talking."

David, who had moved to help, nodded at Felix, strongly suggesting compliance.

Aimer turned back to O and spoke in a calm, quiet tone. "You shot him?"

"Yes."

Felix barked out, "I still think—"

"I only have a couple of minutes. Please, stop talking."

O took a breath. "I was stupid. I was watching at the window. I saw fighting. There were four of them. Then I heard gunshots, and I ran to the door. I went out on the porch like an idiot, and Smoke started running toward me. I ran back inside the doorway, but I had to look. I could see Smoke was wounded and limping badly. Then a bullet hit the door. I guess whoever was shooting could still see me. Smoke ran up on the step."

She white-knuckled the towel. "He spread his arms out wide.... He was shot protecting me." O's face had trails of blood and tears. "He fell on the porch in front of me. I went out to pull him inside... then I got shot."

Aimer put his hand on her shoulder. "Then what happened?"

O pointed. "That bastard said he broke into the office." Her eyes welled with tears. "He said he killed Lo."

"What?"

"I woke up on the floor...I must have been out for a couple of minutes. When I woke up, he had a gun in his hand and was waving it around, bragging about what he had done. He must have thought I was dead." Anger took the place of tears. "He said he felt cheated. He said he had to kill Lo fast, and he didn't get to enjoy it."

A uniform walked into the cabin. Aimer held up a stop sign hand then motioned to the officer to listen. "Doctor, you are stating that this man," Aimer pointed to the Thin Man, "admitted killing your secretary, Loretta Kelly."

"Yes, he said he shot Lo." She wiped the blood from her cheek.

David, Felix, and the uniform were silent.

Aimer continued questioning. "Did he say anything else?"

"Yes. He was talking to Smoke. Telling him that he was a professional and was paid $200,000 to kill me. I saw him raise his gun. Another gun was lying right next to me. So, I picked it up and pulled the trigger. I didn't know where I was aiming, I just shot."

The room was silent.

Aimer looked at the three witnesses. "So, Doctor Bennet, it is your statement"

Felix started to object, and David gripped his shoulder.

"You believed the assailant was here to kill you, and he had a gun in his hand. Is that correct?"

O stammered, "Yes."

"Your statement is that you saw him raise the gun and...then, you shot the assailant."

"Yes, I did."

The Lieutenant raised his voice a little higher. "He had a gun, and he pointed it at you, and you fired."

"Yes..." She nodded, then reacted. "Wait...what?"

He cut her off. "Thank you, Doctor Bennet. I think I have all I need. This is justifiable self-defense."

David and Felix nodded; the uniform shrugged.

"Right." Aimer stood. "The district attorney might want to talk to you, but I doubt it. The report I file will say this was a shooting in self-defense. Now, there is a helicopter about to land and we'll be transporting you and Smoke to the hospital."

The uniform chimed in. "Lieutenant, there's a guy out there with a shotgun wound.

Aimer scrambled. "You find a shotgun?"

"Yes, one of the bikers had a 12 gauge."

Aimer pondered a moment. "Probably, friendly fire, one biker to another."

The uniform asked, "What should we do with him? He was shot too."

"Does he look like he's dying?"

"No."

"Okay. The EMTs that came with us will handle him."

The uniform shrugged indifference. "Okay by me."

The sound of the helicopter landing in the meadow was

deafening. The EMT crew bolted through the door and within minutes had Smoke and O in the air.

Felix and David watched the police process the cabin doing the CSI stuff like the TV show.

Aimer took a break and walked outside.

Felix came up behind him. "Impressive bit of sleuth-like interrogation, Mr. Policeman."

"That's Lieutenant Policeman if you please."

45

Doylestown Hospital, ten minutes from the cabin by chopper, had one of the best trauma units in the state. Fifteen minutes after the chopper hit the ground, Smoke was in surgery. It took two hours to remove the fragments of the bullet from his leg and graft a piece of bone onto his femur. The wound on his arm required a few stitches. There was, however, a more significant problem.

Doctor O was examined and treated for a severe concussion. The bullet had struck above her eye, leaving a seven-inch gash and a groove in her skull. The wound required eighteen stitches and would need the attention of a cosmetic surgeon. However, she was fortunate. The couple of centimeters of bone left intact proved the difference between her current massive headache and death.

In recovery, the wide gauze bandage stuck to her head, and the IV in her arm did not divert her thoughts from Smoke's condition. She stared at the door, willing someone to come in and give her an update.

Finally, the doctor heading Smoke's surgical team, still in green scrubs, walked into O's room. "He's out of surgery and in recovery.

The procedures were successful. He's stable but still critical. The wound to his arm was superficial. The wound to his thigh was also not severe. We removed some bullet fragments and grafted a piece of bone to the femur. The wound in the lower abdomen was a bit tricky, but he was extremely lucky. No vital organs were damaged." She paused a second. "However, there's another issue."

O filled in the bad news gap. "Blood loss."

"Yes, doctor. Frankly, I don't know how he survived. The loss of so much blood caused him to go into hypovolemic shock."

"Coma?"

The surgeon nodded.

O sucked air. "Oh, God."

The surgeon scratched where her surgical mask used to be. "It's a mystery. Frankly, he should've bled out. But...he didn't. The EMTs stopped the bleeding, supplied oxygen, and got him stabilized. That saved his life. The bad news is we had to give him six pints of blood, which, as you know, is more than half of what an adult body contains. His body protected itself and shut down."

O was motionless.

"His body just needs to restart." The surgeon took O's hand. "He'll wake up when he's ready." She gripped O's hand a little tighter. "That's when we'll know if there's any brain damage."

"Can I see him?"

"Of course, but Doctor Bennet, you've suffered a severe concussion. Please remember that you were shot in the head. You know that a severe concussion can be life-threatening as well. Even if you're feeling better physically, there'll be psychological trauma."

Dr. O looked up at the surgeon, "Really?"

The surgeon, embarrassed, muttered. "Ah, yeah...umm sorry, protocol required me to say that."

Smoke looked pale. He lay stiff with his hands rigid at his sides.

There were IVs in both arms and oxygen tubes in his nose. The monitor had heartbeat and blood pressure indicators moving across the monitor screen, mercifully minus mandatory TV movie beeping sounds.

O maneuvered her IV stand and parked it near his, then sat in a chair next to the bed.

She took his hand in hers.

O leaned over and got close to his ear. "I love you." She sat back, looked at him lying there, helpless, then leaned close to his ear again. "If you die and leave me...I will kill you."

46

This day, the sun's appearance began as a single point of light below the horizon. Its gradual ascent marked a slow fade of pastel orange and red that expanded to the underbelly of puffy clouds wearing the color of night on their shoulders. Then, just as rays of light reached out to the furthest point on the morning's canvas, the pastels rolled back from the clouds, drawing in tight, their backdrop changing from dawn grey to morning blue as the single brilliant sphere that gives life to all became the feature star in our heaven—again.

It was near seven o'clock, and the sunlight moved across the parking lot and up the brick walls. When it came through Smoke's window, the beam of light took on dimension and form. It became an elongating rectangle, slowly processing across the floor and up Smoke's bed.

He still lay face up and motionless. The IVs and oxygen were gone, leaving only the LED screen. The series of graphs remained unchanged since he came out of surgery.

O lay awake on a bed crammed in between his bed and the wall. Despite the violation of policy, the administrator accommodated the hospital's recent celebrity patient request for a bed. The administrator was a big fan.

O had not slept well the night before nor any night since the assault, constantly waking at the slightest sound coming from Smoke's bed. She was awake and lay on her side, watching the sunlight come across the floor. Her bed was slightly lower than his, but she could still reach over and touch his hand. O couldn't see his face, but as long as she could touch him, she was good.

Her hand lay still, on top of his.

The sunlight pushed its edge up onto the bed, instantly warming whatever it touched.

O closed her eyes, and she felt the sunbeam touch her hand.

She yawned.

She lifted her head and saw his eyes.

"O." He moved his lips again, but no sound came out.

She threw her blanket off and slid in next to him on his bed.

"I'm here." She kissed his cheek.

"And so are you."

47

F elix appeared in the doorway, wearing a bright yellow tank top and lime green shorts. He mimicked an almost recognizable, Bill Murray impression. "It... Is...Alive."

Smoke and O looked at the man taking up the entire opening.

"I am." Smoke's voice was scratchy and low.

"He is," O added, smiling broadly.

Felix approached quickly and then extended his hand. Smoke slowly reached up, and they gripped like brothers.

Felix, not letting go, leaned over to where O was sitting on the bed and kissed the top of her head.

"David wanted to come too, but he's missed a lot of work and needed a few days to catch up. He'll come down on the weekend."

Felix plopped into the chair next to the bed. "Is this an opportunity to make up a lot of shit you can't remember, or are you 100 percent? To tell the truth, I'm kind of hoping for about 80 to 85 percent. I've been working on some pretty funny stuff, and it'd be a shame to waste it all."

"Some friend." O smiled, dismissing him with a wave of her hand.

Smoke smiled a little, shook his head, then grabbed his water bottle. "I've responded well so far, and my doctor said I'd be fuzzy for a while, but she thinks everything is good to go. Sorry to disappoint."

O took Felix's hand, speaking softly. "You stopped the bleeding. If he had lost any more—"

"I had no choice." Felix kissed her head again.

She looked up, puzzled.

"He owes me money."

O whacked him on the arm.

Smoke beckoned to Felix to close the door.

When he returned, Smoke asked, "I take it that David is an excellent accountant."

"Accountant is incorrect. His title at Goldman is Senior Statistical Analyst."

Smoke grimaced.

O, instantly concerned, said, "We can do this later."

"No. I'm okay." Smoke pointed at Felix. "I'm concerned about security."

O answered. "Robert has taken care of that. Hospital security is on alert and there is an off-duty policeman on this floor. The Doylestown police don't have patient protection in their budget."

Smoke looked curious. "Off-duty?"

"Robert is looking after us. The off-duty police are volunteers from Philly. I told them I would pay. He offered, but they refused. I don't understand."

Smoke nodded at O. "Probably owe him a favor. Don't fret, I'll fix that later." He winced again. "Listen, I think I need to get horizontal."

O stood up and went to the back of the wheelchair.

Smoke stuck his hand out to Felix. "Can you get David here on Saturday?"

"Sure. No worries."

"Good."

Smoke looked over his shoulder to O. "Will you call Aimer and see if he can be here on Saturday too?"

"Certainly."

"What's up, man?" Felix had the same curious look on his face as O had on hers.

Smoke spoke low and clear. "This isn't over yet."

O erupted and came around the chair pointing. "That's enough of that. You need to rest and get better."

Smoke got angry back. "I know you want this to be over. So, do I, but there's no choice in this. We need to end it before they do."

She crossed her arms on her chest, unappeased, and still upset.

He softened his look and his voice.

She remained firm.

He reached up and unfolded her arms then held her hands. "I promise, what happens next has no guns."

Felix diffused the moment. "How's that work, boss?"

"I'm working on it. Felix, do you have the thumb drive?"

"Sure, right here." He took the silver gadget from his pocket and handed it to Smoke.

"Did you look at it?"

Felix scratched his head. "Nope, I intended to but didn't get around to it. Why do you ask?"

Smoke looked at the metal thumb drive in his palm. "So, O and I and You and David are the only ones who know about this, correct?"

O and Felix nodded.

"Good, we need to keep it to ourselves." He put on the serious face. "We can't tell anybody, especially not Aimer or McKee."

O and Felix both said, "Who's McKee?"

"Another co-conspirator."

O and Felix looked baffled.

"She's our legal counsel." Smoke suddenly twisted his body, grimacing.

"That's it, you're done." O grabbed the back of the chair and started wheeling it to the door.

"No, wait." Smoke gritted his teeth and pushed through the pain. He pulled out his phone, found Aimer in contacts, and pushed the button.

"15th District, Sergeant Franco."

"Lieutenant Aimer, please."

There was a pause. "What? No joke, Smoke?"

There was a pause back. "Not today, sergeant. Is he there?"

"Yes, and listen, I was glad to hear you're okay."

"Thanks, but...sergeant, how did you know it was me?"

"See, that's why you're a private dick and not a real cop like me. I have caller ID. Hang on."

The phone clicked, then rang.

"Aimer."

"Bobby."

"Smoke, how youse doin'? Listen, I've been trying to get out there but—"

"Stop, no worries. I'm okay, getting better every day."

"Good to hear."

"I'm going to put you on speaker—O and Felix are here." He pushed the button. "Can you update us?"

Aimer's voice came through the speaker loud and clear. "The NYPD has basically closed the file on the B&E of the Doctor's office. Detective Casey agrees with me that the crew was hired by a person or persons from Philadelphia, making it more my problem than his. Until we get a lead on who hired the crew, the NYPD is happy to get three homicides off their books by putting them on mine."

"Makes sense."

"What about the shootout at O.K. Corral? What are the Bucks County and Philadelphia DAs saying?"

"Neither one is saying anything. Philly opted out because of jurisdiction and Doylestown agreed with my justifiable shoot Incident Report."

O sighed, relieved.

"One thing, though." Aimer stopped talking. There was the sound of footsteps and a door closing. "Felix, you're there?"

"Yep."

"We found nine motorcycle gang members bound up, hands and feet, with plastic tie handcuffs. We brought them in, interrogated them separately, and to a man, they claim they were attacked by between four to six men armed with automatic weapons, smoke bombs, and stun grenades. The officers found tons of evidence. There were bullets imbedded in trees, explosion impact areas, and tons of empty cartridges."

Felix smiled. "But?"

The speaker crackled. "But...the only weapons that were found belonged to the bikers."

Felix was loving it. "That is a real mystery."

"Yes, it is...and... a fortunate one too."

Smoke jumped in. "How's that?"

"So, the dead guy in the cabin, Schmidt the German, was shot inside your house. Inside the house with a registered weapon—clear legal defense—no issues, no charges. The bikers, however, are a different story."

"How so?" Felix seemed mildly concerned.

"If a group of men, with no ties to you, were shot on your property without a clear motive, well, that gets real, complicated, real fast."

O objected. "I don't understand. They were a motorcycle gang who were coming to harm us."

"It wouldn't matter if they were the Taliban. If one of them was shot without a clear motive, it becomes a big problem, real fast."

Smoke eased the tense moment. "So, no one shot anyone. So, no charges there either, correct?"

"Correct."

Smoke tried to bring it back before the pain brought him down. "Can we get past the past and concentrate on the future?"

Aimer acknowledged, "Absolutely."

Smoke winced again and immediately headed off O's objections with a raised hand. "I have to finish this."

She nodded. "Make it quick."

Smoke nodded. "Bobby, do you remember Ignacio de Casas?"

"Ignacio, Hmm. Wait...oh sure, Father Judge High School. He graduated with you, a year ahead of me—an exchange student, right?"

"Correct. Can you find him?"

"I wouldn't know where—?"

"I saw him a couple of months ago. He's back in the neighborhood. Talk to Sister Rose at Saint Anthony's. She'll know where he is."

"Sure, but what do you want me to tell him?"

"Just tell him I need to talk to him and get his number. I'll call him."

"Okay, sure. No problem."

"Thanks, Bobby. I appreciate it."

Aimer lowered his voice. "Smoke, I have to ask—you're planning something, right?"

"Yep."

"So—I gotta ask. Do I get to keep my badge?"

Smoke chuckled. "Why do you always ask me that? You still have it, don't you?"

"Yes—but I live in fear."

Everybody laughed, including Smoke who winced again. "Stop making me laugh. You're killing me."

"That's it. You're done." O started pushing the chair again.

Smoke held the wheels. "We need to act because if we don't, they will." He grunted and gripped his side. "Listen up, stop worrying... because..."

O began pushing the chair out the door.

Felix yelled out, "Because...why?"

Smoke turned back. "Because... I have a plan."

48

S moke sat on the edge of the hospital bed. He was wearing sweatpants and a t-shirt instead of a hospital gown but still looked like a patient. Sleep continued to be an on-again, off-again proposition. The wounds were coming along, but the quick recovery of brain function surprised the medical staff. Despite his miraculous progress, the doctors put caution ahead of expediency and decided against discharge. They advised that any stressful situation might cause a severe relapse.

O pushed an empty wheelchair into his room.

"No way."

"Way."

Smoke waved it out of the room, but it kept coming. Her expression told him disputing the ride was futile. "Let's go, Bucko."

O wheeled Smoke into the sitting room and closed the door behind them. The group stood smiling at him like they were visiting an elderly aunt.

Felix greeted them immediately. "You look ready for the photographers."

"Nice to see you, too." Smoke grimaced.

"Please." Felix waved him off. "You look like shit. I was talking to this walking dream." He made loud kissing noises on O's cheeks. Felix, outfitted like Oscar Madison, wore orange sweatpants and a green New York Giants football jersey.

Smoke reached out and shook David's hand, who was GQ dressed in tan khakis and a salmon-colored golf shirt.

"Bobby." Smoke shook Aimer's hand. "Thanks for your help. We appreciate what you're doing."

"Okay, enough with the love fest. Please tell me what I'm doing here."

Smoke wheeled to her. "Bonni McKee, Doctor Olivia Bennet."

Bonni smiled broadly and reached out her hand. "Very nice to meet you. Big fan."

O accepted the handshake and the compliment with grace and caution. "Thanks. Smoke has spoken very highly of you."

"If he didn't, I'd kick his butt." No laugh followed, but she pushed on. "Aimer called me and filled me in on what went down. I was very, very concerned when I heard that you were shot, and now, I am very relieved to see that you are recovering." She smiled, looking happy with her attempt at being friendly.

"Thanks for coming, Bonni, I know your time is limited, but your presence today is vital."

Smoke rolled his chair to the center of the room to begin the meeting.

"First, before we begin, I want to assure the officers of the court in attendance. What we are going to discuss does not include the commission of any felonies."

Lieutenant Aimer mock wiped his forehead. "That's a relief. However, I am correct to assume a few rules might get bent out of shape?"

Smoke answered, "Depends."

"On?"

"Street rules or cop rules?"

Aimer shrugged.

"Good, moving on, Lieutenant, is there an update?"

Aimer took out a notebook and, in true policeman fashion, began reading. "We identified the DOA found at the cabin. Interpol identified Ralph Harold Schmidt, a German citizen, who was traveling on a Danish passport under the alias of Niels Bohr. Mr. Schmidt was a suspect in four murders, one in Austria and three in Italy. He was questioned and released due to a lack of evidence. The cases are still open."

Aimer looked up, paused, licked a finger, and turned the page.

"The gun he used at the cabin was clean. It didn't match the bullets that wounded Smoke. That could have been a problem."

O looked at Smoke, concerned. "What does that mean?"

Without raising his eyes from the pad, Aimer continued. "Detective Casey, in charge of the NYPD investigation, searched Mr. Schmidt's hotel room. They found several weapons, including the one used to..." he stopped abruptly and looked up at O. "Ah, used in the break-in of the doctor's office. It matched the—"

"Ballistics which matched the gun to the bullet that killed Lo." O finished his sentence.

"Yes, it did." Aimer sounded relieved.

Smoke added the next logical question. "If he didn't shoot me at the cabin, who did?"

Aimer motioned patience. "Good question, I'll come back to that."

Felix curiously asked, "Maybe one of the gentlemen David and I detained?"

"No, but that's a good word, detained. I'm still trying to explain their statements about automatic weapons and the..." he looked down at his pad, turned the page, and tapped a pencil on a note. "Yes... here it is, the grenades."

David looked at Felix, and Felix looked at David. Their performance of shock and surprise would have won a comedy award.

In rehearsed unison, they announced, "Firecrackers."

"Really?" Aimer's face of shock competed for a nomination.

David spoke with a straight face. "Well, a few of the firecrackers were very loud. I can see where they might have been confused."

Aimer laughed out loud.

Felix put on a serious face. "So, other than being fascinated with our mad, scary, soldier skills, did they say anything useful?"

"Yes, something interesting. They were shown a picture of Mr. Schmidt. To a man, they claimed they never saw him before. They did, however, give a pretty consistent description of the guy who hired them." Aimer went back to his book and read the description. "Height, 5′6″, weight, 180 to 200, age fifty to fifty-five, short grey hair, powerfully built."

Smoke immediately pointed at O. "Remember the pictures I showed you of the men watching the office?"

O nodded. "Sure, I remember. There was the Little Round Man and one that looked like a bulldog, stocky, grey hair."

Aimer made a note. "That's good. I'll get the booking mug shots from Detective Casey and confirm that." Aimer flipped to the next page of the notebook. "This is where it gets bizarre. The NYPD detectives are in the lobby of Schmidt's hotel, and that Bulldog guy walks through the front door. Two gold badges are standing in the lobby, asking questions, and the mamaluke walks right into the arms of New York's finest."

O leaned over to Smoke. "What's a mamaluke?"

McKee launched into an explanation. "Mamaluke is Italian slang, which means somebody who does something stupid. But this guy, he's full-time stupid, which makes him a shmuck, which is Yiddish for an asshole."

O whispered to Smoke, "Isn't McKee Irish?"

Smoke whispered back, "Let it go."

Felix chimed in again. "Did the shmuck have anything to say?"

Aimer waved a calming hand. "Don't jump ahead. First, this... mamaluke, unlike Mr. Schmidt, left it all laying out in plain sight. The detectives searched his room and found a bloody shirt and shoes with dirt and fiber. When they scraped his fingernails, they found skin."

His audience was perched on their seats, waiting.

"The priest beaten to death in the park, Father Moreno— the Doctor's last appointment before the break-in."

There were two "Wow's" and one "Oh my God."

O was first. "That is enough. You have enough to book him, correct?"

"Absolutely. He was arraigned on one count of murder two and is being held without bail. There is a ton of forensic evidence, but without a clear motive, the intent is tough to prove. Charges might get pleaded down to manslaughter."

Bonni, who was paying close attention, added a deduction. "So, one could assume, if the DOA—Schmidt—didn't have the gun that shot Smoke or Doctor O, then this Bull guy could have been the shooter."

Smoke weighed in with his eyewitness testimony. "Right. I didn't see another shooter. Which means the bullets that hit us came from the boulders at the edge of the meadow. Though to hit a moving target at a hundred yards."

Aimer made a new note in his book. "It's logical, but it's speculation. Even if we could place the Bull at the scene, which we can't, we'd still need the weapon."

McKee jumped in with advice. "If I were trying the case, I would tell him he was being charged with a contract killing. It's a capital offense with a mandatory death sentence. He'd probably flip and give you who hired him."

"They did that, and it didn't work. The NYPD detectives believe his boss didn't tell him shit."

"Hmmm." McKee nodded.

Smoke pressed Aimer. "You're sure this guy doesn't know anything?"

"Listen, this guy beat a priest to death with his bare hands, and we have him cold. His boss is dead, so he's dying to cut a deal, but he' can't because he's got nothing to bargain with."

Aimer looked to O. "The priest in the park was your last appointment. He tells you he wants you to write a book based on his life. A story he plans to back up with damning information about the Archdiocese of Philadelphia. You refuse to do it. He leaves. A couple of days later, he's murdered."

Aimer takes a breath to make sure everybody is on the same page.

"The Little Round Man who is watching your office also happens to be a priest from Philadelphia. He has a heart attack while acting as a decoy for the break-in of your office. Several days later, somebody murders him in the hospital."

McKee was shocked. "Jesus, Bobby, two murdered priests. You didn't tell me that."

"Sorry, McKee, but wait, there's more. The lease on the unoccupied office used by The Little Round Man for surveillance was in the name of a shell corporation, which, after some digging, led to Campbell Development Corporation."

Smoke's attention was peaked. "And?"

"And... Campbell Development Corporation is currently in front of the Philadelphia Planning Board, seeking final approvals for a large tract of land near the stadiums. If approved, the value of the properties would skyrocket. We also found out that some of the properties included in the tract had been, up until very recently, owned by..." he paused for dramatic effect, "the Archdiocese of Philadelphia."

"Fuck my Aunt Greta." Felix stood up and slapped his thighs.

"How are you surprised? Big corporations, big money, dead bodies, where's the mystery?" McKee was examining her manicure.

Smoke regained control of the meeting. "Look, let's stay focused. This is about bad guys. Let's keep it small."

Smoke asked Aimer another question. "Schmidt's bank accounts have been checked, of course."

"Of course. The detectives got into Schmidt's computer and

email. They found several wire transactions. The last one..." Aimer checked notes for accuracy, "Two hundred thousand dollars was wired to his Cayman account from a Swiss numbered account."

Smoke followed up. "Can they get a warrant to search the land development company records?"

McKee's voice added fact to the frustration. "No foundation for a warrant."

Aimer nodded. "Exactly, there is no connection between the company and Schmidt. Therefore, a warrant without tangible evidence would be—"

"Impossible." McKee finished his sentence.

Aimer closed the notebook and stood up. "Wait, I'm not done yet. This case gets even more bizarre." He continued this time without consulting the book. "One day before the assault upon Smoke Mountain, Lawrence Campbell, the owner of Campbell Development, was murdered by his executive assistant, Nancy Ferris."

"Jesus." O looked shocked.

Aimer continued. "Ms. Ferris stabbed him to death with a letter opener in his office. Afterward, almost naked and covered in blood, she wound up on East 53rd Street, where it took three cops and a stun gun to bring her down. She's currently in Belleview under heavy sedation."

Again, there was a long silence.

Aimer spoke with confidence. "Ms. Ferris was the last possible link to this mess. There's evidence, no connections, and no case."

McKee chimed in again. "He's right," adding with a shrug, "the case is DITW."

Smoke was unfamiliar with the term. "Ah, what does that mean?"

"DITW - Dead in the water." McKee stood up stretching. "Let me try to summarize." She took a few steps, then began. "It's logical that a person or persons unknown, either in the Archdiocese or at the land development company, paid a lot of money to silence a whistleblower to preserve the status quo. It is also logical to assume, if what Moreno stole was leaked, the big land deal would somehow be threatened. But—"

"But," Smoke interrupted, "There is no evidence."

McKee nodded. "Correct. Campbell is dead. His killer, Ms. Ferris, is in a padded room, which means her testimony is most likely inadmissible. Both priests are dead. The hitman is dead, and his partner doesn't know anything, which leaves Doctor Bennet as the only person who could bring even a sliver of daylight to the case. However, whatever she was told by... who was it that stole the stuff? I forget."

Dr. O furnished the answer. "Father Mark Moreno."

McKee nodded. "Thank you. So, whatever he told you is hearsay evidence that will not get into court. There is no way to prove that Moreno was even in her office because the only witness to that event is your Loretta." She lowered her voice. "Who is also deceased." She took a breath and finished. "So, other than the putz in custody, there will be no indictments on anyone on any charge, whatsoever."

Felix asked, "But doesn't that mean this is all over? If the developer dude was the bad guy and the crew is either dead or locked up?"

Smoke answered. "Nope. The developer wasn't the power. He was only the money. The bad guys will replace the money man, restart the land deal, and come after O again."

David broke his silence. "How did you determine the developer wasn't the power and the money?"

"Great question." Smoke smiled. "Answer, the Little Round Man. He was the only player in this whole saga who didn't fit. The crew was professional; they didn't hire him. Somebody made them take the Little Round Man on the crew as a watcher—somebody inside. Somebody who was controlling everything."

Aimer nodded. "That makes sense, Smoke. Campbell had no criminal record, and nothing suggests that he would do murder. But..."

Smoke knew what was coming. "But..."

"But Campbell's CFO told me that the company is on the edge of collapse. The land deal had stretched them to the breaking point."

Smoke put both hands in the air. "Bingo."

McKee perked up. "You said it was a development company?"

Aimer nodded. "Yes."

"Did they only deal with land development?"

"No." Aimer paged through his notebook. "Trucking, and Oil and Gas Fracking, as well as real estate."

McKee continued. "That means there's a board of directors, and I guarantee they're already moving to circle the wagons. They'll consolidate before the assets get bogged down with estate lawyers."

David leaned forward and raised his hand, gaining everyone's attention. "Smoke is right. There is no way it's over. The deal is still intact. Whoever is behind this will contact the development company, make a deal, and it will start again. It isn't over."

Aimer looked surprised. "I didn't pay much attention at the time, but the CFO just told me this morning, he was contacted by a Monsignor who said he heard about the company's misfortune, and he might be able to help. He told the CFO he'd been involved with Campbell in the very beginning, but lost contact after the church signed the agreements. The Monsignor said the church is still interested in the success of the project and that he might be able to recommend a new partner to buy out their company's interest."

McKee pointed to Smoke. "That's the guy."

Smoke was on the edge of his seat. "Bobby, did you get a name?"

Aimer nodded and turned to a page in his notebook. "Monsignor Giuseppe DeFrancisco."

Smoke pressed. "A Monsignor...hmmm...not high enough. Whom does he work for?"

Aimer looked for it in the notes. "He is the right-hand man to the Auxiliary Bishop of Philadelphia, Michael O'Hanrand."

Smoke leaned back. "What is O'Hanrand the Auxiliary Bishop of, pray tell."

Aimer smiled. "The Chancellery of the Archdiocese. It manages all Diocese business."

"Does that include real estate?"

"Yes, it does." Aimer closed his notepad.

"Wait," O spoke up. "When we went into the city to—"

"Get dinner," Smoke interrupted.

"Right...to get dinner. You pointed out the Chancellery because it was where Father Moreno worked."

Aimer smiled. "In the official cop handbook, that's called a clue."

O stood up again, this time looking almost jubilant. "That has to be enough. The men behind all of this are the Bishop and the Monsignor. Am I right?"

McKee responded. "Most likely, but you'll never prove it. It's probably enough to start an investigation, but I don't think it would get very far. I won't repeat my previous objections, which are still valid, but we need to remember who we would be accusing. Two Grand Juries investigated 300 priests for more than 1,000 claims of child abuse, to date, there have only been two convictions. One was for the cover up and one for the theft of almost a million dollars from the parish. They have outstanding attorneys."

There was silence in the room.

McKee stood up and paced in a Smoke-like thinking pattern. "Okay, Smoke, I agree on all but one point."

He answered, "Shoot."

"I have laid out why there cannot be any charges against anyone, and Robert agrees, correct?"

Aimer nodded.

"So, why are you certain they are still after Doctor Bennet?"

Smoke answered quickly. "They think there is a copy of the thumb drive, and they think we might have it or know where it is."

"Wow." McKee stopped, put her hands on her hips, and a stern look on her face. "Are they correct? Do you have the thumb drive?"

Smoke pondered a moment. "They think we have it. So, they will get a new money man, hire a new crew, and come after her." His voice became sincere and determined. "We must stop them before they can regroup."

O jumped up and put her hands on her hips—her face red and eyes wide. "This is outrageous." She pointed at McKee. "You're telling me these bastards are going to get away with murder." She pointed at Smoke. "And you're telling me they will keep coming until..." O turned to face Aimer. "What if there was evid—"

"Stop."

She whipped around and stared at Smoke.

He spoke slowly and firmly. "Bonni and Bobby are officers of the court. If we tell them something, and they are deposed, they must testify to what they heard. You need to trust me. What was on it doesn't prove anything. Even if we had the thumb drive, it wouldn't take these guys out."

O looked at Smoke, then sat, still angry, with her arms folded across her chest.

O's face was redder than before. "This is wrong. Just fucking wrong." She turned to Smoke. "We can't let this happen."

"I know." He regained her angry eyes. "I won't let it."

Her eyes showed pain. "I just want justice."

"Look at me." He gently squeezed her hands. "I promise you will get your shot at them, and Lo will get justice."

Smoke left one hand on hers, then addressed the group. "I think I'll get kicked out of here by the end of the week. We can meet next Saturday at McKee's office. I should have the details ironed out by then."

They milled a bit, then moved to the door.

"Hey Smoke," Aimer suddenly spun around. "Did you talk to Ignacio?"

"Yes, I did. I talked to him, and he talked to me."

Smoke tried a stop-talking look on Aimer, but it didn't work.

"I can't figure why, in the middle of all this, you asked me to track down a transfer student we knew in high school."

"I just lost touch and wanted to reconnect." Smoke sounded unconvincing, even to himself.

"Really?" Aimer didn't buy it. "You needed to find a monk you haven't seen in almost forty years."

Smoke grinned. "Actually, it's only thirty-five years."

O slapped the back of Smoke's head.

"I must be better if you're back to slapping me on the head."

She wasn't smiling. "A monk? What aren't you telling us?"

Smoke rolled his chair to the door, then spun one wheel to face his crew. "I told you guys...trust me. I have a plan."

Felix grinned and glanced around at his fellow conspirators. "He has a plan. Aren't you excited? I am. It's like the ending of The Sting." Felix did a Robert Redford to Paul Newman finger on the nose gesture towards McKee.

McKee used her finger too.

49

For more than eighty years, The Giving Organization held an annual exclusive, black tie, red carpet fundraiser at the historic Morris House Hotel in downtown Philadelphia. There were always last-minute requests for additional invitations, and due to the gala's popularity, were hard to accommodate. However, as a personal favor to the movie star wife of a three-term US Senator, the chairman of the charity granted an invitation to Dr. Olivia Bennet and her plus one. Before the night was through, a few more additions to the soirée would gatecrash the ballroom behind the gold badge of a Philadelphia Police Detective.

Everything on the evening of the gala, including the weather, was perfect. The guests entertained by a three-piece quartet playing Mozart supped on foie gras with hazelnuts, enjoyed poached lobster in a carrot-ginger puree, and sipped vintage Sauvignon Blanc from antique crystal glasses. After the feast, guests casually meandered through a twelve-foot-tall stone archway into the garden where exotic flowers were forced to blossom for the who's who of wealthy patrons and a variety of A-list celebrities.

The event benefited an extremely reputable organization.

Ninety-five percent of the contributions went to causes helping the needy, the homeless, and the sad and the sick. Of course, there is the tax deduction, which is nice.

The invitation came with the expectation of a large donation. The funding goals always achieved meant the usual speeches, and annoying auctions became unnecessary. For some, a gift to their favorite charity resulted in an expensive dinner and photo op with movie stars and politicians who smiled like they were godparents to their children.

Businesspeople and their entourages attended for a type of high-priced, speed dating business meeting. They milled about, waiting for an opportunity to approach the next prospective business rendezvous.

Auxiliary Bishop O'Hanrand and Monsignor DeFrancisco maintained a stationary position in the game. They were not seeking influence. They were selling it. Positioned under an arbor filled with the flowers of Egyptian Star Clusters, they stood almost side by side, the man-in-red slightly forward. The Bishop thought the soft red flowers complimented his floor-length tunic.

Mr. Beaumont Suddath, with an entourage of four, were invited to the event by DeFrancisco to meet the Bishop. They came from Georgia to finalize the purchase of the development rights to a large tract of property that unexpectedly became available.

Beaumont, more commonly known by the family nickname, Blu, was new in the land development business. His father, Forest Suddath was a titan in Atlanta real estate. When he died, he left his empire to his only son, Blu. The now very wealthy CEO, anxious to prove himself worthy, accepted what his father's Philadelphia banker told him was a once in a lifetime opportunity.

DeFrancisco wore a black silk cassock with piping, the exact same color red as his boss. He constantly stroked and smoothed the red silk sash he wore ready for battle.

He saw them on the approach and stepped forward, intercepting the incoming brigade. "Mr. Suddath, please allow me to introduce the Auxiliary Bishop O'Hanrand."

The Man in Red remained posed, chins and nose up.

Suddath glanced at his lawyer, then moved a step closer.

O'Hanrand raised his hand, palm down.

Suddath grasped it and shook.

O'Hanrand pulled his limp fish hand back and frowned.

DeFrancisco tried to repair the faux pa with a subtle reminder to the boss. "This opportunity is like all things, merely a matter of timing. Yours, Mr. Suddath, couldn't be better. Granted, it is a substantial outlay, but God willing, it will return your investment many times over."

O'Hanrand recovered and started his pitch. "The project was days away from final approval. But, as you undoubtedly know, the company seeking approval encountered an unexpected turn of events. Their adversity can be your blessing. Our contact with the CFO has made it possible for you to take over the project. The cost is a fraction of the cost to date."

Blu opened his mouth to speak, but the lawyer grabbed his coattail.

The Bishop paused to puff his sleeves. Satisfied, he continued, "I trust your people have examined the prospectus. I believe it affirms your timing is perfect—perhaps, you're being guided by a higher power."

The Bishop raised both hands, extending open palms in the ritual manner he used to end his soliloquies.

His lawyer nodded, and Blu spoke. "Yes, thank you your eminan...I mean your grace."

The lawyer winced.

"I have, I mean, we have gone over the projections in pretty fine detail, and we agree, this is a great opportunity."

Blu smiled, but neither of the clergy moved.

The lawyer then said what was needed to end the meeting. "We are very grateful for this opportunity."

The Bishop nodded and held out his hand again, palm down.

Again, the young man seemed mystified.

The lawyer leaned over and whispered close to his ear.

"Really?" Suddath looked at the suit, surprised.

Blu's lawyer nodded. He looked back at the Bishop, shrugged resignation, leaned over, and kissed his ring.

"Monsignor DeFrancisco will arrange the details." The Bishop turned his head dismissively.

DeFrancisco moved forward and gathered the crew with an outstretched arm, moving them from the arch of flowers.

The Bishop adjusted his cuffs, reset his pose, and began waiting for the next ring kisser.

DeFrancisco had young Suddath by the elbow. "I'll be in touch in the morning. I have arranged for all of the paperwork transferring the properties and the assignment of Campbell Development's interest."

"Great, we're ready."

"I hope you understand the urgency. No one wants this project held up for years in bankruptcy court." The Monsignor tried to be sincere.

"Yes, we understand." Blu's lawyer affirmed.

"Good, so you are prepared to meet the cash requirements?"

The lawyer responded. "Yes. The property buyout is 3.5 million. The assignment is 7 million. All of it in cash and by the end of business tomorrow."

Blu smiled. "Okay, so we're good then?"

The Monsignor slicked his robe with one hand and took Blu's arm with the other. "I wanted to thank you in advance for your generous donation."

"Excuse me?" The lawyer looked concerned.

"The Bishop and I were so happy to hear that your company had planned to make such a generous donation to Catholic Charities tonight. Three million dollars isn't much in the United States, but it still goes a very, very long way in our African Missions."

Blu stammered. "I'm sorry, I don't understand?"

DeFrancisco let go of Blu's arm quickly like he was throwing something away. "Oh, did I misunderstand? Am I wrong to assume a goodwill donation rewarding our participation in securing your position was forthcoming?"

The lawyer was now visibly angry. "You sandbagged—"

Beaumont took control of his attorney and the situation. "Three million, yes, of course, that's no problem. I'll write a personal check before we leave."

There was a brief stare-down between the Monsignor and the lawyer.

DeFrancisco spoke first. "Yes, your donation tonight will go a long way, but it will need replenishment... every year."

The lawyer took Blu by the arm and tried to pull him away.

Blu turned to the Monsignor, "Can you show me where I can make the arrangements?"

The Bishop was alone, his expansive silhouette framed under the arbors of flowers. He looked powerful and regal.

Several heads in the crowd turned in unison and drew his attention. Several more followed, and soon, everyone was looking at something or someone he couldn't see.

The crowd in front of him parted, and O emerged into his view.

She was magnificent.

About thirty feet away from the arch, she stopped, staring straight ahead. The ladies attending the gala wore expensive, designer-fabulous dresses, but their style was Philadelphia charity-elegant, not Hollywood red-carpet chic.

O wore a gown glowing with sparkling flashes of radiance from the sequence woven into its thread. Slit up one leg from the floor to her hip; it was almost as daring as the plunging neckline. The fabric, suspended on bejeweled spaghetti straps, was glued to her breasts, and a breath away from a wardrobe malfunction. She wore no jewelry save long silver earrings. Her hair was straight and long on one side.

She hadn't broken her stare. Then, as if someone yelled action, she slowly stepped forward, eyes focused on her objective, the Bishop.

O'Hanrand seemed confused. He stood, stoic, in his perfectly pressed, signature red robe with gold fringe. His face locked in stone, his hands resting across his belly and over his crucifix.

His body language was rock-like, but his eyes gave him away. They were darting madly back and forth, side-to-side, as if they didn't belong in his body.

DeFrancisco came back into the room after taking the southern money to the charity table but was far away from his charge.

When O arrived in front of the Red Man, she paused and spoke. "Your Eminence."

The Bishop held out his hand.

Then she bent forward.

There was a gasp from the crowd as a breast bursting out of the dress seemed imminent.

She took the cold, clammy hand in hers. It was wet with sweat.

Instead of kissing it, she bowed her head and curtsied.

He looked surprised as the curtsy seemed too theatrical for the moment.

She knew what she was going to do, but what she wanted to do involved sharp hand tools and an electric drill.

She let go of his hand and stood up, making the long side of her hair fall straight down, covering one eye and half her face. In one motion, she flicked her hair to the side.

A long angry scar accented by dark red scabs where stitches had been was visible for all to see.

The Bishop's face winced, but he didn't break his statue-like pose. Beads of perspiration began to form on his forehead, and the skin under his chins bunched up.

She spoke at normal volume, but because no one else was talking, everyone heard. "I wore no make-up so that you might see my wound clearly."

"Ah, ...aaa."

DeFrancisco was a couple of steps away.

She used one hand to pull her hair away. "Did you get a good look?"

The Monsignor arrived slightly out of breath and immediately whispered in the Bishop's ear.

"This is where I was shot." She dropped her hand and her hair. "And this is so you never forget Loretta Kelly's name."

She saw the Monsignor start to step closer.

Her hand flew from her side, her body turned, and she slapped the Red Man hard across his face.

"Ohhffff." Air burst from his mouth, along with the sound of a whimpering milksop.

The momentum spun her around, and she walked away, head high with an unrestrained smile of fulfillment.

DeFrancisco yelled out, "Dear God. Stop her."

Two uniformed Philadelphia Police Officers arrived immediately after they let O walk away.

Cop 1 grabbed the Red Man by one red and gold sleeve. "We need to get you to a safe place your Eminence."

Cop 2 firmly took the other arm. "Please, accompany us this way, your Eminence."

A few seconds later, the three were moving toward a steel door and the back of the garden.

Cop 3 was waiting at the door and pushed it open for the Bishop and Cop 1 and Cop 2.

Cop 3 stood in front of DeFrancisco, refusing him admittance. "We need to get him in a secure location."

The door opened to the rest of the Red Man's life then slammed shut behind him.

5 0

The hallway of painted concrete walls was lit with yellowed fluorescent lights that also had a soundtrack. It hissed and crackled as the column of blue and grey and black and red uniforms moved to its end. A flush metal double door ended the journey.

Cop 1 slid a key card through a device. It flashed a green light, and the lock clicked.

"You'll be fine here. Go on in." Cop 2 shooed the Bishop inside.

O'Hanrand, rubbing his red cheek, took small steps inside with his head down. Cops 1 and 2 came in behind him, then took positions on either side of the door.

Smoke was standing with his hand resting on the back of an empty metal chair. It was a relatively large space with folding chairs stacked in a corner and metal shelves filled with odds and ends necessary for hotel operations that purposed the room as storage. The lighting was the same as the hall—minus the background noise.

O'Hanrand took small steps, advancing slowly, eyes darting and sweat beading on his forehead.

"Good evening, Your Eminence. Please, allow me to introduce myself."

The Bishop stopped short of the chair and turned to look at the policemen standing guard. They did not look back.

"My name is Henry Smokehouse." He paused then smiled a bit. "You know what, your Eminence? That is the first time I have introduced myself by my given name in a very long time. I usually insist people call me Smoke, but given the circumstances, I think you should refer to me as Mr. Smoke."

Confusion and anxiety penetrated the holier-than-thou attitude as the Bishop stammered, "We don't have... time—"

Smoke jumped on him immediately. "Oh, make time Rev. I promise this is going to be really interesting." Smoke wagged a finger at him, "I am going to have to insist that you drop the third person shit. Saying we instead of I kinda pisses me off, and to tell the truth I'm already pretty pissed off. So, getting me upset about grammar might not be a good thing for you."

He beckoned the clergyman to the chair. The Bishop, short of options, reluctantly plopped awkwardly in the metal chair.

Smoke took out his phone and hit the speed dial. The call connected, but he didn't speak.

The sound of the lock device beeped, and the metal door opened.

Philadelphia Police Lieutenant Robert Aimer came in and spoke to the two guards. "Officers, please carry out the rest of your assignment. When you return, take up a post outside the door. I might need you later."

"Yes, sir." They saluted then left the room.

The Bishop looked curious when he noticed the gold badge clipped to the Lieutenant's belt.

Smoke walked over to Aimer and whispered. "How did it go?"

"Un-fucking-believable. She's a beast." Aimer couldn't conceal his enthusiasm.

"I would've loved to see it." Smoke grinned.

A single loud knock on the door made the Bishop jump.

"Ah, more guests for the festivities." Smoke gestured, and Aimer opened the door.

Cops 1 and 2 brought in DeFrancisco, who was angry and loud. "This is an outrage. We'll have your badges for this."

Smoke unfolded another chair. "I don't have a badge Monsignor. Have a seat. Take a load off."

Smoke rubbed his hands together. "The woman, whom you met in the garden...oh wait, I apologize." With concern on his face, Smoke pointed to the red mark on the Bishop's cheek. "That mark looks like it hurts, maybe we could get you some ice?"

O'Hanrand rubbed his cheek. "Yes, it does hurt, very much."

Then with no concern, he replied, "Good, I'm glad you're feeling better. Anyway, the woman in the garden is the woman you and your buddy have been trying to murder. Her name is Doctor Olivia Bennet."

The Monsignor's mouth opened, but he remained silent.

The Bishop growled, "Grrghmmm. We..." he stopped abruptly. "I mean... I... never—"

"Sure, you did, and the use of, we, would have been appropriate in that context. You and your weasel assistant orchestrated the whole scheme."

Neither of the men in the chairs spoke, their expressions looking stern and resistant.

"But, I digress, we have a lot of ground to cover. So, first, it took a bit of planning to get you two alone in this room. It was time-consuming but not difficult. You see, I have a lot of friends, but more importantly, you, Your Immenseness, have a lot of enemies."

Smoke unfolded another chair and sat down backward. He was concealing his pain. Both hands resting on the top back of the chair eased the pain in his side. "Let me introduce you to the people who made this possible."

Smoke pulled out his phone and hit the speed dial. The lock beeped, and the door opened.

Felix came in first, creating a reduced field of vision for the seated clergymen. At first, they could not see the rest of the entourage. Bonni McKee emerged from behind the shadow and moved to the left of the two men. Next was David, who moved right.

Smoke smiled when he saw O. She had exchanged her fighting outfit for dungarees and a white v-neck t-shirt. He wore jeans and a t-shirt too, but he looked like a mechanic on lunch break, and she looked like a commercial for Cosmo Casual.

When the Bishop saw her, he stroked his still red cheek.

Smoke turned back to the Monsignor and the Bishop and put his game face back on.

"This is Bonni McKee, our legal counsel from Rittenhouse, Rizzo, and Swartz, David Anderson, Goldman Sachs, our financial advisor. Felix Upton Grant is security and special ops. Last but not least, Lieutenant Robert Aimer is here representing Philadelphia's finest."

Smoke put his hand out to O. "Bishop, I believe you've met Doctor Olivia Bennet."

The Bishop shot a glance at DeFrancisco, who shook his head, indicating a don't say anything look.

"I have introduced myself already. My job is to protect Doctor Bennet."

A slight noise, almost a snicker but not quite, came from the Monsignor.

Felix started forward, but Smoke stuck out his stop sign hand.

Smoke took a couple of steps with his head down, looking like he was deep in thought. "Okay, let's stick to the basics: means, motive, opportunity. It is obvious; the dead hitman was the means, the land deal and the dead CEO provided the opportunity... but the motive was a little tricky. It kinda hit a wall, what with me almost dying from bullet wounds. Fortunately, like I said, I have friends."

Smoke pointed to David. "Once we discovered the land deal, Mr. Campbell's business came under scrutiny. David did the research."

David stepped forward. "Campbell Development had several divisions, oil, trucking, and real estate. To protect the divisions from lawsuits, the agreement of sale for the property was in the name of a holding company. That company had eight minority partners which were shell corporations. I traced the ownership of the partners and seven were legal tax shelters for Campbell Development—all but Abisha Limited. That is an offshore company registered in Panama."

Smoke raised his hand. "David, were you able to trace the ownership?"

"Yes. The company, in short, is owned by Michael O'Hanrand."

The Bishop's head was down.

Smoke stood next to David. "And what is the percentage of the minority ownership?"

"Ten percent."

"What would that be worth?"

David went into spreadsheet mode. "Based on the end sales— three million a year over ten years."

The Bishop averted his eyes.

"There's something else. The name, Abisha Limited, seemed odd so I Googled it."

Smoke smiled. "My old friend."

"Abisha is Hebrew and means, gift from God."

Smoke walked up to the Bishop and leaned over to get his eyes. "So, this was the golden parachute. If someday you decide to cut bait and run, you're not beholden to the Vatican to keep you in the lap of luxury?"

He stopped and faced the two men in chairs. "We have means, motive, and opportunity. Now I'll outline the case we would bring to court."

The men sat quietly in their chairs as Smoke wrapped almost every detail of the plan into a nice neat package. Beginning with the land development deal, ending with the slap on the Bishop's face and all the dead bodies in between. When he finished, he stretched, keeping an eye on the clergy, waiting to see if they had a hole card to play. If they did, it would be played right then.

The Bishop seemed to be in shock, but DeFrancisco spoke up. "I think your theory is colorful, but you have no witnesses and no evidence. There is no proof of any connection with this so-called hitman, you will never be able to actually prove ownership of the Panama Company, and we have no knowledge of anything taken from the Chancellery."

Smoke raised his hands, addressing his comrades, "Apparently, these gentlemen don't believe that we have much of a case. They think our conclusions on means, motive, and opportunity are weak and don't support our allegations."

The Monsignor, with a face full of arrogance, spat out, "Non hai niente."

O translated. "He said, you got nothing."

Smoke smiled brightly and shrugged at the clergymen. "My girl... so many talents, fluent in French and Italian."

Smoke turned and faced McKee. "Okay, legal counsel, in your opinion, do we have enough evidence to present to a grand jury, secure an indictment, and convict these two for the crimes I have alleged?"

The Bishop and Monsignor looked at her like they were ready to hear guilty or not guilty.

"No."

The two clergy looked surprised and confused.

McKee went on. "There is an abundance of circumstantial evidence, however, given who we are dealing with and what weapons the Archdiocese has at its disposal, I doubt if a DA would file charges."

DeFrancisco started to get up.

Felix, who had slowly moved behind the seated man, encouraged him to remain seated—with vigor.

Smoke again took center stage. "You know what, you rat-faced prick, you're right. We got, non hi...whatever."

"Non hai niente." O repeated the phrase.

"Yeah, that." Smoke leaned in close. "We got nothing."

The Monsignor's expression went from baffled to outrage. "So, you admit, you have illegally detained the Auxiliary Bishop who is about to be appointed the Archbishop of the dioceses of Philadelphia."

Smoke backed up and put his hands on his hips. "Former."

DeFrancisco spat out, "What?"

"You were almost correct. We have illegally detained the... former... Auxiliary Bishop of Philadelphia."

O'Hanrand's eyes widened.

Smoke hit the speed dial on his phone again.

There was a loud click and all eyes turned to the door when opened.

A tall, thin, bearded man wearing a full-length black cassock tied at the waist with a white rope came into the room. He had a wooden cross hanging from his neck, and sticking out from the bottom of the robe were two bare feet in sandals.

Two equally tall well-dressed men came in next and stood either side of the man in the robe.

Smoke, having let enough drama build, ended the suspense. "Gentlemen, let me introduce Father Ignacio de Casas. We met in high school many years ago. Our worlds drifted apart, but then, like so many other odd coincidences, I happened to run into him a few months ago."

DeFrancisco, still hanging on to outrage, pointed his boney finger. "What does this...monk...have to do with me, I mean us?"

Smoke pointed to the Bishop. "Be careful, Bishop, your faithful servant, almost used I, instead of we."

"Brutto segno." O shrugged. "That means, it's a bad sign."

Smoke addressed DeFrancisco, "Actually, former Monsignor, what you asked is the correct question. This monk has everything to do with youse."

O translated. "That's an abbreviation which means, the two of you, in Philadelphian."

Smoke spun around to suppress a grin.

Smoke put his hands on his hips. "I beg your patience as I do need to tell you why Father Ignacio is important to you. We were in the same class in High School and played on the baseball team. He was an exchange student, and after graduation, I went to college and the army, and he returned to his hometown, in Cordoba, Venezuela."

"So?" DeFrancisco sounded less aggressive.

The Bishop closed his eyes.

Smoke frowned at the Monsignor with disappointment. "I thought you'd have it by now."

"Father, would you like to take over?"

"Thank you." Father Ignacio walked to center stage. "As Smoke said, we go way back. Our friendship began on the baseball team. I helped him with Spanish, and he helped me by... dissuading... a few boys who were bullying the weird foreigner. After graduation, I returned to Venezuela and my home. I also returned to my church where I found I had a calling. I joined the Society of Jesus."

The Bishop let out a sharp gasp of air and the blood drained from his face.

Felix whispered to David. "I think the big one's got it."

"A few years later, I was ordained a Jesuit and received direction and inspiration from my Minister General, Jorge Bergoglio. You may know him as Pope Francis."

DeFrancisco's indignation dissolved.

"Now, even though he is very busy in his new position, he still maintains a connection to his former staff. After Smoke contacted me about events here, I made a call and the Pope asked me to visit him. I left immediately for Rome, met with him, and returned today."

Father Ignacio inserted his hands inside the sleeves of his cassock. "I think it is important to explain why the Holy Father has taken an interest in this situation. A little history is necessary because even though Jorge Bergoglio is the Pope of the Roman Catholic Church he labors under a prejudice against his roots, being a Jesuit. As recently as the 1700s, the Jesuits were deemed too intellectual and too liberal, and banned from many countries. Even Switzerland, who banned us in their constitution, didn't lift it until 1976. Now, despite the worldwide popularity of Pope Francis, he still has many enemies. Inside the organization of the Church is the Roman Curia, which is similar to a parliament or a congress. It conducts the business of the church. Pope Francis wants to change policy and procedure, and his changes are being resisted at almost every level. He has support, but some powerful men in the Curia are fighting hard against him."

The group was listening as intently as the two in the chairs.

The Jesuit looked at Smoke. "Your turn."

Smoke stepped forward. "I was hired to protect this woman. That was my job and I needed to do what I had to do to keep her safe."

He pointed at the two clergy in the chairs. "To cover up your fraud and embezzlement, you were responsible for the murder of two priests." He paused, letting it sink in. "You are here because the people in this room want justice for a woman your hitman murdered and for the woman he tried to kill."

Smoke glanced at the Monk. "You are also here because of a lot of unexplainable coincidences. Things by themselves are inconsequential, but together, led straight to you."

He leaned over and got close to the Bishop. "I'm not a Catholic. I'm not religious. I'm not even sure I believe in God, but I can say this for certain. This group of people acted as an intervention for an unstoppable train of power and corruption. We found the truth, but then discovered we were still powerless to act."

Smoke looked at O. "Then a bullet is a millimeter from taking her life." He faced the Bishop, "I'm shot as well and bleeding out but somehow I survive. Then, in a hospital bed, half alive, I remembered my friend." Smoke pointed to the Monk. "Somehow he is here because I reached out to him with an incredibly, farfetched, even preposterous idea that he might have a key to justice."

Smoke stepped back, and the Monk took his place. "Michael O'Hanrand, in pursuit of an appointment to Archbishop and then to Cardinal, you became a citizen of the Vatican. You are *Status Civitatis Vaticanae* and, as such, you are under its sovereign authority. Because of your actions, Pope Francis has reassigned you to the most remote location in the Catholic Church, the Monastery of Saints George and John Jacob. It was built on an island, centuries ago, where now only a few monks devote their every waking moment to prayer and silence. You will not be allowed to leave for any reason."

The former Bishop fainted.

"Giuseppe DeFrancisco, you are relieved of all duties. You, unlike your former boss, are a citizen of Italy. We contacted the Italian police, and you are to be transported to Regina Coeli prison while you await trial on charges of conspiracy and murder. The charges are not related to crimes here in the United States but are based on your connections to Mr. Schmidt. The Carabinieri suspect you are connected to three unsolved murders they believe were carried out on your order by the man you hired to assassinate Doctor Bennet."

DeFrancisco didn't faint. He began to cry.

The Jesuit pointed to the two men in suits. "The gentlemen who accompanied me here are from the Pope's Vatican guard. They will escort you to a plane that will return you to Italy."

Felix and David pulled the Bishop to his feet and the two suits gathered up their charges and helped them out.

The door closed. The tension broke and the group started talking all at once.

Smoke took Ignacio aside. "What about the thumb drive? Was there anything on it? No one here ever saw its contents."

The Jesuit scratched his beard. "I have been asked, to ask you a question. "

"Shoot."

"Why did you give it to me instead of a newspaper reporter?"

"Oh...yeah, that, well..." Smoke had a blank look on his face. "I don't know why. I guess it would have been great press and maybe somewhere down the road after the lawyers get done fighting, something might have come out of it."

"But?"

"But...I don't know why I did it." Smoke started pacing. "I was hired to protect this woman." He pointed to O, who had separated from the group and was standing a few feet away. "That was my only job. Bringing down the church wasn't in the job description."

Ignacio said nothing.

"You know what happened to me...before?"

The priest nodded.

"I retreated into a hole so deep I couldn't see light. Then...things started to happen. Weird disconnected things brought me to her...to all of this, and I changed. I felt whole again." He put his head down, then shook it back and forth. "She was my focus, but other things happened that led me in one direction. Little things at first—then bigger, like neither one of us being dead. In the hospital, I suddenly realized that everyone involved had been in the right place at the right time with the right information to intervene. Stopping the bad guys was the only way I could protect her. So, that's what I did. My job was to protect her, not take down the Catholic Church. We took out the bad guys. What happens after that...well ...I don't know what that looks like."

The Jesuit stuck his hand in his pocket. "Smoke, what you just said is kind of amazing. The Pope said the same thing to me two days ago. After I relayed what you told me, he said you were not the only intervention. Many others around the world have performed similar acts. He said saving the church from this disgrace needs to happen from the inside out. He said he didn't know what redemption looked like yet, but he had faith."

Ignacio took Smoke's hand. "He gave this to me to give to you." He put the thumb drive in his palm."

"Why would he give it back? Doesn't he need it?"

"No, the information was stolen from the archives in Philadelphia, all which is still there."

"I don't understand. He knows I could give it to the press."

"Yes, you could and maybe you will. If you decide that is necessary."

"If I decide?"

"Yes, you."

"I'm lost. I gave you these two bad guys and you took care of them. I gave you this information and you give it back. Why?"

"Call it insurance."

"For whom?"

"For the Pope."

Smoke looked at the thumb drive, then the monk, then the thumb drive.

"If he can't then I could..." He looked up at the Monk. "How will I know?"

"You'll know." He touched Smoke's shoulder. "I have faith."

Ignacio smiled. "Listen, I promised the Swiss guards Geno's steaks and we have to get to the airport. But you have to come and visit me when I get back from Rome. You'll love Venezuela. Bring your glove. I'm building a neighborhood team. There is some real talent there."

He turned and left, leaving Smoke alone, just for a minute.

51

They met in the lobby of the Logan Hotel. Smoke and O came in last, and together they crowded into an elevator heading for the rooftop lounge and deck. The group was quiet at first, smiling, grinning but silent. Then Felix farted, and the balloon of tension burst. The elevator door opened to everyone laughing hard. Smoke and O walked into the bar like a football team out the tunnel, ready to play.

O shouted over the roar. "Drinks are on me."

The bartender abandoned the few patrons at the end of the bar to service the rowdy bunch. There was a TV above the bar. The sound muted the anchor of Action News, reporting a story. A headshot of O appeared in a split-screen.

Felix shouted to the bartender. "Hey, turn that up. Hurry."

The sound rose. "—event at the Morris House Hotel. The Charity event is not generally known as a red-carpet fashion show; however, Doctor Olivia Bennet, the best-selling author of *Release the Beast*, wowed the crowd in a daring Armani gown."

A still photo appeared full screen. O posed with a hand on her hip and her shield of hair concealing the scar on her forehead.

"J Lo has nothing on you, girl." Felix raised a glass.

"The story wasn't the dress. It was an incident that occurred at the event involving Dr. Bennet and a high-ranking member of the Catholic Church. Let's go to our Around the City reporter, Elaine Costello, Elaine."

"Harry, here at the Morris Hotel tonight, it was reported by several witnesses that Doctor Bennet slapped Auxiliary Bishop O'Hanrand. Philadelphia Police detective, Robert Aimer, was on hand at the scene and witnessed the incident. Lieutenant, what happened?"

The camera panned to Aimer, who was in full cop-on-TV mode. "According to the witnesses I interviewed, the Bishop made several rude comments then inappropriately touched the doctor. The witnesses heard a noise that sounded like a slap, but none of the witnesses interviewed could testify that there was physical contact."

The reporter looked disappointed and pushed the story harder. "That doesn't match up with some reports we heard. Several witnesses said they saw the doctor slap the Bishop."

"Like I said, we have no testimony to those allegations."

The reporter turned to address the camera. "Harry, it appears as if something happened, but no one is talking. From downtown, this is Elaine Costello reporting, Back to you, Harry."

"Pays to have friends in low places, huh?" McKee tipped her glass and looked to Felix and David. "How about another?"

David smiled a bright Colgate smile. "How about several others?"

Smoke took O by the arm and escorted her out to the deck. They sat down on a divan positioned around the flame from a fire pit. It wasn't the same as the stone fireplace at the cabin, but it was close.

They both had drinks, but they weren't drinking.

They were sitting in a conversation pit but not talking.

The only noise they could hear was coming from the traffic on the Ben Franklin Parkway and an occasional crackle from the copper-colored flame.

Smoke looked up and caught her looking down at her drink. He couldn't get a good read through her expression, but he knew it involved deep thought.

O caught him looking into his drink, his face reading deep thought. Her eyes returned to the ice.

With heads down, staring at the ice in their drinks, they simultaneously spoke. "I—"

They both laughed.

"Ladies first."

She smiled and agreed. "It's over, isn't it?"

"Yes, without a doubt."

Again, there was silence between them.

Again, simultaneously, "I—"

She beckoned to him. "Your turn."

"I'm not sure how to say this," he eyeballed his drink again.

Her jaw clenched, expecting a blow. "Say what?"

He raised his head, "We have been through an amazing adventure, that I think it is fair to say was one for the books."

"Agreed." She clenched hers hands nervously.

He was struggling for words, and not knowing where he was going; she seemed reluctant to help.

He stammered, "I... I found you."

Her tension eased.

"But now." His drink became interesting again.

Her jaw tightened. "But now?"

He took a breath. "But now it's done. We were in a life and death struggle ...like on a battlefield. I have been to war before, and when it's over... well, things change."

He stared into his drink again.

She broke the awkwardness of the moment. "Can I ask you something?"

"Sure. Anything."

"What is so fucking interesting about that drink?"

"What?"

"You keep looking into your glass like it was a magic 8-Ball or something."

He chuckled and shrugged.

"And," she paused for effect.

"And what?"

"And, are you stupid?"

He sat up straight. "No."

"Correct. You aren't stupid. You know how I know?"

He stared at her, speechless.

"Well, do you?" She had arms crossed and an angry face.

"No, why?"

Her face went from pretend angry to sincere happy. "Because... there is no way I would ever, fall in love, with a stupid man."

His stoic face almost cracked because of the width of his grin.

The moment was interrupted by the sound of laughter from inside the bar. It was Felix. His laugh was not only recognizable but infectious.

Smoke looked to the door and saw their amigos pointing and laughing, presumably reviewing the replay of the evening's events. McKee was pointing at Felix, who had his arm around David. Both were laughing uncontrollably. Aimer had arrived, and the group gathered around him were hanging on whatever story he was telling.

Smoke turned away and invested in the think-glass again.

O cocked her head. "What's up now?"

He looked pensive.

She just waited him out.

"I have to ask you something that's been bothering me for a long time."

"Okay."

"It's a little thing, but I haven't been able to shake it. Maybe it's nothing."

"Ask already."

"Do you remember the first time I came to your office?"

"How could I forget, and believe me, I did try to forget."

"Funny, but be serious for a minute, please."

"All right." She squirmed, looking uncomfortable with what might be coming next.

"After Felix called and asked me to get involved, the first thing I did was stake out your office. For two days, I watched for anomalies and took pictures."

"I remember."

"On day three, I came into your office, introduced myself and you told me you didn't need protection."

"Correct."

"Then, I put the pictures of the men I saw staking out your office on your desk."

She lowered her eyes slightly and when she did, he knew he was right. "You had a strange reaction when I showed you the photos."

She sat upright.

"When I dropped the pictures, you grabbed them. You looked scared. Then when you didn't recognize them, you relaxed and just dropped them back on the desk. You relaxed even though I told you the guys in the pictures were a real threat."

She dropped her head. "What does that mean?"

He looked at her, not looking at him.

"It means you were afraid of somebody and that somebody wasn't one of the men in the pictures."

"And?"

"And...I think you still are."

Her head was still down.

He took her hand. "Who are you afraid of?"

When her head came up, he could see tears in her eyes.

"I thought it was...that it could have been..." she drew in a gasping breath over her fear. "The man who killed my sister."

He was shocked, but he knew there was more.

A stream of tears ran down her face.

"He killed my sister—my twin sister." She drew a long-labored breath and then sobbed. "He thought... she was me."

Smoke stood suddenly, pulling her up to him, the cool summer evening breeze blew her hair.

He wiped the tears from her face.

She leaned back, her head resting in the palm of his hand.

His eyes met hers and he whispered, "No one will ever hurt you again."

He lowered his lips to hers.

EPILOGUE

Felix Upton Grant and David Anderson.
New York Post - PAGE 6, November 12, 2020

On Saturday night, at Club 312, New York social icon Felix Upton Grant married David Anderson, Chairman and Executive Officer of Philadelphia's newly formed Public Oversight Board (PCAOB).

Upton is a legendary social figure often appearing on Page 6. He and David Anderson are both decorated veterans of Afghanistan and Iraq. Anderson, formally of Goldman Sachs, is heading a new non-profit company that was retained by McKee, Swartz, Talbot, and Juarez to provide oversight on distribution of the Philadelphia Fund for claims of children abused by Clergy.

Judge Paul G. Fenman of the Appellate Division of the State Supreme Court in Manhattan administered the private service. The service and lavish reception were attended by an A list of rich and famous, including Denzel Washington, Alec Baldwin, Cindy Lauper, 50 Cent, Alicia Keys, and celebrity/author, Dr. Olivia Bennet.

Unable to attend was Harvey Fierstein, who sent regrets along with a case of champagne delivered to the couple by a drone that caused quite a traffic commotion.

Bonni McKee, Esq.
Philadelphia Inquirer, November 16, 2021

Bonni McKee, Esq. announced today that Mr. Laurence Talbot, Ms. Rebecca Swartz, and Ms. Juanita Juarez were joining her firm. It will now be known as McKee, Talbot, Swartz and Juarez.

The three attorneys were all formally Associates with Rittenhouse, Bailey, and Stokes as was Ms. McKee, who left the prestigious firm in 2020. The meteoric rise of the McKee firm has been primarily due to McKee's successful bid to become the chief legal counsel for the watchdog committee that will oversee the distribution of the fund set up by the Archdiocese of Philadelphia to compensate for victims of sexual abuse.

Ms. McKee said the new attorneys will administer the firm's pro bono commitments in criminal defense, elderly, and sex abuse and discrimination cases. The Inquirer determined that the firm's dedication to free representation is the most substantial commitment by any for-profit law firm in the country.

Lieutenant Robert Aimer.
Philadelphia Inquirer, January 8, 2021

The Philadelphia Police Department today announced the retirement of Police Lieutenant Robert Aimer, effective January 31, 2021. The highly decorated twenty-five-year veteran is a Philadelphia native. Captain Patrick Ferguson said, "We are happy for our friend Lt. Aimer and sad because the PPD is losing a great detective."

Aimer is retiring from the Police Department but not from the workforce. He has accepted the position of Chief Investigator for the Committee of Oversight for the fund set up by the Archdiocese of

Philadelphia to compensate victims of sexual abuse. He will work closely with the firm of McKee, Swartz, Talbot, and Juarez in vetting claims that had been made by claimants who allege being victimized by those under the supervision and jurisdiction of the Philadelphia Catholic Church.

Monsieur Giuseppe DeFrancisco.
La Republica, August 3, 2022

A statement from the Polizia Penitenziria today announced that Monsieur Giuseppe DeFrancisco, 38, a suspect in three contract murders, was found dead in his cell early this morning. DeFrancisco was being held at the maximum-security facility, Pagliarelli Prison in Milano. The cause of death was not released. However, sources within the prison confirmed to la Republica that the murder was brutal and gang-related.

There has been no statement from the Vatican. However, sources within the Church confirm to la Republica, the Vatican had begun laicization to remove him from the priesthood.

The Carabinieri and Interpol confirmed DeFrancisco was linked by email, phone contact, and money transfers to a German citizen, Ralph Harold Schmidt, who also traveled as a Dane under an alias of Niels Bohr. Schmidt was killed in a failed assassination of the US author and doctor Olivia Bennet in June of 2020.

Sources within the prison also reported DeFrancisco ran afoul with one of the most notorious prison gangs in the world, the Brodraskapet. The source said the gang believed one of their members was murdered by Schmidt at the order of DeFrancisco for reasons still unknown by investigators.

Auxiliary Bishop Michael O'Hanrand
L'Osservatore Romano, August 18, 2022.

The Vatican announced today, Auxiliary Bishop O'Hanrand, 79, died suddenly yesterday at the Monastery of Saints George and John Jacob in Israel. The Auxiliary Bishop left his post in Philadelphia, USA, in 2020 to dedicate the remainder of his life to prayer at the monastery.

O'Hanrand chose to live as an anchorite (one who completely withdrew from all human contact). His daily life of continuous prayer was conducted from a small stoned-walled room at the remote mountain monastery built into the cliffs around 500 AD. An ancient rope pedestrian bridge called Wadi Qelt is the only access to the sixth-century, cliff-hanging structure, which many believe to be Psalm 23's reference to "valley of the shadow of death."

Henry Smokehouse & Doctor Olivia Bennet.
New York Times, Feature Sunday, November 19, 2022.

The long-awaited sequel to Doctor Olivia Bennet's number one bestseller, *Release the Beast,* will be published in the fall of this year. Published by Classic Press, it is titled *Finding Satisfaction.*

Doctor Bennet announced to a packed news conference, she had dedicated the book to Loretta Kelly, her co-worker and friend. Ms. Kelly, a former Marine First Sergeant, was shot and killed during the break-in of the doctor's NY office in 2020.

Doctor Bennet gained national headlines when she shot and killed a man later identified by Interpol as Ralph Harold Schmidt, a German citizen, and gun for hire. Schmidt was confirmed by the NYPD as the triggerman in the break-in of the doctor's office. The motive and identity of the party or parties who hired him and targeted her remain unsolved and an open case.

In her address, Doctor Bennet said she had taken time off from her New York practice to resolve a long outstanding traumatic issue that had been haunting her for more than twenty years. Although pressed by repeated questions, Doctor Bennet would not discuss details, saying the new book describes the investigation and resolution of the incident that had caused her trauma.

"I'm a public figure, and because of that notoriety, I'm subject to scrutiny at almost every level of my life. I've entered into that world freely to reach a larger audience. There are perks that accompany fame but those benefits come at a cost. Recently, I have suffered the devastating expense of public notoriety. In my practice, I advise patients that life lessons can be learned from a tragic event, and drawing on my own advice, I used that tragedy as a catalyst to resolve a devastating event in my past, which I had suppressed. I wrote *Escape the Beast* using real life examples to help those who want to talk more freely about what satisfies their needs."

"I wrote *Finding Satisfaction* using my life as its sole example. It is a cathartic work which draws from my past in the hope of inspiring others to do the same."

During follow-up questions, Doctor Bennet replied to a question about her much rumored engagement. "I choose to be a public figure, so in recognition of public curiosity, I will say that the rumor is true. I will also say to my patients and those who read my work—Hoorah."

It is speculated but not confirmed that her future husband is Henry Smokehouse, who was the only person in the doctor's entourage. Sources inside the NYPD said that Smokehouse, also known as Smoke, was instrumental in the investigation surrounding the break-in and shooting.

Doctor Bennet said her new publisher, Classic Press, indicated pre-orders for the new book, *Finding Satisfaction,* have already qualified it for the NYT Best Sellers list.

THE END

SMOKE

ABOUT THE AUTHOR

Paul Eberz authored Smoke-White Collar Crimes as the first edition of a trilogy. In addition to this series, he is preparing two additional novels for publication, an Historical-Fiction mystery about the death of JFK and a Call of the Wild adventure story set in 1849. Eberz has retired from the construction industry where he held executive positions in Fortune 500 companies and traveled the country working with Native American's. Born in Philadelphia, he now resides in Florida and New Jersey.

Made in the USA
Middletown, DE
10 March 2021